The Rat

KING

Juggernaut

Berlin

KM Stever

Cover design by FRANK GRYNER

KARENSTEVER.COM

PAPERBACK ISBN: 978-1-9994991-6-7
HARDBACK ISBN: 978-1-9994991-8-1

ACCOLADES:

KING JUGGERNAUT WINS BOOK OF THE MONTH!
READ THE INTERVIEW WITH THE AUTHOR:
https://allauthor.com/interview/kmstever/

KING JUGGERNAUT NOMINATED FOR AUTHOR ACADEMY AWARD IN *'BEST HISTORICAL FICTION'* CATEGORY!

CONTENTS

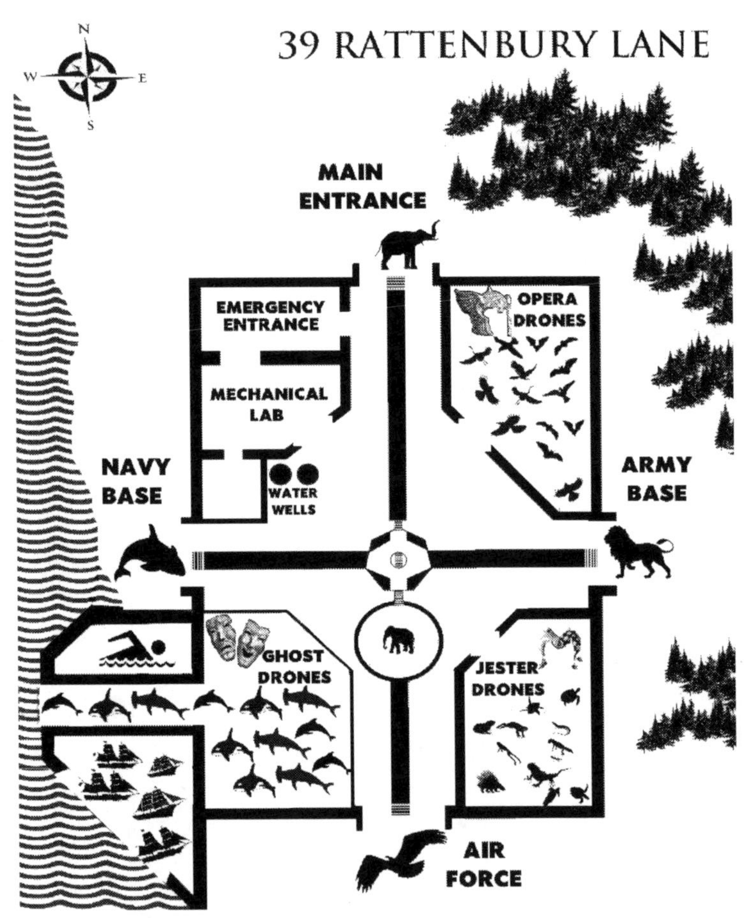
39 RATTENBURY LANE
N
W
E
S
MAIN ENTRANCE
EMERGENCY ENTRANCE
MECHANICAL LAB
WATER WELLS
OPERA DRONES
NAVY BASE
ARMY BASE
GHOST DRONES
JESTER DRONES
AIR FORCE

This is for the liberators of the creatures of Earth.
Your leaders have failed you by not leading with compassion,
and by not shutting off the tap so you can catch up.
Overwhelmed, you get up every day to set the balance again.
Thank you for being light-workers in a dark world.

1 THE GREAT STONE BISON

Don't breathe the air
Make you cough cough cough
Keep your shoes on
never take them off
Gotta run like the horses
Thirty at a time
PANZER! PANZER!
Polish swine!

Rosa paused her hand game poem and inhaled deeply. She was far too young to be living on train station cement.

Her skeleton was trying to hide under bits of charred fabric. It was the same set of clothes she had been wearing since the September Blitzkrieg burned down her apartment in Danzig. She did her best to pull down the cuffs of her jacket so no one would see the pink burn marks on her black skin. The warm hooded coat was given to her by a German dressmaker who felt sorry for her. Getting roughed up by local children made it age quickly and it became as brutal as her fire-singed, grey pleated skirt which **must have been beautiful once**. For her, scars were a point of pride because she helped her father drag the mattress off the bed, pour gasoline on it, and toss it out the window onto a German tank below. The family had just nicely moved to Poland that summer and were not expecting to have any visitors, certainly not unwelcomed ones like Panzer tanks and Stuka dive-bombers.

Rosa was neither Aryan nor German which made it extra tough to pretend she belonged in Berlin. Luckily, she had two things going for her. It was winter, and people could hide behind heavy wools and scarves, and it was Christmas, so generally, the Death Marchers were of good cheer. She moved around a lot and pretended to fit in, but it was awkward for an eleven-year-old girl with African roots to not be seen with a family. Her mother was taken in the Blitz and her father was shot on sight. Seeing her town was being torched, she grabbed her young puppy in her coat and managed to cling on to the back of a German tank...and that was how she ended up living in and around Berlin's Anhalter Bahnhof train station.

Most of the time, she made particularly good decisions and kept her head on a swivel. She would navigate through crowds, and bob and weave when necessary. If she saw the Death Marchers patrolling the sidewalks, she would pivot and position her back to them or stand near a wealthy German family. She had even participated in rallies and held up the nation's flag with the power-spider on it – whatever she had to do, if it meant staying alive.

On this day, Rosa changed from acting with her head to reacting with her heart.

"Shake your finger back-and-forth like you are scolding someone," she directed a young girl who was facing her.

"Mom does it when my tongue hangs out," the girl said, putting her glove on her tongue and shoving it back in.

"I hang my tongue out too...I like catching snowflakes on it. Just tell her you are catching snowflakes," Rosa giggled.

"Every snowflake is different," the girl said.

"Don't be fooled. Every snowflake is different, but they are all white. You get to be white and different," Rosa said, stiffening her lip.

"You can be a brown snowflake, that isn't bad," the girl smiled and then added, "You just can't be yellow!" she said pointing to Rosa's young doggy who was lifting his leg on a cement post.

"NEVER eat yellow snow!" Rosa laughed.

"I never do!" the girl said, laughing loudly.

"Ok, back to the hand-game. You just shake your finger like you are your Mama and say, 'Don't breathe the air!' Alright?"

"Ok," the girl responded, excited to learn it.

"Now, put your hands over your mouth and say 'cough cough cough' – three times -" Rosa said.

The sweet girl forced out three big coughs.

"Don't actually cough. Just say the word cough three times!" Rosa scolded, not wanting the extra attention.

"Cough cough cough cough," the girl said out loud.

"That is four. We will just move on. When you say keep your shoes on, this is tricky... you point to your shoes on the word 'keep' and then put your hands on your hips on the word 'on' - like this... KEEP your shoes ON!"

The girl pointing down and noticed a lace that needed tying.

"Ok tie your boots then, I will wait," Rosa said, folding her arms and keeping watch.

"KEEP my boots ON!" the girl boldly proclaimed.

"Yes! You did that part perfectly! And let's face it, you are right. We're wearing boots not shoes," Rosa laughed ready to continue. "Now stomp your feet, left, right, left when you say, NEVER TAKE them OFF!"

The girl wasn't satisfied with how she tied them and bent down to take a second attempt at it.

"Ok, tie them tightly - that makes sense," Rosa responded in her best Mama voice. "Have you ever ridden a horse?"

"I am a champion," the girl said, confidently.

"Ok, well - show me how you hold your reins then!" Rosa said with her hands on her hips.

"Like this!" the girl said proudly.

"Yes - so that is where you bounce your reins two times and say, 'Gotta RUN like the HORSES' - Yes! Good job!"

"I am a champion!"

"You really are! Now show me ten fingers," Rosa said.

"Two are thumbs," the girl said, looking confused by the request.

"Ok, show me eight fingers and two thumbs," Rosa said, rolling her eyes. "If you flash them three times, that's thirty. You can just trust me now and count them later!"

"Ok, thirty at a time!" the girl yelled.

"You remembered the words! Excellent!" Rosa clapped.

"I am a champion!"

"Can you march like a champion?"

"Yes."

"You just march left then right on the word Panzer," Rosa instructed, stomping each foot.

"PANZER! PANZER!" the girl shouted.

"You are a natural! Good! Now, what do devils have on top of their head?" Rosa asked.

"I think a hat," the girl said.

"You aren't wrong about that - but under the hat are horns!"

"Like a unicorn?"

"They grow like that straight from their skull – but there are two - and you just curl your fingers on your head like you have horns on the word 'Polish'."

"Those guys aren't Polish," the girl said, puzzled.

"It is part of the hand game, silly! You will like the next part - push your nose up with your finger when you say the word 'swine'!"

The girl burst out laughing.

"I am not sure that laughing works in this part, but ok!" Rosa giggled with her. "What is your name anyway?"

"Olcay."

"Ok...well, go ahead!"

"Olcay!"

"Maybe draw it in the snow..." Rosa said. "Use your boot."

Olcay drew her name in big letters.

"Oh! You did a good answer first. How did you get that name?"

"I am a champion."

"At what?"

"At everything."

"So, name something," Rosa smirked.

"Hand games!" Olcay said, proudly.

"We are hand game PIGS!" Rosa said, putting her arm around her.

"Yes! Hand game PIGS!" Olcay shouted, unfortunately alerting the wrong people.

"And what exactly is a hand game pig?" asked a tall German man in uniform.

Rosa turned her face away and had to trust that Olcay would handle it.

"Do you want to learn a hand game?" Olcay asked him.

The man bent down to have a closer look at her.

"Why, you are one of those retarded kids. Where are your parents?" he asked, motioning for another Death Marcher to come over.

"I am Olcay. I am a champion," she told him, shoving her tongue back in her mouth.

"What is the problem?" the second Marcher asked.

"Take a look at this child, what's wrong with her?" he asked as Olcay looked at the ground.

"I will take care of it. Go enjoy the night air," he responded.

As the first man walked away, the second one grabbed Olcay's hood and pulled it up over her ears.

"It is a cold night, little one. Keep your ears warm. Are you waiting for the train? Where is your Mama?"

Olcay pointed to her Mama who came running for her.

"Oh please, please Sir. She is a good girl. We don't want any trouble. Please, I will keep her close!" her Mother pleaded.

"I sent the trouble away," he said pointing to the first man. "I will warn you though... you must keep her on a short leash. I can't protect her forever."

"Christmas Greetings, good Sir! God bless your kindness," the woman said, as she hurried away with her.

Rosa took a very deep breath from behind a pillar near the train rails. She played with danger every day, but Christmas time was busy enough that she could get away with it easily.

It was safer to not have too many friends, but it was desperately lonely for her. She had a routine every day at the station where she could get enough food and money to get her through the day, but Christmas was harder. People were focused on themselves and their families. It was too painful for Rosa to watch them hug and hold hands.

"Come on, Eisbär," she said to her fluffy white pup who was only ten weeks old during the September Blitz. He was growing quickly, but not maturing fast enough. He was quite good on his leash. He blended in with the snow except for one half of his face being burned. The fur never did grow back there. Just like Rosa's skirt, **he really was beautiful once**.

Miss Kraus was one of the youngest teachers in Berlin. She had not married and so without a family of her own, she had plenty of time and energy to mother the school children as they boarded the train. She was always chipper and spent most of her time away from school helping the less fortunate.

The three German children she was with today, Viktor, Charlotte, and Rita were orphaned, and she loved them like her own. She would notice the other parents kissing their children before the last school trip before the holidays, so she would kiss her orphans on the forehead to make them feel included. Viktor was enamoured with her and tried to touch her curly blonde hair every time she kissed him.

"I have cinnamon buns, children! Come and get one!" Miss Kraus said.

Rosa stood nearby wishing she could taste this treat that had taken over the smell of the engines. Eisbär was licking his chops beside her.

Just off the platform, the local church's children's choir had formed a small gathering and were singing Exalted Night of the Clear Stars but was interrupted by sirens bellowing and a recording stopped the hustle and bustle dead in its tracks.

"It is the Drillmeister, children. Please stand at attention and listen!" Miss Kraus instructed.

A Christmas greeting by the Drillmeister played over loudspeaker at the train station...and perhaps every station and household that had reception.

"The flag of the Homeland shall remain proud and free
Know that I am with you, in your homes, in the fields
I am counting on you to remain with me
as I lead you into the rightful victory the Fatherland finally deserves"

Ever trailing behind was Egon.

Unlike Rosa and Olcay, Egon physically fit in. All the kids in the class dressed pretty much the same. Under his overcoat was a nicely pressed shirt and skinny black tie. His hair was trimmed into a choppy blonde boy's cut, and tuffs of it would peek out from underneath his black Panzer wool field cap. His eyes were blue, like the sky on a cloud-free day, and were projected twice the size through black-rimmed glasses. They suited him as his grades were perfect in school. For that reason, Miss Kraus didn't worry about him.

But there were other reasons to worry about Egon.

'Egon *chooses* not to speak'. This was concluded after some bullies at the school told the teachers they heard Egon talking, and that he was faking being a mute. This was not accurate.

Allowing him to trail behind the other children was generally okay. He had been known to wander but because everything was so orderly, it was easy to spot anyone walking out of line. The community did a good job of corralling children back into their groups.

"Egon didn't get a cinnamon roll, Miss Kraus!" yelled Viktor.

"Oh, I have something for Mr. Egon," she said, reaching into her coat pocket and pulling out a plain shortbread cookie. "Would that suit you, Egon?"

Egon took the cookie and placed it in his pocket.

"Who rejects a Christmas cinnamon roll and then shoves shortbread in his pocket?" Viktor asked, filling his face, and licking every finger.

"Children like what they like," Miss Kraus smiled.

Two big army trucks rolled into the train station. Even though the German people were used to seeing them, they still made an impressive, domineering entrance. They were large steel boxes and covered by camouflage tarps. Egon was curious about them, and he walked away from Miss Kraus to get a closer look.

The soldiers who were dressed in their formal uniforms poured out of the trucks and walked to the back. One of the trucks had its rear towards the train station festivities and the other was parked parallel to it, but the back was sitting at the front of the first one. One of the soldiers pulled out a small bugle and blew a few times to get the attention of the people. Of course everyone stopped, even the train conductors, to have a look. As they untied the tarp, many young children ran towards it, excited to see what was inside.

"This is an incredibly special Christmas for the Fatherland, my dear children," the soldier said. "We must remember the many blessings and we will mark this day as victory for our people. May we celebrate this special time of year giving thanks to God and the Drillmeister. We will need you to all stand back, children. There is a large object about to come out of the back and we don't want any of you hurt."

Egon was indeed interested in the surprise, but instead of waiting with the other children, he wandered to the back of the second truck. He could hear movement inside of it and watched while a soldier warned whoever was in there to stay quiet. While it was too dark to see everyone, there were evidently too many poor people packed into a small space. They had an opportunity to beg Egon for help, but they did not. The collective look on the faces he did see was pure terror. They seemed either too afraid or too cold to make a movement.

"WHAT ARE YOU DOING THERE?" came the stern voice of one of the soldiers.

Instead of running away, Egon froze in his place.

"Oh! Did I frighten you?" the man said, instantly changing his demeanour to be gentler. "You are missing the great unveiling. Here, have this!" he said, handing him a small hand flag. "Wave it proudly, son! It is an historic time for our country!"

Egon took it and gazed at the black SS on it. It began to morph into a spider, and he dropped it at his feet and blankly stared down.

"Here you are, son!" the soldier said, retrieving it and sending him back to the rest of the children. "Go on now, don't miss the fun!"

Egon held this power-spider flag stiffly in his hand and walked towards the rest of the crowd.

It took ten to twelve soldiers to remove the massive cargo from the truck. It was uncomfortably quiet until one soldier yelled at the choir to continue their singing.

"Sing loudly so the heavens will hear you, dear friends!"

Out of the corner of Egon's eye, he could see the soldiers guiding the poor people out of the back of the truck and loading them into a train car nearby. They seemed to move slowly in their ratty clothes, huddled closely in some sort of solidarity. It was a bad energy, and Egon was glued to them.

The children at the unveiling were wide-eyed and excited, and many were holding their cinnamon buns in their gloves while big snowflakes came down on their faces. Egon's senses were on overload. He could not take his eyes off the stark contrast of the other truck that had the quiet people in the back. Their faces were all flash-frozen in the same stunned expression.

Someone stole them.

Egon reached inside his winter coat and pulled out a notepad. He began to draw lines which were like the power-spider on the flag, but he added more lines and a small 'x' at the ends of them.

He was then startled by Viktor who said, "That isn't our flag!"

Egon panicked and returned the writing pad to his pocket.

"What is the problem, boys?" Miss Kraus interjected.

"It is the weird little boy again, Miss Kraus. He's making a mockery of the Fatherland!" Viktor tattled.

"Egon doesn't even speak, Viktor. This isn't even possible!" she quipped. "All eyes should be on the surprise in the truck!" and she turned both their shoulders to watch.

"I know what I saw, Egon. You are ashamed of your heritage, but you ought to be ashamed of yourself," Viktor whispered. "You WILL get what's coming to you."

Egon pushed his black-framed glasses up his nose and opted to move away from Viktor. As he navigated through the crowd of children, he tried to get closer to the front where he could see properly. He wasn't the average height of other children - he was quite a few inches shorter.

"Alright my children, we are going to start clapping very slowly. Can you all give me just one big clap on the count of three?" one of the soldiers asked. "One - two - three!"

Hundreds of children responded with a very muffled clap.

"The heavens will never hear this! Take off your mittens and we will try this again, all right?" he laughed. "One - two - three!"

That did the trick. Everyone else at the train station stopped and looked over.

"You got their attention, children! Now, follow me as we clap together!" and he started very slowly, then built up faster.

As the clapping built, he added in his feet.

"Stomp! Stomp! Stomp!" he yelled over them.

The other people at the train station applauded with the children and it erupted into a fury. Then the chanting began.

"SIEG HEIL!

SIEG HEIL!

SIEG HEIL!"

Olcay liked all the stomping and she joined in with that. Her Mama tried to keep her tucked in closely because it was always risky having her in public.

"Are you ready to see, children?" the soldier yelled.

"Yes! Yes! Yes!" the children responded back.

"Alright! Count backwards from five! Altogether now!"

They all joined in.

"Five! Four! Three! Two! One!"

On 'one', several soldiers removed the large tarp to reveal a stone eagle statue. Its wings were spread as wide as the front row of the crowd directly in front of them. They cheered so loudly, Olcay's mood changed instantly, and she covered her ears, then hid her face in her mother's coat.

Viktor was cheering the loudest. He turned to Egon and demanded, "Let us hear your cowardly voice. This is your country, Egon!"

Egon said nothing. He raised his hand-held flag just enough to blend in with the others.

"Come, children! You may touch it. It belongs to all of you," the soldier encouraged them.

Egon reached in his pocket and pulled out the shortbread that Miss Kraus gave him. It was cut into the same shape as the statue. He slowly put the cookie up to his mouth and instead of taking a bite, he held it on his lips as he looked at the statue. The eagle's grey eye went from stone to pale yellow glass and looked directly at him. Colour began to saturate the stone face and the cement feathers became real. Brown continued to bleed down the body and yellow and black filled out the legs and talons. Egon was uncomfortable with how close everyone was, and he stepped in to push each child off, either protecting them or protecting the great bird. Some children began to push back.

"Stop pushing!" one yelled.

"We all get a turn, crazy boy!" screamed another.

Viktor took it as an opportunity to really push Egon, as he had been dying to. A soldier scolded Egon by putting his finger in his face and Egon returned the gesture by biting it.

“Someone control that boy!” a woman from the crowd yelled.

Egon’s glasses were knocked off his face and he stumbled around trying to find them. Just then, an enormous vulture, twice the size of the stone eagle, flew overhead and swooped down. In one swift pass, it knocked the eagle backwards breaking off one of the stone wings. The crowd began to scream, unable to process what just happened.

“Was that a bomber?” someone asked.

“It was definitely the enemy in some way!” another man answered.

The soldiers abandoned the eagle, which was now flat on its back, had returned to stone, and one of the wings were broken off at the shoulder.

“Are you looking for these?” a voice said to a very blurry-eyed Egon who had his hands out in front of him. “I think there may be a chip out of the frame, but otherwise, I believe they are alright,” she added.

As Egon put the glasses back on his face, he saw Rosa standing in front of him, scratching her frizzy hair and eating his cookie.

“It fell on the ground. I didn’t figure you would want it after that. It’s fine for me, though. It is quite good. Whoever baked it did a good job,” she smiled.

Egon didn’t seem terribly upset by that.

"Let's call it an even trade. You get your glasses back, I get your cookie!" she said, extending her hand to shake.

Egon didn't do things like that.

"No worries. I can be your friend from over here," she smiled.

"Egon, are you ok?" Miss Kraus asked, but swiftly ran to other children in the chaos.

The soldiers guarding the second truck ran over to join the soldiers at the stone eagle.

"So - your name is Egon. That is a good name. Come on - come with me," Rosa whispered to him.

He seemed pleased that somebody was being kind to him, and he followed behind her.

"Come on, Eisbär!" she called to her dog. "Don't mind his face. He was burned in a big fight."

Rosa grabbed Egon's arm and pulled him behind one of the big pillars.

"I know what I am doing. You always need to keep your eyes open. The Death Marchers are busy right now, so we have a big opportunity! We just need to wait a bit," she said pulling a book out of her coat. "Sit with me, Egon!"

He seemed really interested in whatever she had to show him. He tucked himself into a tight little ball beside her and Eisbär tried to lick his face.

"Just say no and SIT!" she directed.

Just like that, the dog sat staring at them.

"Eisbär is my best friend, Egon. I wrote a poem for him. Want to hear it?" she said opening her writing pad. "I write and create hand poems. I draw pictures, and in the summertime, I am planning on being a street performer. I feel like I could make some money from the rich people. Are your parents rich, Egon?"

Egon folded his arms over his knees and hid his face.

"Oh. You might have a story like me, then. We do not have to talk about that. Would you like to hear my poem about my doggy?" she asked, not entirely concerned with him answering. "Here it is! Ready, Eisbär? This is for you!"

Eisbär fell flat on his belly in the snow and listened.

"*Then our Bear-Puppy friend caught his first fish.*
He held it in his paws as it went squish-squish.
But the curly-tailed guppy looked awfully thin.
So, he bid him farewell - and he tossed him back in."

She patted Eisbär on the head, and he smiled with his tongue out.

"You love that poem every single time, don't you my sweetheart? What about you, Egon? Do you not speak because you have nothing to say or are you just not ready to? Well, never mind. I hear people talking all day long. It's pretty nice to have an interested listener!" she smiled, seeming content with her new little friend.

"Would you like to see some of my art?" she asked as she flipped through her pad. "This one is from my old-old country

- two countries ago. Everyone wore bright fancy colours. That is my Father, that's my Mother and that's our dog Jo-Jo. She died of old. **She really was beautiful once**. And this picture is from the country I was in just before this one. This is our apartment - it was on the second floor just above the main door so I could see all the people coming in and out. Once a week, the mailman would come - and sometimes, I would get a postcard from my aunt in the old-old country telling us how Grandpa and Grandma were doing. This is my favourite postcard from her. All the girls learned to walk with big pots on their heads. Isn't that funny? Someday, I'm gonna make my way back there and learn to walk with a pot on my head too."

Egon reached inside his coat pocket and pulled out a notepad of his own.

"Do you draw too? Wow, Egon! I think we were meant to be good friends - maybe even best friends. Would you like that?" she said putting an arm around his shoulder.

Egon wasn't exactly comfortable with affection, but he seemed to like Rosa enough to stay there.

"May I look in your book? I take it very seriously, you know. Artist to artist, our work is our soul!" she said, acting like an experienced aficionado.

He handed her the book and began to pet Eisbär.

"Oh - hmmmm - okay - uh, Egon, I – I don't really understand it. There are a lot of lines and numbers and maps. Oh! Are you an explorer? Egon - you might be one of those people who find new land! That is very noble!" she smiled, not knowing exactly how to respond to the madness in his book.

"Alright! I think the coast is clear. We can go explore right now!" she said, getting up and walking over to the truck with the people in it.

"I saw you looking in it! Come on! Come on, Egon the Explorer!" she giggled.

Egon followed behind and Eisbär trotted along. Luckily, the soldiers were busy attending to the broken eagle.

"Eisbär, keep watch! And for heaven's sake - keep quiet! Well, at least his white fur blends in with the snow," Rosa said, approaching the truck with caution. "I have done this before. Are you nervous, Egon?"

Egon seemed horrified that she was doing something in defiance like this and he stood frozen.

"Ok! Watch and learn, then!" she said, grabbing a long bar that was securing the back doors of the truck. She pulled it sideways ever so carefully so it wouldn't screech.

"Just one tiny squeak! Not bad!" she said, winking at Egon.

As the doors opened, she whispered to a young scared man just inside, "Why didn't they take all of you out? Never mind that. You are all going to want to run fast. You cannot run in a group. You need to quietly exit and then you need to scatter. After this, you are all on your own. Do you understand? Anyone who doesn't want to get shot at, can stay in the truck, but you'll be going to your death! Your choice!"

With that, the mothers, fathers, and their children stepped out of the truck quietly and did exactly as she instructed. They scattered.

"Be ever so quiet but go as swiftly as you can!" she whispered as they exited.

As they ran, soldiers spotted them as they disappeared into the thick of the crowd.

"What did you think of that, Egon? Rather good, huh?" Rosa said. "Most times, they load all the people in the trains. I don't always get a golden opportunity like this! Now we need to disappear!"

Eisbär began to growl just past her.

"They saw me, didn't they?" she said, not turning around.

Just behind Rosa were two soldiers with their guns pointed at her.

"Just because you might get caught, Egon, doesn't mean you shouldn't do it. Remember that!" and she turned to face them.

"A black kid! Of course it was a black kid!" one of them said.

"What do you want with me? I am just a child!" she said boldly.

"You let those people go? They were violent criminals!" the second soldier said.

"Pretty young kids in there to be violent criminals. Or was their crime not being one of YOUR kind?" she disputed.

"Where are your papers?" one soldier demanded.

"You know I don't have papers," she challenged them. "Now what? Now what are you going to do?"

"Put her in the back of the truck until we find the others," the soldier said.

"That is quite the Christmas spirit that you have, kind Sirs!" she mocked.

As they approached her, Eisbär stood his ground, growled then barked.

"That is one ugly dog," the second soldier scoffed.

"Wait! Don't hurt him. He belongs to a local shop owner," she lied.

"Oh yeah, which one?" he demanded.

"Give me a minute - uh, oh yes - Mr. Ziegler from Ziegler's Shoes. Take him there, he'll tell you," she said.

"Put him in the front, we'll sort that out later," the first soldier said. "And who is the boy with you?"

"That kid? I don't know him, but I saw him with Miss Kraus' class," she smiled at Egon.

"Alright, son - come with me!" he said, motioning for Egon.

Egon was paralyzed with shock and went along. He looked back and Rosa smiled confidently, waved at him, and went into the back of their truck.

"Oh - would you permit me my writing pad? It fell on the ground," she asked.

The second soldier picked it up, and quickly leafed through it.

"You cannot keep this book. It has colours that are not in nature. This is not permitted. Rules from the Drillmeister," he said, walking it over to a trash can.

"No, please! It is all I have!"

Egon heard her confidence turn to pleading, and there was nothing he could do.

"Is this boy part of your class?" the soldier asked Miss Kraus.

"Oh yes! Thank you, sir. We will not let the children wander off again! Everyone was scared! Are we under attack?" she asked, ushering Egon to the group.

"We aren't sure yet. Please do what you can to keep the train trip normal for your class," he instructed.

"We most certainly will!" she obliged.

Miss Kraus was having a rough time mobilizing the children for their Christmas train trip. Everyone was frazzled, but it was important to maintain order and remain festive.

"You seem like you have your hands full," a friendly voice said to her.

"Oh! Yes - children - say hello to the Lokführer. He drives our locomotive!" Miss Kraus said, still trying to round up children.

Everyone did their best to say hello to him, but they were trying to board the train at the same time. Egon was quite a few feet behind everyone else and he remained fixed on Rosa's truck.

"Egon, come along now," the Lokführer said to him.

Egon was confused that a train conductor would know who he was. The Lokführer bent down close to his face and said, "Do you want me to retrieve Rosa's book for you?"

Egon didn't know what to do with that information, and he just looked down at the ground.

"Miss Kraus, Egon left something behind. We'll be along shortly. I will make sure that he gets on the train," he said. "Walk with me, Egon! I noticed they pitched it into the trash. Oh yes, there it is!" he said, pulling it out of the bin. "There you are!" and he handed it to Egon, who quickly put it inside his coat.

"You are quite taken with Rosa! She has lived at this station since September. I have watched her do magnificent things. I have seen her make people laugh and help many others like she did today. She moves to the beat of her own drum. She knew the risks," he said, not really making Egon feel any better. "May I give you something to cheer you up?"

The Lokführer was a tall man around seventy years old with a big white handlebar moustache and matching bushy sideburns. His eyebrows were unruly, and his nose was extra-large on his face.

"Here you are, I hope you like it," he said, handing him a Waffen SS Berlin identification tag. "It belonged to your father, Egon."

Egon didn't want to take it but was clearly interested in what he just said.

"You look like him!" he said to no response. "May I slip it in your pocket?"

Egon just let him do it with no reaction.

"Hmmm, Yes - you don't speak. I do know you write some very intriguing things in your notepad! I know all sorts of things about you. I know you have an extraordinary gift and have perfect grades in school. I know that you play the akkordion by ear. I also know you are staring at something just past me that others do not see. It's a stone animal, isn't it? Wait – let me guess – I am quite good at this – hmmmm a tiger, - no wait – hmmmm – bigger than that – let me see, let me see, is it a bear? No? Bigger still – let me think, is it a bison? YES!" and he turned to see a stone bison at the edge of the station. "Hey look at that! Ha ha! Well, do not be too impressed. I already knew it was there. Isn't it magnificent? Do you want to go see it?"

Egon walked slowly in that direction, and then turned to see the chaos created from the broken eagle.

"Oh. You don't want another incident. Shall we get you back to the train? You have an incredible journey ahead of you, Mr. Egon Savant!" he said, patting him on the back.

Egon stepped a few feet closer to the bison and looked into his eyes. Thankfully, nothing was triggered. He suddenly became overwhelmed by what just happened, and he hurried ahead of the Lokführer to get to the train.

Miss Kraus was getting a bit perturbed and called for Egon, "You are going to miss the train!"

"No worries, Miss Kraus. It cannot leave without me!" the

Lokführer laughed.

"I suppose not, but we still need to remain orderly," she said.

"Hmmmm, yes - order. There has been a lot of talk about order," he smiled at Egon as he took his place behind the group.

Egon looked over to Rosa's truck, but nothing was materializing. He boarded the train, took a seat with the other children, and stared out the window. As the train slowly moved out, Egon looked over at the bison. It was coming to life and slowly stretched and moved. Then, it began to walk alongside the train. He looked to see if anyone else saw, but they were all too involved in the candy Miss Kraus was handing out. As the train gained speed, the bison began to trot – and then run – and then gallop as fast as it could! Steam was coming out of its nose and snow was flying everywhere.

"Would you like some?" Miss Kraus interrupted Egon, but he would not take it.

"First no cinnamon bun, and now no candy!" Viktor chimed in. "Weirdest child alive!"

Egon locked eyes again with the bison and it finally had to give up as the train gained too much momentum. It stood there breathing heavily for a moment and then sat down in the field. It was far too wild to be lying on train station cement.

2 THE SKELETON FOX OF TIERGARTEN

"A criminal transported, or an alien deported?"

Egon was rattled after meeting Rosa. She was an alien in the country, but it wasn't known if she was being deported back to her old country or her old-old country. Certainly, just like the children in the back of the truck, she was too young to be a criminal.

Egon's parents were both German. His grandparents on both sides were German. Between having perfect grades in Math and his dominant lineage, he was safe from the train transport that went in the opposite direction of Tiergarten - where his holiday school trip was heading.

In such a short time, he watched a vulture attack a stone eagle, met a burnt-faced dog, saw stolen people escape, made a best friend, and lost her, and some old man knew all about him. Not all his days had been this eventful, but they were mostly chaotic since his parents died. Orphans were treated fairly, but not lovingly.

It's also not every day your train is chased by a massive bison. This rattled him too. It seemed to have more layers of fur than the average German woman had wallpaper. Snow stacked neatly on top and perhaps cooled him down after such a violent run. Perhaps, it missed the next train to the Annual Bison Family gathering. It was a short trip - only six minutes by train. What else did the bison have going on? If he wanted to go, he could have arrived there eventually.

Each snowflake coming down was the size of a coin and Egon was hypnotized by them and the pine trees whipping by in the countryside. The predictable view was a contrast to the day so far and he melted into his seat.

Charlotte and Rita were inseparable. They were the type of girls who couldn't go to the bathroom without one another. They were wearing their school uniforms and were both so happy to be away from their families on a school trip. They joked and giggled the whole way.

"Did you see how angry the soldiers were when the big stone eagle lost his wing?" Charlotte laughed.

"Oh - my precious bird, my precious bird! Their faces were horrified. One time, I watched a pigeon poop right on the head of the one hanging from our balcony!" Rita whispered.

"You are so lucky! I have prayed for that to happen to ours. I have nightmares about that thing attacking me in my bed!" Charlotte responded.

"Talk about an unveiling going wrong! But what about that thing that swooped in and broke its wing off? What do you suppose that was?" Rita asked.

"THAT was the ENEMY!" Viktor chimed in. "You two need to take this more seriously. The Fatherland is under attack. Do you want your homes blown up?"

"Oh Viktor," Rita said. "You are FAR too ominous. It is Christmas! Stop being so serious all the time!"

"This isn't like any other Christmas. Don't you feel the change? Don't you feel the shift in control? The enemy has plans to confuse us. They are infiltrating. If we do not stop them, you will never have another Christmas or a train trip or a cinnamon bun or candy!" Viktor warned. "And you both will end up being the only two German girls left in the country! Let that sink in!"

Charlotte and Rita both looked really confused and turned to look at each other - then burst out laughing.

"You are nine years old, not nineteen, Viktor!" Charlotte mocked.

"You actually sound ridiculous," Rita added.

"One is never too old to begin their training. You would both do well to start thinking about how you are going to serve your country," Viktor preached from a pulpit he wasn't even tall enough to stand at. "I have already qualified to join the Youth movement."

"To do WHAT?" Charlotte said, having just about enough of his nonsense.

"To FIGHT! To DEFEND! To PRESERVE! And when I am old enough, I will throw the two of you into jail for your dissension," he sternly warned.

Both girls gave that a dramatic moment of thought and then

simultaneously laughed right in his face.

"Keeping dreaming of the day, Viktor, you are a big JOKE!" Charlotte mocked.

"Maybe it is because he knows that no girl will go anywhere near him - you have ZERO chance of having a wife, Viktor! Your heart is BLACK!" Rita scolded.

"Keeping laughing," Viktor said, folding his arms as he turned to watch the landscape.

"Keep your mouth shut, Viktor," Rita warned.

"Yes - it suits you better. Be more like Egon!" Charlotte teased.

"Like that COWARD? NEVER! He is weak! He will be trampled!" Viktor said, his face turning beet-red with anger.

"Did you see the poor people scatter through the train station?" Rita continued her conversation with Charlotte.

"I LOVE when they get away," Charlotte smiled.

"You love when who gets away, children?" Miss Kraus interrupted.

"Oh! We are just passing the time, don't mind our silliness!" Rita deflected. "Are we almost there?"

"Are you excited? Oh, children - you are all in for such a treat!" Miss Kraus said, happy to be their teacher and sort of part-time mother.

Most of the children on this trip had no parents and she was aiming to make it special for them.

"Make sure you have gathered all of your belongings. We won't have a lot of time to exit the train and it is important that you stay close together," she instructed.

"These girls know nothing about staying together," Viktor barked.

Both girls rolled their eyes and went back to chatting. Viktor was staring a hole into Egon, as he was an easy target. Egon did not stare back. He remained patient that this ride would soon end. He put his hands under his glasses and rubbed his eyes. He was not used to staying up late at night like this.

Upon exiting the train, each child stopped abruptly at the bottom of the steps causing other children behind them to bunch up.

"Keep moving along, children!" Miss Kraus said to them, their eyes as big as saucers.

What they saw was truly special. Tiergarten was magnificent. It was a lush forest with sidewalks crawling through the park and the Recreations' Department spared no expense at Christmas time. The smell of baked goods was greeting their train, and there was music playing, and glittering lights. The children's choir arrived in a separate car. They were like Olympians before the final competition. Many were jumping up and down squealing.

"We will all head through the Elephant Entrance. Stay in the group and always be aware of where I am," Miss Kraus said, waving both of her black gloves above her head.

"Look at me, Charlotte. I am an elephant!" Rita said, pinning her shoulder to her nose and swinging her arm like a trunk.

"Me too!" Charlotte mimicked.

The whole class thought this was funny and they all did it, waving their arms out in front like a celebrating herd.

"The Elephant Entrance was built in 1899. The two Asian elephants are carved from Sandstone -" Miss Kraus said, spinning around with joy, thrilled to be with her children.

The children's faces were twinkling with exuberance. Sadly, two of these little bulbs were not like the others. Viktor was a broken bulb. Well, no one was sure if Viktor ever had a light. Egon's bulb was dim and barely contributing to the festivities. He was stuck on the two elephants and wandered away from the group.

Egon looked at each elephant on either side of the gate. They were on their bellies when he first saw them - now they were standing up. He put his mittens up underneath his glasses and rubbed his eyes. They were both looking up at the sky. He turned to look around to see if anyone else was witnessing this, and when he looked back, they were stretched out on their bellies once again. Egon reached inside his coat and pulled out his writing pad and began to sketch.

"You would think you could do that at home," Viktor snarled.

Egon saw Charlotte and Rita and joined them. They knew how to put Viktor in his place if need be.

"Stand back off the road, children. The procession is about to begin!" Miss Kraus announced.

Egon tucked his face between Charlotte and Rita's shoulders, and felt temporarily safe from Viktor. The first thing everyone heard was the foot soldiers. Their heavy boots were crunching on the fresh snow, and in the distance, a marching band could be heard. The trombone and tuba were especially loud.

While parts of Tiergarten were sufficiently lit up, the road the children were standing on was quite dark. Still, visitors were lined up on either side of it expecting a parade.

Hundreds of men were marching and carrying torch lights chanting, SIEG HEIL! The crowd cheered them on - except for Charlotte and Rita who were clearly uncomfortable but trying to fit in. Viktor cheered the loudest, as expected.

"SIEG HEIL - to the Drillmeister and the Fatherland!" he yelled out, feeling powerful and vindicated.

Egon was stunned and added some notes to his book as Miss Kraus continued being their tour guide.

"This was a moment of valor," Miss Kraus explained. "After the hounds distracted the great bison, the hunter delivers the final blow! This monument was so well constructed, it will live on for multiple generations past your great grandchildren!"

"VALOR!" Viktor yelled from the back.

"Hmmmm - Yes. I do appreciate your enthusiasm, Viktor. Let's go see the next one, children!" Miss Kraus said with some concern.

Egon stood there as the children moved on. The hunter's spear was deep in the rib behind the front quarter. He couldn't stop staring at it. The hounds at the bottom of the statue were enthusiastically helping a hunter. He made sure the class was busy at the next statue and he took a few steps toward the bison. He looked into the eyes of one of the hounds, and the stone turned to glass just like the eagle at the train station. As he looked at the other hounds, their eyes were doing the same thing - they were coming to life, and the wild melted away into a relaxed state of humility. Each dog stepped away from the bison and collapsed on his belly staring at Egon. They seemed very ashamed of themselves.

The puncture hole where the spearhead stabbed began to bleed. Egon cautiously put his hand on the cement fur, and it felt warm.

The sound of Miss Kraus' voice jolted him back to reality when she said, "Egon - please stay with the class!"

After looking at her and then looking back, the statue had returned to its state, so he stepped away to join them. Just behind the statue in the thick of the bushes, was the snow-covered bison. It was staring at him, steam coming out of its nostrils.

"Egon! Now, please!" she added.

He reached inside his coat pocket again to pull out his notepad. He sketched a few things and then returned to the group.

The hunting theme continued as the children viewed other sculptures.

"This is what a hare-hunting party looked like," Miss Kraus began. "This was built in 1904 and as you can see, the dogs are plenty enthusiastic - and this one had to be held back by his collar because of his excitement!"

Egon stuck his fingers under his glasses and began to kick the snow as they walked.

"Why are we not viewing that sculpture over there, Miss Kraus?" Charlotte asked pointing at a statue with a male lion.

"There is only so much time - you could be here for days!" she said, dismissing it immediately.

"Let's go see it," Rita whispered. "If we are purposely avoiding it, it must have significance."

"I'm with you - are you coming with us, Egon?" Charlotte motioned to him.

The last thing Egon wanted to do was stay with Viktor by himself. The girls were his wolves and it was safer exploring with them.

Rita threw her hands up to her face and gasped. Charlotte's eyes filled with tears.

"That is simply horrible," Rita said, crossing her arms and fully disgusted.

"It is more than horrible. How can the same people who put up hunting sculptures be fine with this one too?" Charlotte said.

Egon stepped in closer to have a look. A male lion was standing over top of a dying lioness - an arrow impaling her. The look on his face was a husband in love swearing to stand by her side but promising to seek revenge if she passed. The look on her face was a mixture of defeat and shame but mostly pain.

Egon looked into her eyes and they came to life long enough to stare into his soul. She inhaled a deep breath and expanded her ribs in and out, then she exhaled, closed her eyes, and rested her head on the foot of her husband.

Egon put his lips on her paw but was met with the ferocious growl of the male.

As he stepped back, he noticed she had two cubs lying with her, and he respected the distance.

"Awwww, look at Egon kissing her paw - that is really sweet," Charlotte said.

"It's just a sculpture, Egon. For all we know, the lion killed the hunters, she got better, and they raised their cubs as a happy family," Rita added.

Egon reached inside his coat to sketch something down, and then returned it to his pocket.

"Egon, is that your book of big ideas?" Rita asked.

"They say that every famous artist or author has a book of ideas," Charlotte added. "If you're ever famous someday, your sketchbook will be famous too!"

Egon turned and trotted back to the group. When he got close to Viktor, he turned to see if the girls were coming along - and they were.

"I don't know if I can look at any more statues today," Rita said.

"Yes, I thought this was supposed to be Christmas. I sure hope this ends soon," Charlotte concurred.

"This bronze group on a boar hunt was presented to the German Emperor by the Berlin Tramway Company in 1904..." Miss Kraus began.

"Oh, make it stop!" Rita said to Charlotte, covering her ears and looking at the ground.

"I don't think this ever stops. Look there!" Charlotte said, pointing to Egon who had already moved on to the next sculpture.

He sat himself on the ground hugging his knees and looking up high. Several hounds were circling a hunter standing beside his horse. He had a horn on his coat and in his right hand, he was holding a dead fox high for the heavens to see.

"Why?" Rita said. "Why must we see this at Christmas?"

"Why must we see this at all?" Charlotte said back.

Egon reached forward and grabbed some snow off the bottom block holding the sculpture. As he put it in his mouth, a mother fox with a kit came out from behind the statue. They were not covered in fur. They were skeletons. It may seem unimaginable that a skeleton could have emotion, but it was clear that this was their husband and father held high above the hunter - and Egon couldn't do anything for them.

The curious Skelekit (which seems like an obvious name for it) wandered over to Egon and rubbed up against him like an affectionate house cat. Egon looked at the mother fox for approval and then ran his hand along its spine. The mother came over and touched his hand with her boney nose and then touched the forehead of the kit.

Egon waited for a moment and then she ran off, leaving the baby in his care. He thought if he got up and went back to the group, that the Skelekit would join its mother. Instead, it followed Egon.

"Why is he looking down beside him as he walks?" Rita asked.

"He is such a mysterious boy. I do feel the need to protect him, though," Charlotte said.

"Well, he'll never tell us!" Rita said. "You are right. We need to keep him safe from Viktor."

It was an awful lot of walking for children between the ages of eight and eleven. It was also getting late and past the bedtime of the little ones. The snowflakes along the Budapesterstraße were large and beautiful but the air was cold. The children were getting to the point where they weren't even chatting anymore, and the only sound was the snow crunching under their feet.

"My nostril hairs have icicles on them," Rita whispered to Charlotte who was about to respond but was interrupted by Egon running to the front of the group, ahead of Miss Kraus.

When he got there, he turned to face them, put both hands straight up in the air, motioning for them to stop in their tracks. The Skelekit followed him closely and sat by his foot.

"What is the matter, Egon?" Miss Kraus asked, putting her arm out to signal the children to wait.

Egon turned around and reached down.

"Oh!" Charlotte said. "I think he noticed something under the snow that was about to trip us!"

"Yes, I think there's a fallen tree branch," Viktor said, as though he was the man of the group. "This is no job for a skinny-armed little boy!"

When Viktor moved to the front of the line to take over, Egon fearlessly stepped forward, with square shoulders to block him.

"Egon got brave!" Charlotte said with delight.

"I believe Egon would like the opportunity to move the branch off our path, Viktor," Miss Kraus intervened. "Perhaps we should let him."

"Oh I would love to see this!" Viktor laughed. "Please! Everyone! Give the braaaaave soldier some space!"

Some of the children snickered, while others rolled their eyes at Viktor.

Egon grabbed a black pointy end and began to pull. There was a better chance of his arms breaking off at the shoulders than him clearing the path. Viktor saw a wide-open door to mock him.

"Oh, please Miss Kraus. Do let me assist the boy. It's ever so sad."

Egon faced Viktor again and stood his ground between him and the obstruction.

"Now, that is just sad," Viktor ridiculed. "Move, boy! Let a real man do this!"

"Viktor - be kind!" Miss Kraus said. "I am sure, we can all assist in clearing our pathway. Don't feel bad, Egon. You made a valiant attempt!"

"Just get out of the way, you -" Viktor began but was knocked clear off his feet.

The children laughed hysterically, while Miss Kraus broke a smile but then reverted quickly to help him.

"Wait - did Egon do that?" Rita asked to a confused Charlotte.

"I just slipped on some ice," Viktor assured everyone, but he looked around to see what could have done that.

Only Egon saw what knocked him off his feet. Wild skeleton boars began to dig the snow on the path and Egon quickly joined in. Even the young Skelekit did its best to dig. Once the object was dug out, the boars began to pull it off the path. Egon grabbed it a foot from the tip as the biggest boar had a grip on the end. Once it was moved off the path, the children all cheered.

"Egon dug the branch out and then pulled it all by himself!" Miss Kraus said, seeing it as a teaching opportunity. "Let's show him our appreciation!" and she began to clap.

Viktor folded his arms in a big huff and moved to the back of the group to blend in.

Egon went and sat under a tree, pinned his knees to his nose and rocked.

"Miss Kraus, I believe we embarrassed him," Rita said, sitting beside him.

"He doesn't have many friends," Charlotte said. "I don't doubt that he will be extra afraid of Viktor the Meany now!"

"Why don't the two of you sit with Egon until he feels better. I will take the group to the Aquarium," Miss Kraus suggested.

"I think this is an excellent idea," Charlotte responded. "We would be happy to."

As the class began to walk, Viktor furrowed his brow and put a fist up to Egon as he walked by. Both girls put their arms around Egon to warn Viktor. Once the class had left, Egon reached in his coat to pull out the book.

"Do you mind us watching? You can trust us. As you can see, we protect you!" Rita smiled.

Egon began drawing the shape of four crocodiles on the page.

"You ARE an artist!" Charlotte laughed! "Those look great!"

The Skelekit, who was only seen by Egon at this point, hopped through the snow and jumped up on top of the dead frozen crocodile Egon helped pull out.

"Wait, I think that big tree branch does resemble a crocodile. Is that what inspired you to draw your art?" Charlotte said.

"Oh, it does kind a look like a crocodile! You have quite an imagination, Egon!" Rita added.

They were good little Mamas.

"I think we better go join the group now," Charlotte suggested. "I would like to see the aquarium before we go home!"

"Me too," Rita said. "Shall we go now, Egon?"

Egon got up and the Skelekit danced around him all the way there.

"I want to thank you both for how you handled yourselves back there," Miss Kraus said to Charlotte as they entered the aquarium building.

The ceiling was mostly glass with multiple exhibits of creatures from yesteryears and yesterdays who **may have been beautiful once.**

"The group is inside! Come get warm!" she said, guiding them in.

"What are you looking at, Egon?" she asked, as he was looking down at the Skelekit.

Unwilling to answer, or ever speak, really, Egon hurried inside and the Skelekit remained at his feet. Miss Kraus smiled and closed the door behind them.

"There are tour guides who will show you the aquariums," Miss Kraus explained. "Egon - you, Charlotte and Rita can go to the left and join that group right there - I will be with this group on the right."

"Look, Egon! They are showing the alligators and crocodiles! You will like those!" Rita said, wrapping her arm around him and ushering him in.

Egon looked for Viktor and spotted him in Miss Kraus' group.

"Poor Viktor! Nobody to bully," Rita said, rubbing her eyes in a cry-baby motion to Viktor who frowned at her, and then moved on to see the fish.

"Look at the size of this croc, Egon!" Charlotte said.

Egon walked up to the enclosure and stared at him. The class moved ahead, and he stayed behind. He looked up at the arched glass ceiling at the snow falling and wandered outside. He began to walk around the building. The cement walls had engravings of various reptiles and he wiped away the snow off the face of a crocodile.

Overhead, vultures were circling. They were oversized like the one that broke the eagle's wing. Egon watched them form a circle around the middle of the roof. He took his notepad out and scribbled a few things.

"Egon! There you are," Rita called out. "Nobody knows you left! Come back in!"

Then, she saw the vultures flying.

"Oh! Did you see them through the glass ceiling? Do you suppose there's something they want?"

Egon kept watching them and writing.

"Are they - speaking to you, Egon?" Rita said, walking outside to get a better look. "Say, are you like an animal translator or something? Because you don't speak yourself and they don't speak..."

Egon just kept going.

"Egon, we really need to keep with the group, now. Please, come in," she asked gently.

Egon put his book bag into his coat and returned inside.

"We need to go now, children!" Miss Kraus said, clapping her hands. "It is getting late and we still have a train to catch!"

"We could spend days and days here," Charlotte said.

"Most certainly! We will come again someday!" Miss Kraus said, motioning for everyone to keep going.

It was another crunchy, quiet walk to the train.

"Jack, would you help me pass out cookies? The Children's Choir is going to sing a good night song for us before we go!"

The children arrived at the Elefantenpagode - The Pachyderm House. It resembled an Indian temple that probably wasn't an accurate replica, but an overexaggerated cultural misrepresentation. In the summer, the area outside the House was usually filled with tourists looking at the elephants. This Christmas, they were all inside except for one baby elephant and her trainer.

"Christmas Greetings from Odin!" he said, and the children all yelled, "Christmas Greetings, Odin!" back to the baby who was covered in Christmas ornaments and a wreath around its neck that looked too heavy for it.

"Odin loves to hear music! Shall we sing?" the trainer asked the Choir Director in their semi-rehearsed dialogue.

"What kind of treat did you get?" one child asked.

"A chocolate soldier!" another responded.

"Lucky you! Look at my wheel cookie!" a girl interjected.

"Oh here, I can trade you for my eagle," her friend offered.

"Where is your cookie?" one boy asked Egon.

Egon was looking at Odin and then down at his feet. The Skelekit had taken off towards the entrance of the Pachyderm House with his cookie.

The Choir began to sing,
"Silent night, Holy night,
All is calm, all is bright.
Only the Chancellor stays on guard
Germany's future to watch and to ward,
Guiding our nation aright."

Egon followed the Skelekit into the building and it wasn't long before they saw an angry elephant inside who was clearly missing its baby. It was pacing back-and-forth in its pen. It was running its tusk along the bars which was upsetting the other elephants. Egon was cringing and blinking at the volume of the sound, but he approached the cage, dropped his head down and slowly extended his hand towards the bars. The elephant let out a big trumpet and walked over to Egon who didn't look up, but felt the trunk touch his hand for a moment. Then, the big male walked away. When he looked up, all the elephants in their enclosures were calm. The large male picked up a carrot off the floor and brought it over to Egon. They stood for a few moments looking at one another and then he accepted the gift. The elephant waited patiently for Egon to do something with it. He finally raised it to his mouth and took a bite. As soon as he did this, he dropped it on the floor and ran out of the House. The Skelekit retrieved the carrot and ran after him.

"Are you alright, Egon?" Rita asked.

"Yes - you look as though you saw a ghost!" Charlotte added.

Egon rubbed his eyes and ran back towards the train.

"May we, Miss Kraus?" Rita asked.

"He is not having a good night, please go with him. We are going to wrap up the festivities, anyways," she said.

"Before you leave, children, we have a Christmas ornament for each of you," a soldier said.

"This has been the best night ever!" a young girl shouted.

"I am so happy that you had a nice visit," the soldier responded.

"I plan on helping the Youth," Viktor said, standing tall.

"Very proud of you -"

"My name is Viktor Emmanuel Voigt!" Viktor replied.

"I look forward to training you, Viktor Voigt!" the soldier said.

He handed out ornaments which were not usual Christmas angels and snowmen. These were Panzer tanks, zeppelins, soldiers, and the power-spider from the flag.

When a soldier tried to hand one to Egon, he rejected it.

The soldier bent down close and said, "Please take it, it is a gift."

Egon did nothing.

"This ornament is an exact replica of the latest Panzer tank in our army. You should be proud and most certainly lucky to have one of your own," he said.

He still did nothing, so the soldier abruptly grabbed Egon's chin and raised it.

"You will keep your chin UP. You will keep your shoulders SQUARE and never SLOUCH," he warned.

Egon continued to look at the ground.

"CHIN UP, I SAID!" he warned again, and squeezed Egon's mouth.

Egon responded by biting his hand so hard that he locked onto it. The soldier grabbed him by his coat at the back of his neck and pushed him into the bush. The children heard a lot of scolding and a hard slap.

When they returned a few minutes later, Egon was holding the side of his face. Rita and Charlotte ran up to him to console him.

"DO NOT make him weak!" the soldier yelled, instantly killing the festivities. "War IS coming children. You need to learn to be grateful for our protection. We are teaching you invaluable lessons that will save you from the enemy. Your teacher extended kindness to you as she knows most of you do not have parents. Be grateful to her as well," he lectured, and then he stormed off.

"Can we go now?" Rita asked Miss Kraus.

"Yes," she sighed. "Please board the train."

Charlotte and Rita bookended Egon on the train and burned a hole into Viktor.

"Listen, children..." Viktor began. "These are important times for the Fatherland. We had an opportunity tonight to celebrate what makes us so great. And your childish acts ruined it."

"Viktor," Charlotte began. "Shut your mouth."

"Yes," Rita supported her. "We just had our share of lecturing."

"And don't call us children. You are nine years old!" Charlotte added.

"CHILDREN!" Miss Kraus snapped but tried to quickly calm her impatience. "I do not mean to be irritable," she said, sitting with them. "The soldier is correct. War is coming. We wanted to give you something lovely tonight but as you know, we must move all of you out of the city. It breaks my heart so much," she said, fighting back tears. "Egon, I know you have become good friends with Charlotte and Rita. But considering what just happened, I think I need you to come home with me tonight, and we will talk tomorrow about what to do with you."

"Oh, please!" Rita pleaded. "We can watch over him."

"It isn't a debate, girls. We will be at the train station shortly. We will meet your guardian there and they will accompany you outside of the city where you will be ever so safe," she said, having to get up and leave so they wouldn't see her cry.

They all stared blankly, even Viktor.

Rita looked at Charlotte, "When we step off this train, do not let go of my hand."

"Glad you said it - don't let go of mine," Charlotte said.

Egon looked really lost.

"It is only temporary, Egon," Rita said, trying to console. "You get to go with Miss Kraus. Hold her hand, alright?"

That was a problem for Egon. Handholding was not his thing.

Viktor really tried to cover his fear with meanness.

"I would stay in the city and fight if they'd let me - but YOU, Egon? YOU are going to DIE!"

Charlotte had enough and gave him a swift kick to the chin.

"Go ahead and tattle! I will tell her what you said!" Charlotte urged.

Viktor responded back with a stiff upper lip, "I am a man - I can take it!"

"You are a cowardly little boy!" Rita said with her arm around Egon.

The Skelekit tagged along without anyone seeing, and had nestled into Egon's feet, where it curled up like a dog with its owner. It seemed to transition from its Mama to Egon nicely.

Perhaps that Mother fox wanted her baby kept safe too. It was neither a criminal nor an alien. This little skeleton baby was a stowaway at this point. The good news was that only Egon saw it and it felt safe for the time being – and it went to sleep.

3 THE CHICKEN THAT FELL DOWN THE CHIMNEY

"Will we ever return to the Blisse?" Rita asked Miss Kraus.

The Blisse was what the children called The Blissestift, the children's home in Wilmersdorf where they felt like prisoners most of their lives, except for when they were with Miss Kraus at school or on special nights like this.

"I didn't think you would ever want to return there," Miss Kraus joked with her.

"It isn't my favourite place, but I don't understand where we are going," Rita said concerned.

"If we are going to this place where you promised our safety, why were you crying?" Charlotte interjected. "Do you know that we will be safe? What about you? Will you be safe?"

"Of course! I am young! I can move quickly! It isn't so easy moving children!" she laughed, trying to keep the spirits high.

"I would like to personally keep you safe, but that isn't possible, I know," added Viktor, whose cowardice was on full display for the whole class.

"Oh Viktor – will you write to her every day?" one child teased.

"Perhaps you can take her handkerchief and keep it in your pocket!" another poked fun.

All the children laughed as Viktor fumed with embarrassment and rage.

"It would seem to me," Charlotte said. "That Egon is deemed the strong one – who will stay in the city with Miss Kraus. Oh, dear Viktor. That medicine has to be so bitter to swallow."

Viktor stormed onto the train as the children continued to laugh at him.

Miss Kraus couldn't help but snicker, but gave a couple quick claps and said, "Everyone into your new seats. Your train is heading out shortly."

"For a little boy who wandered off all evening, you have been very good about standing in one place," Miss Kraus smiled at Egon.

He should not have been given so much credit for staying. The Skelekit was sitting on the top of his shoe, trying hard to catch a few winks where it could between the disarray. Egon was simply letting it sleep.

Miss Kraus stood in one place and regrouped. She took a deep breath in and exhaled.

"I guess we go now, Egon. I am sorry to have divided you from your friends. I'm not certain that you would get to stay with Rita and Charlotte. I don't even know if they will stay together yet. We will go back to my apartment for a sleep and figure out next steps tomorrow. You may not understand this now, but the fact that you do not speak works against you. I cannot just send you off like that."

Egon was more concerned about the little stowaway on his shoe. It was good nobody else saw it – and really – how can one hurt something that is already seemingly dead? Still, the baby's Mama entrusted the Kit to him, and he took this responsibility seriously. So, he scooped it up, still curled in its ball, and tucked it inside his coat to keep it warm from the crisp air.

"My apartment isn't far from the station," she said. "I know you walked a lot tonight, but it is only five or six minutes to get there. It will be a good way to wind our brains down."

Egon kept his face down and stayed close to her.

"I normally love my walk home from the train. It is my time to reflect on the day and think about how I will plan the class for the next day. You can see all the shops and stores I see along the way."

Egon spent the walk trying to keep the Skelekit warm in his coat.

"Here we are," she said, stopping at a door between a bakery and a dressmaker. "It is never smart to put a woman between food and clothes like this. My whole paycheck is spent before I ever get it."

Egon looked in the display window that had fresh buns and bread.

"Are you hungry? I will get you something when we get upstairs!" she said, unlocking the door.

As they entered, a friendly orange cat came to greet them.

"That is Miezekatze. When you live alone, they make great company."

The cat came over to Egon and rubbed against his leg. Then it stretched up to sniff his coat and hissed.

"He never does that!" she said, surprised. "Of course, it isn't often I have company."

Egon held the Skelekit closer.

"Take off your coat. I will try to find you something you can wear to bed tonight. I have a bunch of clothes I gathered for the orphanage. I am sure I can find you something. I have some soup I can heat up for you. Would you like that? Make yourself at home."

As she went to the kitchen, Egon tried his best to keep the cat off the Skelekit. He tucked himself into the corner of the couch and waited.

"Ok, come into the kitchen!" she said, putting some bread on the table. "The soup is warming."

Egon stared at the bread. They didn't have anything like that at the children's home.

"That is from the bakery downstairs! Go ahead!"

Egon took it and smelled it for a time.

"That smell is the smell of home, isn't it? I wish I knew more about your home, Egon. I am sure your parents loved you. I hate that they were taken from you so young. Life isn't very fair, is it?"

He began to eat the bread.

"I think the soup is warm enough," she said, setting it on the table.

He kept eating the bread and ignored that. He rubbed his eyes and yawned.

"I have many nights at the end of a long day where I have to decide if I am more tired than hungry," she smiled. "Now, I only have one bedroom, so the sofa is yours tonight. You can use the bathroom to get changed – it's over there. Let me go find you something."

She returned a few minutes later with some oversized pajamas meant for a boy a few years older.

"They are big but clean and certainly comfortable for sleeping. I have a knitted blanket on the sofa, and you can use the other pillow off my bed. I do have an extra toothbrush."

About ten minutes later, Egon came out of the bathroom with his cap still on, the pajamas dragging way past the toes on his socks, and his coat on. He was still nestling the Skelekit.

"If your coat makes you comfortable, that is fine. You can set your hat on the end table."

Egon seemed happy to get under the blanket and have his head on a decent pillow.

"Sleep well, little man. I hope you are not too lonely. Come get me at any hour of the night. Things may seem complicated for you. Never forget that nature too goes through violent shifts to maintain balance. Adults have much to sort out. **It all used to be beautiful once**. Our class will be reunited again. You will see Charlotte and Rita. I never knew how much I loved all of you until tonight. You are truly my world - every single one of you."

She kissed him on his forehead and clicked out the lamp. The cat sat on an ottoman and stared at Egon with its tail snapping for a time until Miss Kraus called him into her room. Egon seemed pleased by that, held the Skelekit close and eventually fell asleep.

In the morning, Egon woke up to the smell of breakfast cooking and he stretched.

"You sure sleep heavy. I have been awake for hours! I thought you might sleep all day! It doesn't seem to matter what time I go to bed; the sun still greets me at six am," she said in a perkier tone than what he was able to handle.

"I have sausage and eggs – come eat!"

The Skelekit decided to venture out of his coat at some point in the night.

"Aren't you hot in that thing?" she asked.

He realized he didn't need to have it on now and so he removed it and hung it on the back of his chair.

"I have been on the telephone with a few people this morning. As much as I would like you to stay here, my days are going to change. They are using the Christmas Holidays as a time to sort out where the children without parents will go to be safe. They would like me to come for a different type of training. Germany needs extra help right now. We found a family in the country to take you," she said, a bit disappointed.

Egon looked up at her when she said that.

"You only know the city! The country is very peaceful. You are a peaceful soul, Egon. I think it will suit you perfectly. The man I spoke with knows you have perfect mathematical skills. I think he took a keen interest in that as well. He too is a mathematical wizard. I suspect he will be a good mentor for you with some of his projects. Your talent shouldn't be wasted in an orphanage."

That was too much to process and he stared at the bread in the bowl on the table.

"Isn't it the best bread on the planet? I am so fortunate to have access to the bakery like this. Help yourself. But please, eat some of the other food too. You have a big day ahead of you!"

Egon just ate the bread. It was nothing like the terrible slop thrown into his bowl at the children's home meal after meal. Once he was done, he raised his hand.

"You have never done that in class! That is hilarious. You don't need to do that here. But yes, you may be excused," she smiled.

Egon got up and went to the bathroom to change back into his clothes. When he came out, he handed her the pajamas perfectly folded.

"That is lovely! Thank you, Egon! You are a fine boy! I think we had a lovely stay. Wouldn't you say?"

As Egon bent down to tie his shoe, he saw the Skelekit under the sofa hiding. It saw Egon and came out and jumped into his arms.

"Did you see the cat under there? It has gone into hiding since you arrived. That was the first night it slept under my blankets!"

Egon tucked the Kit back in his coat and followed her out the door.

At the bottom of the apartment stairs, a car was waiting for them. A man jumped out of the driver's seat and ran around to open the door for them.

"Hello, Henry," she said. "This is Egon who I told you about. We appreciate the drive! I take public transit everywhere, Egon - so I don't have a car. Henry offered to drive us."

"I am more than happy to do it!" Henry said. "We are all doing whatever we can for the children. It is a time to show our kindest selves, wouldn't you say?"

"I absolutely agree," she said, a little bit flirty.

"Hop in wherever you like!" he said.

"I will ride in the back with Egon – I think that would keep him at ease," she responded.

"Does he have a suitcase?" Henry asked, looking around.

"No, he has nothing. I put together a small bag with a few

items I had – but it isn't much. Irene said she has some things for him from another boy who was there. I think we are all doing what we can."

"I practice gratitude every morning," Henry said, closing the back door of the car for them.

"That is a healthy attitude!" Miss Kraus smiled.

"If you force it a few times, it eventually sticks!" he laughed.

"That is too true!" she laughed back. "We have plenty to be grateful for, right, Egon? Like bakery bread!"

"Ah! You tried Becker's Breads? Their donuts are out of this world too!" Henry said with delight.

"Oh chocolate anything is divine!" she added.

Egon shoved himself as tightly into the corner as possible and gazed out the window as the city buildings began to disappear.

"How long is the drive?" Miss Kraus asked.

"Around half an hour or so - not too far," Henry added.

"I never get to be in a car. We can just enjoy the sights, Egon!" she said, watching the scenery.

"You should get out and try new things!" Henry suggested.

"I think it is hard to do in these times," she said, a bit deflated.

"Fear is useless," Henry said. "Action has to happen from a place of calm. Like today! You are doing something positive!"

"Your kindness is a lighthouse in the current storm of anger,

Henry!"

"The storm can't stop us from flying. I believe we are called to a greater purpose during uncertain times," Henry reassured.

"Don't compromise your character, my friend. It is really all you have control of keeping!" she said, looking out at the snow falling.

If Egon's job was to be a statue for a whole ride, he accomplished that. He didn't flinch a muscle until their arrival.

"Here we are!" Henry announced.

"Oh, this can't be right. Mr. Swartz said 39 Tiefer Bach Road," she said, checking her paper.

"The sign says exactly that! This is it," Henry pointed out.

"But this seems – are you sure? Maybe I wrote it down incorrectly."

"When you said Mr. Swartz was impressed with Egon's grades – and then you told me the address – well, I figured you knew what you were doing..." Henry said, a bit lost.

"But he is supposed to be staying with Irene. Maybe drive up to the front gate and we will ask," she said.

"Good idea," Henry obliged.

The black iron gate sat between cement pillars which were attached to hundreds of feet of stone walls. Above the walls were barbed wires.

"Let's ask this soldier. He at least must know the area and can

Egon as she picked up the bag the soldier dropped in the snow.

Egon just looked at it.

"Oh – I forgot. You don't speak. So much for them sending me some useful company! We'll make do," she said, taking off her coat and hanging it up. "Come get warm by the fire."

Egon's eyes were in the rafters. The whole house was made of logs and it smelled like a burnt piece of toast. There was a stack of cut wood near the fireplace, and it looked to be a full-time job feeding the flames.

"I am Irene," she began. "Eugen is in the barn with the pigs and chickens. You might as well know, we both live here, but we are not married. I don't even like him."

Egon was more interested in the hound dog sleeping by the fire.

"I can tell you that, because who are you going to tell?" she laughed. "Oh, that is Aldo. If you wake up one night and he's dead, it is because he is over one hundred in dog years. He has been everywhere with me. I suppose it is good of the High Command to let me keep him. We have lived in eight places in four years, but we have been here this full year."

Egon looked at the sofa.

"Oh, sit wherever you like. I don't even know what to do with you. That is up to Eugen and Swartz," she said walking to the kitchen which was part of the open space. "Would you like a snack? It's a bit early for lunch."

Egon sat on the sofa and the Skelekit jumped onto his lap. Aldo, the hound dog, shot his head up, got up with audible bones cracking, and came over to Egon for a sniff.

"Well thank you, guard dog," Irene snickered. "Egon has been here for four whole minutes and stolen everything we own."

The Skelekit hid inside Ian's coat as Aldo sat with his head in Egon's lap.

"Well, someone made a friend. That's nice," she said, tying a kerchief around her short brown curls.

Hound dogs can look sad at the best of times, and this old dog was a depressed soul. Egon grabbed a long ear in each hand and stroked downwards. He seemed to like that.

"So I understand you are good at Mathematics?" Irene asked, putting a plate of carrot sticks in front of him. "I had perfect grades in Math my whole life. Eugen too. He is a horrible man, but a mastermind. Go ahead and eat."

Egon was perplexed looking at the carrots.

"Oh, you are a city boy. Oh – and from the orphanage. That's right. There are no vegetables there. I grow these on the farm. I will show you the cold cellar sometime. The carrots, potatoes and onions are all down there. Go on, take one," she said getting up to put a kettle on.

Egon took one and gave it to Aldo who took it back to the fireplace and put his head on it. On the sofa beside him, he noticed a ball of yarn and some knitting needles.

"I didn't put those there, they did. They said it makes the place look home-y," she shrugged. "The same with the horse puzzle on the table, the throw blankets, the pictures of family on the walls. I don't know those people. Today, they dropped off that akkordion – with no explanation. I don't play. Props!"

Egon sat there doing nothing.

"Well, you are a quiet, seemingly well-behaved boy. This shouldn't be too bad. You don't like the carrots? Your taste buds were most likely ruined by the orphanage. They just toss you bread and porridge, right? Maybe barley soup if you are fortunate? I wanted to make some fruitcake back in the Fall. You must make it a few months before Christmas for it to be moist enough. I did it with my Mama growing up. I asked for those supplies then. Every day I see the soldiers, I ask them for something. As you heard – they always say tomorrow. If Eugen asks for supplies, they get it to him the same day. I am basically invisible."

Egon's eyes were fixed on the akkordion case.

"Oh – maybe that is for you – do you play – hmmmm, it does look children's size now that I look at it. Do you want to have a look?"

Irene brought the case over to him, opened it up, pulled it out from under a red velvet cloth and put it on Egon's lap.

"Hohner! It is a beauty! Here, put the straps on," she said dressing him like a doll. "If you do play, I would love to hear it. I am starved for entertainment here."

While it was Egon's size and did fit him perfectly, he didn't play it.

"That is yours for sure! Well, we just met – why would you play for me? I will haul it up to your room. You might as well give it a go. Nobody else is going to touch it."

Egon took an opportunity to stuff some carrots in his pockets.

"You don't have to hoard food here – we eat well," Irene said. "I suppose we need to go tell Eugen that you have arrived. When you go into the barn, check first for flying tools. I had a monkey wrench nearly hit my head."

With that, Egon took a step behind her and the Skelekit took a step behind him and they headed out to the barn.

As predicted, they could hear many tools being tossed and a whole lot of yelling.

"Just wait here – I will tell him you are here," she warned.

Egon looked around. From the outside, it appeared as a typical barn constructed from grey wood boards and a steel roof on top. The floor in the area where he was standing was a combination of straw and dirt, much like you would see from any farmer tracking mud in and out. The smell was strong and was a combination of chicken and pig. He was shivering from the wind blowing between the slats.

"The majority of that time was waiting for the right time to even say something," Irene said, returning after several minutes. "If I was married to him, I would have divorced him – and then I would marry him again – just so I could divorce him again. Come on in."

That seemed like an awful energy going in, and Egon wasn't quick to move.

"It doesn't get better – just view it as a challenge. Head on in," she said with her hand on his back.

Egon walked in very slowly with the Skelekit on his heels. While the inside was certainly insulated, and it seemed Eugen had everything he needed to work, it was chaotic. Every inch of wall had a tool of some kind hanging from it, and there were steel shards blanketing the floor like sawdust. The middle of the room had a workstation that was at least twenty feet in length and there was a mass of metal that looked more like a Frankenstein creation than something for the farm.

"This will be the death of me – or of someone else!" Eugen exclaimed, as he began to pace around the room.

Egon looked at him and then took a walk around the massive table.

"It all *technically* makes sense, Irene! Look here – look at the plans. We went through this so many times!" he screamed with lava shooting out of his ears.

"It isn't a good start to scare a child, Eugen."

"Do I LOOK like I CARE about a CHILD right now? If this doesn't work in even a model capacity tomorrow, we will all be hiding in fear!" Eugen said, pacing frantically.

Egon continued to walk around it. As he reached inside a mass of bolts and wires, Irene stepped forward, "Oh please, Egon – don't touch anything!"

"He can't hurt it – it is going to be scrapped," Eugen flung his hands up in defeat and slunk into a big, dirty chair.

Egon reached further in and fiddled with some wires. He grabbed a wire and touched it to something causing a spark, then a zap.

"What did you do?" Eugen jumped up from his chair.

"You said he couldn't hurt it!" Irene reminded him.

"No. WHAT DID YOU DO?" Eugen said again.

Egon showed him where he reconnected wires and rerouted them to new places.

"How do you do that? I have been trying to figure that out for days!" Eugen said, quite elated.

Egon went over to the chair and sat down, while Eugen grabbed his welding mask and continued to reroute.

"Well, how does it feel having a child that is smarter than you come in and fix your mess?" Irene taunted.

"He did nothing extraordinary. And you will NOT mention this to Swartz when he arrives tomorrow," Eugen said, suddenly embarrassed and fearful.

"Swartz is the one who sent Egon!" Irene giggled. "Oh – now, that is rich!"

"Well that is just grand! So they already believe I am underperforming? So much that they send a child? You stay clear of me, child!" Eugen warned.

"His name is Egon – you were just grateful to him a minute ago! He isn't going anywhere - unless you would like to confront Swartz!" Irene barked back.

"Get him out of here," Eugen said, putting his welding mask down and lighting the torch.

"That was a very good start, don't you think, Egon?" Irene said, guiding him out, suddenly loving that she had someone to help her get under Eugen's skin. "We should be good friends!"

The Skelekit suddenly went down into a hunting stance when it saw a black chicken walk in front of them.

Egon stopped to look at it. It was super friendly with some long gorgeous black feathers that looked a bit blue from the light hitting them.

"We call it Soot. She is the chicken that fell down the chimney! The white ones have beat her up and taken many of her feathers. **She used to be beautiful once**. She believes she is a human now. She gets very nosey and wants to be in the middle of everything," Irene laughed.

Soot stormed straight at the Skelekit who was too small to take on something twice its size.

"Soot, let Egon be. He just got stormed by Eugen. It is too early in the day for your nonsense," Irene said, heading back to the house.

Egon stood and stared at Soot.

"Feel free to wander around and get to know the place. I ring a bell at lunch and dinner – even though Eugen ignores me," she said, walking into the house. "Oh and I can see why Swartz wanted you here," she turned to say. "That is quite a talent you have! Don't mind Eugen's ego. He will just take some getting used to."

Egon began to kick through the snow with no real place to go. He had never been given this kind of freedom and he was terrible at using it. The Skelekit jumped and played in the snow and Egon just watched him. Soot walked in front of Egon every time he took a step. Irene was right that she wanted to be right in the middle of everything. It was endearing at first, but it soon proved to be quite unproductive! Every direction Egon tried to go, Soot was under his feet. It wasn't until he headed towards the chicken shed that Soot let him walk. It was odd that he was corralled there, as it was a place of fear for Soot.

He opened the latch and walked in. The inside of the shed was only five chickens across and maybe fifteen chickens deep. The clucky birds were all white as Irene said, and were either pecking at the floor or at their water feeders. He looked back out at Soot in the snow who seemed like a poor kid trying to catch a glimpse of rich kids by the pool.

At the back of the shed was a handle on the floor which the Skelekit was scratching at. It was covered in bits of straw and manure. Egon kicked it sort of clean and then grabbed the handle with his mitten. Soot had jumped up on boxes to see in the window and was sort of cheering him on.

The main shed door flung open and there was Irene.

"I saw Soot by himself outside the shed, so I figured you were in here. It is just a chicken shed, Egon. Nothing special," she said. "I've come to tell you Mr. Swartz will be coming for lunch today, not tomorrow. Nothing is ready for his arrival. Can you come inside now?"

Egon abandoned the handle and walked quickly past her and back outside.

"They expect us to be dressed properly and have a proper greeting. I need to set the table accordingly too," she said, rather flustered. "Please do help me with this. We cannot anger them."

It was clear people here were prisoners just like Egon's Wilmersdorf home at The Blissestift Orphanage – even if they were wandering free like Soot, they were not leading their best life.

4 THE ABBOARDION'S BELLOWS

It looked like Soot had a wee crush on Egon and she followed him back to the house. The Skelekit kept rushing her like a jealous girlfriend which made Soot cluck and jump all over the place.

"How did you get so skittish? You are behaving oddly around Egon," Irene laughed. "No-no - you aren't coming in!"

Soot always tried to get past Irene.

"She's determined! Eugen would lose his mind if he saw a chicken in the house. We won't have her. The chickens won't have her. I am shocked she is not dinner at this point. Someday, I suppose her time will be up!" Irene shrugged as Egon stopped and stared at her.

"Oh - you like her?" Irene said, folding her arms. "Well, if you would like to keep her alive, I would suggest you keep her away from Eugen's work - and his feet!"

Soot listened in as if she understood. Her head tilted left and right.

"You know what you can do to help me? Grab that shovel and

clean the snow off the steps and front porch before Mr. Swartz arrives," Irene said, before scurrying inside.

Egon just stared at the shovel. He had never used one in his life. Still, he grabbed it and pushed it around to move the snow. The Skelekit thought this was great fun and chased the scoop, which caused Soot to join in. She couldn't fly like other birds in the sky, but if she flapped her wings enough, she could get up several feet at a time. She got herself up to the shovel's handle and Egon let her stay on. It seemed like she had perched for her first time ever next to a friend. He held the handle close to his chest so she could lean on him. Her eyelids closed upwards instead of down, and Egon watched in fascination. He stroked the feathers between her eyes, and she started to doze.

She was almost completely asleep until Irene yelled out the front door, "Egon, can you come help – oh no, you haven't shoveled! We are so far behind!" and she came barreling down the stairs as Soot flew off the handle – just like Irene was about to.

"Give it to me – you go inside, take your boots off and set them neatly to one side. Hang your coat on the coat tree and then go wash your face and hands. I will be right there," and she shoveled snow madly.

So far, nobody noticed the Skelekit except for other animals. Hanging up a coat was an easy task, so he took it off and hung it up. He set his boots nicely to one side and headed to the bathroom.

It wasn't a large space – just enough room for a tub, toilet, and sink. There was a pile of books beside the toilet and he stacked them up to get a look inside the medicine cabinet behind the mirror. Irene didn't wear any make-up, so there was nothing for her in there. It seemed to be taken over by Eugen and his shaving supplies.

He grabbed the shaving brush and swept it across his face. He then took a tube of shaving soap and squeezed it onto his hands, and then put it on his cheeks. Egon was at an age where most boys would watch their daddy shave, but there was no father to show him.

In the other room, Irene could be heard welcoming some visitors.

"I hope you don't mind the mess. Our concentration has been on the project. Had I known you were coming, I would have increased the effort to -"

"Please don't," a man's voice interrupted. "It shouldn't matter who shows up here. It should always appear you are a devoted housewife. Where is Eugen?"

"His priority has been on the project. He is in the big barn," she said nervously.

"Go get him," the man instructed another soldier. "Now, where is Egon?"

"He is washing up for lunch," she said. "I will tell him you are here."

She knocked on the bathroom door.

"Egon, Mr. Swartz is here. Can you come out now?" she said to no response. "Uh – I am coming in – ok?"

When she went in there, Egon had shaving cream on his *entire* face.

"Oh! No! Egon – that isn't soap. Oh – hold on, I will grab a towel!"

With one swoop, she smeared all of it off, removed his hat and tried to brush through the dirty blonde mess.

"That will have to do. Let me adjust your shirt," she said, quickly ushering him out the door.

Down below, the Skelekit rubbed cream off her nose and followed Egon out just before Irene closed the door.

"Here he is! Such a handsome boy!" Irene said, awkwardly.

"Come here, Egon," Mr. Swartz said.

Irene pushed him forward. "Go on," she said.

Egon sheepishly walked towards him and the Skelekit hid under a chair.

"Do you know why you are here? I will take your silence as a yes. You are very safe here. Do you know this? Did your akkordion arrive?" he said holding Egon's chin in his hand. "You smell of shaving soap! You wanted to try?"

"It won't happen again, Sir. Yes, his akkordion is in his room," Irene answered for him.

"SILENCE, WOMAN!" Mr. Swartz blew up. "DID I ASK YOU?"

Mr. Swartz was Oberkommando of the Army. He stood head

and shoulders over everyone else and was plenty intimidating.

"It's just that he doesn't speak, Sir. He is a mute," Irene said.

He took a few steps into her face.

"You are now educating me on the child that I sent here. Laughable," he mocked. "Go to the kitchen and prepare our lunch."

"Yes, Sir," Irene said, and fluttered away.

"Just because you do not speak, Egon, does not mean I will disrespect your intellect. You understand everything going on around you. You did not achieve your grades in school by not recognizing the teacher's expectations of you," he smiled. "Now, my interest in you is not that you accomplished what was asked of you, but that you were achieving things which were not asked of you. This is of great interest to me. Did you know that even Miss Kraus did not understand your calculations? Yes! This is true!"

Egon was distracted by the Skelekit under the chair.

"Eugen and Irene are a pair of toads," he whispered. "They are currently the smartest toads we have. You can learn from them, but they will learn from you as well. Just ignore their quirks. They would be destroyed if harm ever came to you - so, they are no threat. They are simply an annoyance."

Eugen came rushing in, sweating and dirty.

"Why is everything so chaotic with you, Eugen?" Mr. Swartz sighed.

"We have had a breakthrough today," he started to say, but Mr. Swartz had no patience.

"Come eat, Eugen. I am sure our guests are famished," Irene said, trying to keep things moving along.

"Come sit next to me, Egon," Mr. Swartz said, directing him to a chair.

Eugen grabbed a chair to sit.

"Irene, do you always invite the swine to the table? Go wash up!" Mr. Swartz snapped.

Eugen hurried off to the bathroom.

"The breakthrough came because of Egon," Irene whispered. "Eugen was frustrated. Egon sorted it out within two minutes of his arrival."

"Is that a fact? I was not wrong about you, my boy! Irene, I will be taking Egon with me this afternoon, after you eat of course – the Doctor has asked to see him. Please retrieve his akkordion," Mr. Swartz instructed.

"Yes, of course," Irene said, jumping up.

"After lunch," he replied, and she sat back down.

"My apologies for the delay," Eugen said, joining them.

"Shall I say grace?" Mr. Swartz asked.

"That would be lovely," Irene answered.

"God nourish our bodies and protect the Drillmeister as he

leads us into victory...Amen. Let us eat!" Mr. Swartz said. "An update, Eugen."

"Like I mentioned earlier, Sir. I had a breakthrough today. It was rerouting some wires. That did the trick. I believe we are well on our way," Eugen lied.

"You rerouted some wires?" Mr. Swartz asked, lifting soup to his mouth.

"Yes, uh, a simple adjustment really," Eugen stammered.

"Wow. Your intellect has no bounds!" Mr. Swartz baited him.

"Thank you, Sir," Eugen said, looking down at his soup.

"It would seem you don't require help from the boy, then."

"He is welcome to stay here – for safety and all – I don't require his help," Eugen said, grabbing bread and not looking at him.

"You know, Eugen. You could at least look me directly in my eye when you lie to me," Mr. Swartz said, very calmly.

Eugen's hand began to shake.

"I would never lie to you," Eugen lied again.

Irene jumped up and said, "I will get more bread."

"You will SIT DOWN, WOMAN!" Mr. Swartz fumed. "Take Eugen outside," he instructed the soldier at the door. "Eugen requires some clarification on the truth, and we do not need our lunch disturbed."

"No wait, I swear – I would not lie to you – please, Sir," Eugen stammered, trying to save himself as the soldier removed him.

"Would you like some bread, Egon? You don't seem to want the soup," Mr. Swartz said.

Egon took the bread and began to eat.

"Children from orphanages are not going to eat fancy food. They don't know any different," he said, patting Egon on the back. "He is starving. Pay attention to his needs."

"I will do better, Sir," Irene said, continuing to eat her soup.

The cries from Eugen outside were hard to ignore, but Mr. Swartz was a master at it.

"Like I said, the Drillmeister wishes to see you. We want you to join the Reichsmusikkammer. It is a children's music group, Egon. Music feeds intellect. It will be good for you."

"That sounds wonderful," Irene gushed.

"I hate to cut our lunch short, but now would be a good time to retrieve his akkordion. I do not wish for Egon to suffer any more of the negativity Eugen is exhibiting today. I trust he will be better when we return later?" Mr. Swartz said, handing that responsibility to Irene.

"He will be aligned by then, I am sure," Irene said, going to get the akkordion.

"Wonderful!" Mr. Swartz clapped. "I do appreciate alignment."

Eugen entered after taking a brutal beatdown.

"Go to the bathroom and clean up. We are finished lunch," Mr. Swartz said. "I will return again later today. I will be looking for improvement and truth. Can you handle this?"

"Yes, Sir," Eugen said.

"Perfect!" he clapped again. "Shall we go, Egon?"

"Here you are, Egon," Irene said, handing him the case. "Let me grab your coat and boots."

"Let me ask you, Irene. Do you think a nine-year-old boy who just fixed Eugen's mess requires you to retrieve his coat and boots for him?"

"No, Sir," she said.

Egon marched over and put on his coat and boots quickly. The Skelekit retrieved his hat from the bathroom and Egon put it on.

"And a bonus hat! Well done! A little respect goes a long way," he boasted. "Shall we?"

The Skelekit ran alongside as Mr. Swartz ushered him out.

"Oh and Irene," he said on the way out the door. "Please make sure the soup is hot next time. It is winter."

"Will do, Sir," she said.

Egon seemed happy enough to get out of there and he gladly jumped in the car to go anywhere. The Skelekit made it in before the door closed. It was about a fifteen-minute drive north to the music school. The roads were slippery, but not busy due to everyone being home for the holidays.

"You must feel a bit lost," Swartz said, sitting beside him in the back seat of their car. "You have some exceptional abilities, I understand."

Egon stared out at the big snowflakes hitting his window.

"Mathematics. Geometry. I liked both of those in school. No two snowflakes are alike – but each one is perfectly created. Even if they look different, they are still the same colour. They accumulate with the same substance. Do you notice when rain is introduced? The snow melts and loses its beauty. People are like this too. The rain wants to melt us. We must keep the snow pure, Egon. We must protect this. I am excited that you are going to help us do this."

Egon did not respond and spent the remainder of the ride watching each tree pass by until they arrived at the Music Institute which was an old building that had taught many generations.

"Here we are! Let's get in and get warm," Mr. Swartz said. "Your case."

Egon grabbed his akkordion from the car and they walked in.

"Please meet Mr. Bergmann, your conductor," Mr. Swartz said to Egon. "This is a fantastic boy! He causes no grief – and a star pupil both in Mathematics and Musical Theory classes. Ms. Kraus in Berlin called me as he is an orphan. The entire Blissestift orphanage was moved by train, as you know for their safety. We have identified the music pupils who would be an asset to the Children's Reichsmusikkammer. Ms. Kraus let me know that Charlotte Pfeiffer, Rita Graf, and Viktor Voigt were all from the orphanage as well - and are musically gifted.

We intercepted the train and retrieved those children."

Egon was wide-eyed and looked around for them.

"Isn't that lovely that your friends will be playing music with you?" Mr. Bergmann said.

Egon sat on his akkordion case, and the Skelekit jumped up and sat next to him.

"I understand Dr. Goebbels is coming today to hear the children play?" Mr. Bergmann asked, guiding Mr. Swartz away from Egon.

"Indeed, along with Mr. Heinz from the Reichskulturkammer. A piece by Haydn or Wagner, perhaps?" Mr. Swartz advised.

"Very good, Sir!" Mr. Bergmann said. "We will run through several and I will choose the strongest."

"Something that lauds German virtue," Swartz said. "Have you received the recent list of banned material? We do not need a repeat performance of what happened with Furtwangler five years ago."

"I am honoured to have the esteemed Doctor visit today," Mr. Bergmann gushed. "We are happy to comply with all changes for the benefit of the Fatherland."

Charlotte and Rita walked by them as they were talking.

"Who is Fritwaggler?" Charlotte asked Rita.

"I have no idea. Do you suppose this Waggler man played *degenerate* music?" Rita asked back.

"His proper name is FURT-WANGler," Viktor interrupted. "He was vice-president here for only one year. Everyone was excited for him because he was so renowned – but he made a fatal error, refusing to adhere to the ban."

"How can music be banned – it's just a string of notes," Charlotte said, folding her arms.

"I will play any music," Rita said to Charlotte. "At least we are together – well, it had to be with Viktor, but at least we didn't get broken up."

"I know – our entire class looked like they were on a train to nowhere," Rita said, with big sad eyes.

"Hello children," Mr. Bergmann interrupted them. "Would you please join the others and get set up?"

Viktor grabbed his stand-up bass and marched over to the group. Rita played violin and Charlotte played the flute. They grabbed each other's hand and joined the rest.

Egon didn't move from his akkordion case. He was petting the Skelekit who was now inside his coat.

"Have you heard about the Swingjugend trend?" Charlotte whispered to Rita.

"You mean the boys who are growing their hair?" Rita asked.

"And the girls wear short skirts – and put paint on their nails," Charlotte dreamed for a moment.

"Oh! I didn't know that was what they were called, but I have seen them," Rita laughed.

"Someday, I am going to ditch these braids and wear my hair down and flowing like theirs," Charlotte said, getting her flute out of the case.

"I am with you! My bun is so tight my skin is stretching!" Rita grumbled with her violin.

"We will move to Hamburg and be show-girls! You and me!" Charlotte suggested.

"You are one year away from the Jungmädelbund -" Viktor warned. "You are German Maidens. You would be best to mind your imagination."

Rita put her fist right in Viktor's face and said, "I will shove your nosey nose right up into your brain if you don't stop eavesdropping! It is creepy!"

"I intend on joining the Deutsches Jungvolk next year. I have already begun rifle practice," Viktor said, trying to impress them.

"When can you use a rifle when you are so busy getting in everyone's face?" Rita said. "When does this mysterious rifle practice happen, while the rest of us sleep?"

The two girls laughed as Viktor opened his bass. "Laugh now!" he said, taunting them. "I will be fighting for you both."

"Because you love us sooooo much," Charlotte teased.

"Charlotte!" Rita interrupted, pointing across the room.

"Is that Egon?" Charlotte asked.

"I think it is!" Rita said, running over.

Egon was still sitting on his case with head down when Rita scared him with a big hug that nearly knocked him off.

"Bet you didn't see that coming! So happy you are here! Quickly, grab your case and come get set up before you get in trouble!" she said, guiding him back.

"Egon!" Charlotte exclaimed, hugging him as well. "Did Mr. Swartz pluck you out too? Where are you staying? I wish you could tell us!"

"We are staying in a group home nearby," Rita added. "They said they want us near the Institute. They gave us meat and vegetables, Egon!"

Egon sat back on his case and the Skelekit sat at his feet.

"Egon, you are going to be in deep trouble. Here. Let me help you get it out," Charlotte said, as Egon got up.

"Ms. Pfeiffer...Egon can retrieve his own instrument," Mr. Swartz called from across the room.

"Yes, Sir," Charlotte conceded. "You have to do it now," she whispered to Egon.

Egon froze and locked eyes with Swartz who folded his arms and waited. Luckily, Swartz was distracted by Bergmann and they began to chat. The Skelekit jumped up and unlocked both sides of the case, stuck her nose in and flung the lid open which caught Swartz' attention.

"Lovely enthusiasm, Egon!" Swartz called out.

Rita and Charlotte looked puzzled.

"Take it out of the case, Egon!" Rita warned. "It's ok! I know, this is all new to us as well."

Egon tipped the case on its side and lifted the red velvet blanket. The Hohner wasn't in great shape. Most of the instruments the children had from the orphanage were donated. The keys and body still looked ok, but the bellows had a few holes and it took more effort to get noise from it. Still, it was Egon's size and he was good at it.

Charlotte and Rita had their flute and violin ready and motioned for him to come sit on a stool next to them.

"I've been ready for an hour!" Viktor said, disgusted at their clumsiness.

"Where is your trophy for that?" Rita laughed.

"Don't you know? Viktor is SO good, his bass plays itself!" Charlotte giggled.

Rita stretched her neck behind Viktor's bass.

"What are you looking for?" Viktor asked.

"The chain. I was certain you had it tied down. Otherwise, it would run away from you!" Rita joked.

"You are a disgusting witch," Viktor scorned.

"You better watch I don't cast a spell on your bass and turn it into a SERPENT!" Rita cackled in her best witchy voice.

The Skelekit was feeling especially bratty and grabbed Viktor's bow while they argued. She dragged it behind Egon's case.

"Alright, children!" Mr. Bergmann clapped. "Tannhauser!"

"He's trying to put us to sleep already?" Rita whispered to Charlotte.

"WHERE IS MY BOW?" Viktor said to the girls in his loudest, angriest whisper.

"I don't have it!" Rita said. "I was arguing with you."

"I didn't take it," Charlotte said, poising her flute to wait for her turn.

Viktor turned red as he panicked to find it. He spotted it behind Egon who was sitting on the other side of the girls. He ran behind them to grab and it and gave Egon a hard shove off his stool and quickly assumed his position. Egon fell forward and he landed on top of the akkordion.

"Egon! Return to your seat!" Mr. Bergmann stormed.

Charlotte grabbed his elbow and helped him up but then jumped back on her stool.

"I look forward to turning you into a toad, although - then, I'd just feel sorry for you!" Rita whispered to Viktor.

Mr. Bergmann raised his baton and waited for silence. Then he took a deep breath, and everyone began. Rita was right, it was a real sleeper, and Mr. Swartz pumped the brakes.

"Is this a funeral procession? Please, something more uplifting!"

"Another from Wagner – perhaps Symphony in C Major?" Mr. Bergmann asked.

"That sounds like a triumphant song for the esteemed Doctor!" Swartz agreed.

Mr. Bergmann raised his baton and the children frantically swiped through their sheet music. As he snapped both arms down for the first simultaneous note stabs, a young German Youth teenager came running in and whispered to Swartz, which, of course, caught Viktor's eye.

"Silence, children!" Mr. Swartz called out, stopping them mid-song. "Please form a line left and right. Dr. Goebbel's car has arrived!"

"Who is Dr. Gobble?' Rita whispered to Charlotte.

"Do NOT make me laugh right now," Charlotte said, trying hard to hold it in.

"Is he the Christmas turkey?" Rita continued.

"Rita! STOP!" Charlotte said, about to burst.

Mr. Swartz laid a hand on each of the girls' shoulders. "I did say 'silence', did I not?"

Both girls pressed their shoulders back and stood still. Egon fumbled to lay his akkordion on his stool and was noticeably late to the line-up. Viktor of course was in-line so quickly, it might as well have been last week.

"SIEG HEIL!" Swartz called out as most of the children raised their right arm. "Say it back to me, children!" and they all exclaimed "SIEG HEIL!" in unison.

"Very good, double that enthusiasm when the Doctor enters,"

Swartz said, applauding them.

"Egon, what are you doing?" Rita whispered. "You need to salute when they enter. I know it is stupid, but we don't need the hassle!"

Egon was not meaning to ignore it, but the Skelekit was running around making a nuisance of herself and Egon was distracted.

"We welcome Dr. Goebbels, Kommandeur Kroeger and Hauptmann Hesse! It is an extreme privilege and we are honored to have the Ministry visit us!" Mr. Swartz announced as he extended his arm to salute. "SIEG HEIL, children!"

All the children responded with a loud "SIEG HEIL!" as the three men entered.

"SIEG HEIL!" they saluted back.

"So lovely to be in your school today, children! I am Kommandeur Kroeger," he said, smiling at each of them. "This is Hauptmann Hesse. Now please salute the Doctor. SIEG HEIL!"

The children were very intimidated and responded accordingly. Egon was still watching the Skelekit run excitedly between all the children's feet.

"SIEG HEIL!" Dr. Goebbel said, with an exceptionally stiff arm and hand.

His tear-drop shaped head was pointed at the chin and massive at the top like an alien. His hair was slicked back with a fine comb – and potentially car oil. He used a walking stick and looked into the eyes of each child in the line.

"You are proud of the Fatherland," he said to Viktor.

"HEIL TO THE DRILLMEISTER!" Viktor eagerly responded, standing like a soldier.

"Lovely," the Doctor noted and moved along to Rita and Charlotte who were noticeably annoyed but stayed adequately in line.

"Tighten up your braids, yes?" he pointed out, touching Charlotte's hair.

"Yes Sir," she cringed.

He passed by Rita and stood at Egon's feet.

"I have so many questions for you. Where do I begin?" he said, as Egon looked at the Doctor's shiny knee-high black boots. "Where are your eyes?"

Egon did not look up, so Goebbel put his dark glove under his chin and pulled up.

"You do have eyes! That answers one question. Now, who permitted you to wear a hat?" he said close to Egon's face. "I said, WHO PERMITTED THIS BOY TO WEAR A HAT?"

Mr. Bergmann came running across and grabbed the hat off Egon's head and ran back to his position.

"You have eyes and hair. Where is your arm? Why is this child missing so many body parts?" he asked in a very condescending tone to the group.

Rita motioned for Egon to raise his arm, which he didn't. She inhaled and held her breath.

"We only have one body part left to find. Do you also own a tongue?" he said, about to grab his face.

"He is a mute, Sir," Swartz burst out.

"And so, why is he – here?" Goebbel asked.

"This is Egon," Swartz answered.

"Oh. I see. My sincere apologies. Happy to have you here, Egon," Goebbel said, and he moved along.

"Would you like to hear the children play?" Mr. Bergmann asked.

"Very much so," Goebbel responded. "What a glorious time of year, children. The Fatherland is entering a magnificent time in history and you are all part of it! Isn't this fantastic? People will be inspired by you."

"Please assemble," Mr. Bergmann said as they each grabbed their instruments. He then raised his baton and the children began Wagner's Symphony again – everyone, but Egon.

The Skelekit began tugging on the overcoat of the Kommandeur who could not figure out what was irritating him. Egon just stood and blankly stared.

"Egon!" Rita scolded. "You will have us all in trouble! Grab your akkordion! He will send you away if you aren't perfect!"

Egon snapped out of it and picked it up. Rita shook her head and just looked over at Charlotte who seemed anxious as her fingers shook on her flute.

"Why is this child permitted to stay?" Kommandeur Kroeger leaned into Dr. Goebbel.

"Is it enough that I say so?" the Doctor said in a monotone voice, barely acknowledging him.

"It is enough," the Kommandeur conceded.

The children's song was lovely and went on for several minutes while the men chatted.

"Most of the children here are orphaned, but they are all documented as descendants of the master race," Swartz began. "The orphanage did well to keep them disciplined on their instruments."

"They are not children of fathers and mothers, but of Germany. They are children of Germany," Goebbels said. "This is their home. They will be in our protection. Is this understood?"

"Of course, Doctor," Swartz said.

"There are four boys that I would like moved to the Jungvolk," Goebbel said pointing to Viktor and three others. "Their hearts are already all in. It won't take long for their bodies to follow."

"Certainly," Swartz said. "Consider it done."

"The girl in the blonde braids – who is that?" Goebbel asked.

Swartz was uncomfortable answering but did anyways, "Charlotte Pfeiffer."

"Put Charlotte in our car when we leave today," Goebbel whispered to Swartz.

"Is she the only one? There are others who would be fit for the Jungmädelbund as well," Swartz said, clearly fishing as to why he wanted Charlotte.

"I don't recall saying she would be going there. DID I?" he snapped back at Swartz.

"You did not," Swartz said, stepping back. "Consider it done."

"Nothing resets the holiday spirit like children playing, don't you agree?" Hesse said, hoping to change the tone.

None of the other children noticed that Goebbel was watching Charlotte, but it certainly made Egon uncomfortable. His right hand became shaky on the keys and he hit them harder as he became anxious. Instead of playing the Wagner song, he began to peddle on three notes. It went, 'Low, middle, high, middle, low, middle, high, middle…' in a dizzying sequence that he peddled on for several minutes.

"Get it together!" Rita whispered to him.

One of the keys made a horrible noise when Egon hit it and the group all looked at him. When he went up a couple octaves, something sharp cut him and he jumped. Between the B and C on the keyboard, where there isn't a black note, something long and pointy began to grow out. He tried to continue playing, hoping nobody saw, but another sharp pointy object came out between the keys a few octaves lower. They were ivory like the keys and appeared to be horns which grew out over a foot long each on his right hand. Another pointy object grew out the opposite end with the buttons but looked like a skeleton tail. The bellows began to turn into a rib cage, and Egon was now holding the skeleton of an animal **which used to be beautiful once**. He quickly pulled his arms out of the straps and dropped the bones to the floor in a loud thud which stopped everyone from playing.

The rest of the bones had now formed a wild boar and wild it was! This AbBOARdion took off running around the room knocking children off their feet and Egon tried to chase after it to catch it.

Mr. Bergmann yelled out, "EGON! STOP! WHAT ARE YOU DOING?"

From their perspective, Egon had a hold of the straps and was whacking everyone with his akkordion. They did not see what he saw. The Skelekit, of course, delighted in this, and joined in the fun. The pair of them banged into Viktor, Hesse, and Kroeger and then they both barreled into Goebbel, who fell backwards into a table. He rose to his feet and grabbed Egon under the chin. Egon bit down hard on his hand.

"VAMPIRE!" Goebbel screamed.

Mr. Swartz seized Egon and shook him, "Why would you do such a thing?"

Mr. Bergmann ran over to Goebbel, "Are you hurt?"

"Get your hands off of me!" Goebbel said, rising to his feet. He slicked his hair back into position and announced, "We are finished here!"

"Egon is a sick boy," Viktor kissed up. "He is not a good

choice to represent the Fatherland, Sir."

"BACK OFF of him," Goebbel said, to everyone's surprise. "Swartz, may I speak with you privately?"

"Of course," Swartz said, following him into another room.

"See that no harm comes to Egon. He cannot remain with these children. They are a bad influence on him, clearly. Please take him back to the farm," Goebbel said.

Swartz seemed shocked by the response but allowed him to save face.

"Absolutely, Sir! Consider this done."

Goebbel stepped back in the room enough to motion for his men to follow – and they left.

"You made me miss my chance!" Viktor stormed Egon, going for his throat.

"Get off of him!" Rita said, pulling Viktor into a choke hold.

Mr. Bergmann broke them up and Swartz yelled, "BACK IN LINE – NOW!"

They all scrambled to their position.

"I don't know what happened here, but you can be sure your chances to play for the Drillmeister have been ruined," Swartz said, disappointed. "Mr. Bergmann, spend a few weeks and come back to me with your assessment. This may have been too soon."

"I will," Bergmann said, completely embarrassed and flustered.

"I am glad you 'missed your chance', Viktor," Rita mocked. "You deserve NOTHING you want. EVER!"

Meanwhile, Charlotte was hugging Egon tightly around his neck, crying.

"Thank you," she whispered.

"Come with me, Egon," Swartz called out. "Oh, put your instrument back in the case."

Egon looked down at the akkordion lying in a heap on the floor.

"May I help him?" Charlotte asked.

Mr. Swartz was quietly relieved that Charlotte was left there in the chaos, and he nodded for her to help.

"Do you see Rita's hair, Charlotte?" Swartz asked. "I think you would suit a bun like that." He then leaned down to whisper, "It would keep the greasy mitts off of it."

"Thank you, Sir," she said, fighting tears.

"And never cry in front of men. It shows weakness," Swartz warned. "You were lucky today."

"Thank you, Sir," she said, putting her chin up. "I am counting my fortunes."

"I am taking Egon with me," Swartz said to Bergmann. "Please see the children back to their group home. Remember, they are our treasures. Treat them as such."

"Understood," Bergmann said.

Swartz and Egon headed out to the car as the driver put the case in.

"I made a bad choice for you today, Egon," Mr. Swartz said, sitting beside him in the back seat as Egon stared out the window. "You are best to focus on helping Eugen on his project. You saved Charlotte today. Had she gone with the Doctor – well, she didn't. So, you went there for a reason. Sometimes the Universe calls us. But enough of that. Tonight, get some rest. Tomorrow, you will be in the barn with Eugen. He is a terrible man. Try to learn from him, correct him when he is stuck. You will hate it, but it will be for the good of Germany. You will see."

As they pulled in the driveway, Irene greeted them.

"Did it go well today?" she sheepishly inquired.

"Get him fed and well rested," he said, purposely ignoring her. "He is to be in the barn with Eugen tomorrow, understood?"

"Understood," she said, guiding him in.

Mr. Swartz got back in the car and left.

"Alright then. Kick your boots off at the door and put your hat and gloves on the box there," she said going to the kitchen. "You know what? I am not raising you – I am just watching you. There is the refrigerator. Take what you want, and I will show you your room."

Egon stumbled over to the kitchen and opened the refrigerator door. The Skelekit looked more excited than him, so he grabbed a few items. He shoved a bun of pumpernickel bread under his arm, a few carrot sticks and a handful of blueberries.

"That seems better than your lunch," Irene snickered. "Your hands are full, I have your akkordion. Let's go."

They headed up a short flight of stairs.

"Your room is on the right. You can get adjusted and eat your food. I put out pajamas. I will come check on you in a bit," she said, closing his door.

Judging by how cold this room was, it was obvious why the hound dog was stuck to the fireplace downstairs. Egon threw all his food onto the bed and walked over to the akkordion case which Irene set down at the end of the bed. He laid it on its side and opened it up. It was just an akkordion. On the bed, the Skelekit was playing with a blueberry. Egon walked over to her and stroked her nose. He then took the pumpernickel and broke off a piece. He jumped up on the high bed and his feet dangled. As he ate the bread, he looked around the room. The entire structure of the home was a log cabin, so his walls were giant logs too. The floors were big planks and even his bed was made from the forest trees. It smelled of pine and not much else.

When he finished eating his bread, he changed into the pajamas. They were a bit big, but he didn't really seem to mind. Even the slippers were too big that Irene left on the floor for him – but he never wore slippers before – so this was interesting. As he wandered downstairs, Eugen was warming up by the fire. One side of his face was clearly swollen and bruised. He said nothing to Egon.

"There is a toothbrush in there," Irene said, pointing to the bathroom.

Egon shuffled along, looking back at Eugen.

"Stay out of the shave soap," Irene called out.

While Egon was in the bathroom, Irene asked Eugen if he wanted a compress for his face.

"No," he said. "I want a gun."

"You talk a brave talk," she said. "Where would that get us?"

"Just stop talking," he said. "My head is pounding."

They sat in silence. They weren't married, friends or barely even roommates. Even Aldo, the hound dog was awkwardly quiet.

The toilet flushed and the bathroom door creaked open.

"Oh good," Irene said, relieved to go anywhere else. "Bed-time!"

Aldo got up and followed them.

Eugen leaned back in his recliner and put a blanket up over his face to sleep.

"Are you going to sleep on Egon's bed?" Irene said to the dog. "He'd probably like the company. Well, good night," she said with no motherly instincts, then closed the door.

Egon and Aldo stared at each other for a few minutes, then Egon got into bed – mostly because he was cold. Aldo moved up beside the bed and sat. Egon grabbed some bread and tossed it on the floor. Aldo didn't want it and jumped up on the bed. He curled in next to him and went to sleep.

It was as though the dog was showing him how to quickly adjust to a situation he was thrown into. Aldo was a professional at it after years of practice.

Egon was comfortable with Aldo keeping him company – and keeping him warm. The Skelekit was not – and did the same thing she did to Soot, the chicken. She started rushing the dog like a jealous girlfriend and Aldo completely ignored her. Seeing as this did nothing, the Skelekit saw the dog as a heat source and curled into his ribs and fell asleep.

5 THE BURNT TOAST WEASEL

"Tap. Tap! Tap-tap. Tap-TAP! Tappity-tap-tap. Tappity-tap-tap-TAP! Tappity-tappity-TAPPITY-TAPPITY-TAP-TAP!"

Egon was woken up by something tapping on his bedroom window. He rubbed his eyes and tried to pull his legs out from under a heavy dog. He jumped down on the floor and moved like a zombie over to the window.

"Tap. Tap-Tap."

It was Soot!

Egon stretched up on his tippy toes to look down at the chicken footprints in the snow. She could fly enough to jump on a barrel, then the windowsill of his room. She had a layer of snow sitting on her black feathers and was eager for someone to wake up.

He tapped back to her and she eagerly cricked her neck left and right. She was clearly awake a long time ago and the bright light was burning Egon's eyes.

Aldo barely cared. He was a sleeping-in kind of dog. Well, he went to bed early too – and loved long afternoon naps. It would be easier to list the times he was awake – maybe to pee.

The Skelekit jumped off the bed and stretched into a play-bow stance. Then, she rushed the window, causing Soot to fall to the ground. Proud of herself, she returned to her warm spot with the hound while Egon looked down at Soot who curled up against the side of the building.

He looked at the other two who had now stretched out to take over the whole bed. He wasn't getting back in there easily now. He opted to wander around his room. There wasn't much in there. The bed was made of logs like the cabin-style house and there was a dresser with an attached oval mirror which had three big heavy drawers and two smaller ones stacked side by side on top. He paused to listen for Irene or Eugen, then opened the bottom drawer first. It had sweaters. The next one up, a wool blanket. He took that out and tossed it on the foot of the bed – it would come in handy later that night. The top big drawer had socks, underwear, and pajamas. The top left small drawer had an assortment of things. There was a jackknife, a bottle opener, candlesticks, and lamp oil. The other drawer had a couple books and some papers.

He was stopped by his own belly making a noise and so he ventured downstairs. Aldo and the Skelekit could not have cared any less. They stayed put.

Irene was awake and sitting in a chair reading. She looked up enough to say, "Morning" and put her nose back down. He paused for a moment, possibly to assess etiquette – or simply to wake up. Irene wasn't a mother, guardian, or friend. She seemed more like another patient waiting at the Doctor's office. Egon was dropped into this space the same way she was. They weren't even roommates. They just occupied similar spaces.

"Mr. Swartz seems to think you have it all sorted out," she said abruptly. "Based on what happened to Eugen, I am not going to push my luck. Everything you need is in the kitchen. Just holler if you can't find something."

He stood there blankly at the bottom of the stairs.

"Oh. You don't holler. I do love that. Well, tug my arm or raise your hand up or something."

As she went back to reading, Egon wandered into the kitchen. For all the places he had found himself in, free to work in a kitchen was not a luxury he had been afforded. The kitchen at the orphanage was run by staff – who generally just cut up bread and provided a sticky, goopy porridge. He saw Irene open the fridge once before, so he started there. It was full of fruits, vegetables, breads, juices, milk, butter, and eggs. Without knowing how to prepare any of those, and not having tasted over half of them, he went straight for the pumpernickel.

"It's really nice toasted with jam – knives are in the top – oh – yes, I am not supposed to assist you. Never mind. I need to go shovel," she said, and she started to get dressed to go outside.

Egon opened the utensil drawer to see neatly stacked forks, knives, and spoons with bigger blades sideways in the front. He was a bright boy who could fix or build anything, so cutting some bread wasn't hard. With some fumbling around, he cut a decent couple of slices and got them into the toaster.

While he waited, he noticed the big walnut table was covered in paper. It must have been rolled up at one point, because it had a book holding down a corner, a couple of candlesticks on two other corners and a can of soup holding down the fourth. It appeared to be blueprints for a boat from the Kriegsmarine.

Egon ran over to his coat on the hall-tree and reached into the inside pocket to pull out his book. He feverishly drew some things but then his nose crinkled up. He looked around at what the awful smell was.

BURNT TOAST.

He ran back and popped up the toaster, then dropped it on the ground as it scorched his fingers. He tried again with two new slices.

While that was cooking, he took his book and the two burnt slices off the floor over to his coat and stuck it all on the inside pocket. Then he marched back to the toaster and waited for it, so it wouldn't burn again.

"Well, that is a dreadful smell," Irene said from the doorway. "It doesn't pop up on its own. I have wasted more of my life just staring at it. It isn't fixable, and they won't bring me a new one. Eugen is waiting for you in the barn, whenever you are ready. If he doesn't report that he spent time mentoring you today, Swartz will – well, let's not worry about that. Once you are dressed, come on out."

The second time worked better. The pumpernickel toasted well, and Egon headed upstairs with one slice in each hand. Aldo opened his eyes and yawned, then his sniffer started going. Egon handed one of them to Aldo, broke off a corner for the Skelekit (who mostly just played with it) and then Egon nibbled away at the rest of it himself while he got dressed.

He was a small nine-year-old, and while the clothes were probably for an eleven or twelve-year-old, Egon seemed happy to put on something clean. Working in the barn only required farm clothes, but he picked out a pressed green shirt and black pants. They were a bit long, so he rolled them up – same with the shirt sleeves. In the side of the sock drawer was a long skinny black tie and he flawlessly tied it and then put both hands on his hips to show Aldo who was still licking his face from the bread - but seemed to approve.

Egon waited for Aldo to clean his face so he could make the bed. When he was done, it looked like a staff member of a hotel did it. He then went downstairs, and Aldo and the Skelekit followed.

In the bathroom, he brushed his teeth and then did one smear of the brush to push his dirty blonde hair sideways. He rubbed his glasses on his shirt and stuck them back on his face.

Aldo went back to the fireplace to assume his daily position. Sleeping with Egon was a nice break for him.

On the way to the door, Egon stopped at the blueprints on the table again. The door flung open again and Irene yelled, "Eugen is calling for you! He is paranoid Swartz will show up and you aren't out there!"

She saw Egon at the table.

"Oh my – I am glad you noticed those. I completely forgot to put them away. It is our next project – but if a stranger shows up, they cannot be lying around like that! Thank you, Egon! You saved me!" she said, quickly removing the weights and rolling it up. "Can you imagine Swartz seeing that? Let us NOT imagine that!"

Irene unlocked a drawer in the kitchen and put the plans inside. Then she put the key in a draw on the other side of the kitchen.

"Well, shall we get you out there?" she said, hustling over to the door. "I don't even care if you contribute. Just stand near him in case Swartz comes, alright?"

Egon followed along and so did the Skelekit. Aldo gave a big yawn as if to say, "I will be toasty right here, if you need me."

Eugen was a nervous worker ever since the incident with Swartz. He seemed frantic to finish his job, and his patience was waning. However, Swartz found favour with Egon, and Eugen needed to in some way as well.

"I was where you were once," Eugen said, not turning around but sensing Egon was there.

Egon was standing in the doorway with no direction.

"Go on in," Irene said, giving him a nudge. "Just stand near him, learn what you can, help him when he is stuck – I guess."

"HOW DO I GET THIS FINISHED AND MENTOR A CHILD?" Eugen exploded.

Egon dropped his head, the Skelekit hid behind him, and Irene stepped inside to address the issue.

"You haven't let me help you in weeks. You are not where you are supposed to be – and Swartz knows this. However angry he is with you, he has people who can take a strip off him too."

Egon walked over to the table Eugen was working at, looked inside for a moment, then pointed to a wire and a connector.

Eugen looked at it, stood back and folded his arms for a few moments and then said, "Oh!" before grabbing his welding mask and getting to work.

"I guess I will leave the two of you to it, then," Irene said, winking at Egon. "Egon saw the plans on the table, Eugen."

"Oh. Good thing he is a mute," Eugen said, going back to work.

"He can probably help us fast-track it, no?" Irene suggested.

"I can tell you this - your talking slows us down!" Eugen barked.

"You could at least explain what needs to be done. He is probably feeling lost," Irene said, leaving the shop.

Egon reached in his coat and pulled out his book to jot some things down.

"She is the worst. What's that book all about?" Eugen said, putting his welding mask up on top of his head. "I had a book of data and schematics too. It does help the mind release some of the pressure. Some kids counted sheep. I was the kid who tried to get to the end of all numbers every night. The sunrise would beat me."

Egon put his book away and sat on a shop stool.

"So you truly are a mute, huh? I do not trust Irene. I cannot have her in here. For all I know, she is a spy. But you? You can't tell anybody anything," Eugen began. "She knows what we are building. It is a submarine. She knows they are for patrolling the deep seas. Think of it as an underwater shark with men inside. Except, our shark has to have a brain so it can talk to other sharks a whole ocean away."

Egon just listened.

"We can make our brain talk to other brains – but then we have to change the brain every month – because someone intercepts the messages. Someone must deliver the new changes from the big brain to the smaller brain - but how do you trust the messenger? It's a conundrum."

"Wolf-pack," a voice interrupted.

It was Swartz, stealthy and slow. His knee-high shiny black boots tapping on the cement floor towards them.

"I beg your pardon, Sir?" Eugen said, looking at the floor.

"Sharks are highly skilled hunters, Egon," Swartz said, circling Eugen. "There is no doubt about this. They have outstanding receptors that detect vibrations. A shark can feel when someone is flailing or in distress – they swim closer to investigate. They have small pores in their snout which allows them to detect electrical impulses emitted by other creatures," he said, his nose close to Eugen.

"They are indeed formidable," Eugen said, nervously.

"But a wolf-pack, Egon," Swartz continued. "That is a team effort. A shark cannot control a territory. They are solo hunters. Wolves can take on dangerous prey and protect one another. They also form an intense loyalty in the pack. Don't you agree loyalty is a top trait of wolves, Eugen?"

"Yes, Sir," Eugen agreed.

"They make up for their size by their intellect and collaborating with the pack. These wolves are loyal to the Fatherland, Egon. They are establishing the territory – and together will take down the larger prey. Eugen here – is a shark. He is a devastating hunter, but his solo mentality will be his demise."

"I wish to work with the pack," Eugen submitted.

"Then STOP your arrogance and INCLUDE him!" Swartz roared.

"I – I – I – I will, Sir," Eugen said, shaking.

"If you expect the pack to hunt successfully OUT THERE," he said, pointing to the outdoors, "then you will enact a pack mentality IN HERE!" he said tapping his walking stick twice on the cement.

"I will," Eugen said.

"WE!" Swartz corrected.

"WE will!" Eugen adjusted.

"Lovely," Swartz instantly calmed. "You have a family, Egon! Isn't that perfectly lovely? Now, please, Eugen. Continue explaining the conundrum."

"We have added an additional rotor. The problem, Sir...is setting the intervals at which we scramble and reset new codes. The – uh, ALPHA can communicate with the, uh... PACK. The pack knows what to do... until the uh, PREY learns the tactic, then the tactic becomes obsolete. I - I mean WE are estimating the prey would need the better part of a month to unscramble, so the suggestion would be to set a new code monthly. The problem is, getting the new monthly message from the Alpha to the pack without compromise or interruption."

"Hmmm, I see," Swartz said, pacing the floor. "Radio would be interrupted. It would have to be by carrier, I imagine."

"I don't see another way. It would require a deep loyalty to the Fatherland, Sir," Eugen advised.

"The loyalty of the Alpha crew is not a problem. The loyalty of the pack is not an issue. We will have to develop touchpoints in between," Swartz said. "Leave this with me."

Egon rubbed his eyes under his glasses.

"I am happy the two of you will work together. Egon showed me a fierce loyalty yesterday, didn't you? It was to a girl, but still – it is in you, Egon!" Swartz smiled.

Egon blushed and hid his face.

"Will we see you soon?" Eugen asked.

"I come and go," Swartz said. "Do your work, teach the boy, work together."

Swartz went to leave and then turned around.

"Mind your behaviour, Eugen. If I do not bite, Egon will," he said, tipping his hat and closing the door behind him.

Eugen walked over to the wall and slumped to the floor. He drew his knees into his chest and tried to slow his breathing down. The Skelekit jumped onto Egon's lap to take advantage of the silence and get some pettings.

Irene quietly wandered in.

"I saw Swartz leave. Is everything satisfactory?"

"He is evil," Eugen muttered, not picking up his face.

"Well, this we know," Irene agreed. "What is next?"

"I am to teach the boy. He is to assist me. I am overwhelmed. I need a break," he said, jumping to his feet, then grabbing his hat and coat.

After he left and slammed the door behind him, Irene walked over to Egon.

"You really are unaffected. Or numb? Either way, good job. Want to help me with the chickens?"

Egon hopped off his chair and walked to the door.

"Not a bad boy. Obliging and quiet!" Irene smiled, and they walked outside together.

Soot showed up.

Well, she never went away. She was the farm lurker...or outcast...or comedic relief. Every time Irene went into the chicken coop, Soot was right there. She gave up trying to get in ages ago. She just wanted one tiny peek inside to see how the other half lived. Egon stood and stared at her as Irene entered the coop.

"Even if I picked her up and put her in, the other chickens would chase her out," Irene said. "It's survival of the fittest for most of us lately."

Soot jumped up on some boxes and looked in the window. It was at least something to pass her time.

"You can start cleaning at the back," she said, putting corn out for the flock. "It is warmer there – no draft from the door opening. Just grab a shovel and put it in this wheelbarrow."

Egon began but then eyeballed the trap door in the floor.

"I used to work with Eugen," Irene began, obviously needing a friend or therapist. "I am a scientist, you know. I never married. I was excited to come work here at first. Now, I am reduced to cleaning chicken pens."

Egon was still looking the floor.

"We were all told we were making a difference – at first – oh yeah - some difference."

She managed to cover the floor in corn before giving up.

"I'll be back out in a bit, I have a few things to do in the house," she said, without really contributing anything to the cleanup.

The Skelekit, as one would imagine, was interested in chickens – the smell of them was grand even to a skeleton with no sensory receptors. Egon snapped the shovel down in front of her to establish a boundary. She sat scolded in the corner until he grabbed the handle of the trap door.

Under the floor was a dirty set of stairs leading into darkness. Unable to see a thing, (and wearing glasses did not help) he put the door back down and looked around for something to illuminate. There was a brass oil lantern, but it was just out of his reach. He would have to wait until he could find a flashlight or way to get the lantern down.

A scuffle started in the front of the henhouse, so he abandoned the trap door to go see. The chickens were trying to fly up to their roosts and feathers were flying everywhere. Even Soot was upset, and she was safely outside!

The Skelekit jumped in on the fun. It was simply in her nature. It was an awful racket, and Egon grabbed the shovel and waved it around to break up the bedlam.

There stood every chicken farmer's nightmare – a weasel.

He was skinny and agile, slippery, and cunning. He ducked and dodged Egon's shovel, even though he wasn't trying to hurt him – simply corralling him out of the henhouse. Egon remembered he put the burnt toast into his pocket and offered that up as an olive branch. He opened the entrance a hair, tossed it near the doorway and the weasel went for it. It paused for a second and then darted.

A deep, husky man's voice could be heard outside.

"Good boy, Frecher! No chicken today!"

That was a new voice, so Egon peeked out the open door.

There was an old man twice the height of Egon patting the weasel on the head. This weasel named Frecher dropped the toast on the man's knee-high, shiny black boots, and he bent down to pick it up. He was clearly elevated in the German ranks, but his highly decorated uniform, complete with iron cross at the bottom of the high starched collar, was worn by Hussars or Feldmarschalls twenty years prior in The Great War. The fur busby hat on top of his head had a skull prominently in the front which mirrored the furrow in between his overrun eyebrows bordering a deeply creased forehead below. While he was a striking character, nothing was physically as fantastic as his salt and pepper moustache which parted in the middle and was twisted on both ends.

"Did you find this unidentified object in a war zone?" he asked Frecher, sniffing to figure out what it was. "Do you suppose there is still food under it?"

The old man took out a jack knife and scraped the black dust off.

"Someone gifted this to you! They must have taken a fancy to your larger-than-life personality! Is that what it was? You were just sooooo irresistible? Who is this strapping young lad, all sprightly and willowy coming for dinner? Oh, it is a weasel! Everyone loves those! Let us give him toast and hope he returns!" the man joked.

Frecher stretched up clapping to ask for the toast.

"There you go, naughty boy. You may want to remove the chicken feather from your fur before making your case to me," he said, shaking a finger at him.

Frecher ran with it behind the chicken coop, and that is when Egon promptly tucked his face back inside.

The old man pretended not to see him. Instead, thought he would play for a bit.

"There once was a weasel, who ate all my cheese-l!
I kicked him outside, but he started to freeze-l!
He stole all my blankets, ate fish from my tank-ets...
SO, next time it's geese-ls, OR bees-els, NOT weasels!"

Frecher tried to sneak past the man by going around the back of the coop.

"I see you, you can come out," he said.

Egon stood frozen.

"Come out, come out, come out Mr. Wolff," he said, as Egon looked around. "Yes, I mean you," he laughed, walking over to the coop door. "Hello, Mr. Wolff."

Egon was confused but comfortable enough to walk outside.

"You haven't heard that name in a long time. Are you confused why I am calling you that – or perplexed that I know it?"

Egon looked down at the Skelekit who perched on his boot.

"Hello, Skelekitty!" he said, which made Egon's head snap up. "How are things at the Garden? How is your Mama doing? Good, I hope!"

Egon looked up at him and down at her and back at him.

"Ah. I am the first one to see her besides you. I can see how that could be unnerving. It is not a superpower. The rest of the world has no vision, that is all."

There was no reaction, good nor bad.

"Egon Wolff," the man continued. "It is your name."

Egon leaned sideways to look past him.

"Frecher. His name means 'naughty'. He comes by it honestly," he said, still looking right at Egon. "And he NEEDS TO COME HERE THIS INSTANCE!"

Frecher came over with something tucked into his belly.

"Give it to me, Frecher," he urged.

Frecher looked disappointed and handed him an egg.

"Weasels and eggs!" he laughed. "Frecher isn't actually a weasel, he is called a stoat, which are larger than weasels. In the summer, his fur is light brown. This white coat you see is his winter fur. Isn't that funny? He is like two different animals."

"And speaking of chickens, my name is Kluck – with a K. August von Kluck. Here is your egg, Egon. See that Soot gets it back. It is all she has."

Egon took the egg and looked around for where Soot might be.

"She isn't a fan of Frecher. You will find her behind the coop," Kluck pointed.

Soot had dug out a hole in the ground under the floor of the coop and lined it with pine needles and feathers. She was sitting in there shaking. Egon looked down at the egg in his hand and then tucked it under her. She adjusted herself and sat proudly.

"Frecher has never actually harmed a chicken. He talks a big talk. He wants the eggs. He knows he gets hers once she realizes they will never hatch. She needs to come to this conclusion on her own. Frecher is not a hunter, he is an opportunist."

Egon was not interested in that conversation, and walked back to the coop.

"That was your father's name too," Kluck called out. "However – he had no middle name, so your mother wanted you to have a proper one. You are Egon Engel Wolff. It is a surname **that used to be beautiful once**. Isn't that brilliant? I just love it."

Egon stopped, turned around and faced him.

"Reach in your pocket," Kluck urged.

Egon reached in and pulled out his book but held it close to his chest.

"Oh no, I do not want your book. You cannot take a boy's book! Didn't the Lokführer gift you something?"

Egon reached in his upper pocket and pulled out the Waffen SS tag.

"When a soldier dies, they take it off them. I think you already know this," Kluck said, solemnly. "Your father was captured.

Nobody wanted to tell you this at the orphanage. They see it as a point of shame...of weakness. The weak are the ones who have never marched in those boots and cast judgment."

Egon didn't react. He just rubbed the tag.

"Smart like you. A soldier ...a data scientist. He took great risks because his family was in danger. I can at least say that about him."

Egon still didn't react.

"Say, that abboardion incident was really something, was it not?" Kluck said, changing the topic. "It is always great fun to watch ego-driven men lie flat on their backs because of a child."

That made Egon look up.

"Oh yes, that was you. Your akkordion changed to help you protect Charlotte."

This changed the colour in Egon's cold cheeks.

"My aim is not to embarrass you. Charlotte and Rita are great friends. They are safe. Rosa is not safe. Other children are not safe."

Egon walked up to Kluck and looked way up at his busby hat and uniform decorations.

"It is a horrible hat. I know. However, I can get into all sorts of places others cannot. Just this week, I marched beside the Drillmeister. He didn't question me at all."

That made Egon turn and march back to the chicken coop,

visibly unimpressed.

"The Reich is seizing this moment. But evil cannot be taken down from the outside alone. I need you on the inside too, Egon!" he called out.

Egon ignored him.

"What about Rosa?"

And that made Egon stop.

"You can stay here and help build weapons of war – or you can come with me and set this all straight."

The Skelekit tugged on Egon's leg, and the weasel offered his burnt toast back to him.

"Germany is about to do terrible things - and terrible things are coming to Germany. Don't be part of the terrible, Egon."

Egon turned and looked at him.

"I want to take you to the Grunewald Forest. I have ever so much to show you. Everyone has forced you to do things. They have placed you in situations. They do not give you a choice. I respect you enough to allow you to choose. I will say this. Saying yes can be scary, but it does remove one ugly thing – REGRET!"

The Skelekit kept tugging on his pants.

"Why is it that only you and I see her? Does this not intrigue you? Say! I have something for you. It plays chords like the akkordion," Kluck said, handing him a harmonica.

Egon took it.

"Blow into it," Kluck said.

Egon put it in his pocket.

"Come on! Try it! Just blow one time into it!"

Egon took it out and awkwardly blew into it and it sounded like it struck multiple chords.

"You will get the hang of it. Blow in for one chord, breathe in for another. Concentrate on just one square."

Egon did this and made a nice chord blowing out and another one breathing in.

"That is technology! I thought you might like it! Do it again!"

Egon did it again and Kluck pointed up.

"Look who you have called!"

Up above was a black eagle circling. It passed by the sun and cast a shadow over them.

"That is Düster!" Kluck clapped.

Irene came out of the house.

"General Kluck! I am honoured to have you – but what has brought you here?"

"Oh come now, Irene. You are not honoured. You are disgusted. You don't have to pretend," Kluck said, taking on a stricter tone with her.

"This is Egon -" she began, but he cut her off.

"Egon is currently making a choice, aren't you, Egon?" Kluck said.

Egon looked up at Düster flying.

"Can you saddle up a horse for me – and a pony for Egon?" Kluck requested.

"Right away, General," Irene said, and ran to another barn.

"I am a tall man, don't give me a short horse!" Kluck called out.

"I will dress Reiter," Irene said, rushing off.

Egon noticed Soot away from her nest, curled up beside the shed.

"Her egg was no good after all, Frecher," Kluck shrugged.

Frecher wasted no time and ran around back to retrieve it.

"Well, she made her choice."

Frecher handed the egg to Kluck.

"I will tell you this, Egon. If a woman wants to be in my life, she better love me more than this weasel," he said, sniffing the egg. "Oh Frecher! That thing is rotten. I can smell it on the outside! You can have it."

Frecher took it back and ran in circles with it.

"We better get Irene going on those horses. Are you coming, Egon?" he asked, walking over to the barn.

Egon followed.

"Wonderful," Kluck said.

At the barn, Irene was working double-time to saddle Reiter and the pony.

The blanket and saddle were sitting on top but not fastened, and she was tightening the saddle of her shiniest black stallion.

"Breath-taking, Irene. Thank you."

Egon grabbed the stirrup from the pony and tugged the whole thing, blanket, and all onto the ground.

"Does that mean he doesn't want to go?" Irene asked.

"Perhaps," Kluck said, helping her with Reiter. "I am guessing he doesn't want Spickz to have all that junk on her. It is how he thinks."

Egon walked out of the barn and looked up into the sky. Düster was still circling, and he followed.

"No! He's going!" Kluck laughed. "I am too old to walk. I will still take Reiter."

The pony wandered out of the open barn door.

"Oh no," Irene said.

"Let him go, he is following Egon... listen!" Kluck said, putting a hand to his ear.

Egon was blowing in and out of the harmonica as though he was communicating with Düster up above. Spickz the pony walked directly toward the sound as Egon followed Düster into the woods.

"If Swartz comes, tell him General Kluck took Egon…or some Feldmarschall you saw. I outrank him. He cannot say anything to you. Is this understood?" Kluck said, helping her finish up the saddle.

"Understood, General," Irene said, smacking the rear of the stallion to guide him out.

"A step, please," Kluck asked.

"Oh, of course... here you are!" she said, placing a box beside Reiter.

"Thirty years ago, I could leap onto a horse several hands taller than this one!" he said, mounting Reiter and adjusting.

"I will need a carrier attached to the saddle – somewhere my weasel can ride," Kluck said.

"It's on there," she said pointing to the back.

"Oh yes – uh – my eyes aren't what they were."

"General, I don't know what you want with Egon – but he is a good boy," Irene said, concerned.

"Egon is not a *good* boy, Irene. He is exceptional. Just relay my message to Swartz," Kluck said, riding off after Egon.

Just ahead was the Skelekit and Frecher.

"A pied piper!" Kluck laughed.

Tappity-tap-tap-TAP! Tappity-tappity-TAPPITY-TAPPITY-TAP-TAP!

Soot was tapping on the chicken coop window.

"Are you coming, Soot?" Kluck yelled out to the black chicken.

Soot snapped her head around and ran as fast as she could, flapping to get caught up.

Irene ran after the chicken and snatched her up.

"Can I put her in the saddle bag, General?" Irene laughed.

"You don't hear that question every day!" Kluck smiled and nodded. "Irene," Kluck said as she was walking away.

"Yes, Sir?"

"You are doing very good work in the chicken coop," he said with a wink.

Irene was taken aback, but she didn't have to respond because he kicked his heels in and rode off.

"You found your family, Soot!" Irene muttered and smiled to herself as she went back to the chickens.

Soot pecked on the side of the bag.

"Tap. Tap-Tap."

6 THE GRUNEWALD GORILLA

Düster's black wings against a cool winter sky were easy for Egon to see. The snow was crunchy under his feet. The only other visible movement was the weasel's black tail. The rest of his body was white like the snow. The Skelekit, while only visible to Egon and the General, was already white. Spickzettel was brown with a shaggy white mane and a dirty white tail. She had two white socks on the front and one on the back.

"I guess the black chicken wanted to ride on the black stallion!" Kluck called out. "Or she is partial to my name?"

Egon kept walking straight ahead.

"Frecher, want a ride?"

Frecher ignored him.

"Frecher, want a ride with a chicken?"

Frecher turned around to see Kluck up high and he ran towards him. Reiter's ears went back as the weasel climbed up with little effort and started immediately sniffing the chicken in the saddle bag.

"You ride on the other side! This will be a lesson in RESTRAINT!" Kluck laughed.

Never in recorded history has there been a chicken and a weasel riding on the same horse together. There was some tension.

The Skelekit ran happily around Egon's feet, almost tripping him at times because Egon's eyes were mostly up at Düster.

"It's a long way. Spickzettel will certainly carry you. You don't weigh much!" Kluck offered.

Spickzettel walked right beside him, without pressure, but made herself available.

"Boys love adventures, Frecher. It reminds me of my first time in the forest. I was close to his age," Kluck said, feeling sentimental. "You are walking quickly, Egon!"

He was hoofing along and Spickzettel was walking a steady pace to keep aligned with him.

"Is this how you thought you would spend the Holidays? All of Germany is celebrating – and here you and I are in the woods – with horses, and a weasel, a chicken and a Skelekitty!"

Egon wasn't having the small talk. He was simply watching Düster. A whole hour went by and he remained vigilant in following the bird.

"I have pumpernickel," Kluck finally called out, disturbing the silence. "Frecher, take this to Egon!"

Frecher jumped off the horse and ran up to Egon and gave

him the bread, but not before smelling it.

"Give him that, and I will get you one – go on!" Kluck said sternly.

Frecher handed it to Egon who took it and began to eat.

"Do you want water?" Kluck asked.

Egon stopped.

"I suppose you do!" Kluck said, retrieving a flask for him.

Egon halted because Düster stopped flying and came in for a landing at his feet.

"Such a fine specimen," Kluck observed. "Depicted for evil, but really the opposite."

Düster was a fine bird indeed. The sun had come out and was hitting his black feathers showing an emerald, bluish tinge. His wingspan was several feet across, and his feet were big like snowshoes hovering effortless on top of the snow as he walked ahead of Egon, guiding him toward water.

"You don't require my flask, do you?" Kluck smiled.

Even though December was a brutally cold month, and the lake was mostly frozen, there was a stream running into it that remained flowing, and Egon mirrored Düster in getting a drink by cupping his hands like a soup bowl.

"Birds don't need flasks," Kluck said, dismounting and drinking from his own. "Be a dear and fill mine up, would you, Frecher?"

Frecher waited waaaaaaaaay back in line, nervous of the daunting eagle.

"This is the Grunewaldsee, Egon. It is the water that feeds into the Hunting Lodge just ahead," Kluck warned.

Egon looked right at him for the first time in their journey.

"The Jagdschloss Grunewald," Kluck said, sadly. "Please tuck your Skelekitty in your coat."

Egon looked down at the Skelekit who looked unnerved.

The forest surrounding the Jagdschloss was a mix of winter pines and maples. The sun was hitting them, highlighting the crystal feathers from the previous night's frost. Even the long dead grass was covered in icy bits. The Grunewaldsee was not a safe lake this time of year. Parts were thin and bubbled.

The hunting lodge itself was a massive castle around four hundred years old. The building was three floors high with a lot of arched doorways set against white paint under a red roof. A sign on the fence said, "CLOSED FOR THE HOLIDAYS – SEE YOU IN THE NEW YEAR!" The fresh snow in the courtyard had no footprints and it was safe to assume nobody was here.

Kluck slowly walked Reiter into the courtyard – ever so gradually and circled around. There were a few outdoor lights on, seemingly for security but it was adequate for Egon to see deer antlers mounted above an arched entrance and he was frozen by them.

"Egon," Kluck said. "Look to me."

Egon looked up at Kluck.

"It takes superhuman strength to remain calm when you are a justice seeker. You don't need to worry about who *they* are. The strength is in knowing who *you* are," Kluck said, as Egon looked back to the antlers. "Do not be immobilized by one set of antlers now, or you will be rendered useless when the horrors grow in front of you. For now, it is a thing."

Egon's jaw clenched and it was so quiet, you could hear his teeth grinding.

"You didn't bite the Doctor to stop him, did you?" Kluck said, and Egon snapped his head towards him. "Oh yes, I know why you bite. I did too. I understand your frustration with that."

Kluck's eyes turned to see a large-antlered buck standing on the edge of the forest watching them. The buck was peaceful, snow building on its brown fur, enjoying the Christmas Holidays perhaps, but loving the abandoned grounds.

"Have you ever watched animals play on school grounds during the weekend? Humans have set the hours when it is acceptable for them to come out. That is not sharing the world. That is not integration. Nature acts according to nature. It does cleanup and maintenance in harmony. We both cause the mess and subsequently are in the way during cleanup. And forget maintenance. Nobody moves unless it causes enough of a detriment to themself to care. **It used to be beautiful once.**"

The Skelekit stepped forward and like her little fox self, slinked low in the snow towards the deer. She had spotted an entire herd behind the one, except they were Skeledeer.

"Careful, Kit," Kluck said. "We don't want to scare them off – but my, are they gorgeous!"

They truly were. There was a mix of mothers, fathers, and their assortment of babies. Their off-white bones were a nice contrast against the snow and the Skelekit was smitten. She ran up to one of the babies and instantly wanted to play. She hadn't seen another skeleton since Tiergarten, and she felt immediately at home. A fawn stepped out to greet her and they circled each other. Then, a second fawn stepped out to join them. There were a lot of play bows and tumbles on the fresh snow.

"There is nothing quite like watching babies play," Kluck said.

Egon wasn't entertained and his teeth grinding became harsh as he looked around the premises. The Skelebabies were having a great time until the Skelekit playfully took one down. The buck was having no part of this and he put his head low to the ground and chased her off, then cornered and pinned her inside the jail bars of his antlers. Soot was hilarious. This was perhaps the warmest she had ever been in winter and she basked in the coziness of the saddle bag she was in. She peeked her head out enough to appear concerned and then tucked back down.

Frecher was not a hunter but a thief – a sugary sweet one, mind you – but he was really looking for opportunities. These Skeledeer had nothing to offer him and so it was his primary focus to stay away from the trampling of hooves.

Egon walked towards them and pulled out a carrot. Then he offered it at the ground where the buck's nose was.

"That was my trick as a child. I had everyone believing I ate a great assortment of food, when really, I only ate pumpernickel for the longest time - stuffed my pockets for the animals," Kluck laughed.

Egon gave him a stern look.

"Oh, don't be sour. Who would I tell?" Kluck giggled.

The buck sniffed the carrot from Egon and then raised his head off the Skelekit who tore back to the group and hid behind the weasel.

"Let them come to us," Kluck said.

The buck thought about it for a moment and then snapped off a bite - which echoed through the air.

The peace ended abruptly by the sound of a hound barking, which set off an entire pack barking. It was a faint forest echo that grew louder by the second. Reiter snorted and kicked his front hooves up and turned out of the way just in time to not be hit by a wild animal. It tore a line straight through the fresh snow and disappeared around the side of the building.

Egon's eyes grew wide as the Skelekit hopped into his coat and the weasel jumped into the saddle bag. Kluck got Reiter back in line but kept him pinned near the wall as the hounds flew in like a hurricane. Like most hounds, they had a strong scent that made their sniffers go crazy, and they practically ran each other over to get around the building. One must wonder how they could smell anything because they were pure bones – Skelehounds.

Egon tore around the side of the building to see where they

went but it all happened so fast and there were so many nooks and crannies in the courtyard to play chase in.

Just behind the dogs were horses – also Skelehorses...nothing covering them but a saddle and their riders – also Skeletons.

"You aren't freezing out here?" Kluck yelled as they flew by. Then he followed up with "Don't catch a cold!" to a straggler at the end.

Frecher barely popped his head out, but his two big brown eyes peered over the edge of the saddle bag followed by Soot's beak opposite him.

"Ah, it never gets old, does it? You doing alright, Soot? You still do not care – you are finally WARM! Ha HA!" he joked. "Well then, let's go see if Egon is fine, then."

Egon was fine but he was running now on the heels of the hounds and was breathing hard. The horses blazing by him made him toss himself out of the way, and he fell hard onto the ground.

Kluck and Reiter caught up, and Spickzettel trotted behind.

"Are you injured?" Kluck asked, but Egon rose to his feet and dusted the snow off.

Frecher and Soot looked alarmed.

"I believe he is fine, perhaps a little perturbed he is now behind," Kluck laughed.

Egon straightened his glasses and fixed his hat and then stormed off after them.

"Stay in one spot, Egon! Listen!" Kluck yelled to him.

Egon stopped and listened. They were coming back the other way. The animal they were chasing jumped up into the air and onto a nearby platform. It was a Skeleboar, much like Egon's Abboardion but without the instrument. As it hit the top of the cement box, three hounds jumped up and bit into it. When Egon saw it, he threw himself into the middle of them and they instantly turned into bronze, frozen mid-fight...now a sculpture, and not Skelecreatures anymore.

Egon was very still, one of his hands grabbing the back of a hound neck, the other arm pushing one back.

"You gave no thought to the consequences, my dear boy!" Kluck said, in total shock. "What did you think you were going to do? Break up a boar hunt?"

Egon dropped both arms down at his side as big snowflakes hit his face.

The Skelehorses and Skelehounds were nowhere to be found.

Frecher crawled out of the pouch and calmly wandered up to Egon. The Skelekit was hiding behind the platform, and Soot – well, she was a chicken. She stayed in her bag.

"I wasn't sure if you would see the sculpture come to life or if it would go from life back to bronze. It was the other way for me – wasn't it Frecher?" he said to a confused little weasel - errr stoat.

Egon turned to face them all. He was not happy but not upset. He looked off into the distance at what just transpired, then hopped off the platform.

As he stood in front of it, Kluck said, "Turn around and wipe the snow off the boar's hoof."

Egon furrowed his brow and turned to do so.

"What does it say?" Kluck asked, knowing Egon wasn't going to answer, but gave him a moment to process it.

"What does it say, Mr. Wolff?" Kluck asked again.

The carving plate said, "WILDSCHWEINJAGD – F.W. Wolff".

"What do you think of that?" Kluck asked.

A peripheral creature stepped out of the shadows. It was an unusually large black wolf.

"FRECHER! UP NOW!" Kluck warned.

Egon locked eyes with this gorgeous beast who was double the size of the rest of his pack. The parts of his body that were metal were shimmering through his shiny, thick, black-as-coal fur.

"That is Blackguard! Egon, remain calm," Kluck said nervously. "He is a bit - unpredictable."

Egon bowed his head and sat on the ground. He hugged his knees and hid his face. Blackguard stepped forward to sniff him, growling low and deeply in his chest. While Egon wasn't scared, he was playing it smart. Blackguard put his snout up to his jaw where the grinding of Egon's teeth could be heard.

Frecher looked at them and then up at Kluck with unease.

Blackguard then sat in front of Egon, puffed his chest out, put his face up to the sky and howled the most blood-curdling howl anyone had ever heard.

Egon remained in the same position, waited for the howl to be over, then extended his hand like he was asking to shake a paw. Blackguard sniffed his hand, ears, and face, then turned and walked into the woods.

"Well, that just happened!" Kluck said to Spickzettel, who was hiding behind Reiter. The horse and pony turned to look at each other as if to say, "Wow."

Egon took a few more moments to process it, then he got up and stormed off to the Lodge.

Kluck gave him some space and time. When he did approach him, he was shaking behind a rain barrel. Perhaps he was cold, perhaps he was upset, but appeared to want to be alone. His teeth must have been worn off from grinding them, but because he never spoke, nobody really saw inside his mouth. It just made a noise as unsettling as nails on a chalkboard.

The Skelekit was beside him, stuck to his leg, belly flat out.

"It is getting cold, Egon. Should we keep moving?" Kluck said but there was no movement. "Then, we wait."

A few minutes passed and Düster flew overhead. That made Egon get up.

"Spickz will still carry you - it isn't a problem for her."

The pony walked up to Egon and put her nose down. He touched her nose and kept walking.

"Sometimes, I think children have the right idea, Reiter. But I still appreciate you carrying me."

The air was getting colder as they were losing sun. That was the problem with a December adventure. The sun disappears before dinner.

"Would you like more pumpernickel, Egon?" Kluck said, after a long trek along the river. "Frecher, take these mittens to Egon. The sun isn't going to help us now."

Frecher ran up and handed the gloves and bread to Egon, and he took them. They looked big on his hands but were warm. Spickzettel still walked with him, but Egon wasn't taking her up on it. This was the first real journey he had been on where he was leading it, and he was on a mission. Düster soared when he needed to and landed on branches to show Egon the way.

Kluck needed to cut the silence.

"You were very brave with Blackguard back there," he said, trotting up beside him. "Not too many people have survived his hot breath on their face."

Egon kept a swift pace in his step and ate his bread.

"I am not certain that you found that to be a disturbing encounter with a wolf. Do you suppose he knew your last name?" Kluck chuckled. "Maybe he knew your middle name was Engel."

Egon was starting to get tired. The walking seemed to go on forever and it was cold. Düster landed on a branch and Egon was forced to stop.

"This doesn't seem right, Düster. This is the same landscape we have seen the whole time," Kluck said, looking around.

Düster hopped off and sat at Egon's feet and looked at him. Egon decided to sit.

"Düster is telling you to rest? Is that what we are to do now?" Kluck asked.

Düster hopped over to Spickzettel and scratched the snow in front of her. Spickzettel walked up beside Egon and kneeled her front legs down.

"It really is fine. She is offering, Egon," Kluck urged.

Egon looked at Düster who planted himself firmly in the snow and waited. Egon begrudgingly tucked the Skelekit in his coat and ever-so-gently climbed on her back.

"They really don't mind the friendship. They just don't want slavery, just like anyone," Kluck smiled. "Reiter and Spickz are happy to be out of small pens. They like adventure too."

Egon barely moved on her. He may have been cold, or he may have been afraid of hurting her. Düster returned to the air and they could finally move swiftly.

The river to their left turned to railway tracks, but the falling snow covered them quickly after trains passed. Because of the holidays, most people were in Berlin already, so not too many trains were running. Düster landed on a nearby brick wall of a train station and began to preen his feathers. Egon seemed to take that as a signal he could move freely, and he jumped off Spickz. Frecher and Soot stayed in their individual saddle bags and kept warm. Weasels – errr, stoats - are so lovely when curled up like croissants. Soot's thin eyelids going up instead of down was adorable too.

Kluck dismounted and did a big stretch.

"My bones sound like your teeth grinding! Aging is NOT for the old. We can't handle it!" Kluck laughed.

Reiter and Spickz trotted off to a small shelter where a few other horses were parked. There were water buckets and hay inside.

"Does it seem like you were just at a train station? Do not worry, I don't plan on going on one tonight. However, Düster wanted you here," he said, shrugging his shoulders. "Should we at least take advantage of the warmth?"

Egon looked at Düster who was quietly content to groom himself. He saw the arched doorway of the station and a sign above which read, 'Berlin-Grunewald'.

This train station had way more of the Orpo, or Order Police wandering around. The employees kept their chins low to their chests and didn't speak out of turn.

"We will reserve number seventeen," a high-ranking Orpo said to two others in uniform. "Please keep German families away from this platform as it will be for the chosen people in our population movement program."

"Very good, Sir!" a station employee responded.

A wealthy Jewish couple tried to slink by the soldiers, but they were detained.

"Show your identification," an Orpo said.

"You know I do not have what you want. It is Christmas, please. Just look the other way," the man begged.

The wife started crying and pleading with them. "We do not want any trouble! Please, Sir. Please!"

"Please take them into room four, I will be along shortly," a young General instructed.

"His parents think he is too young," one of the soldiers said, continuing a previous conversation. "Of course, he is not."

The man and wife continued to beg and plead as they were put into a detainment area.

"I joined at age sixteen with only four months of military training before I volunteered to serve on the Western front," a young General responded. "I was awarded this iron cross for bravery and it changed the entire trajectory of my life. I have no use for coddling. I have spoken with these boys. They are not just willing, but anxious to serve. It builds a man. After joining the regiment full-time, I received the first-class iron cross. I have no regrets."

"What is a General without regrets?" Kluck intervened.

"Good point, Feldmarschall," the young General said, with great respect. "Where did you serve, Sir?"

"Where did I NOT serve – that would be a shorter list. We must remember not to own these awards. No war is won – or lost – by one man, General," Kluck said sternly.

"Certainly not," he concurred. "What brings you here, Feldmarschall? Your time has passed, no? You can curl up with a good book and just pass the time now!" he laughed to his friends.

"We must also remember what is best for our country, not our ego," Kluck stated.

"Oh we are doing that, aren't we men?" the General laughed.

"STAND UP STRAIGHT when you address me," Kluck pulled rank.

"Sieg Heil!" the man said, correcting his misstep.

"It's alright, I was young and overly confident once, Kurt," Kluck smiled.

"You know who I am," he said, surprised.

"You have managed to make everyone know who you are, no?" Kluck said, snidely.

"I worked hard," Kurt smirked.

"I couldn't help but hear about this 'population movement program'," Kluck said. "That seems like a slippery agenda, no?"

"It will be a smooth implementation. It will be closely monitored," Kurt responded. "Again, you are at a grand part of your career – you don't need to concern yourself."

Kluck laughed. "Yes, I suppose this is true. I enjoyed today, for instance. I came in by horseback. Cold, but a wonderful way to clear one's head."

"By horseback you say?" he laughed with the group. "Forgive me Feldmarschall, but does it get, uh tricky to get on and off the horse? No disrespect, I am simply curious."

"Because of my age, I see," Kluck said, sharply. "I spent the day mentoring a young German boy. It was quite rewarding. You should try spending time with children. You can also learn from them. Do you have any of your own?"

"I do not," Kurt said. "Perhaps, one day."

"This boy came from an orphanage," Kluck began.

"Very kind of you," Kurt said, bored of the conversation. "If you will excuse me, Feldmarschall."

"When a boy is taken to an orphanage – with no explanation. When that boy is lied to by the adults in the room – with no consideration for his feelings. When that boy's past is covered up, or even manufactured, that boy has a right to know where he came from – so he can heal – so he can find his place – his purpose!"

"That sounds like a noble thing you are doing," Kurt said, attempting to ignore him.

"I would love to think I am noble. It is obedience to my calling," Kluck said.

"Listen, Feldmarschall, I am ever so happy to have met a distinguished hero like yourself, but I really must get back to my conversation. I do not wish to be rude to present company. I am sure you understand," Kurt said.

"Oh please – do carry on. It isn't my job to break up your

plans," Kluck grinned.

"Lovely meeting you, Feldmarschall," Kurt said. "Sieg Heil!"

"Let me conclude by saying, the iron cross will indeed change the trajectory of your life – in ways you couldn't imagine," Kluck smiled.

"Thank you, Feldmarschall," Kurt said. "Good night to you."

"Good night, General Wolff," Kluck said, and turned to walk past Egon, who was frozen staring at the man.

"Let's go, son," he said to Egon. "Egon, are you coming?"

Egon was stuck somewhere between the detained couple and General Wolff's name.

"You saw *him*, he does NOT need to see *you*," Kluck turned Egon's shoulders and guided him out.

As they exited the building, Egon's anxiety turned into a massive teeth-grinding session.

"Will you come sit with me for a minute, Egon," Kluck asked.

Egon's eyes were everywhere. He kept looking inside the station. His eyes danced between the Skelekit dancing around his feet and Düster still grooming himself. He finally sat in the snow beside a bench and hugged his knees, teeth still grinding away.

"We really must get you to a dentist to make sure you still have some left!" Kluck joked, then sat on the bench. "Your mind must be on fire now. I mean, never mind that you had two lifetimes of things happen to you before we ever left the farm!

Just know, I am with you on this journey, alright? He is a seriously flawed man, Egon. I am unwilling to say if someone is beyond redemption, but he is planning to execute an evil – a brand of evil this world has never known," Kluck said with his face in his hands. "Are you cross with me?"

Egon's eyes were on Düster. He showed no signs of anger.

Düster stretched his wings, jumped off his perch and hopped along the snowy train tracks. Egon got up to follow. Kluck stayed on the bench as the Skelekit followed but maintained a safe distance from the black eagle.

There was the number seventeen that they heard General Wolff discussing. It seemed just like any other platform, but it wasn't as visible to the public. If the Waffen were planning a 'population movement program' like they discussed, they could get away with it here quite easily.

"There are two types of vulnerable people, Egon. The kind who are stolen in vulnerable situations. Cats are set loose on cornered mice. They have no hope. They try sticking together in a bigger group or they scatter, and everyone takes the 'survival of the fittest' approach. Then, there are the vulnerable people who do not know they are vulnerable. They are the cats who have suffered hardships and wish to live like the other cats. They have never tasted power – but are promised access to power. This current brand of evil makes them feel like they have it even if it is an illusion."

Egon walked close to the wall of the platform, his right hand dragging along the cold brick as his eyes combed over the tracks to the left. He was suddenly stopped by his hand hitting something warm. As soon as he hit it, it jumped up and ran.

The snow was coming down in extra-large flakes now, so it was difficult to see what the figure was.

"Well, there he is," Kluck whispered. "I believe a big reason Düster brought you! Let's go get Reiter and Spickz!"

It seemed that Egon knew he would never catch up to the creature unless he got Spickz, because he hurried after Kluck to go retrieve them.

Reiter and Spickz had full bellies and Kluck thanked a station employee, then tossed him a few coins.

"Must go now! Uh – can you give an old man a boost up?" Kluck said to the worker, and up he went.

Egon easily mounted Spickz again as she bent down for him.

"Fancy little thing! Bareback too! Quite a new skill you have there!" Kluck said, proud of him.

There were enough tracks still in the snow to see where the creature went, even if they could not see him. Frecher and Soot peeked up again, trying to catch up on everything that was happening. It seemed like a long ride again. Every tree passing them looked the same, and the train tracks morphed back into forest. Without Düster and these large creature tracks, they would have no direction at all.

Finally, there was a building – a tower really. It was red brick and went straight up. Düster flew high to the top which was over fifty meters high. Reiter and Spickz moved slowly towards the tower. Both Kluck and Egon had their eyes on Düster, but they really should have looked down.

It was Soot who alerted them by clucking away. She was unnerved, but not enough to get out of her bag. Frecher started screaming, and the Skelekit dug herself deep inside of Egon's coat.

"Oh my," Kluck said, caught off guard.

It was a gorilla. He stood at the bottom of the tower, just a few steps from the black iron gate and stared at them all. He was hot and panting.

"Alright, it is alright, Zusa -" Kluck began but was cut off by the gorilla opening its jaws wide to SCREEEEEEEEEEEAM and then it pounded its chest hard.

Egon bowed his head. Kluck looked at Egon and mirrored him. They stayed quiet.

The gorilla stepped towards them and stood between their horses. Then, he gently touched Reiter and Spick's faces. He then looked up at Kluck but ignored him. He looked up at Egon who was not looking back. He reached up and put his hand on Egon's leg. It took a few moments for Egon to touch his hand, but he did, just on the tips of his fingers.

"Stay calm, Egon," Kluck whispered without looking up. "This is the magnificent Zusa!"

Zusa screamed at Kluck and then grabbed Egon off the pony. Egon went stiff as a board. He set him down onto the ground and then signaled for Spickz, who followed him to the black iron gate. It was at the bottom of a dozen or so steps with short pillars on either side. Zusa turned to Kluck and signaled for him as well. The Skelekit turned to wait for Egon, and Zusa growled for her to go too, so she obliged.

"Whatever communication animals have between themselves remains a mystery," Kluck smiled.

Egon was left in the snow confused while everyone else went through the gate, up the stone stairs and in through the arched doorway. In a few moments, Zusa came out for Egon. He sat on the step and waved for him to come over. Then he did something wonderful.

He hugged him.

He picked him up and set him on his lap and cuddled him as the snow came down. Nobody else saw it. Egon was never held before and it was hard to tell if he even liked it, but he *needed* it. Zusa pet his head and kissed his face and rocked for several minutes. Egon did not fight any of it. It was an amazing gesture.

Düster was watching them and circling the tower, avoiding the SS black eagle plaque on the high parts of the tower.

Zusa set Egon back on his feet and looked in his eyes. Egon's anxiety was gone. He was calm. He reached inside his coat and took out his book again. He handed it to Zusa who leafed through it quickly. He stopped at the page that had the crocodiles from Tiergarten. He tapped each of them on the page and looked at Egon who said nothing. Zusa closed the book and tucked it back in Egon's coat. Then he touched Egon's face and extended his hand. Egon took it. He didn't do that with people.

Egon looked up to see Düster's black wings against a cool

winter sky. As they walked past the gate and up the stairs to the tower, the snow was crunchy under their feet.

7 MORRIS THE WOODPECKER

Kluck was inside waiting patiently for Zusa and Egon to return to the Tower. Frecher and the Skelekit were becoming good friends, and Soot remained in Reiter's saddlebag.

"Would you like to stretch your wings a bit?" Kluck asked her. "Come on out!" he said, setting her on the diamond-shaped tiled floor. It was a mixture of white, black, and burgundy and was interlocked with precision.

The walls were red brick like the outside of the tower and the windows were extravagantly arched like a cathedral. The ceiling was vaulted with intertwined patterns of gold-leaf and greens between the red brick. This room had only one item in it. It was a marble statue of King Wilhelm I, the first Emperor of Germany and King of Prussia. The Grunewald Tower was built as a memorial to mark his one hundredth birthday. It did not appear to serve any other purpose except for the observation deck, some fifty meters up, which overlooked the Havel River.

Zusa and Egon finally came in.

"Thank you, Zusa - for the food for everyone," Kluck said, while standing in front of Wilhelm's statue. Reiter and Spickz were munching on oats in buckets. "It smells like Christmas!"

Zusa was holding Egon's hand in the doorway and staring at Kluck.

"Oh, I suppose you need me to move - right away!" and he stepped aside.

Zusa looked down at Egon who was holding tightly to his arm.

"I suppose you had a conversation," Kluck smiled, tearing up over their instant connection. "Egon looks relaxed again. It was a terribly tense day for him. He has been grinding his teeth so much."

Zusa pulled his arm away and squatted down in front of Egon. He put a finger on his bottom lip and Egon dropped his jaw open. Zusa examined his mouth and ran his finger along his molars. He then put his hands on his own cheeks showing Egon how to relax his jaw. Egon mirrored him. Then, he walked over to the statue. With one giant shove, he pushed it back to reveal a door in the floor.

"I love you, Zusa! Who would you like to invite down?" Kluck asked.

Zusa pointed to Egon, who immediately grabbed his hand again with so much enthusiasm, it was like trying ice cream for the first time and wanting more of it. Zusa then pointed to the Skelekit, who stood behind Egon, naturally. Frecher ran straight up to the gorilla and boldly asked to go with begging eyes. Zusa pointed behind the Skelekit, and Frecher ran there.

"No Reiter and Spickz?" Kluck said.

Zusa shook his head 'no'.

"I can see how that wouldn't work," Kluck laughed. "Well, I guess they can wait here. They are sheltered anyways," Kluck said, walking to the door in the floor.

Zusa jumped in front of him and stood an inch from his face, blocking his way.

"I will wait, Zusa. It was rude of me," Kluck said, bowing his head.

Zusa put a finger under Kluck's chin and looked him in the eyes. Then, he grabbed the fur busby off his head, sniffed it, and set it on the floor.

"Oh. My apologies. I must wear it, or they will suspect, Zusa. I get into all sorts of places most people don't."

Zusa kicked it to the wall by Reiter and Spickz, then played with Kluck's messy hair.

"I know its a nightmare," Kluck laughed. "I never know when you are playing with me. It always makes me nervous!"

Then, Zusa instructed Kluck to go down.

Clucking at his feet was Soot. Zusa picked her up and kissed her all over. She did not know what to do with all that love, but there she was getting it. Zusa carried her under his left arm and reached out for Egon with his right. Egon took his hand again and down they went, Frecher and the Skelekit running happily between them. Zusa let go of Egon's hand and closed the door in the floor behind them.

It was unclear whether this secret passage was constructed at the same time as the Tower, or afterwards, but it was very intriguing to Egon. He was not a fearful boy and found a wonderful new group of friends who seemed to like adventure. The hallway was dark, nearly black for several meters, and the walls and floor were rock and dirt.

Zusa instructed them to all be silent by putting his finger up to his lip. Then, he knocked three times on a wooden, arched doorway. It took some time for all the locks to be unlocked. It sounded like there were five of them. On the other side, was an old woman, kerchief on her head and a Christmas apron against her red checkered dress, who was drying her hands on a green tea towel.

"Who do you have, Zusa?" she asked. "Why, General Kluck – good to see you again. And who is this?" she said, looking at Egon.

"Hello Mrs. Winter – it is indeed Winter!" Kluck said and kissed her cheek. "I smell oranges and cinnamon!"

"Oh yes, this is the only Christmas you will find without the SS on every ornament," she laughed. "Come in! Get warm! So glad to have you!"

They all went in except for Zusa. Egon walked back out with him.

"It's alright, Egon!" Mrs. Winter explained. "Zusa is going back up. He gets too hot down here!"

"Speaking of that, can you grab blankets for the horses? Zusa already gave them bedding," Kluck said.

Egon wanted to leave with Zusa, but he picked Egon up, hugged and kissed him all over, and then set him back down.

"He takes pride in his guarding, Egon. He will see you soon," Kluck added. "You are one of his treasures, he must keep you safe."

"Here are the blankets for the horses, Zusa," Mrs. Winter said, handing him heavy wool.

Egon turned and faced the wall in the corridor. Zusa touched his head and went back up. They all heard the marble statue scrape along the floor, presumably back to its position.

"Come in when you are ready, Egon," Mrs. Winter said. "The other children are having dessert."

Mrs. Winter and Kluck went inside and the children all cheered when they saw the General. Egon stayed in the hall and pulled out his book to look at the crocodiles.

"I missed you too!" he could hear Kluck call out to them cheerfully. "I see new faces! And what is your name?"

"We have a new boy named Egon!" Mrs. Winter said.

"I was scared to come in too," a young boy piped up.

"Oh, I doubt Egon is fearful, I think he just loves Zusa! He doesn't speak, so I am not entirely sure," Kluck said.

"Everyone loves Zusa!" another girl laughed.

While everyone was getting to know one another, a girl with

leg braces got up and hobbled out the door. She had sandy blonde hair cut just below her ear and the bangs were held back with a clip and silk white flower. She was wearing a school uniform and skirt so you could see her braces up around her knees.

"I stood out here for a whole hour when I arrived," she said to Egon. "It was the most peace I had in months."

Egon kept his nose in his book.

"Did he hug you and kiss you and rock you?" she asked. "He did that to me too. It is like being in heaven."

Egon looked at her legs.

"Yes, I am broken. So are you," she said. "Everyone is. So, I hear you don't speak. See? It is because you are broken. I keep saying it. Everyone is broken."

Egon put his nose in the book and ran his fingers over the crocodiles.

"I am Anna, by the way. I am almost ten. The children here were all stolen...and now we have been stolen from the thieves. It's never going to end," she said, sliding down the wall beside him.

"May I see what you are looking at?" she said, peeking in his book.

Egon showed her the page.

"Are you an artist? They are nice looking crocodiles. I cannot draw anything. I do not even know what I am good at. I am good at hiding...and running, well on these stupid things."

Egon closed his book and put it back in his coat.

"I am good at thinking, though. I spend a lot of time thinking...by myself. They treat us kindly here, but we must hide for now. I do understand. I just think I was meant for something bigger. You know what I mean? But how do you know where you are supposed to go when you are not allowed to go?"

Egon was exasperated and hugged his knees.

"Look, Egon," she said, pointing to her braces. "I can't even bring my knees up like that."

She sat with her legs straight out.

"See? I am basically a dolly you put on your bed," she joked, dropping her head to one side, and making a blank face. Then she laughed at herself. "There's not much to do here, sorry to be the bearer of bad news."

Kluck tucked his head out in the hall.

"Are you sure you two don't want to join us? Mrs. Winter made a lovely meal! The children are having plum pudding, but she can heat up anything you want."

Egon kept his face in his knees.

"I'll have pudding," Anna said, getting up like a stiff tin man. "I am going to invent better ones someday."

"I am sure you will, you are a very bright girl, Anna!" Kluck smiled, patting her shoulder as she went back in.

Kluck walked over to Egon and said, "You are with friends now, Egon. You can feel safe coming in. Zusa must protect the outdoors. It is his great purpose in life. He does it on his own. It is his choice."

Egon looked down the hall where Zusa went.

"There are a couple people you will want to see, Egon!" Kluck tried to entice. "No? Ok, I am sure Charlotte and Rita will understand."

That made Egon shoot his head straight up and jump to his feet, although he stopped just inside the door to look around. There was a whole harvest table full of children and it seemed a bit too much to walk into. It was a lovely big room with fire burning, a pine wreath bordering the fire with red berries set in it every few inches. There were candles lit and everyone was cheery and chatty.

"Egon! How did you? What happened?" Charlotte said, dumping her pudding and dropping her chair on the way over. She flung her arms around his neck. "I didn't think I would see you – well, after the incident with your akkordion! Where on Earth did you go?"

"They know each other?" Mrs. Winter asked. "How delightful!"

"Egon saved Charlotte – and they became such good friends, I thought they should see each other at Christmas," Kluck said.

While Egon did not show much emotion, he pushed his chair right into hers and sat down. Anna sulked about this and left the room.

"Anna will be fine," Mrs. Winter said. "She just requires her alone time more than the others."

"Let me go speak with her," Kluck said.

Rita was on the other side of Egon, chucking food in front of him. "Mrs. Winter cooked the best meal! I think I ate all of her glazed carrots, though!" she laughed.

"You ate yours and everyone else's I think!" Charlotte laughed.

Meanwhile, Kluck knocked on the bedroom door. "May I come in, Anna?"

"Yes," she said faintly.

"The beds are getting closer together in here," he sighed.

It was a long underground bunker with dozens of bunk beds, some three high. Anna was about halfway down on the bottom of one of them. Kluck looked at them all as he walked.

"You children make your beds nicely! Great work!" Kluck said, stopping at Anna's bed. "I am too old to sit," he laughed. "I tried to ride a horse today. Between you and me – that was rough!" and he sat on a bed opposite to her.

"I would love to ride a horse. Breathe the open air. I do not know what to do in here. It's making me crazy," Anna pouted.

"I wish I could explain how lovely this is in here compared to how it is going to be out there," Kluck began.

"I would be willing to risk it," she said.

"Where did you come from, Anna?" Kluck asked.

"I was stolen from Poland," she said, flopping herself down onto her pillow.

"Where are your parents, Anna?"

"Maybe dead," she said, with tears in her eyes.

"I see," Kluck said. "You want to find them."

"Yes," she said, crying now.

"Let me be upfront with you. I do not lie to children. If they are dead, what do you think they would want you to do?" Kluck asked.

She thought about this for a moment.

"If they are dead, their opinion no longer matters to me," she said, becoming angry.

"Anna, if they are dead – if they are alive - their opinion can be heard, but ultimately, at some point, and frankly, it may be sooner than later, you will have to make very pointed decisions really quickly. These decisions must come from you. They must be to further your life but more than that, they must be for the betterment of all. I am certain they would have liked to have had more time with you to teach you this, but time is going to elude you now. I must fill your tank quickly. You must get yourself from zero to one hundred FAST! I do not tell you this to steal your emotions, but we brought you here to try and protect you – because we need you safe."

"I want to be useful!" she said, hitting her pillow.

"The Universe hears things like that – and even a big Universe like ours cannot ignore a little girl's massive heart. There is much work to do! Be patient. You are so loved!" he said, trying to get up.

"Do you hear those bones? Terrible. I am ready for one of these beds right now," Kluck laughed. "Will you help an old man to his feet?"

"You do realize who you are asking," she said, looking at her braces.

"I love you AND your braces, Anna!" Kluck said, hugging her. "Everyone is broken, right?"

That made Anna smile and they walked out to join the rest of the children.

"Can I see the horses?" she asked.

"We'll see if it is safe!" Kluck smiled.

Anna quietly returned to the group, a tiny bit better than when she left.

"I am so glad you could have Christmas with friends, Egon," Kluck smiled.

"Glad Viktor didn't come!" Rita whispered to Charlotte.

"We are concerned about Viktor. He was plucked out and taken for training. We have not given up on him," Kluck said to Mrs. Winter.

"We do not give up on anyone," she responded.

"The German soldier who is part of his Viktor's training is also the man who sent you and Charlotte here, Rita. Without him, I am not sure where you would have gone," Kluck informed her.

"I'm sorry, General," Rita said, hanging her head.

"Don't be ashamed, I value your feelings about Viktor. Please continue to be open and I will do my best to add clarity," Kluck said, patting her head.

"There is a lovely mixed bag of children here, Egon!" Mrs. Winter explained. "Edward from Belgium, Mila, Julia and Anna are from Poland, the twins, Ivan and Illia are from Russia and Filip is from Czechoslovakia..."

"Egon will be overwhelmed if we try to name everyone tonight!" Kluck laughed.

"I miss my school," Filip said sadly.

"I miss my bicycle," Edward added.

"I just want to play games," Charlotte said.

"Yes, no more marching and flag-waving, day in, day out," Rita said.

"At least living underground, no military parades!" Charlotte said.

"I want my name back," Mila said. "I don't like Helga!"

"Think of it like a secret agent! Or a pen name! You can be you in here and a special agent out there," Mrs. Winter laughed.

"How about you, Anna?" Kluck said. "Do you want to share?"

"I don't belong here," Anna said quietly with her head down.

Mrs. Winter bent down and held Anna's face.

"You belong wherever you go! Your environment does not make you! You are a strong girl. You will walk into any room and demand that it belongs to you. You are ANNA! Someday, you will be responsible for great things! I see this in you!"

"Not just someday - TODAY!" Kluck added. "You helped Egon with his transition TODAY. You bravely walked out there and shared yourself with him. You absolutely belong here, lovely lady!"

Egon's eyes were everywhere on every child, but mostly petting the Skelekit inside his coat.

"Egon does not speak, children. I am hesitant to speak for him, either," Kluck said. "I can safely say, Egon was not brought here from another country like many of you. He has not watched his parents killed in front of him, like some of you. He has his own story. He has a reason he is here. It is important we accept one another despite the country we are from. You are only some of the children. There are more. There will be more. We are going to help whoever we can. If you were brought to this location today, it is because we believe you are powerful enough to change the course of this terrible war. What happened to you, your parents, your friends, your siblings...they have plans to do this to hundreds of thousands. I am not telling you. I am asking you to help us. Do as much as you are able. Keep speaking about your feelings. Come to me, come to Mrs. Winter. Look out for each other – and above all else – be ever so patient. This is a marathon, not a sprint," Kluck concluded.

"I do not belong here!" Anna said boldly.

"Give it time, Anna," Mrs. Winter said. "It is Christmas Eve, let us not be so gloomy! How about some games?"

The children all cheered as Mrs. Winter retrieved a box that had card games, dominoes, and checkers. Some stayed at the table while others moved to the floor by the fire.

"We have to extinguish the fire soon, it was special tonight, but we cannot have it alert anyone," Mrs. Winter said.

"It is well routed to a safe area," Kluck added.

"You know me, can never be too safe! They are my lovelies!" she smiled.

"It's a cold night. The airpipe doesn't help," Kluck said. "Where are Frecher and Soot?"

"I put them in with the others while you were speaking to Anna," Mrs. Winter said, washing some plates.

"Egon, would you join me?" Kluck waved for him to go to another room.

Egon didn't seem interested in games, so he got up to follow Kluck. On the other side of the heavy metal door were the sounds of multiple animals in pens. Egon began to walk by each one.

"They complained about the killing and experimenting of animals, and yet we found these creatures at the Schakal Haus Institution. The doctors had to try things on animals before they do it people," Kluck said sadly.

Egon tried to open the cages of the rabbits.

"They are hurt and resting, Egon. Think of it like they are in their hospital bed. We need better assistance for them, but that will come."

Egon looked in the cage of a Beagle and reached through the bars to touch it.

"You have been taught about Germany protecting the animals. They protect Germans too. They protect whoever is superior. Wolves and horses are always saved. It is why we can leave Reiter and Spickz above ground. Hopefully, they are quiet enough to not alert anyone, but they will never be killed. However, it is important to note – and I was taught this at the highest level – the extermination of people who are not Aryan can effectively be implemented due to the experimentation on animals who are also not deemed superior. Most of these animal laws are made so they have an excuse to send people to camps... or immediately to their death."

Egon simply didn't like them in there.

"Would you like to hold the Beagle? You need to be careful. She is so old. She has known no other life."

Egon stepped back to let him open the cage.

"I don't even know why we lock her in. She has never tasted freedom. She wouldn't know the difference," Kluck said, lifting her out.

She was a rag doll. She barely opened her eye to acknowledge them. Kluck set her gently in Egon's arms, and the Skelekit jumped out of the way.

"We got her just before they were going to inflict her with a gangrene wound," Kluck began.

Egon's teeth began to grind, and he walked away from Kluck.

"I tell you because you are ever so crucial to the reversal of so many horrors, Egon. I tell you because I know you have a big job ahead of you. I was lied to as a child. I will not lie to you. If you understand, you will be better equipped to deal with the cruelties - and the overall mentality we are up against. None of this is meant to upset you."

Egon cuddled her close to his chest. He learned a quick lesson today from Zusa in identifying those who needed love and cuddles.

"We will fix who we can. Those we can't, we will get professionals to help – when we can," Kluck said. "Would you like to see how we will leave here someday? It will need your help, though!"

Egon didn't want to set the Beagle down.

"Can we let her rest in her hospital bed?"

Egon thought about that and then kissed her head the way Zusa did. He set her back inside her cage, and before closing it, he touched her head the way Zusa touched his.

"You are learning how amazing it is to give love! Zusa is an exceptionally good teacher. Thank you, Egon!"

There was yet another set of doors leading to a new area. It looked more like an airplane hangar than a room and had only one thing in it - an enormous TANK. It was outrageous. It was over six metres high, three metres across and a monstrous thirteen metres long. It was one hundred and twenty ridiculous tonnes.

"How did it get IN, you may ask? How will it get OUT?" Kluck laughed.

Egon stretched out his hand and began to walk the whole length of it as Kluck followed. It had the typical roller-type track system with iron crosses every meter and was fitted together in six modules.

"I oversaw its creation at the War Ministry in 1917. After the Battle of the Somme, I was part of a committee to investigate tank development. It is where the initial Panzer unit was created."

Egon stopped and looked at him.

"The money that poured into that research could have fed a whole country ten times over for a year. However, the naval blockades stopped access to raw material, so everyone pretended they were dishonorable weapons – and the money went into U-Boats."

Egon pulled out his book.

"Oh yes, you saw the current plan. Eugen is working on the next monster. Between those and the elite infantry – plus the stormtroopers, they will be unstoppable. Would you like to see inside?"

Egon seemed disinterested in stepping in.

"Twenty-seven. That is the number of crew that could work in there. Seven gunners operating the MG08 machine guns – and that is just the fighting room – never mind the control room or engine room. It could go seven and a half kilometers per hour!"

Instead of going inside, Egon walked to the front to have a look at the where the main gun normally was. Instead, it was a hardened armoured elephant trunk, mostly metal but three-quarters rusty.

"It was the world's first super tank. There was only two of them – and they were meant to be destroyed. As you can see, that didn't happen."

Egon gave a very stern look.

"I was like you, Egon – in an even uglier time. They knew I had the talent to do this. My childhood was mostly forced labour and terrible experimentation. We don't have to talk about that now. What do you think of the elephant trunk? That was my own personal modification. Kind of fun, no?"

Egon looked up at it and his teeth began to grind.

"I thought that might speak to you," Kluck smiled. "I call it 'The JUGGERKAMPF'. What a colossal failure," he said, looking up at the mammoth. "Well, over the last two decades for me, it has passed the time."

Egon put his nose back in his book.

"I hope someday, you will feel safe sharing your thoughts with me. Perhaps by me sharing my projects with you, you will be inspired."

Frecher and Soot were frozen in the doorway. They wanted to know what was going on, but they didn't.

"Shall we head back out?" Kluck said, guiding Egon back through the double doors.

Frecher ran into the animal room and onto the Beagle's cage.

"He is doing fine, Frecher. If nothing else, he can carry out his final days among family. He can experience his golden years restfully."

Tappity-tap tap – TAP – tap - PITY tap —tap - pity TAP!

"Oh! Soot got herself locked in the room!"

Tappity-tap tap – TAP – tap - PITY tap —tap - pity TAP!

Egon walked over to the door to let her out while Kluck fought with Frecher over latching and unlatching the cage.

Tappity-tap tap – TAP – tap - PITY tap —tap - pity TAP!

Egon placed his ear against the door and listened intently.

"Are you going to let her out?" Kluck asked, still fumbling with the cage.

Egon slowly opened the door and Soot came flying out.

"Why Soot! Were you scared my girl?" Kluck laughed, picking her up.

The Skelekit stayed close to Egon as he walked halfway into the room and looked up.

DAH-dit-dit dit-DAH DAH-dit DAH-DAH-dit dit dit-DAH-dit was the sound of tapping on the ceiling above.

Egon ran out past Kluck through the animals' chambers, through the room where they ate and back out into the hall. Anna got up and immediately tore after him.

Kluck after hearing it himself, ran out to inform Mrs. Winter.

"Morse code in the ceiling of the hangar– DANGER!" Kluck said. "Do not scare the children, get them inside the Juggerkampf – but do not create panic. Close the door behind you and wait for my knock and ONLY my knock. Understood?" he said, helping the children.

"Yes! Come children, everyone grab something from the table – everyone grab a game – If you have an extra hand, grab any other stray item," she said, extinguishing the fire with a pail of dirt and looking around for straggling objects.

Up top, Zusa picked up Kluck's busby hat which **used to be a beautiful animal once**, and smelled it, disgusted that is was fur. He ran his finger along the front skull and touched his own face. He looked inside and then placed it on his own head. He stood up tall like Kluck, turned like a stiff soldier and saluted Reiter and Spickz. They did, as one would expect, nothing. It was something for him to do.

Anna knocked on the exit door with the same three knocks Zusa used when he brought the children down.

"He responds immediately – every time – he is not responding, Egon!" Anna panicked.

"Everyone into the Juggerkampf – quickly!" Mrs. Winter whispered.

The children were well trained at this and did so efficiently, not leaving a trace of their presence anywhere.

"What is that tapping above?" Charlotte asked Mrs. Winter.

"I believe that is Morris the Woodpecker. He is a great lookout soldier!" she said, hurrying them along.

Zusa also heard the woodpecker tapping, so he grabbed both horses and hurried them down the steps and around back where he hid them behind the brick wall encompassing the Tower. He tried to ignore Anna's knocking, but finally had to move the statue to stop her. He opened the door under it, and she came running up and into his arms.

"I want to help! Please let me help!" she begged Zusa.

He slammed the door down onto Egon, grabbed her in his arms, and hid her with the horses.

Kluck ran out as the door came down hard, and he saw Egon fly into the hallway wall from the jolt. He ran over and picked him up.

"If Zusa slammed that door, you MUST go hide with the others!" Kluck urged.

Egon kept looking up.

"Egon! NOW!" he stormed in a voice a parent only uses when their child is about to be struck on the road.

Egon kept looking up at the door and then went with Kluck back down, through the kitchen and they locked the door to the animals' chambers.

They went into the room with the tank and Kluck could still hear the Morse code above signaling danger.

"Into the Juggerkampf!" Kluck instructed.

Egon ran in, Skelekit still glued to him...and Frecher and Soot hurried with them. Kluck was the last in and closed the door.

"Is everyone accounted for?" Kluck asked Mrs. Winter.

"I thought you were bringing Egon AND Anna with you? Where is Anna?" Mrs. Winter asked.

Kluck got up to go find her, but Egon grabbed his arm. He grabbed his book and began to sketch a gorilla and then he pointed to it.

"Zusa has her?" Kluck asked. "We can't risk going up. If Zusa has her, she is safer than us."

The tapping stopped and they all waited patiently.

"Who is Morris the Woodpecker, General?" Charlotte asked.

"Like Mrs. Winter said, he is a fine lookout soldier," Kluck added. "We need to lock the door of the tank. They cannot hear us if it is closed."

"How will we know it is safe to go out?" Rita asked.

"I don't know the answer to that. We just wait," Mrs. Winter said, putting her arm around her.

"If it all goes properly, we should get an 'ALL CLEAR' from Morris," Kluck explained.

"Like, he will tap it to us – oooooooh – he knows that code!" Rita said, a lightbulb going off over her head.

"Morse code!" Kluck said, patting her shoulder. "Well done, Rita!"

"Morris code!" she laughed.

"Yes, Morris code today, anyways!" Kluck laughed. "I suppose it is Soot code too!" he said, petting the chicken. "Soot alerted us first! I knew there was a reason you came along today!"

Rita was pleased with herself as she got all the children to laugh in a scary situation which unfortunately, Anna was unable to do back at the horses.

"You look so funny in Kluck's hat!" Anna whispered as loudly as possible.

Unamused, Zusa took it off and set it under Reiter.

"Zusa, I will fight with you! Tell me what to do and I will do it!" she said fiercely.

Zusa motioned for her to stay put and she curled herself into a ball by the wall. She didn't even know what she was fighting. Everyone was waiting – but they didn't even know what for.

"Today, Soot stretched her wings and came out of her bag," Kluck laughed. "She had a job to do – and she did it. Take note, dear children, your lesson today came from this chicken."

"Saved by the chicken!" Rita exclaimed.

8 THE GOLDEN EAGLE SWARM

Zusa stretched his hand out and the woodpecker landed on his finger. It was no ordinary woodpecker. Its body was mostly there – bits of white and black speckled feathers and a pointy red head. Its beak was reconstructed by someone. It was a shimmering silver, sharper than the point on a nail. Its metal wings were also added on – like it was part of a scientific experiment or was an alien half-breed. Zusa just loved him and ran a finger down his back lovingly.

Anna slowly tiptoed over to watch them.

"May I hold him, Zusa?" she whispered. "He is ever so beautiful."

He looked around nervously and then walked the woodpecker over to her. She sat on a step and with his free hand, Zusa took Anna's hand and turned it so her palm was facing down. The woodpecker stepped out onto her hand.

"DIT-DAH-DIT-DIT DAH-DAH-DAH DIT-DIT-DIT-DAH DIT" the woodpecker tapped on her leg brace and then flew off abruptly.

"What does that mean, Zusa?" Anna asked, giggling.

Zusa drew a heart in the snow with his finger.

"Love? Does it mean love?" she said, amazed by him.

Zusa nodded yes.

"In sign language, you just cross your arms like this on your chest," she said.

Zusa crossed both hands over the middle of his chest.

"Yes! That is it! We all work well together! You don't get lonely out here? If I can get warmer clothes, I could help you. Look at my legs! They have bits of metal too!" Anna laughed.

Zusa picked her up and set her on his knee - then hugged her.

"You love children so much. Did you have any children? I mean, before you got here."

Zusa tapped one fist on his chest.

"Your heart is broken," Anna said, sadly.

The woodpecker really meant what he said on the first notice and he warned them again.

"DAH-dit-dit dit-DAH DAH-dit DAH-DAH-dit dit dit-DAH-dit" they heard on a metal pipe close by.

Zusa picked up Anna and put her back with the horses.

The Grunewald Forest was thick at the best of times and hard to navigate through on such a snowy night. A group from the Order Police parked their car and six men poured out of it. Even though each of them was carrying a flashlight, it made it difficult because of the large snowflakes.

"Someone saw a gorilla running from the train station in this direction," one of the officers said to a team of others. "Hopefully, we can wrap this up quickly. I wish to spend time with my family tonight."

"Another man said they saw an elderly General following him," a second officer said.

"So many good men from that war lost their minds, but I have never heard of them wandering off and chasing monkeys through the bush on Christmas Eve!" the first officer said, and they all laughed.

"It was a Feldmarschall. General Wolff spoke with him at the train station just before. After hearing that an eyewitness said an elderly General was following him, he is indeed concerned that he has gone mad and wishes to have him brought in for assessment," the highest ranking official in the group said. "And the gorilla is entirely possible as they have been looking for Zusa from the Zoo since the Fall. Take your post seriously. Let's split off – we will cover more ground."

The group split into three each. Zusa needed to make a bold move as they were too close to the Tower. He moved quietly away from the Tower and then purposely broke a branch to distract them.

"There is the gorilla!" one of them yelled and three of them took off on foot.

Zusa could move quicker than they could and with the snow coming down, it covered the tracks almost immediately. He made some good gorilla noises and they followed. Just as they thought they were getting closer, he would speed up and lose them.

"He is running right back to the train station. We will alert the Zoo about the gorilla. I am not going to chase him all night. Our families are waiting," the head Orpo said.

Anna got sick of staying behind the wall. She had been waiting in a bunker since the Fall Blitzkrieg in Poland – and she had enough! She quietly moved out and saw the second group of three men circling the Tower. Because it was red brick and enormous, it was the only thing they could see – and one of the only landmarks in the Forest that people recognized.

She patted Reiter and Spickz.

"Death Marchers," she whispered to them. "You can tell by the spiders on their arm. Don't make a sound. Zusa will come get you soon!"

She kissed them both on the muzzle, then walked the opposite way around the Tower.

"I am so glad someone found me!" she yelled and waved.

"Child, why are you in the middle of the Forest? There is a gorilla on the loose!" the head Orpo said.

"I was – uh – going for a Christmas Eve stroll in the woods and lost my way. Can you point me back to the train station?" Anna lied.

"All by yourself? In the woods? And you wish to return to the train station?" he laughed.

"I am admittedly a bit of an adventurous type," she said. "I wasn't anticipating the snow would cover my tracks so quickly."

"What is your name?" he demanded.

Anna's last name was Nowak, but she quickly offered them her German spy name.

"Anna Schmidt," she boldly offered them.

"Alright, Anna Schmidt. What happened to your legs?"

"Born that way, Sir. As you can see, they don't stop me. I am preparing for the Maidens. I am almost ten!"

Anna had done some homework. The Jungmädelbund was the youth section of the Band of Maidens, but you had to be ten to enter it.

"Hmmmmmm, I would say you may be pretty enough to join the Faith and Beauty Society when you are older!" he said.

"Thank you - very kind, Sir," Anna replied.

The head of the first group blew a loud whistle signaling the end of their search.

"Have you seen an elderly General? He was wearing a busby – very tall – would be hard to miss," he asked her.

"No, but the visibility isn't very good tonight," she said.

"You are coming with us, child," he said.

"Thank you very much. I really appreciate it," she said, rather impressed with her own manipulation.

"She is fair-haired. Even if she were not born in Germany, she could be trained," one of the men whispered.

"The leg braces are a problem," one of them whispered. "We can sort it out when we get back."

The man blew his whistle back and they caught up with the group and headed back to their car parked on the side of the Forest. Anna got in and strained to look through the snow.

"A gorilla?" she joked. "That is so funny! Alright – WE ARE LEAVING YOU, GORILLA! THANK YOU FOR NOT EATING ME! YOU CAN GO BACK TO – UH – BEING A GORILLA NOW," she laughed, trying to get the men to laugh and alert Zusa at the same time.

The men did smile – and Anna grinned at how she swayed them. She just didn't have a follow-up story yet.

"Should someone go check on Anna?" Charlotte asked.

"Absolutely not – not until we get an ALL CLEAR message from Morris," Kluck warned. "It could put the entire group - and this bunker at risk. I will leave the tank door open a crack so we can hear."

"You are a good soldier," Mrs. Winter told her.

"Oh yes," Kluck agreed. "A good soldier looks after the team – but always has to be strategic and clever about protecting the core group and hiding spot. What is the first thing one should do when someone else is in trouble?"

"Help?" Filip from Czechoslovakia asked.

"Very good, but that is number three," Kluck said, patting his leg. "What is number one and two?"

"If I was helping someone who was drowning, I would put on my own lifejacket first," said Edward from Belgium.

"Very good, Edward! You and Filip would make excellent teammates! That is number two," Kluck cheered.

Illia, one of the Russian twins, piped up and said, "Breathe?"

"And why would you say that?" Kluck asked.

"Because when I am frightened, I stop breathing," she said, taking a deep breath.

"It is exactly what you do. It is number one. Nice work, Illia!" and he touched the tip of her nose and she smiled. "Fear takes our breathing first. Our own lungs need help first. Never forget this."

"Breathing helps me to think clearly," her twin brother Ivan added.

"Yes – and once you can breathe, you can help," Mrs. Winter added.

"*Once you can breathe, you can help*. A lovely way to summarize it," Kluck smiled.

Soot interrupted them and tapped on the floor of the tank.

"Oh! Listen, everyone!"

DAH-DIT-DAH-DIT DIT-DAH-DIT-DIT DIT DIT-DAH DIT-DAH-DIT

"CLEAR!" Kluck exclaimed. "Anytime I heard that in my life was a grand moment! Thank you for your patience, children! And you got in here in record time! Now, you will know that if it happens again, you can probably even beat your time! What a FINE group! Ever so proud of you!"

Kluck walked out, and Frecher ran close to his heels. He tapped on the door and then heard the statue move. There was a sad Zusa standing with shoulders drooping, petting Morris, wearing his busby hat.

"Zu-sa," Kluck managed to get out through a lump in his throat.

As he walked up the steps, he said, "Zusa – look at me!" and then touched the gorilla's face.

Zusa had lost his confidence and looked ashamed, he took off the hat and set it on Kluck's head.

"Thank you – but where is Anna, Zusa?" he whispered to him.

Morris the woodpecker stepped off Zusa's finger and sat on one of the short pillars beside the steps and relayed this message by tapping on it:

DAH-DAH-DIT DIT DIT DIT-DAH-DIT DIT-DAH-DIT-DIT
DAH-DAH-DIT DAH-DAH-DAH DAH-DIT DIT

"Girl – GONE." Kluck said, unable to breathe. "Zusa help me – who took her?"

Zusa banged his chest and pointed up. A great swarm of eagles, birds not known to fly in groups, was circling the Tower. They were not black like Düster. They were gold from the tip of their beaks to the ends of their tails.

"They were here," Kluck said with great concern and he immediately ran back down the steps.

"May I speak with you, Mrs. Winter?" he said, directing her out into the hallway.

"What is happening?" she asked.

"They snatched Anna. Zusa is out of breath, so I will assume he either played his decoy game or there was a struggle. Either way, he wouldn't just hide and let her be taken," he said.

"Well, we can't just let them take her! With her braces, they will transport her somewhere awful!" Mrs. Winter said.

"That is a real possibility! I will not lie to the children, but we must continue to teach them about patience and approach. We must implement the strategy and stay on course. Egon is here now, this will accelerate it," he said putting an arm around her and guiding her back in.

"She is a spunky girl – and smart as a fox," Mrs. Winter said, trying to find a bright light. "She will survive this. Look what she has already been through!"

"She said she didn't belong here – perhaps she didn't," Kluck said. "Let's trust her instincts for now. Let's trust our patience too – it has worked for us in retrieving each child so far."

"Shall we go explain to the rest of the children?" she asked.

"Yes - be calm - show control," he said, as they walked in.

"WHERE IS ANNA?" and "YEAH – WHERE IS ANNA?" and "DID THEY TAKE ANNA?" is how they were met as soon as they walked in.

"Please children, sit down," Kluck began. "What is the first thing we do?"

"We breathe," Illia, one of the Russian twins said.

"Why do we breathe?" Kluck asked.

"So we can think clearly," her brother Ivan added.

"We are going to breathe through our nose for five seconds one...two...three...four...five," he instructed. "Very good and count to five as we exhale slowly one...two...three...four...five. Now before we begin discussion, feel how calm you are right now. Be conscious of your breathing as we discuss. This requires us to be calm."

The room was silent.

"The Order Police have taken Anna," he began.

"Death Marchers!" Rita exclaimed as everyone gasped.

"How do you know this?" Charlotte asked.

"Because the Golden Eagle Swarm was above," he said. "And Morris said GIRL GONE."

"We need to go get her!" Julia called out...and everyone agreed.

"BE CALM.... and breathe!" he said. "Now, it is important that we begin with gratitude. We need to be thankful to Zusa and Anna. Also to Morris the Woodpecker and to wonderful little Soot," (who clucked a little thank you) "We need to be happy that this bunker is still safe. Anna is super smart. She is wired for extreme adventure. Her sharp mind will be planning something bigger. We WILL track her down just like we found each of you. They still believe I am on their side. This works to my advantage. I would have thrown out this awful hat years ago, but like any good spy, I am playing the part. We are great actors on this stage – and some terrible evil is coming. We are just going to act our way through it."

"Anna ran out! Why would she do that?" Ivan asked.

"Because her heart is the biggest part of her," Kluck said.

"I think it is time for bed, children," Mrs. Winter said.

"Tomorrow is Christmas," Julia said, sort of happy, sort of sad.

"I miss Christmas in Poland," Mia said.

"You children have seventy to eighty more Christmases awaiting you once this is over. The goal is to live through this one and free everyone to be able to be reunited. We can do this!" he clapped.

The children all got up and started to prepare for sleep as some used the bathroom while others splashed water on their faces in the kitchen. They eventually all settled into their bunkbeds in the other room.

"I think that went well. They are all maturing so quickly," Mrs. Winter said.

"A little too fast for my liking," Kluck added, removing his busby.

Some of the children were having a pillow fight when Kluck came in the bedroom. Others were quiet in their beds.

"Alright, time to settle in! You need to wind your bodies down if you ever hope your busy brains will get tired!"

"Can you tell us about the woodpecker?" Charlotte asked.

"Yes – where did he come from? Who gave him the name?" Mia asked.

"Who taught him Morse code?" Edward added.

"Once you are all in your beds, I will tell the story!" Kluck said, which made them all hurry under the covers.

"I was a Field Marshall in the Great War, some of you may know this. There was, just so you all know, NOTHING great about it. It was to end all wars. It did no such thing. I made great friends, learned invaluable lessons...built a camaraderie with teammates that would have lasted my whole life, had they not been taken in battle. War is very lonely at times. Fighting is lonely. Hiding is lonely, right?" and the children nodded yes to that. "We often found friendships in the strangest places. There was one time our horses were all tied up for the night, we were sleeping in the woods, taking turns so we always had a lookout - and it was my turn. It was the longest few hours of my life from about three am until dawn. I felt myself nodding off and then I heard DIT-DIT-DIT DAH-DAH-DAH DIT-DIT-DIT over and over."

"That is SOS!" Edward said.

"It is indeed! A common phrase in Morse code. So, I jumped to my feet to go see and I found Morris, laying in the grass beside the tree he was pecking with a broken wing. I was so amazed that he knew this code...so honoured that I was there to find him."

"How did he know it?" Julia asked.

"My best guess is that he heard it and mimicked it. But I believe he was destined...like any of us with special talents."

"What happened next?" Charlotte asked.

"I took him under my care, wrapped his wings, fed him some bread crusts and he stayed with me until we returned to base – almost two weeks! The problem was that the story got around and they decided to teach him some other phrases. It started off innocently, but then it became abusive. His poor beak couldn't take the experimentation and I knew I had to get him out of there."

"Where did you take him?" Rita asked.

"Oh Rita – somewhere fantastic – somewhere I wish to take all of you someday!"

"Jagannatha? To see the King?" she asked with wide eyes.

"We did indeed go there...but the King was not there. There are people there who fix creatures all day long – but it has been so long since I have been. The last time I was there, Morris got his brand-new shiny beak and his new set of wings. They are angels."

"Where is the King?" Charlotte asked.

All the others wanted to know too.

"Maybe we will save that story for another night!" Kluck said to the children's disappointment. "But as for Morris, he forgave me. When I asked him to come with me on this journey – he came. The woods were a scary place for him. It was where he broke his wing...but he returned better than ever. He can peck all day long and never tire. His wings don't get tired or cold. He is a super-bird now and he saved our lives tonight."

The Skelekit was tucked in with Egon in his bed. He was watching a cellar spider on the ceiling, who was not in the least bit entertaining. Those types of spiders are known for their do-nothingness.

"Do you ever wonder why the others don't see Skelekitty?" Kluck whispered, sitting on the edge of Egon's bed with Frecher on his lap. "Oh Soot! I didn't see you there! You have two ladies competing for your attention!" he said laughing at Soot maintaining her distance from the Skelekit. "As for me, I have this cheese-eating weasel!" he joked as the lovely little white fellow looked up at him. "Alright you are a stoat, not a weasel – excuuuuuse me!" Kluck laughed, as Frecher curled himself into the shape of a croissant in his lap.

Kluck looked at Egon for a moment and took a big breath and exhaled.

"The other children are also woodpeckers - the Mauerspechte...each one will peck a hole until it all falls. You are the Makadee ka Bachcha! The Spider Child! See?" he said pointing to the ceiling. "You dream about spiders, don't you?"

Egon tilted his head and looked at him.

"I know this because I have dreamed of spiders since I was a boy. I still do," he said as Egon looked back up. "Spiders with fangs on them!"

That made Egon look back at him and he began grinding his teeth.

"You dream of spiders with fangs too! What did Zusa say about your jaw?"

Egon thought for a moment and then put his hands on his face and slid them down.

"Yes, relax your mouth," Kluck smiled. "You don't want to keep the children awake all night!"

Egon put his hands under his glasses and rubbed his eyes.

"May I put them under the bed for you?" Kluck said, gently removing them. "WOW! May I CLEAN them for you?" he laughed as he rubbed a handkerchief on them. "How do you see through them? Hmmmm.... maybe you have been too busy."

Egon was distracted in his thoughts.

"The Zoo is not safe from war. Zusa knows this. He is not just any gorilla. Zusa was called. Just like you are, just like I am. We all have things we can see that others can't. We know bits of information which is mostly a burden. People like you and me dream of spiders and elephants...some of it beautiful, some of it ugly. **Germany was beautiful once**. It will be very ugly – and then it will be restored."

Egon strained to look under his bed.

"Yes, your glasses are there – on your book. Is that what you were looking for?" Kluck said, grabbing it and giving it to Egon. "Did you want to look in it?"

Egon put the book under his blanket and looked back up at the spider.

"He showed me," Charlotte interrupted. "He will show you when he is ready, General." Then she added, "Good night, Egon – so happy you are here now," and she rolled over.

"Nothing makes me happier tonight than knowing you have been reunited with your friends. I don't need to see in your book. I had my own book as a child. It slowed my thoughts down to a pace where I could process them. It was mine. You don't have to show it to anyone."

Charlotte jumped out of the bed and came over to Egon. "May I hug you good night?"

Egon sat up and Charlotte hugged him. He wasn't big on hugging back. Then she went back to bed.

"Charlotte," Kluck said. "I know what Egon did for you."

"We are friends. That is what friends do," she said, pulling the covers up.

"I see you are wearing a bun now like Rita. May I tell you something? You wear your hair however you want. Nobody has a right to comment on it OR touch it. It belongs to you. You hear me?"

"Thank you, General," she smiled.

"Friendship will be the thing which glues us all together through this. Good night, Charlotte! Look for the beautiful moments in the chaos. They are there! Good night, Egon – may your dreams this Christmas Eve relieve you of crocodiles and octopuses."

Egon's eyes were wide as he held tightly to his book.

"I know you, Egon. You are me. Never forget how very loved you are!" he whispered as he patted his leg.

Outside, Zusa had both the horses laying down in the bottom of the Tower with blankets on them. He was sitting against the wall with the busby hat on and Reiter's head was in his lap on the right of him while Spickz's head was on his lap to the left. Morris was tucked in close on his belly, ready for a well-earned night's sleep night. They could finally relax as everyone was home for Christmas and the snow was far too heavy now for travel. Zusa loved having the company and was about to wake up on Christmas with his first true family.

Düster was on self-appointed lookout duty, but he even came to realize no threat was coming in this weather and he wandered in to be with the rest of them.

When morning came, Mrs. Winter was busy making stacks of pancakes and putting them in the warm oven when Charlotte tippy toed out before the rest of the children. She walked past Mrs. Winter and quietly sat at the table.

"Good morning, Charlotte!" Mrs. Winter whispered. "Oh! Look at your curls! I didn't know you had such beautiful golden curls!"

Charlotte replied, "Do you think it is too much?"

"Now hold on," Mrs. Winter said, drying her hands on a tea towel. "Let me tell you something!"

She walked over to the table and sat at the corner near her.

"Let me get one thing straight. You are CHARLOTTE! Nothing about you – not a thing – from your curls to your toes is too much! You are enough!" and she tapped the edge of her nose.

"I am enough," Charlotte smiled, as the other children began pouring out of the bedroom.

Rita sat beside Charlotte and said, "Your curls are amazing!"

"Try taking your bun out!" Charlotte said.

Rita dropped her dark brown curls down.

"Now, shake it!" Charlotte said, "Like this!"

Rita shook her curls and they both laughed as Mrs. Winter smiled at them.

"PANCAKES!" Ivan yelled out.

"Everyone sit! We have maple syrup today!" Mrs. Winter announced.

The children sat down and were happy and chatty eating up all the pancakes when Kluck and Frecher came in.

"I am late to the party!" he said, dusting off the snow. "I was spending some time taking care of Zusa, Reiter and Spickz. Are there any pancakes left?"

"Oh yes, sit down! However, the children are done and anxious!" Mrs. Winter said, washing dishes.

"Oh please! Do not let me stop you! Go ahead!" Kluck said, pulling up a chair.

"You each have a paper bag with your name on it," she said, putting each one in front of them. "Let me disperse them all first, then open them all at once!"

The children waited patiently until all the bags were shared.

"Ok, go ahead!" Mrs. Winter cheered them on.

"Chocolate!" Rita said. "And popping corn!"

"A toy truck!" Ivan said.

"I got a red car!" Mia said.

"I hope you trade the toys around each day, so they belong to everyone!" Kluck said.

"The chocolate and popcorn are from a candy store in Berlin. Because they are not German, their business has been suffering. So, when you eat those, you can remember you are supporting them!" Mrs. Winter told them.

"That is crazy – this chocolate melts in your mouth!" Julia said.

"If you close your eyes, it is like you are on a tropical beach, it is so good!" Edward said.

"Yes, it is a shame someone's hate makes them blind," Kluck said.

"Who is this letter to me from?" Rita asked.

"I received one too!" Illia squealed.

"You all did! They are from your pen pals!" Kluck said proudly.

"We have pen pals?" Filip asked.

"Yes! You will also see writing supplies in your bag too," he explained. "These children are all away from their original homes like you are. I thought it would be good for you to correspond with others throughout this time. It will help them and help you pass the time and gain perspective."

"You will deliver them?" Charlotte asked.

"Oh yes, I have helpers everywhere!" Kluck laughed.

"You really do!" Ivan said, biting into his chocolate.

"Now, I have a set of envelopes to hand out and so does Mrs. Winter," Kluck said walking around the table.

Each child was handed an envelope with their name on it.

"Alright! Does everyone have one? Go ahead!" Kluck said.

Egon put his on his lap under the table.

"How did you get these?" Rita asked.

"Because of my rank. I can get in just about everywhere," he said with a wink.

The children each received pictures of their parents or family photos...and the room went dead silent.

"It isn't meant to be gloomy," Mrs. Winter said, consoling each child. "Be hopeful!"

"Oh no," Rita said. "These are tears of joy. Thank you so much!"

"I love having this again," Edward said. "Of course, it is very sad."

"They brought you to this Earth – they set you on your path – if they are gone, you can still be grateful for them having you because we are every so happy you are with us!" Mrs. Winter smiled.

"They are chapters in your book – for better or for worse," Kluck said.

Egon didn't look at his bag. Charlotte went to say something to him and Kluck looked at her and put a finger to his lip.

"Everyone can look at theirs in their own time," Kluck said. "I know for many of you, Christmas isn't celebrated, or it is on a different day...I don't care about any of that. In the true spirit of Christmas, we will love one another, help one another, look out for one another. Name one other household in all of Europe that has a gorgeous mixed bag of children eating together like this on Christmas Day. You won't find it. You are leaders...examples of what could be. We aspire to this level of kindness and friendship everywhere!"

The children all smiled at each other – they were proud of themselves and all sat up a little taller.

"Shall we give them their last present?" Mrs. Winter asked.

"I stayed up most of the night thinking about this! I may be more excited than you!" Kluck smiled ear to ear.

Mrs. Winter reached in her apron and pulled out a large stack of envelopes.

"More letters?" Rita asked.

"Oh no," she said. "These were handcrafted especially for you!"

Mrs. Winter walked around the table and handed each child their envelope.

"Now, don't open them yet, wait until everyone has theirs and then we will open them together on the count of three," she said.

Each child was handed their envelope with their name in a fancy script on the front.

"Look at the beautiful writing!" Charlotte said.

"Ok, shall we all count to three together?" Mrs. Winter asked. "Ready?"

The children were all smiling at each other in anticipation.

"ONE – TWO – THREE!" they all spoke in unison and then opened their envelopes.

Each envelope had varying degrees of dirt on papers.

"What are these old papers?" Rita asked.

"Mine has my German name on it," Edward said puzzled.

The children were confused.

"So does mine," said Julia.

"Does this mean – is this – our pretend documents?" Charlotte asked with a tiny lightbulb going off.

"That is exactly what these are!" Ivan said with a bigger lightbulb above his head.

"Can we – GO OUT?" Illia said with her eyes popping out of her head.

"ARE WE LEAVING?" Mia asked.

"General, are we leaving here?" Charlotte said.

"Even German children are getting rerouted, so let's not get too excited - we can't go out often, but maybe some field trips to start when I see some safe opportunities!"

"But Rita and I are German – why do we have papers?" Charlotte asked.

"To keep you both safe from terrible people like that Doctor. You can teach the other children German ways with your new German names," Kluck said.

"Don't be mistaken, they will also help us to free others. They are kind of like your work papers too," Mrs. Winter said.

"I want everyone free. Once they are free – we will be free," Charlotte said.

The children all jumped up and down practicing what they would say if they were asked for documents.

Egon was sitting halfway down the table petting the Skelekit in his coat.

"Where is Egon's?" Charlotte asked.

"Egon doesn't require new documents," Kluck said. "In fact, the highest leaders controlling this country already know about Egon."

"Then, they know he is missing?" Charlotte said, very worried.

"They will soon enough," Kluck said. "With yesterday being Christmas Eve and today being Christmas, not much attention will be on him – which is why, sadly, I need to take him back today."

"But - we just got back together!" Charlotte raged.

"I wanted him to have Christmas with his friends. I never said Egon was staying. He is safer than any of us wherever he goes. You saw for yourself, Charlotte – when he protected you – the high Doctor demanded nobody touch him – even though Egon was responsible for knocking him down. He must go back, or they will be looking for him. We cannot have that."

"It doesn't matter, Charlotte!" Edward said. "We are all getting out of here!"

"Mind your expectations, Edward! I said a bit at a time – when it is safe!" Kluck warned.

"Well, it is HOPE!" Rita said. "Who did this for us?"

"I will introduce you someday, but I cannot divulge their identity right now. Just know they love you very much!" Kluck said.

"Well they are very talented – they look real!" Rita said.

"Yes, they look as though we have been carrying them around for a long time too," Charlotte smiled.

"Very authentic!" Edward said.

"It is all about you knowing that information on the papers if they take the papers and test you!" Kluck said. "Make sure you practice!"

"I am going to hide these under my bed!" Julia said, running off.

"You may for safe-keeping but hiding them will not matter if they find this place. German children would never hide underground. You have to start thinking like them," Mrs. Winter said.

"If they did find us, could we make up a story – like we were stolen and put underground?" Ivan asked.

"Let's do this. You children put your heads together – as a team – come up with a solid story if this happens – and we will discuss it. Sound good?" Kluck suggested.

"I have ideas already!" Edward said.

The children all started to group off like children do at Christmas, reading their pen pal letters, eating their candy and practicing their false heritage stories. Egon sat still at the table and Mrs. Winter sat beside him.

"You already know what is happening in Germany, don't you son," Mrs. Winter said to no response. "The expectations on you are a lot. My heart is with you, dear Egon. Trust destiny!"

She kissed his forehead and circled around to watch the other children. Egon got up and went back to the bedroom and changed out of his nightshirt into his clothes. Soot was still snoozing on the bed, and he gently picked her up and brought her into the other room.

With the Skelekit by his feet, Soot under one arm and his Christmas bag in the other, Egon stood at the doorway near the hall and looked at Kluck.

"Oh. I see," Kluck said with a big sigh. "You know it is time to go now, Egon?"

Charlotte got up from playing cars on the floor and ran over to Egon and hugged him.

"I don't understand your work, Egon," she said. "I wish you could tell me things. I don't know where you are going or when I will see you again. But we keep connecting – so why wouldn't we connect again, right?"

"Whatever happens after today," Kluck said. "You two have made the loveliest connection of any children I know! Hold that in your hearts!"

Kluck turned to speak to the children.

"We must go now – but I will return to you. I will always return to you!"

They all got up and rushed him. He nearly fell over from the love!

"I love you all. Mrs. Winter, can you come out in the hallway, please?"

"That was a great evening and morning for them!" she said in a whisper.

"It was the loveliest of loveliness. You did such a wonderful job – and you continue to. I will take Egon back to the farm. You must listen for Morris' tapping. Even if you do not understand the codes, which I know you do, don't wait – get the children into the Juggerkampf at once."

"Oh yes, they know the drill!" she said, patting his arm.

"If I get back in time, we can take the children for a short forest hike. Shall we, Frecher?" he said, looking down at the weasel.

Egon was already walking down the hall to the door. Kluck followed him, tapped on the trap door, Zusa opened it, and out they went.

Outside, Düster was soaring overhead on a clear Christmas day. The Golden Eagle Swarm was gone, and he had the sky to himself. The sun was hitting the glistening snow and the crisp air made their noses scrunch up when they breathed it.

Zusa stretched his hand out and the woodpecker landed on his finger.

"I cannot thank you enough, dear friend. Keep a watchful eye. If they even caught a glimpse of you, they will be back," Kluck warned.

Zusa just loved Morris and ran a finger down his back lovingly. Reiter and Spickz both had their ears pressed forward looking at them.

"Are you sure you don't want to leave Soot here?" Kluck asked Egon.

Egon walked over to Reiter and handed Soot to Kluck who then placed her back in the saddlebag.

"Your choice!" Kluck laughed.

Egon shuffled over to Zusa and looked up at him. Zusa let the woodpecker go and picked Egon up. Then he sat down on a step where he hugged him and kissed him all over.

"That is a true Father's love," Kluck muttered to himself. "I just wish your real one was a better man, Egon."

Egon didn't want to leave Zusa's arms.

"Well, shall we go?" Kluck called out.

Egon got up and touched Zusa's hand and looked in his big dark eyes. Then he looked up at Düster who was still soaring above them. Zusa touched his cheeks and pulled down to remind him not to grind. With the Skelekit skipping behind him, Egon headed off into the woods.

"Give an old man a push up, will you Zusa?" and up onto Reiter he went with Frecher in his arms.

Spickz caught up to Egon and walked beside him, patiently waiting to see if he needed a ride.

9 THE KARTOFFEL PIG BOMB

It was an easier ride back to the farm than going to the Tower, although the heavy snowfall had presented a few challenges for Reiter and Spickz.

Düster stopped soaring and landed on top of the chicken coop. Irene was overwhelmed with the amount of snow on the porch and was taking frequent breaks, but it was a clear, sunny day. As she lit a cigarette, she looked at the forest and saw Egon riding Spickz. She put her shovel down and walked out into the yard to meet them. Reiter, who was carrying Kluck, Frecher and Soot, was not far behind.

Egon jumped off Spickz and walked around the front to pet her face. Then as he turned to look at Irene, Spickz walked away and he stood there motionless. Kluck wasn't far behind and he called out to her.

"How are you this beautiful day?"

She seemed a bit confused by his jovial demeanour but responded, "I am well, General. And you?"

"Very well," he said, awkwardly dismounting Reiter. "Are you alone?"

"Yes, General. Eugen is in the barn."

"Did anyone come around?" Kluck asked.

"Swartz was here yesterday evening. I believe Eugen told him you had Egon, like you asked us to."

"And how did he feel about that?"

"He said very little, General," she said, extinguishing her cigarette on the ground with her foot.

"You do not love yourself," Kluck said. "Have you quit caring?"

"I am fine, General."

"I see."

"How was your time with Egon?" she asked, changing the topic.

"Caring about Egon's time seems admirable – but ultimately does you no good. You would be best to attend to your health – both physical and mental," Kluck said, blocking her.

"I will, General."

Kluck was not about to offer any information that could get back to Swartz.

"Please see to it that the horse and pony are washed down and fed well. They were very loyal. As for this chicken, it should not live outdoors despite Eugen's issue with it. Egon needs to feel content here. He likes the creature and it should sleep in his room. I do not want to see it making unfertilized nests under the chicken coop which only serve to disappoint her after suffering a long unrewarding sit on them," Kluck scolded. "If Eugen takes issue, he can take it up with me."

"This is understood, General," Irene noted.

It wasn't Kluck's intention to be curt with her, but he needed to play his part. It was also not his intention to stay and make friends as he needed to be very safe about all information leaking back to Swartz.

He walked over to Egon and whispered, "I love having adventures with you. Remember how very loved you are. The road ahead is long, but you are protected by both sides here. You may just get bounced back and forth for a time. I have great faith that you can handle this! Take good care of Soot – she has a lovely knack for Morse code – brilliant little thing!"

Soot clucked away beside Egon and still maintained her distance from the Skelekit.

"Take good care of Egon," he said to the Skelekit.

"Are you speaking to me, General?" Irene said, confused by him looking at the ground.

"I am speaking to the chicken," he said quite seriously. "Egon is good with chickens. You really should have him work more in the coop with you. Don't you think?"

He looked for her reaction to that – which was uncomfortably covered up.

"That would be fine, General," she said, looking down at the weasel.

"Frecher is coming with me – you do not need to be concerned," Kluck said.

"I do not feel concerned, General," Irene said.

"The chicken is still alive, no?" he laughed as he walked out the laneway.

"Do you need a car, General?" she called out.

"I am a high-ranking officer. These things are of no concern to me, but thank you," he said, adding a tiny bit of sugar onto the end of their conversation.

Irene went back to shoveling but noticed Egon standing there.

"Are you hungry? Would you like to rest? Maybe just come inside for a bit?" Irene said, realizing the importance of making sure he was happy, but she was terrible at parenting. It was the equivalent of handing a carrot to a newborn baby because they are hungry.

Egon followed her inside and took off his hat and boots. He was still carrying his bag with the chocolate and popcorn. Irene looked at it but was careful not to impose. She was now paranoid around him.

"I see you received a Christmas gift, maybe? Does it need to be in the refrigerator, or do you want it in your room?"

Egon just held onto it.

"Alright then," she said, looking down at Soot. "I guess I will put newspaper down in your room for the chicken. Would it be alright if Soot stayed in your room? I mean, just so it, you know, contains the mess?"

Egon said nothing as usual.

"That seems like a good idea," she said shaking her head and grabbing some old newspapers from a pile by the fire.

Egon walked up to his room with the Skelekit and Soot following. Soot was hilariously hopping one step at a time behind him and it was enough to make Irene crack a small smile before tossing the newspapers down.

"Just scatter them about the floor – but then be careful where you step," she laughed before leaving.

She was some help.

Aldo, the old hound dog, had followed Egon up and jumped up on his bed. Egon went over and looked in his big droopy eyes before holding his extra skin in his hands. He was slobbery but relaxed. Egon placed his hands on either side of Aldo's face and pulled his cheeks down. Then, he did the same to his own face – just like Zusa did to teach him to relax his jaw. Egon pulled up one side of the dog's mouth to look at his teeth which were old and ground down. He ran his finger along them, and Aldo just let him. He was that old and trusting. Egon then ran a finger along his own teeth, perhaps assessing how much he had worn down his own. Aldo started happily panting and Egon scrunched his nose up reacting to the dog's breath which had that aging/health-breaking-down smell to it. He grabbed his paper bag and pulled out a few bits of popcorn – as though that was going to help – and gave them to the dog. He happily ate them.

Aldo was already acquainted with the Skelekit, and probably with Soot, albeit through the window. He was one of those amazing hounds that seemed fine with just about anything. Soot was clucking away at his feet, extremely interested in this popping corn – or any corn for that matter. She was willing and available. He tossed a few down to her and she pecked them into obliteration. She could have spent the rest of the day trying to find them in various places around the room!

Speaking of messy bedroom floors, Egon spotted the stack of newspapers and remembered to put them down on the floor for Soot.

The first one he picked up had a recent date with a headline on the front of the weekly *Der Stürmer* newspaper which read, 'The Judan Are Our Misfortune'. Every column seemed to be reminding the German people of how great they were, how victorious they were, how in control they were of the battles, the economy and overall how superior they were to everyone other country. It didn't take him long to identify this edition as a great addition for Soot's, uh soot. He placed it in the corner of the room, the farthest distance from his bed and Soot went over to it, pecked at some politician's face, and then did his business immediately. Soot then kicked a few times and walked away.

Seeing as he did it on the first try, Egon wasn't in a hurry to put paper down everywhere. He walked over and turned on a small radio on top of the dresser, even though it was staticky.

'Do you stand for the Fatherland, for the Drillmeister, for victory for Germany? As a proud German citizen, will you work the necessary hours

each day to give your all for this victory? For the Fatherland to win, it must be total commitment..."

It was background noise. Egon barely paid any attention to it. He took his book out and jumped on the bed with Aldo. Soot flapped her wings hard enough to get on the bed and cautiously introduced herself to the dog. Aldo let out a big sigh and put his head down to nap. Clearly, his previous fifteen years of solid napping wasn't sufficient. Soot moved slowly and then nestled herself into Aldo's warm ribs. The Skelekit tucked herself under Egon's arm. The room was cold compared to the room down by the fire and he pulled the wool blanket onto his feet. He didn't seem at all upset to have his alone time with his animal friends. On the contrary, he seemed to embrace it. It gave him a chance to freely spend time with his book. It was a confusing heap of content! Egon's book was neither chronological nor logical – at least to someone picking it up for the first time. Most people write in a book starting at page one. Egon would write on whatever page he felt like at the time. The first few pages were blank at the beginning and so were the last few. He tended to fill a page as full as possible and then leave some pages blank. Some of the pages had scribbled mathematical equations, some had maps that didn't resemble anything on Earth, and other pages were random drawings - mostly of animals.

His most visited page was the one with the crocodiles on it. The Skelekit was the only one who saw his inspiration for that drawing. She put her front boney paw on that page and patted it. Then, she stretched out on it and went to sleep. It must have been a comforting memory of her time at Tiergarten. He didn't want to move her, so he reached in and slipped out Rosa's book which he had tucked in the back of his.

Her book **may have been beautiful once**. It went through rough times recounting her days at the train station. The first picture he looked at was of her fluffy white dog, Eisbär. He was sitting happily with his tongue out, one side of his face scorched. The next photo was an ideal looking German family – Father, Mother and children holding hands and waiting for the train. She had realistic sketches of the train itself and pages and pages of people in various poses at the train station. The last page was a partial sketch of Egon. He stared at that for several moments.

Had it not been for the Lokführer retrieving Rosa's book, he wouldn't have it. He reached in the pocket of his pants and pulled out the Waffen SS tag. It was the first time he had a chance to really look at it.

He was startled by a knock at the door. It was Irene popping her nose in.

"Oh. Glad you are having a rest. Can you come help Eugen in the barn?"

It didn't seem to matter that it was Christmas. There was no sign of anything festive there. Egon shoved the Waffen tag back into the pocket of his trousers and went to follow Irene out. He paused and grabbed the flashlight he found in the dresser and put that inside his shirt until he could transfer it to the inside of his winter jacket. Aldo slid off the bed, half asleep and followed them down to sit by the fire again. Soot was an indoor/outdoor chicken now – so she went wherever Egon and the Skelekit were heading.

"Would you like a leash for her?" Irene laughed as Soot hopped down each step with a wee cluck on each.

Egon put his coat and boots back on, then tucked his book inside his coat pocket.

"Did you have a Christmas out there? Is anyone doing Christmas festivities?" she asked, as though she had been locked away for half of her life. "I was in a department store years ago," she recalled. "It was a few days before Christmas. Everyone was shopping for socks and ties. I wonder if that still goes on."

Egon wasn't listening to her. He was watching Soot and the Skelekit playing on the way out the door.

"I swear that chicken has developed a shadow. That is such bizarre behaviour," Irene said, shaking her head, unable to see the Skelekit. "Well, she's your chicken now."

When they got outside, Swartz and another man were standing in the snow.

"You are here on Christmas, General," Irene said, surprised to see them. "I thought you would be with family."

"Where did they go?" were the first words out of Swartz's mouth.

"I am sorry, where did who go? It is just Egon and Eugen here with me."

"Where did Egon go yesterday and over night?" Swartz demanded.

"As I am sure Eugen already mentioned. We do not know," she said, her voice shaking.

"Eugen said Kluck took him," Swartz said, getting angry.

"His rank is above you, General – so we respected the rank and did not question it," Irene said.

"Did they leave by car?"

"No, by horseback," she responded. "He requested I prepare them -"

"You PREPARED horses for them. This seems like quite the involvement, Irene!"

"No involvement, General. Like I said, I had to respect the rank. I didn't know what else to do."

"What did Egon return with that he didn't have when he left?" Swartz asked.

"A paper bag, but I didn't look inside," Irene said.

"We entrust the boy in your care – and you do not inspect a foreign bag he comes home with after being gone over night?" Swartz fumed.

"I apologize, General," she said.

"No matter," Swartz said, changing his mood. "You are here now. Egon has become a – popular boy. Moving forward, Irene. The boy is to remain under your care unless I say otherwise. My orders come straight from the top. This is above Kluck. If he shows up again, you will stall for time and contact me immediately. Is this understood?"

"Yes, General."

"If a single hair is harmed on this boy's head, you and Eugen will be finished. I mean this quite literally. Let that sink in," he warned.

"I understand the consequences moving forward, General," Irene agreed.

"This is Professor Wissen. He will be working with Egon today," Swartz said. "Please welcome him to the farm."

"So kind of you on Christmas," Irene said, awkwardly inserting small talk.

"I am alone at Christmas, this doesn't matter to me," Professor Wissen said with a dry tone.

His crooked black bow tie poked out and it was hard not to stare directly at it. He was tall and skinny in a cheap brown suit under his overcoat. It wasn't an attempt to be formal, as he was disheveled despite his academic standing. It was an untailored outfit - and someone as lanky as him really could have used a good tailor.

"Shall we find a building where you can set up?" Swartz suggested.

"I can set up anywhere," Professor Wissen said. "It doesn't need to be a big area. In fact, smaller is better."

"May I suggest the smaller workshop beside Eugen's barn? There are any amenities you may require there," Irene proposed.

"That will be fine," Professor Wissen replied, carrying a large briefcase that Egon couldn't stop looking at.

"Right this way," Irene said, guiding them there.

When they all got inside the workshop, Swartz said, "That will be all, Irene. We will call on you if we require anything."

Irene was noticeable uncomfortable with leaving Egon and she said, "I am not busy – I can certainly stay and be available for you?"

"No thank you, Irene," Swartz said sternly. "Oh and Irene - Toss that chicken back outside. We don't need the distraction."

"It was General Kluck who said the boy should have the chicken. I suppose he feels it is good for his state of mind," she said, nervously.

"Did he now? Raising German boys to have chickens as pets can't possibly be good for their state of mind," Swartz snipped. "IF I am instructed to get him a pet – and only IF I am instructed to get him a pet – it will be something noble like a Shephard. Did you not even consider how ludicrous that scenario comes across?"

"It is indeed ludicrous. I will remove the chicken," and she picked Soot up before anything bad could happen to her.

"That is all, Irene," Swartz said, closing the door on her before quickly reopening it. "Oh Irene, retrieve the bag he came back with."

"I will look for it, General," she said, rushing off.

"I apologise you had to endure such nonsense, Professor. Now, Egon - I understand Feldmarschall Kluck was here and took you for the night?"

"I was told he does not speak, General?" Wissen asked.

"You are correct," Swartz agreed. "I just want to make sure Egon understands something. If the Feldmarschall comes again, you are not to go with him. He is indeed a high-ranking General – and well respected – but he is retired – he is not working with us now. He is a lovely gentleman – but the war was not kind to him. He truly has lost the sharpness of his mind. He is currently best described as a dull pencil."

"He was not always so dull," Wissen said. "It was said he was the brightest mind in all of Germany during the War."

"His time has come and gone. We have new minds to work with now," Swartz said, smiling at Egon.

After a few minutes of the men going through the briefcase, Swartz said, "Alright, Professor. I will leave you to it."

As he walked outside, he was met by Irene with the brown paper bag.

"It seems to only have some chocolate in it, General."

Swartz snatched the bag from her and pulled out the chocolate bar. He looked at it and sniffed it.

"That is black chocolate from a Jewish Bakery," he said.

"I swear I didn't hear a thing, General," she said, scared out of her mind.

Swartz handed the bag back to her.

"Please put it back where you found it. Egon doesn't know. This isn't his fault," he instructed.

"I will do, General," she said, as he walked away.

"And do not interrupt Professor Wissen."

"Certainly not, General," Irene said, like the robot she was.

Egon and the Skelekit were standing in the middle of the workshop. It was a dusty, unused space. Perhaps Eugen came looking for extra oil or some nails the odd time, but not much else. Professor Wissen spoke with his back to Egon as he rummaged through his bag.

"I spoke with Miss Kraus," he began. "She told me you were a perfect student. She even suggested school was so easy for you, you had to be put into older grades. Then, you became bored of it. She told me that one time you finished your Mathematics test, which was several grades above you, so early, you played with a bug on the floor for the remainder of the testing. She says you went on to write down the chemical compounds used by that bug for defense - on paper – in full form - before the remainder of the class was done."

As he turned to speak to Egon, the Skelekit jumped onto the table and pulled some papers out of the bag ever so quietly and brought them to Egon, who stuffed them in his jacket quickly and went back to his motionless self.

"I am under strict order here. I have come to see for myself if you can do this, then I will be leaving."

Egon was unaffected.

"As you know, our troops are courageous and going into harm's way every day for the Fatherland. It is our duty to protect them whenever possible. My group has been studying diseases so we can keep them safe on the field. They are out there with the swine, as you know," he said pompously. "There are two parts of war: offense and defense. We are doing well defending our soldiers from illnesses, but until we cut off the source, we will always have a hole in the bucket. Now, you may be wondering why you have been brought to such a place of secrecy. The enemy must never know what is coming. Surprise offense is always the best tactic. We have approximately four months to put our offense into action. It is when the snow will be melting – and we must adapt to the changing weather systems," he explained, grabbing a jar. "Here is something interesting for you to see up close," he said, casually handing it to Egon.

Egon looked up at him and then down at the jar. His glasses knocked against the walls that were housing a confused hornet.

"Take this paper. Show me your reaction on paper like you did in your classroom," Wissen ordered.

Egon held the jar in his hands and his teeth began to grind. Wissen winced his eyes at how loud and screechy Egon's grinding was, but he let him do it.

Egon drew out a blueprint for the hornet. He started off with the typical eye, thorax, and abdomen, along with wings, antennas, and legs, but then inside each of those parts he added random compartments.

Professor Wissen reviewed Egon's work.

"Operation: Hornet Nest. You are looking at the first female fighter pilot to accompany the Luftwaffe. They are already brilliant, using material at their disposal to build intricate paper nests – and are brutally defensive of their hive. Like us, they only attack when stepped on or met with aggression -"

He stopped there when he noticed Egon inserted something extra.

"You've made a modification. What is this?" he said, pointing to one of the antennas.

Upon closer inspection, his face lit up.

"You have made it so she can differentiate! Hmmmm, will have to think on that. Perhaps one antenna identifies the enemy, while the other keeps it from attacking its keeper."

Egon's design modification looked like he could have done it in his sleep...and he was getting bored and tapping the jar.

"The Drillmeister was in New York this past Autumn on business. He brought home some souvenirs. If you are behaved and do well, I will recommend that you are part of the first team to view them. I hope this gives you something exciting to look forward to," he said, packing up his bag.

Wissen's job was done and he abruptly packed up and walked out. This left Egon and the Skelekit confused in the middle of the workshop. There were times when Egon lived in places like the orphanage where he was under constant scrutiny and then other times where there is nobody to tuck him into bed. It was an inconsistent life but at this point, he didn't know anything 'normal'.

The Skelekit scratched at his leg as if to say, "Now what do we do?" and Egon reached in his pocket to have a look at the papers the Skelekit fetched from the Professor's bag. There were some rough blueprints on one page, some calculations on another. Egon became engrossed in them as he wandered out the door of the workshop.

"Perhaps you didn't bring them?" Irene called out as Professor Wissen ran back into the workshop.

Egon saw this and ducked quickly into the pig barn with the Skelekit in tow. He tucked the papers in behind a large potato sack. He then put his ear to the door and listened.

"THEY WERE HERE – HELP ME FIND THEM!" Wissen yelled to Irene.

"Why the yelling?" Eugen asked, coming out of his work area.

"The Professor was working with Egon in the small workshop and he has misplaced some of his very important papers," Irene said, going in after him.

"I will look for Egon," Eugen yelled. "Perhaps he was curiously looking at them?"

"Not from my briefcase, he wasn't. I was with him the whole time. That is impossible," Wissen said, fumbling through his bag again.

"Perhaps back at the camp then?" Irene suggested.

Meanwhile, Egon was standing in the middle of the pigs, and they were frozen upon his arrival, having never met him before. There was an assortment of them, mostly pink, presumably, under the muck. There were varying sizes from large to newborn forming a sniffing circle around Egon, even though the strongest smell understandably came from them.

The Skelekit made a point of smelling each of them, which caused the piglets to smell back.

Their inquisitiveness may have been boredom. Egon went back to the potato sack and opened it up, crinkling his nose at the rotting smell. This was probably why this bag was out here. It had gone bad and was now fit for the pigs. He did his best to find some which were decent and started rolling them to the middle of their pen. As he did, the little ones would pounce like a fox, which seemed to impress the Skelekit! She would pounce on them, teaching them the professional way to do it.

Irene popped her head in.

"Oh! There you are!" she said, looking back out at the men. "Did you take the Professor's papers?"

Realizing he couldn't answer, she reached into his jacket which only had his own book.

"My apologies for being intrusive, but that will be better than if they do it," she said. "You like the pigs? You should say hello to Blumen in the back. She has a new baby named Gras."

Irene left, and Egon noticed a wooden door near the back of the barn, so he went off to explore.

"I found Egon," Irene said to Wissen and Eugen. "I checked on his person. He does not have them. He is feeding the pigs."

"There was no way he would have them anyways. He was never near my bag," the Professor said, leaving in a huff.

There was a simple latch on the door which led to an extra-large pig pen. In fact, it was unreasonably big for the single black sow and her baby. Surely, Eugen and Irene were not so compassionate as to give this mother and baby so much room!

Blumen and Gras did seem to love the room and/or quiet from the craziness on the other side of the door. Blumen lived like a celebrity back here. It wasn't a tall room, maybe two and a half big pigs, but it was long and narrow, measuring around nine to ten pigs in length by three to four pigs across. The floor was immaculately clean but covered in fresh straw and the far side of the room had it stacked up close to the ceiling as though the workers were way ahead in their chores.

The Skelekit saw the little black piglet and began to run circles around him. Gras was around the same size, and they greeted one another like children at daycare – cautious at first, warming up quickly.

Blumen walked over to Egon and sniffed him. She didn't smell bad at all. She was remarkably clean. She was so well fed and cared for, that there was clean water in the bucket completely untouched. Egon reached out and touched her face and she let him. She was very relaxed near him and he stroked her floppy ears, touched her big bushy eyebrows and he even stroked her big double chin with both hands. Blumen loved the attention. He ran his finger around her snout, and she made circles in the air. It might have been the first time she had any real fun. It was doubtful that Eugen or Irene would have played with her.

She opened her mouth with a nice big piggy smile as if Egon told her to say aaaaaaaaaaaaah. The canines and incisors at the front were not too sharp as she was getting older and they were ground down. She surprisingly let him run his finger along her back molars. This caused Egon to grind his own teeth and when she heard it, she closed her mouth and touched her snout on his cheek. It was a good reminder for him to relax his jaw like Zusa taught him.

Blumen then walked over to the big straw pile and started tossing it like spaghetti. She now had a friend and could have a bit of fun. Egon grabbed some straw and threw it up in the air too. Gras and the Skelekit joined in and straw was flying everywhere creating such a dust that Blumen sneezed.

A shiny object caught Egon's eye. He pushed the straw away to uncover a smooth metal surface. He pushed more away and revealed more and more as he walked down the room.

"The Falcon," a voice said at the door. It was Eugen. "There are others in there too like the 'Wren'."

Egon zoomed past him out of the room.

"Hold on a minute!" Eugen called out. "Don't you want to see the Sea Devil which carries them?"

That made Egon stop.

"I thought so," Eugen said. "Come with me."

Egon followed him back through Blumen's pen and through yet another door at the end of that long room.

When Eugen unlocked this door, he said, "This wasn't as easy to cover up with straw. You like elephants? Lock that door behind you."

Egon was all eyes. Even the Skelekit sat up straight.

Eugen grabbed several tarps and began pulling them down. It was massive and took up most of the space.

"The pigs built it," he joked, perhaps for the first time in his life – to no applause.

It was a submarine...in the barn. The full length was around fourteen meters.

"This holds two men - has both gasoline and electric motor. There is the propeller - two caterpillar tracks there. It should go about ten knots, maybe eight underwater. We shall see."

Egon looked back to Blumen's room.

"Oh yes, it will carry two of those at a time. Has a periscope, radio antenna – the challenge is, once you fire the torpedoes, they know where you are. She is the Elephant Sea Devil - The Elefanteufel."

Egon had enough. He stormed out straight past Blumen and Gras, through the rest of the pink pigs and marched outside.

"Weird boy," Eugen said as he put the tarps back on.

Outside, Egon stopped as he saw Düster flying overhead. He breathed the cold air deeply and pulled down on both cheeks to stop the teeth grinding. Düster passed through the sun on every rotation and each circle around came closer to Egon like a funnel downwards. He finally settled on the roof of the chicken coop. Egon looked around and nobody was there. It was a good time to go have a look inside.

10 PANGOLIN BABIES LOVE ANT HILLS

It was already getting dark on Christmas Day.

The farm was relatively quiet, and the chickens were slowing down for the day. A few were still pecking at the odd vegetable peeling on the floor while others were starting to roost. Irene had fresh sawdust and straw scattered and it didn't look like there was going to be any more activity tonight.

Egon pulled out the flashlight he got from the dresser in his room. Luckily, the trap door was not heavy. He lifted it up and could see down the dirty set of stairs underneath. It was a dull light, but it illuminated a few feet in front of him. The Skelekit was still sniffing at the chickens – again – with no logical sniffer due to being a – skeleton. Ian tapped the flashlight on the edge of the floorboard, she snapped out of it, and ran down behind him. He gently closed the door above his head.

There were only a half a dozen stairs down, much like the storm doors that farms use in case of tornados - just enough so a person of average height could stand. The steps and walls were a combination of red brick and stones. It felt more like a dugout tunnel than a hall, but it was leading somewhere.

The wide hall was made narrow due to being lined with dirt boxes. When he looked in them and tossed the earth about, he saw carrots, potatoes, and turnips for winter storage. Egon walked about ten meters before hitting another heavy rusty metal door. It was locked. He flickered the flashlight around the walls and ceiling, but there was nothing that was going to help him unlock it. He started to make his way back to the trap door and heard footsteps above him. He waited just under the door at the top step until the footsteps stopped. When they did, the trap door flew open and there was Irene.

"I thought you would be right there. The door didn't have any straw scattered on top – so I knew you were down there," she said. "You are in no-man's land."

Egon bolted past her to leave.

"Egon, did your curiosity die?" she said, which stopped him at the door out of the coop. "You'll need this."

She was holding a key, and Egon seemed surprised that she maybe wanted to give it to him. He walked back slowly towards her and stood still.

"We work for terrifying people, Egon," she began. "Eugen and I live very well compared to some. Remember one thing," she warned. "You are German. You are brilliant. You have skills. You clearly have the attention of the highest leaders in the land. If you do as you are told, you will live well. I have seen what has happened to equally brilliant minds who do not follow rules. Don't let things upset you, alright?"

With someone like Egon who had heightened awareness and intellect, it was easier said than done to accept and follow. Still, he kept staring at the trap door and Irene was his way down there.

"Come along then," she said, pointing down.

The Skelekit got down just before the door closed on the floor. Irene had a better flashlight with her, and Egon saw his own breath in front of it. After a short walk to the locked door, she pulled out her key and unlocked it.

Before opening it, she turned to him and said, "Just move quietly."

Egon was a professionally quiet boy. That was easy. Irene opened the door slowly to reveal another long hallway. This hall looked more like the inside of a hospital, except it wasn't clean. It was cold but not like the winter cold outside. It was a damp cold. The floor was wooden slats pressed together and the earth was still visible between them. Still, not bad for underground.

The end of this hall had three doors. One that went straight ahead, one to the left, and one to the right. The one on the left was a half barn door you could look over except the top half was sturdy gridded wire. Egon stood way back.

"Move slowly so you don't startle them," she said, her flashlight down by her side.

Egon walked over and readied himself to look in. Irene lifted the flashlight ever so slowly to reveal a room with square, boxed-in compartments stacked on top of each other. They were each about forty centimeters high with wire doors on the fronts of them. When she dragged the light across each one, all

Egon could see was some straw poking out through the wires.

"There's one, look there!" she said, pointing to one box in the middle of the top row.

Egon rubbed his eyes under his glasses, trying to understand what he was looking at.

A sweet little brown eye with a long scaly snout looked at Egon for a moment but then tucked her head back away from the light as though she was ashamed of herself. **She may have been beautiful once.**

"Let's let them sleep. You can look at the ones who are still awake," she said, going to the opposite door in the hall.

This was a similar door, wooden on the bottom, stiff wire on the top half. Irene offered her flashlight to Egon.

"Go ahead and have a look," she said, but he was nervous to take it.

Egon saw dozens of scaly creatures with extra-long tongues foraging in the dirt of a massive indoor, zoo-like replica of their home in the wild. It looked like a mini city was built from varying sizes of anthills. The plants looked well-watered but lacked the sunlight to make them deep green. It was a contrast to the bitter winter going on above ground.

"They are called pangolins. They don't have teeth. See the long tongue? It goes deep into the anthills and pulls out bugs and termites. The end of our tongues end at our throats. Their tongue ends at their stomach. They are being - studied here," she said, condensing many potential questions into one insulting answer that didn't satisfy Egon, as he put his back to her and them.

Irene looked around to see who else was there.

"Listen, son. I am not good at any of this. I am just trying to get through the day, you know?"

Egon waited, not knowing where to go next.

Irene scratched her head and then asked, "Do you want to hold one?"

Egon turned around and was interested in that.

"Walk behind me. They can be vicious if they are preoccupied with food," she said, walking through the door slowly with the flashlight scanning the floor. "Hmmmm – they all look busy."

As they walked through, the Skelekit, who was still loyally trailing Egon, stopped to say hello to one just sitting by itself. Irene's light barely hit it, so Egon tugged on her coat and pointed.

"Oh. Yes – that would be a good one to hold. I named her Hoffnung – Hoffie for short. She is leaner than the rest as they pick on her. Sometimes I stand guard at a hill so she can forage for a bit," Irene said, picking her up. "See how she curls around my arm immediately? Put your arm out."

Egon touched her scales. They weren't as pronounced as the others. She wasn't a wee baby, but she wasn't fully grown yet either. She was noticeably thinner than the others. She had kind brown eyes which were adjusting to the light, and her tongue zipped in and out of her mouth like a lizard.

"Put your arm out, she will curl onto it like a tree branch," Irene said, still looking around nervously.

Hoffie immediately clung onto Egon and he placed his arm against his chest. She curled right into him. He noticed her wrist, one of the only parts on her body without big scaly, armoured plates, had a metal ring pierced through it like a bullring. The yellow tag hanging off it read, "43". The Skelekit was like a nosey big sister and wanted to see. Egon squatted down on the floor to show her.

They were both startled by the third door opening.

"Oh! Hello, Irene. I didn't hear you come in," a man in a white laboratory jacket said. "Who is your guest?"

"This is Egon," she said. "Egon, this is Mr. Wirdstaub."

"I didn't know you had family here," he said.

"He is a guest of General Swartz. He wants me looking after him. I am trying to keep him amused," she said, hoping the conversation would end there.

"Any guest of General Swartz is a guest of ours! If he has you here, you must be under protective order!" Wirdstaub said, pushing the heavy lens on his glasses back up his pointed nose.

"Well, I guess I am a woman," Irene complained. "So, I need to look after children."

"It is war-time, Irene! Everyone does what they need to. Stop being so sour that you are not used for inventing right now!"

"I am not sour, I am under-performing," she grumbled.

"Well, you are welcome here, dear Egon! I see you have 43. It would be nice for Swartz to know you had a good experience here. Let's show you around then!" Mr. Wirdstaub said, inviting them in.

"We haven't had dinner yet, maybe another time?" she said, trying to end it there.

"Don't be silly. You are here now! Come on in, Egon. Do you like 43? She is a gentle one," he said. "She isn't quite a year old."

"Egon doesn't speak, he isn't being rude or shy," Irene said.

"A quiet child is never a problem with me!" he laughed. "Did he see the stables?"

"We put a flashlight in, but they are all sleeping," Irene said. "We saw one peek its head up, so he did see."

"Nonsense," he said, opening that door. "Come on in, Egon."

As they went in, Mr. Wirdstaub had his own light and he began to introduce Egon to them.

"They are just babies in here," he said, running his flashlight over them.

Egon walked along the boxes and looked in at them. They seemed cold and lonely, confused, and agitated.

"They sleep a lot right now," he said.

Each of them had the appearance of scales coming in, but not hard and armoured yet. They were all tagged with numbers. Egon walked further down on his own, trying to see in a slightly larger box.

"Oh that is 43's mama. She is ready to give birth again. It is a three-hundred-day gestation and it is quite painful in the last day or two."

As Egon walked closer to her compartment, Irene flickered her flashlight over it so he could see in. Hoffie's sniffer started going and she made a few tiny noises. This agitated her mama who made the equivalent of a hissing noise at her. Hoffie started to struggle and Egon pulled her in close and walked away quickly.

"You can see how the weaning process here can get complicated," Wirdstaub said, following him. "You have to break a few nature rules to get things done."

Egon stood in the hall comforting Hoffie with a concerned Skelekit at his feet.

"We can show you the next area," Wirdstaub said, opening the third door.

"We really can't stay," Irene said, looking as though she was beginning to regret having a guest down there.

"It won't take long. You can bring Hoffie in, Egon!"

Egon moved slowly through the entrance. The floor was no longer wood and dirt, but tiled. The lights were brighter and the doors to the rooms in this hall were metal with glass windows in them. Another man wearing a lab coat came out of one on the right.

"Good evening," he said quickly, and disappeared into another room.

“Come on in,” Wirdstaub said, inviting them into the room the man came out of.

“Please keep it light,” Irene suggested. “He is just a boy. This is new to him.”

“How does a boy become a man when you ‘keep it light’ as you suggested?” he said, disgusted by that.

Irene said no more, she knew her place.

This room was a lab. It was cold and well-lit. There was a metal-top table in the middle and the outside perimeter was lined with glass-fronted cupboards. It smelled like strong chemicals, and Egon’s nose immediately curled up.

“This is where we examine the powder,” he began.

Egon looked at him and then up at Irene.

“Does Egon know what we do here, Irene?”

“I told him it was for study,” she said.

“Oh! So your first-time seeing pangolin dust, then?”

Egon became flush. He instantly looked too hot.

“Let me grab a jar to show you,” he said, pulling one out of a cupboard where they were lined up in rows.

“They are their scales that were shed. They are like your fingernails,” Irene inserted.

“Alright! THAT isn’t exactly accurate, Irene. I will take you to where we remove -" he said but she cut him off.

It didn't matter. Egon was teetering on passing out and his teeth were grinding away.

"Egon, sit! Here, sit here," she said, offering him a chair.

She ran over to get a glass of water from the lab sink and gave it to him to drink. He clutched the baby tightly in his left arm while he drank the water with the other.

"Like I said, it is dinner time. He is light-headed. Just give him a minute to adjust!" she snapped as she folded her arms and waited for Egon to gain the colour back in his face.

"You KNOW there is nothing magical in these scales," Irene whispered to Wirdstaub.

"You are way beneath this, Irene. Don't speak of things to which you have no direct knowledge."

"I am a scientist. Of course I have direct knowledge about that," she said.

"Except, not all decisions are based on science alone," he claimed.

"Or science AT ALL!" she clapped back.

"Oh! So you know about the Drillmeister's trip to New York City this past October?" Wirdstaub asked.

"What about it," Irene said.

"You don't know. I didn't think you did," he said, putting the jar back in the cupboard.

"Why would I care if the Drillmeister went there? Was it in the paper?" Irene asked.

"Absolutely not. But your overconfidence shows you make decisions based only on a few facts in front of you, and you ignore the larger picture. All I will tell you is he brought back something to Germany that will change the future of the Fatherland forever," Wirdstaub boasted.

"So you complain I make decisions based on partial facts, and you tell me a partial story – oh, that is so helpful. I learned nothing," she said, feeling Egon's head.

"See how that works?" he laughed.

"I am not laughing," she said.

"I work in a lab underground, Irene. Afford me a bit of fun!" he said, poking hard at her ribs.

"At my expense, how lovely," she said.

"Listen, I don't mean to tell you a partial story – the story is just beginning to unfold. What he brough back is a partial piece of a partial story. We will all know soon enough," he smiled.

"You are perfectly awful," she said, waiting impatiently for Egon's fast breathing to slow. "This is upsetting him. Just stop talking for now."

"The Fatherland has been under the feet of the world long enough. It is time to restore its greatness. The Drillmeister is destined to do this for us," he said proudly.

Irene ignored him. Egon was staring at him now.

"Well, I am glad one of you is interested in what I have to say," he laughed. "It's a good thing I like my own company!"

Irene reached down to feel Egon's head again and whispered, "He is like a hamster on a wheel. He will just go on all night if we allow it."

She then straightened up and said, "Shall we go get dinner, Egon – it is so late now."

Irene walked right to go back, and Egon walked left to continue down the hall.

"Egon, are we leaving?" she asked.

"Curiosity is a good road for a boy to be on. Our children must know the reality of their environment and how some of us are correcting it," Wirdstaub said, following him out.

"Correcting it. Yes, this is correction," she said, rolling her eyes.

The hallway ended up at yet another door that blew in a cold shot of air when Wirdstaub unlocked it. It was still underground but didn't feel as professionally insulated as the lab areas. There were poor people wandering about, some lying on bunkbeds. They were all wearing similar filthy striped uniforms with triangles. The men had matching striped caps, while the women wore kerchiefs on their heads and heavy long skirts. They looked dirty, tired, overworked, and underfed. A few looked perpetually fearful, while others were blank. The look they gave Egon was neither welcoming nor intimidating. It was nothing.

"Mr. Wirdstaub, may I speak with you?" a soldier guarding the workers said.

"Certainly," he said. "Irene, tell Egon what is happening here. I will be back."

This infuriated Irene who hated it here to begin with. The last thing she wanted to do was be a tour guide for slavery.

"Here is my advice to you," she said, getting close to Egon's face. "Do not allow anything to upset you. This is our reality now. I will try to get us back above ground as quickly as possible, but you need to go confidently too."

Irene then tried to paint the picture as fast as she could with a big wide brush.

"Those people work here. They transport various substances from the lab to the loading zone over there. Other people put it in trucks, and they take it to other people who want it," she said.

Egon held Hoffie tightly in his coat and the Skelekit stayed close.

"They are having their five-minute break. Yes, they receive five-minute breaks. Isn't that impressive? Most likely from something breaking down." she said sarcastically.

Egon took a walk through their beds and looked at each one of them. They may have been confused why this young German Prince was taking a night stroll, or they may have been puzzled why he was cradling the livestock with such tenderness when their job was the opposite.

"They wish they could be you," Wirdstaub said, returning to

the tour.

"They wish they could go home," Irene whispered to Egon.

Egon stopped to look at an old woman lying on the bed. A guard saw Egon looking at her and he walked over and put a whip just under her chin.

"You have a child of the Fatherland in your presence, woman. Sit up and show some respect!" he said, putting a knee into her back.

She was so crippled up with arthritis, and clearly couldn't lift another finger today.

"She is not worth wasting the food on," a high soldier said to the guard. "Remove her."

"NO!" a younger man cried out, lunging to save her.

"Oh! An admirable hero in our midst!" the soldier said to the other guards – and they all laughed. "You seem to have valuable energy tonight! You can work after the others go to bed then," he said, jamming a stick deep into his back.

Egon walked away quickly, most likely so he wouldn't cause any more harm. The Skelekit ran after him and so did Irene. He then entered an open storage area that had hundreds of containers in it. In each box, were dozens of sugar beets. There were also large cylindrical canisters that had skulls on them signifying poison.

"You aren't allowed to eat the beets," a young boy said. He was so malnourished and his skin, like the rest of them lacked vitamin D. They were all pale. "Don't eat them. You need to quit looking at them. Say no to the beets."

Egon turned to look at this robotic, monotone voice. He wasn't anywhere near these precious beets.

"You aren't allowed to hold the livestock," the boy said. "Don't eat them. You need to quit looking at them. Say no to the livestock."

It was like his thoughts were jammed. Egon walked straight up to him and looked down at Hoffie.

"You are not allowed. You are not allowed," he continued.

Irene intervened.

"Noah, nobody is eating or looking at anything," she said, turning his shoulders away. "Maybe you can see if that man is looking at anything over there."

Noah grew concerned that someone was looking at something and off he went.

"Noah is still alive because if you give him a job to do, he will do it all day long," Irene said to Egon. "He has become comedy for the soldiers. If he wasn't, well...let's not talk about that."

As she said that, the soldiers were pointing and redirecting him to other people... and he repeated the same warnings to them – to not look at anything, to not eat anything.

"Have you seen enough? We can go now," Irene said.

Egon was interested in all these supplies.

"There is a good part of sugar beets and then a bad part. The bad part becomes a really bad part. That is about all you need to know," she said.

"We feed people, we take care of pests, we have industry which is helping the Fatherland to recover from decades of unfairness," Wirdstaub added. "That seems like a good summary, right Irene?"

"I suppose we are still identifying who the real pests are," she said with her arms crossed, anxious to leave.

"You brought him down here! I didn't send a formal invitation!" Wirdstaub snapped.

Their arguing allowed Egon to look closely at these big cannisters. They indicated that they were a pesticide for killing mice and rats. Egon's teeth began to grind. He wandered over to the loading zones where there was a truck fleet at the mouth of a tunnel. There was indeed a whole underground industry here. There was one truck coming in with a roof full of snow, and one getting ready to leave. The one coming in was packed tightly with people like he saw back at the train station before his Christmas trip to Tiergarten. The truck that was being prepared to leave contained bags that looked like flour. Egon was trying to understand what was in them.

"Pangolin dust! Those scales may as well be gold coins!" Wirdstaub said with way too much joy.

Egon held Hoffie tightly and marched back to the lab area.

"I think you need to separate yourself, Egon. You will get soft," he called out as he followed.

They got back inside the lab area and Wirdstaub corralled him back to where he picked Hoffie up.

"It's time to put it down now," Irene agreed. "Let's head out."

Egon reluctantly set Hoffie back down on her ant hill. As he went to turn away, he took a better look at this wee hill. It was shaped, or she had shaped it, like a bigger pangolin – perhaps her Mama. It may have been a monument to her, as though she died in battle. Maybe it was to make other pangolins think she had security, and they wouldn't try to bully her. Most likely, she needed to feel less alone in the cycle of her life where she wouldn't have been alone had the natural course of a Mama/baby relationship not been stolen from her. A mother weans gradually, not abruptly.

Egon's teeth were grinding loudly. It was the scratch of the Skelekit at his leg that made him reset his face the way Zusa taught him to.

"Listen, Mr. Wirdstaub. I don't want to pass the Pangolin barrier any longer. I prefer to stay on this side of the door," Irene said, mustering up enough fierce bravery to say it.

"You prefer? You are a worker who now prefers to say how they work?" Wirdstaub laughed.

While they were arguing, Hoffie scratched the anthill (or pangolin monument!) which made the Skelekit sniff too. Egon looked at Irene and Wirdstaub who weren't paying attention, then squatted down to watch them play in the ground. Hoffie was using her claws to remove dirt, but not using her tongue to find any ants or termites. The Skelekit joined her in digging and the pair of them made quite a hole. Egon spotted something shiny and he began digging too. It was a tarnished gold skeleton key with a sideview of an elephant head with its mouth open on the end. Both Hoffie and the Skelekit stopped digging and sniffed at it. Hoffie even shot her tongue out at it like a frog catching a fly, maybe just to taste it.

Egon looked at Irene and Wirdstaub again and then shoved the key in his coat. He picked Hoffie up and boldly walked to the exit door with her.

"We are leaving now. I have said my peace," Irene snipped, and followed Egon.

"Pangolins don't leave, Irene," he said.

"You grind up hundreds of them into useless dust," she said, exhausted by his arrogance. "You are going to miss one?"

"That isn't your property. Egon, return 43 to the pile, please," he said, pointing back to the anthills.

"I told him I named it Hoffnung. A number like that to a child seems cold," she said.

"They aren't pets. Here, let me make this easy for you," he said, removing Hoffie from Egon's arms and marching her back to the pile.

Egon stood frozen watching Hoffie go back, and she looked at him as though it was her first time experiencing love.

"Let's go, Egon," Irene said to no reaction. "Egon, we should just go."

Mr. Wirdstaub closed the pangolins' door and locked it.

"That is why we explain the truth to children, Irene. They do not need to become attached to livestock," he said, and left through the lab door.

Egon was left stranded in confusion and upset. Irene had to physically turn his shoulders around to guide him out. The Skelekit even seemed sad as she was witnessing Egon's disappointment at almost every step in his day.

Irene was walking a normal pace back to the trap door in the chicken coop floor, and she still had to wait for Egon who was dragging his feet with no real hope in his step.

"Welcome to my life. Did you know I have the same education as that man? Here I am taking care of livestock. It wouldn't matter if I waved my degree in his face, he would see me as the woman who cleans the pens," she said, lifting the trap door. "I am so tired of the condescension."

Egon was slow to come up out of the ground, and the Skelekit jumped up just before the door closed.

"Let's try to be quiet. The birds are sleeping," she said, shoving straw back over the door and exiting slowly through the coop.

As soon as they got outside, they saw Swartz.

"Are the birds not sleeping, Irene?" he asked.

"Yes they are now," she said, still recovering from one narcissistic man.

"Egon, would you go in and gather your belongings," Swartz said.

"He hasn't had dinner yet, General," Irene said.

"Grab something to go when you come out. I will wait," he said.

Egon went inside while they talked.

"Based on Wissen's report back to me, we are going to have Egon stay with the Kriegsmarine," he explained.

"Oh. I see," Irene said.

"You weren't growing – *attached* to him, were you?" Swartz giggled.

"I just follow orders, General," she said passively.

Egon grabbed some pumpernickel and headed upstairs. When he opened the door, Soot was on the bed. Irene put her there to appease both Swartz and Kluck. She began clucking away when she saw Egon and resumed her game with the Skelekit to win his affection.

"Did Ian see underground?" Swartz asked.

"He did, General," she admitted.

"I see. In the future, ask if that is allowed. This child doesn't speak, so no harm in him repeating things he sees, but you may get other children here – and you MUST follow the rules. Is this understood?"

"It absolutely is, General," Irene agreed. "It really is not a place for a boy. But he found it himself."

"Oh he had a key?"

"Well, no," she said, her face going red.

"I thought as much. I do agree. Our children don't need to be down there. Egon especially must be protected. None of it matters now. His new how will be at the Kriegsmarine with some of the best brains in the world. I am thrilled for him. Depending on his response to it all, he may do extraordinarily well," Swartz said.

"I don't know what any of that means, but it sounds wonderful, General," she said, trying her best to sound happy.

Egon dug through the dresser and found extra batteries for the flashlight and added those to his pockets. He grabbed a random bag and shoved a few clothes from the dresser in it.

Soot's newspapers on the floor needed changing, so he crumpled up the used ones and put new ones down. She still just used the one farthest away from the bed, even though Irene put them everywhere – along with a nice bowl of water. Maybe Irene would let her stay – if she feared the wrath of Kluck, she would. Egon broke off a piece of the pumpernickel and tossed it on the bed for her, stroked her lovely black feathers and then left with the Skelekit.

"Look at that," Swartz said when Egon came outside. "No resistance. What a fine boy!"

Egon peeked up at the bedroom window and saw Soot staring down. He quickly looked away so Swartz wouldn't see.

"Thank you for your efforts, Irene," Swartz said, guiding Egon to his car.

"Will he be returning?" Irene called out.

Swartz turned to look at her and said, "You will be the first to know."

It was now pitch black out on Christmas Day – a day that felt like a dozen days long. Swartz and Ian navigated through the deep snow and got into the back of the car to leave for the Kriegsmarine. Irene waved at them and Soot was still sitting in the window upstairs. Egon just had to trust that Irene would look after her. He pulled out his flashlight and didn't seem too worried about Swartz. He was, so far, no threat to any adult he encountered.

"I understand you had a trip underground, Mr. Wolff," Swartz grinned. "How would you like to take a REAL trip – but under the SEA?"

11 THE U-39 GHARIALS

Egon kept looking around for the entire trip. Not only were they driving slowly, there was a huge truck transporting an attached load following closely for their whole ride. Swartz noticed Egon looking back.

"They are with us," he said. "We need to drive cautiously. The weather is clear but that is a big load!"

Egon continued to fiddle with his flashlight – an object every young boy should always have on him.

"When a boy has a flashlight, he owns the whole world!" Swartz said, striking up a one-sided conversation.

Egon continued to watch out the window.

"I'm not cross with Irene, but that is no place for you. German boys don't live with the rats. We have been trying to find a place for you. It comes straight from the top that you are to be protected. Your stay with Irene and Eugen was temporarily fine, but General Kluck should not have taken you from there. We are just assuming he also saw something special in you. I apologize if you have felt tossed about on the waves of war.

Between this reason and Professor Wissen seeing great promise with you, it should only make sense that you go somewhere better suited - and where you are protected."

Egon was still working on his pumpernickel.

"You will learn to eat again. This is normal for orphanage children to be malnourished. That will come."

The rest of the trip was quiet, and Egon nodded off from the snowflakes hypnotising him.

It was still dark when Egon's eyes opened, and Swartz's hand was patting his knee.

"That is what our men do too," he said. "They catch a few winks when they can. You never know when the enemy is upon us."

Egon looked all around.

"No enemy upon us. You passed your first drill though! You are instantly alert! There will be times on the base that this is not a drill. We will teach you what to do in situations like that."

The driver got out of the car and opened Egon's door, and Egon stared at him.

"He has not been treated properly," Swartz said to his driver. "Thank you for this proper introduction of respect. You will be respected here, Egon."

"You can come out, Egon," the driver said.

"While he is on base, he will be addressed as Herr Wolff. Is this understood?"

The driver corrected quickly. “Your door, Herr Wolff.”

“That is wonderful,” Swartz said. “Please walk ahead and alert the officers,” he whispered to the him. “It is important for his upbringing that he is addressed this way.”

Egon was more interested in this giant transportation that had been following them.

“One of our workers saw Eugen showing you something he wasn’t supposed to. He was not instructed to do so. This is of no concern as it was ready to come here anyways. The Holidays are a good time to do covert activities as everyone is celebrating with family,” Swartz said.

“Will you need me to take Herr Wolff back at some point?” the driver asked.

“You may not have understood. Herr Wolff is not going back. Eugen made a huge error today. Irene made a larger one. They will be of no use to us now.”

“Very good, General,” the driver said.

The driver did as he was told and gave a quick instruction to the officers ahead. They nodded and he returned to the car.

“I have let them know,” the driver said. “They will communicate this to the others.”

“Very good,” Swartz said. “Shall we, Herr Wolff?”

Egon gripped his flashlight and followed Swartz.

“Admiral Prentzel will guide us,” Swartz said. “You won’t need a flashlight, but keep it in your coat,” he smiled. “Ah, there he is! Sieg Heil, Admiral!" Swartz saluted with his arm straight out.

"This is quite an honour to have Herr Wolff with us!" the Admiral said. "I see grown men all day long. It will be a welcome change to mentor you! I have received reports of your brilliance. You seem to have passed Professor Wissen's test with flying colours!"

"Herr Wolff is a welcome addition to your wolfpack, Admiral," Swartz said. "Perhaps I will accompany you on the tour – you understand – to help with his transition. He has been, unfortunately, thrust into chaos."

"Chaos! We specialize in the transformation and ascension above chaos! We deal in order. You are at the right place. Your training here will be dignified, productive - and of course, orderly. You are at one of our many fine ports. We are protected here by the entirety of the Wehrmacht – by land, by air and of course, by sea. You will not find a safer place on this planet – or any other for that matter. The Kriegsmarine shall be your home. I believe you will love it here. Service is in your blood!"

"He was recovered from an orphanage, Admiral. He does not yet understand his heritage."

"Yes, I understand Herr Wolff's – turbulent past. We also specialize in navigating turbulence, isn't this great news?" Prentzel laughed.

Egon let out a yawn. The Skelekit yawned back.

"Are we boring you?" Swartz laughed. "He napped on the way.

It might be best to show him to his bed tonight and start fresh in the morning?"

"You were right to bring him here, General," Prentzel said. "Our leaders were specific about keeping him safe - and guiding him properly."

"Do they wish to see him?" Swartz asked. "I haven't had the impression they want that."

"I do not have this impression either," Prentzel agreed.

"Egon?" a man's voice called out.

Egon turned to look, recognized him, and went running over to him. He stopped at his own self-imposed boundary line. He never asked for affection, and never reached out. He did get a big bear hug, though!

"Wait until Miss Kraus hears that I saw you!"

"You know Herr Wolff, Henry?" Admiral Prentzel asked.

"Wolff? He is a Wolff?" Henry asked, a little shaken.

"Please address him as Herr Wolff," Swartz said. "After speaking with his teacher, my orders were initially for Herr Wolff to go to Tiefer Bach Road. She suggested a mutual friend, Henry to drive them there."

"We have not readied permanent accommodations for Herr Wolff, but -" Prentzel began but Henry cut him off.

"Sir, if I may, Sir. He can stay with me – well, even just for tonight until he is situated, Admiral," Henry said.

"I think that is an excellent idea," Prentzel agreed. "May I speak with you privately, Henry?"

"Yes, Admiral, Sir," Henry stammered.

"I know you are a cook here. I know you are relatively new here. You are to respect rank. You will mind your place in the conversation. Is this understood?" Prentzel said, without expression.

"Understood, Admiral," Henry agreed.

"Herr Wolff's last name, or his personal circumstances are not your business. You do not have permission to discuss this with him. Is this also understood?" Prentzel added.

"Understood, Admiral," Henry agreed again.

"Very good," Prentzel said, returning to the others. "It will be good for Herr Wolff to have a familiar, happy face on his first night here. Henry sleeps in the crew cabin. In the event the Wolfsboot gets a call, Herr Wolff is to be returned to base before departure. It is a quiet night, though – and sleeping with the crew will be a good first taste of life here. Herr Wolff will have a proper tour tomorrow, and I will have his permanent room assigned and prepared on base, according to further orders I receive."

"That sounds great," Swartz said. "Henry is trustworthy, and Herr Wolff is clearly comfortable near him."

"Welcome to the family, Herr Wolff. I trust you will have a wonderful new life here," Prentzel said, patting his head. "I must go now."

"I must go as well," Swartz said. "Thank you once again, Henry. Please take your mentoring seriously. This is an incredibly special boy to us. As you can see, we have gone to great lengths to secure his place. Please continue to be responsible."

"He is one of us now, General. Happy to have him!" Henry said.

Swartz kneeled in front of Egon.

"A boy who consistently feels tossed about like an ocean ship will ultimately feel at home on the water. Let the water guide you, son. Have a wonderful sleep. Keep your flashlight handy!" Swartz said.

He tapped his nose and walked away.

"Look at this!" Henry laughed. "Never did I think that I would be dropping you off at Tiefer Bach and then run into you again at my work. Oh, Miss Kraus will be so thrilled. She has been worried about you!"

Egon gazed into Henry's big brown eyes and seemed safe there. He was instantly liked by anyone who met him and radiated kindness.

"Shall we?" Henry said, pointing ahead. "Six am comes quickly and it's cold! We should get going."

They walked a long icy dock to get to there. The winter was not kind this year. Snow was falling faster than the men shoveling it could handle and they looked ready to give up. The chunks of ice floating on top of the water seemed like they were taunting them. Even the ocean had given up on trying to melt them.

"This is our dock," Henry said. "Here, take my hand and I will help you up. Steady on your feet, now!"

Because of the snow falling, and bitter wind, Egon had no time to understand where he was, or what he was walking on. He was tired and cold, and happily followed Henry to wherever he was going!

He opened a big metal porthole and said, "Want to venture down or follow me down?"

Egon was so cold, he went first. The Skelekit jumped on his shoulder for the ride down.

"A man of adventure!" Henry laughed. "It's a ladder. You turn yourself around and go feet first. Hold on to the sides on your way. There is a small drop off the last rung – you can safely hop off."

When Egon's feet hit the floor, a man's voice met him with, "And who are – oh you are with Henry."

Henry was closing the door and following down the ladder. He came dangerously close to crushing the Skelekit who jumped out of the way at the last second and clung to Egon's feet.

"Herr Wolff is staying with me tonight. This is Navigator Becker, Captain Klein, and Helmsman Meyer."

"Herr Wolff? Is he related to -" the Captain asked.

"I was only instructed to have him sleep here this evening," Henry said, concerned about answering questions.

Egon was in the control room and there was plenty to look at with all the pipes, cogs, wheels, tanks, gauges, and wires.

"I believe the Admiral would like to conduct his own tour with Herr Wolff in the morning. It is late, and we are going to get some sleep," Henry said.

"Glad to have you, Herr Wolff," the Captain said.

"Please say hello to our Meteorologist and the First Watch Officer," Henry said, passing them by. "We will speak more in the morning. Herr Wolff needs to get some sleep. He can barely focus."

"Herr Wolff?" he heard the men whisper.

They went through a hole in the wall into another room which was the crew cabin. Beds were staggered boards coming out of the walls and the men were crammed in there like sardines.

"When they are in here, we try to be quiet. Rest time is sacred. Of course, you are the best at keeping silent!" he smiled, quickly putting together a blanket and pillow for him on one of the boards.

Egon was the easiest boy on the planet. Not only did he not speak, which for most people there who believe 'children should only speak when spoken to' is preferred, but he also was adventurous enough that he was obliging. The truth is that Egon had five hundred adventures on Christmas Day, and he was too tired to do anything else but rest on this board.

"You have a true friend here, Egon," Henry whispered, stroking the hair from his forehead. "Rest well, sweet boy."

Egon's body was done for the day as he fought hard to keep his eyes open. As he was falling asleep, a cabin rat was under the board of another crew worker munching on some breadcrumbs. The Skelekit watched this mini pirate for a time but nestled into Egon's chest - and the two of them drifted off.

Morning did come quickly for the crew on the Wolfsboot. The sun was barely up.

"Are you hungry?" Henry asked when he saw Egon open his eyes. "I am the cook here, so I can get you anything you like!"

The kitchen was essentially part of the crew cabin. It was the smallest partitioned area.

"He is used to breads and pumpernickel. This will change, but at his own pace," a familiar voice said. "That is a sleepy looking boy! I trust you rested well!"

It was Swartz, standing there with the Admiral. It was a lot for Egon to take in. Having rested, he could look around his surroundings better and there were so many men coming and going. It was a controlled environment, but people were working steadily. He sat on the edge of his bed-board where he received a piece of bread from Henry.

"I believe he did, General," Henry said.

"I am here to give you a tour of this Wolfsboot," the Admiral said.

Egon lit up.

"Yes! You are inside one of the many wolves that travel in the wolfpack," Prentzel continued. "I don't believe your last name is any coincidence. It makes sense that you should be in the Wolfsboot."

All the men surrounding the Captain stopped to look at Egon.

"Yes, this is Herr Wolff, everyone. Enough whispering and gossip. This is all you need to know about him. Go back to your posts," the Admiral said...and they did.

"You will see more men than usual. We normally have two dozen crew – it is more than double that because of the times we are living in. Shall we begin in the middle?" the Admiral smiled.

"Seems reasonable," Swartz laughed.

Egon walked straight ahead of Prentzel, back into the Control Room where he first arrived.

"A boy with initiative – good blood in that one!" Prentzel said to Swartz.

The Captain greeted them and offered to take over the tour for Egon.

"That would be fine. This is your ship!" Prentzel said to Captain Klein.

The walls of the control room were covered with the mechanisms for guiding the boat, and the valves were the only thing illuminated. They controlled the flooding and venting of the tanks. There were varying sizes of poppy red and green grass wheels which the crew would turn upon the Captain's order to dive. The background colour behind all of it was a mossy tank green.

"I see you eyeing up the periscope. Would you like to see?" Klein asked.

Egon looked around and then slid a box over and stood on it. He put his left and right hands on the handles and looked through.

"Has he done this before?" Klein asked them.

"Not to my knowledge, but as you know, it is either in you or it isn't," Swartz said with a big grin.

Egon looked through, saw a vast ocean, and then took both handles and clicked them up into a storage position. He jumped off the box, went over to the navigator's table, took a compass, and started calculating a course.

"Oh those are my papers, no -" Becker said walking forward, but the Captain stopped him.

"They are papers. Anything can be fixed. Let him go," Klein said.

The Captain and Admiral looked over each of Egon's shoulders as he adjusted their route.

"That is quite the emergency pivot! Becker, look and see if you are seeing what Herr Wolff is seeing or if he is simply role-playing for fun," Klein ordered.

"Yes, Captain," Becker said, looking through his periscope.

He walked back to the table and looked at Egon's work and said, "He's just mimicking the adults. It is quiet out there."

"Herr Wolff has shown some exceptional work. It would be

dangerous to ignore him. Maybe this is clear, but do not pass it off as role-playing or mimicking in the future. He has some special skillsets," Swartz warned.

"And where did he learn this? Has he been on a boat before?" Klein asked.

"Let's continue the tour," Swartz said, ignoring the Captain. "So, you are in the brain of the boat. I am sure Herr Wolff would love to see the engines, no?" Swartz suggested.

They walked back through the circular opening in the wall and through the crew cabin where Egon slept.

"You are standing on top of the ammunition, Herr Wolff. Did you know that as you slept? Do you feel the power under your feet?" Klein said, patting his back.

Egon's teeth were grinding as they walked back through the kitchen area.

"We call it diesel food," Henry said, pointing to the sausages hanging up. "It starts to taste like diesel after a long trip."

Egon moved away from this summer-sausage/diesel-fuel stench, and quickly moved into the Engine room where the two large sets of six-cylinder diesel engines on either side of the walking space had dozens of jointing limbs working with one another.

"Each engine is fifteen hundred horsepower. We run these on the surface of the water. They need air and the exhaust must go somewhere. While they run faster than the electric motors used for below the surface, the electric motors make no noise," the Captain boasted. "We need to be silent while hunting convoys."

"A good wolf moves silently," Swartz agreed, and he winked at Egon.

"And they work at night to avoid detection," Klein said. "Think about this, Herr Wolff. When you are part of a wolfpack, you need to figure out how to tell the others without the prey knowing it!"

"Shall we go outside and gain perspective on what you are inside of?" Swartz asked. "It was dark and blustery last night when you arrived."

Egon didn't wait for further instruction, and he zipped up the ladder.

"Oh let me help you with the door!" Henry said, climbing up after him.

Egon probably didn't need help with that either. His curiosity was driving him now.

"This is the first I have seen him come to life," Swartz said. "I think he is home!"

When they all got outside, Egon looked out from the deck of this grand submarine known as the Wolfsboot. It was a clear day, but not sunny. They were slightly above water in the harbour, and black smoke was bellowing out the top. Chunks of ice were floating on the dock's water line and it made the ocean look as though she had white scales that rippled with the waves. On the main dock, dozens of young men (boys, really) were practicing marching orders with accompanying flags. What stopped Egon in a deadpan gaze was the Fatherland's flag hanging proudly above. There was the black power spider many had grown to revere, fear, or steer clear of.

"He was home before he ever arrived," Admiral Prentzel said.

Out in the water, he saw men loading the two-man sea devil that Eugen showed him – the Elefanteufel.

"It had to come here. When Eugen and Irene broke our trust today, we removed it – and them," Swartz said, coming in behind him.

The Skelekit jumped onto Egon's foot when he said that – and Egon snapped his neck around to look at him.

"Well, removal sounds harsh. Is relocation better?" he smiled.

"Everyone gets relocated – some below ground," Prentzel laughed.

Egon's blood shot up to his face and his breathing started to labour.

"It is of no concern to you. There are always loyal German workers to work the farm and do what we need done. It will be a fresh start for some lucky recipient!" Swartz said, patting Egon's back.

The Skelekit wasn't comfortable like she was in the Grunewald Forest. It was a disciplined atmosphere not exactly conducive to rogue skeleton fox babies playing full-time. She always had one boney foot on Egon's boot. What could she possibly be afraid of? Nobody saw her here.

Well, somebody did. Up above, circling high, was Düster. It's a wonder the Kriegsmarine didn't shoot him out of the sky because he managed to infiltrate the no-fly zone. Perhaps they thought he was there to see them because Swartz exclaimed, "A black eagle!" as though Düster was proud to be on all their flags, equipment, and clothes.

All eyes were proudly watching as though the Universe sent him to give its approval. He began to circle down as they stood tall, and proud to be in his presence. As Düster came closer to them, he landed on a post right beside Egon. He extended his wings, showing just how majestic his wingspan was, then closed them and sat still. His rank was clearly above the Admiral's.

"You are home," the Admiral said, walking up to Egon to shake his hand.

Düster was not having that, and he lunged at the Admiral's hand. Prentzel pulled back quickly and laughed.

"You are not only home! I believe this is YOUR home!"

"Herr Wolff is apparently home wherever he goes," Swartz said.

Düster then shot off the post and flapped his wings at all the men. It was so violent, that it knocked their hats off their heads and then he screeched and flew away.

"I believe that was our lesson in humility," Prentzel said. "The Fatherland has spoken."

Swartz walked over to Egon and whispered. "There is a great power in you. We will protect you, son."

"I believe the future was just handed to us, my friends. SIEG HEIL!" Prentzel said with a salute.

"SIEG HEIL!" they called out in unison.

Egon's eyes were still on Düster who disappeared into a black dot in the clouds.

"Shall we show Herr Wolff the very special project we are working on?" Swartz asked.

"I think it is safe to do so. If we had doubts before, they just flew away," Prentzel said, looking where Düster went.

Henry put his hand on Egon's shoulder and said out loud, "Good day, Herr Wolff. It was a pleasure having you as our guest."

Then he leaned in and said, "I will tell Miss Kraus I saw you. She worries about you. Come find me if there is trouble, alright?"

As the men laughed about their experience with the black eagle, the Admiral said to Egon, "Shall we, Herr Wolff?"

Egon quietly followed along, looking back at Henry who was waving with a big smile. As they walked along the dock, they were stopped by a sign:

AUTHORISED PERSONNEL ONLY.

It was attached to a double iron gate. The men guarding the entrance saw Prentzel and Swartz coming and opened it for them before they could even ask. These two elite men were known in every area of the Wehrmacht: The Heer, The

Kriegsmarine (where they were) and The Luftwaffe had a handful of top leaders that were revered right across the unified armed forces.

"Are they planning to transfer today's delivery in?" Swartz asked one of the guards.

"They are, General. It will be set up in the main shop next to the aquarium," the young naval guard said.

"Very good," he said, as they ventured in.

Egon looked at the guard when he said "aquarium" and ran inside the gates. The Skelekit was hot on his heels.

"No fear there!" Prentzel remarked, and they followed Egon who seemed to know where he was going.

Most aquariums were known for tour guides and replicated areas that were supposed to make creatures feel like they were still in the wild. While this place was state-of-the-art, it was not for tourists. It was for science and study. The ceilings might as well have stopped at Mars, they were so high. It was a curved dome, sliced into pie strips with glass in between bent steel beams that were dotted with reinforcing round bolts all the way up.

"You are inside the Seeigel," Swartz said, pointing up. "The Sea Urchin is a living, breathing space where we use the power of nature to battle our enemies!"

"It is as though we are on the ocean floor here, Herr Wolff," Prentzel said. "This is the very best of the German minds, congregating together here – at our command – to construct an underwater army that will strike with such a devastating force, THEY will not only be sorry – but ASHAMED to have awakened the monster."

Egon began to walk through this Urchin with life swimming all around him. It was like being shrunk and put inside a fish tank, except there were halls carved out where he could walk. The corridors were not straight, they curved and veered off left and right. When he and the Skelekit walked down the right squiggly corridor, water surrounding them, he began to explore some of the creatures.

"Those are Sea Pens," Prentzel said, tapping the glass where purple, yellow, and peach coloured feathers were fastened to the floor and swaying in the water. "They call them that for obvious reasons. They are like writing quills, you see? Our goal is to place them in various ports. They are no ordinary Pens standing tall in the silt, bored of life, they will have the ability to alert us to incoming enemies. Their outer layer makes it impossible for the enemy to detect the electrodes inside of them. See the one in the back? It has grown to two meters."

A Leafy Sea Dragon floated by.

"Their snout is like a straw. They suck up bits of enemy cells for us to analyze and return it to us. Oh, Herr Wolff, would you like to see the Vampire Squid?" Swartz asked, calling his attention to the aquarium on his left. "Get your flashlight out. They prefer the dark."

Egon retrieved his flashlight from his pocket and began to shine it through the glass. There he saw mini footballs with bat-winged fins swimming past one another.

"They are in the very bottom of the ocean because they need it to be dark," Prentzel said. "They are our messengers. Oh look! We startled it. It turned itself inside out like folding your socks!"

Egon walked ahead still with his flashlight.

"This area has the Winzig Panzers," he continued. "Tiny for a Panzer tank, giant for isopods. Imagine crabs that have their small legs tucked under them. Between them and the armoured snail – a creature whose shell we are studying to determine what the substance is made from as it appears impermeable – we are creating an underwater tank division which will pierce small holes in enemy ships. Sometimes death by a thousand cuts is the preferred tactic."

Up ahead was an ominous creature. It had the head of a shark, body of an eel and big fins along the edges.

"One of our scientists discovered the Frilled Shark in the late 1800s," Prentzel said. "Some think it is a sea serpent. It has a high sensitivity to microscopic movements of prey. We are reprogramming it to detect movement from thousands of kilometers away."

Egon put his flashlight away.

"They are all parts of our wolfpack. They will interact with our ships. Our men will be in constant communication with them," Swartz said. "You will grow up with them and learn how to communicate with them too."

Egon walked away from all of them and marched down the left corridor. He found a door that was away from the rest of the aquariums and opened it slowly. Prentzel followed him.

"You now understand the Wolfpack. I want to show you our latest adaptation. You are one of the very first people to see what we are working on in here," Prentzel said. "If you watch closely, you will see small bumps on the water. Those are babies."

The water was not in a tank but looked more like a shallow lake. Their habitat here was a close replica of the wild.

"We find them in shallow riverbeds, but they are programmed for ocean water," the Admiral noted. "They are growing accustomed."

Egon looked closer to see them cutting ripples through the water as they swam.

"They are hovering above their father – who undoubtedly won't like any of us here," Swartz explained. "Shall we take him under?"

"That is exciting, Herr Wolff!" Prentzel clapped. "Are you excited?"

Egon walked to the right of the waterbed where he saw a square opening on a moss green tiled floor. Just like he had learned to do in the back of the chicken coop, he grabbed a handle and pulled straight up. He looked back at them and then he and the Skelekit disappeared into the floor.

"I suppose Irene was right when she said he found it on his own," Swartz laughed. "Shall we try to get ahead of him, Admiral?"

The two of them hurried down the steps behind him.

At the bottom of the stairs, one might expect to see another rectangular door, but this entrance was curved with grey rows of round scales at the top fading into yellow rows of square scales towards the bottom. It appeared like a stone mason had fit these together like pieces in a puzzle.

Egon placed his hand flat in the center – and the door was...breathing.

"The Unterghar! Want to go *inside* of him?" the Admiral asked. "If we stay calm, he may remain still while the babies are above."

He was indeed alive but a completely immobilized version of his former self **who used to be beautiful once**. Egon was both apprehensive and curious.

"The offspring will have an easier time than him. They were born here and don't know any different. He is a combination of nature and science. Now, Herr Wolff. Tell me if this looks familiar."

The Admiral pressed his hand on an area of scales where a door handle would normally be. After pushing in, the side of the Unterghar became a door.

Egon walked into a control room with a periscope. There, they introduced Egon to a Captain, Meteorologist and the First Watch Officer just like in the Wolfsboot. He immediately looked at the walls which were breathing in and out. The workers seemed unreasonably calm.

"Herr Wolff, gentlemen. He will be raised on this base. We are giving him a tour!" Swartz said.

The Captain tipped his hat. "A wolf is always welcomed here!" he said, sitting at his worktable. "This is the most excited I have been about a project. The Unterghar 39 will ultimately not be dependent upon diesel or electric."

Egon saw a portal door and peeked in to see identical sleeping quarters that were in the Wolfsboot. They were making a Wolfsboot/Gharial hybrid. It was disturbing at best.

"He was already in the U-boot, so this must seem like he is dreaming this," Prentzel said.

Up above sounded like squeaky toys crying out for a parent.

"The offspring congregates until they are too big. Then, they are moved to another area where they are operated on. Our scientists will be constructing rooms inside them which will grow as they grow. My niece called them miniature doll houses!" the Captain explained, as they all laughed out loud.

Egon was noticeably upset, and his teeth were the loudest grinding they had been. His hands were shaking and forming fists. The Skelekit stayed close to him as he ran to the other side of the room and looked in that door. It was another room with men working.

"Exact same set-up! When they dragged this beast here, he was only a third of the size. Now, with a little help from us, he is virtually the same size as the Wolfsboot."

The babies began to squeak loudly which caused the Unterghar to become restless.

"Calm the children," the Captain radioed to someone. "I repeat, CALM THE CHILDREN!"

Everyone grabbed a hold of something to steady themselves.

"Just some turbulence," the Captain said to Egon who was turning green. "Imagine the stomach upset our crew will have testing at sea!"

The Unterghar calmed down for a few moments until the babies started chirping again.

"What seems to be the problem up there?" he radioed in again.

Just then, a red light on the wall of the Unterghar began to blink on and off which alerted the crew.

"We need to leave!" Prentzel said with urgency.

He grabbed Egon's arm as they all poured out of the Unterghar and marched up the steps, down the curly walls of the aquarium, through the Sea Urchin and back out to the entrance they came in.

Outside, war sirens were blaring so loudly, they could barely speak to each other.

"Everyone to your post!" the Admiral exclaimed.

"Come with me!" Swartz said, tugging at Egon.

As Egon ran with him, he looked up. There was Düster circling down. He reached for his flashlight – indeed, an object every young boy should always have on him.

12 THE FEATHERLESS FLOCK (WAR BY AIR)

Egon put his hands up to his ears.

The war sirens were on high posts close to him and Düster was still circling him.

"Herr Wolff, we must go!" Swartz yelled to compete with the noise.

He didn't want to move while the bird was still circling. This was the same bird that led him to the Grunewald Forest. The Skelekit was frozen, waiting beside him. Düster finally came down close to him and flapped his wide wingspan in his face seemingly to push him back. Egon covered his eyes so the feathers wouldn't hit him. Düster seemed particularly upset about the dome roof of the aquarium. He circled it a couple times and then landed. He looked down at Egon and then began to tap loudly against the glass on each sliced panel.

Swartz attempted to grab Egon as he tried to run back into the aquarium, but he slipped through his hands and darted back inside. He ran down the curved corridor towards the

Unterghar with the babies. Without any fear, he jumped into the water and began to grab as many of the little gharials as he could. The Skelekit waited, not wanting to go into the water.

Two men jumped in to grab him. One got a hold of him from behind under his ribs while the other removed the babies from his hands and returned them to the Unterghar.

"They are safer here than anywhere else," one of the men said, tossing them back in. "If you detach even one of them, it will upset the Unterghar - and this entire aquarium will be turned upside down!"

Soaking wet, Egon was corralled down the corridor and pushed back outside. The two men slammed the doors shut and locked them, leaving Egon to frantically bang on them.

"There you are," Swartz called out. "The aquarium must remain in lockdown during drills. Parts of it can potentially withstand a direct hit. We must count on our defense systems to protect all of this. You must come with me now!"

The chaos outside had increased. A large group of men grabbed the General and quickly ushered him away from Egon. They didn't even take the time to let him speak. He became a top priority that they needed to protect and there was no conversation to be had over such loud blaring sirens and bodies running in all directions. Düster got himself in between the men who snatched the General and Egon. He continued to flap his wings, herding him like a border Collie with sheep. It didn't seem to matter which way Egon would step, the bird didn't want him to move. He stood there soaking wet and freezing, watching people run around him as though he was a tree stump. The Skelekit was mirroring his steps and finally settled on top of his boot, shaking, nervous and cold just like him.

"We are sitting ducks! They can't stay in there!" a man yelled.

"I am the Captain, STAND DOWN!" Klein yelled from the top of the Wolfsboot.

"Permission to limit the staff to essential personnel only, Captain!" someone yelled.

"We will keep essentials here to fire at bombers. I will remove the others!" the Captain hollered as he ran back down the ladder.

Egon's clothes were freezing stiff. Düster was keeping him in that position.

Inside the Wolfsboot, Klein called out, "Essentials only! Everyone else needs to get off the boat and into the ground! Enemies are flying in!"

"We see them on radar, Captain," Navigator Becker pointed out.

"How many?" Klein asked.

"Looks like six so far, Captain," Becker responded.

"Let's hand it off to radio, you need to go get underground," Klein urged. "Combat men ONLY! We aren't out at sea firing torpedoes!" he yelled, clapping his hands. "GO! GO! GO!"

It was only a few moments that men started to come up out of the boat in single file. As soon as every one of them hit the ground, they covered their ears and ran into holes in various points around the Kriegsmarine base. At least two dozen men ran close to Egon, and none of them noticed he was there. He became like any other post on the property. Düster stayed immediately in front of Egon, flapping away.

Up above, the men on the deck could see tiny dots in the sky - dozens of them.

Düster moved from Egon to the Wolfsboot. He flapped frantically to stop the Captain from closing the door from the inside.

"Someone get this bird off of me!" he called out. "I can't close the door!"

Several men tried to shoo Düster away, but he was good at his job and was too overbearing for them to make any progress. He consistently flapped cold snowy air into their faces. Holding them back was enough for his friend to escape the U-boot. There was the rat from under the bunk – and it ran straight to Egon. It only stopped long enough to circle back a few steps to grab the bun it had been nibbling on.

The Skelekit drew her front legs up into her belly at the sight of a rat coming at them. This tiny stowaway zoomed inside Egon's coat. Düster then let the Captain close the door.

"Yes! Get off my boat!" Klein yelled at it, and he slammed the door down.

Düster was calm now. He flew back over to Egon and stood on the ground in front of him. They connected on a level most people wouldn't understand. It was silence and peace between them while the Kriegsmarine was preparing for an imminent assault.

Düster looked up to see an entire flock of geese coming in their typical V formation. They were maneuvering well through the wind and snow to move this boy out of his marble coma. Nobody else was doing it. The V inverted at the last landing moment and Egon was in the middle. The leader had stopped at his feet and each goose landed on either side of him. They began honking loudly, their flippers were smacking off the ice, and their wings created a flurry like a butterfly migration. People walking by wouldn't be able to see Egon standing there simply from the confusion they created. They bullishly moved him towards a building that nobody else seemed to be going into. Egon's senses were overloaded, and he was rendered immobile. Because they were herding him to a door, he was forced to open it. In he went, Skelekit in tow, rat in coat – and they followed him. Once the flock was inside, Egon closed the door and peeked out a small window to see what was going on.

This dirty repair shop smelled like oil and diesel. It was most likely used by the local mechanic for naval officer vehicle repairs. The leader of the flock walked all the way around Egon and the rest followed in a circle. Once the ring was complete, one by one they all sat down and waited. Egon looked at them from his center and then sat down, careful not to sit on the Skelekit and extra careful not to squish the little fugitive in his coat.

The rat poked his head out and saw the geese and zipped back inside. Egon reached in to force an introduction, and he was peaceful in his hands. He still had the bread in his mouth which Egon took from him. He broke off equal portions of the bun and tossed a bit to each goose. It wasn't a meal, but it passed the time.

It was next to impossible to stay calm with the blaring sirens in the background, but this flock was doing a great job keeping him focused and grounded. Three of the geese were preening each other and the rest were cleaning themselves after a presumably long winter flight.

It doesn't matter how many generations try to replay, then relay war horrors to their current generation, nobody can explain or prepare a person or team for the impact is of a bomb. Half the people on base were sent running for cover while an elite selection had to stay to defend their fortress. Egon was thawing out and the heat from the birds was helping take the shiver out of his skin. Even though his days were full of adventure and surprises, the devastation from the first plane's gift to the harbour sent a wave through the entire Kriegsmarine that nobody had previous experienced. They were used to being wolves. They were convinced they were apex predators. They believed the Universe was siding with them and wanted the world to be a pure race, guided by their ideologies and self-proclaimed enlightenments. Of course, they were an intelligent group who didn't just bathe in the confidence of offense. Their base was fortified to take the hits from their enemy. They banked on having stellar radar detection and defensive teams. They were about to deploy all of them in response to twelve Vickers Wellington bombers that were intent on decimating the harbour.

The German Freya-radar systems identified them early, however the communication between the air surveillance departments was sluggish at best, when every single second counted. It turned out to be more helpful if someone on the ground spotted them coming – then would run and tell everyone else. This wasn't exactly an ideal strategy, but it got most of the people underground when they hit.

When the first wave came in, the geese all stood up and honked. The first impact was like experiencing a massive earthquake. The ground shook under them, everything in the room fell off the shelves, the windows blew shattered glass against the flock, and a burst of snow stormed in and covered over half of them. A British bomber had levelled a German warship. Men were screaming "run for cover!" and "get underground!"

The second, third and fourth attacks were insulting because there was no time for anyone to recover from the first. The geese were still honking loudly, either to communicate with each other or simply to express their gut-wrenching emotional reaction. They formed a safety canopy of wings around Egon on the floor, even though the blasts were making it difficult to do so. Not every bomber struck a ship or strategic target, but they created chaos and did incredible damage to the base.

Egon was curled up in a ball under this makeshift goose-tent, trying to protect the rat in his coat, and the Skelekit, who so far seemed to survive everything – even death. If any animal sound on Earth could compete with bombs and air raid sirens, it was angry honking geese. After all, car horns 'honking' were patterned after them!

Egon kept his hands on his ears until they finally settled down and began to dissipate from the shelter around him. After they all settled back in seated positions around him, Egon was able to assess the damage. They were no longer in a sheltered space as part of the wall was pushed in and there was no glass in the window. This was not upsetting. The real damage was to the geese.

It had to have been the leader who was lifeless on the floor because the rest of them seemed lost, and a goose who appeared to be second in command was honking to get the rest to calm down, but was visibly upset itself. Two other geese were yanking at glass shards pierced in their bodies – and a few others were helping them. It felt like a war zone hospital springing into action.

Surprise attacks are not only shocking, it is hard to know when they are done. However, when the next wave of bombers came in, the harbour began to fire back. It makes sense that if an attack is planned in broad daylight, the target is going to watch for subsequent waves. This was the failure of the Wellington Bombers. All airfields were informed, and they sent in several Me 109s Fighters and Me 110 Destroyers. When a Messerschmitt can reach 560 km/hr and can carry four machine guns and two machine cannons each, it becomes a lopsided battle.

The Golden Eagle Swarm that Zusa had spotted flying above the Grunewald forest made it through. Düster spotted them coming in and he soared into the shop where Egon and the geese were. He landed at the foot of Egon who was cradling the large goose. It was all he could do to hold it up. Düster looked at his condition and then pivoted to the next in command who honked back at him, and they flew out together.

Henry was among seven crew members who initially came up from under the ground. He was a cook, not a fighter. They all split off to assess damage and recalibrate. Henry was stopped by a boisterous goose who yelled at him until he followed.

"What is going on? What is your problem?" Henry said, rushing along to see where he was going.

He brought him to Egon, who was sitting on the ground, cross-legged, and still cradling the fallen leader.

"Egon! Why are you not with crew members?" he said, rushing to his side. "Look at that! You are tending to a wounded soldier."

As Henry tried to look closer, the remainder of the healthy geese rushed him and backed him right off.

"Oh no! I am not hurting anyone," he said with his hands up where they could see them.

Egon awkwardly pushed himself up to a standing position and walked the heavy bundle over to him. Henry looked around to make sure it was safe.

"I am not here to upset everyone! I can help!" he said, taking the goose from Egon.

The geese all fell silent and stretched their necks up to look. It was heart-breaking to see such concern for one of their own. In this case, their leader.

"Egon, this looks bad. I am sorry. I am sorry everyone," he added.

One by one the geese honked in disapproval.

"Alright! I won't give up. You need to let me tend to him. If I just leave him with all of you, he will die for sure," he said.

They all fell silent and stretched their necks again to watch.

"I will need to take him out of here, alright?" Henry said.

They all began honking their disapproval again.

"I cannot fix him here! You can all come along, alright? I am just not sure how I can travel discreetly with an entire flock."

He looked over to see a goose tugging glass from its body and flipping it away.

"I guess everyone needs a post-war check-up then. Alright! You cannot honk, though!" he said, looking quietly through the hole in the wall while they quietly stared a hole through him.

The rat peeked out of Egon's coat.

"Oh! You have Hausratte!" Henry laughed. "Only one other crew member knew about him. Klein would have burned the whole boat down if he knew of his presence. He slept me with me many nights!"

Hausratte seemed pleased to see his friend Henry and ran down to greet him. He ran up his leg and over the goose and sat on his shoulder. This concerned some of the other geese.

"He is one of us. It is alright, everyone!" Henry laughed. "Getting out of here will be tricky, Egon. We need to go out the door and then quickly move towards the Sea Urchin. It is the only place I know that has supplies to help our friends here."

Still holding the fallen goose, he slowly opened the door and they all slithered out unobtrusively except for their webbed feet pattering along the snow. Egon stopped to assess the damage in the same place where he stood frozen prior to the geese showing up. Henry stopped to whisper to him.

"The U-47 was so lethal. It took down the Royal Oak and killed seven hundred and eighty-six of her crew," Henry said. "Of course they are seeking retaliation! Come with us, Egon – we can't be seen."

When they reached the door of the Sea Urchin, Henry grabbed the handle and it was locked. The geese, who were used to moving in a straight line were a bit lost and wandered aimlessly in their circle.

An aquarium staff member opened the door.

"The Urchin must remain closed and locked until we get an all-clear from the Admiral," the man said.

"I am with Herr Wolff. Let us in at once!" Henry said in his best commanding voice, even though he was a gentle spirit.

"Oh, Herr Wolff! Yes, come in!" the man said, revering the name immediately.

"This flock belongs to him," Henry added sternly. "The leader is injured and requires medical attention."

"Alright, I guess!" the man added, then awkwardly let them in and locked the door again.

Henry was leading the flock down the curly corridor. Well, their leader was in his arms – so technically, they were following him. They were hilarious. Their flippers were fwap-

fwap-fwap-fwaping on the tiled floor and they were thrilled to see the marine life inside the glass walls. They were acting like tourists at an aquarium. One stopped to tap the glass like he was grabbing a fish.

"You are Ben, right?" Henry asked.

"That is correct," he said.

"Thank you for helping us, Ben," Henry said. "Herr Wolff loves these birds."

"Is Herr Wolff -" Ben started.

"Do you love working here?" Henry asked.

"I do, it is always interesting," Ben said.

"Working with creatures must be fantastic!" Henry said. "Is this the room?"

"It is," Ben said. "I believe Herr Wolff was in here before the blast."

They were back where the gharial babies were. Egon stood looking at them hanging out on top of the Unterghar.

"You can bring the injured in here – the rest can wait over -" Ben began but he was cut off by them all honking and jumping in the water.

"I suppose a goose knows what to do with water," Henry laughed.

Once they hit the water, they were calmly floating.

"They seem peaceful there," Ben said. "Right this way."

Ben took Henry into a room where he put the bird on the table. They both got to work on his belly where most of the blood was.

Meanwhile, the rest of the geese had stepped up their water game. They were splashing about and curious about the gharial babies who were too large to be food, so they became entertainment.

Ben received a call to which he only replied, "Understood, Admiral."

"Everything alright?" Henry asked.

"The Urchin is remaining locked down until Command says otherwise," he said.

"We are safe for now and out of the elements," Henry said.

The gharial babies were not playing. They always had a big pool of water to themselves, and a black and white goose was not the best introduction to another species. Still, the Mommas in the goose group were gentle with their curiosity and treated the babies as they would their own. These wee ones hadn't seen their mommas since hatching from their eggs and they soon understood they were no threat.

Egon got lost in the moment of a Mother goose tapping the back of the one of the baby gharials as though it needed cleaning.

"You never knew your Mother, did you?" Henry said, startling him a bit. "Sorry about that! Ben wrapped the leader and is letting him rest. We don't know how it will turn out yet. We wait and see."

Egon went back to looking at the Momma goose and gharial baby.

"My Momma was wonderful. Miss Kraus is a lot like she was," Henry said, smiling.

Egon looked at him when he said that.

"She knows you are here. I communicated with her," Henry said.

Egon ran his finger along Hausratte's head after he returned to his coat.

"If we ever get out of here, would you like to see her sometime?" Henry asked.

Egon looked back at the Momma goose.

"I think you might," Henry smiled. "Say, do you want to go back inside? Ben thinks you went for a quick tour."

Egon marched over to the door in the floor and yanked it up.

"I guess there is no asking you twice!" Henry laughed.

They went down the steps and Egon stood looking at the scales of the Unterghar.

"Do you know how to get in?" Henry asked.

Egon watched the breathing for a moment and then placed his hand where the Captain did. The Unterghar's door then became visible and opened for them.

They were back inside the control room. The Captain, Meteorologist and the First Watch Officer were gone – in fact, everyone had abandoned this post.

"Nobody is here," Henry said, looking puzzled. "I suppose everyone went underground after that first blast."

Hausratte peeked out again and jumped out like he found somewhere familiar.

"Look how good a rat's sniffer is!" Henry giggled, pointing to Hausratte nabbing a piece of pretzel. "He sure liked my scraps on the Wolfsboot."

Egon walked around freely with nobody here and was curious about this periscope. He flipped a box of papers over and stood on it to get tall enough to see out. At the other end, he could see the geese feet paddling away and the wee feet of the baby gharials.

"May I see?" Henry asked. "If he is called the Unterghar, would they be Uberghars?" he said, laughing at his own joke.

Egon felt right at home behind the periscope.

"I would love to get you a telescope someday. If you really want to discover something that **I believe used to be beautiful once**," Henry said, losing himself in a moment. "What if you, me and Miss Kraus went on a road trip that went somewhere beautiful. Would you like that?"

Egon dropped both his arms down and turned to face Henry from the box.

"I would like that too," Henry said, his eyes filling with tears. "There is so much ugliness surrounding us. We must remember about hope."

The Unterghar's walls sucked in gradually and exhaled slowly.

"It's still alive you know," Henry said. "Word is they have stolen him from India. One of the villagers discovered one that was larger than normal and sold him to Germany for a bit of food and money for his family. While he was abnormally big, he was never this size. They made him grow. It's a cruel process."

As they spoke, the Unterghar breathed in again.

"I believe he hears us, Egon!" Henry smiled.

Egon hopped off the box and put his hands on the walls. His teeth began to grind as he felt the breathing. He immediately left the control room through the door leading to the sleeping area and kitchen. Henry followed.

"It is the same design as the Wolfsboot," Henry said, as Egon passed him coming back into the control room.

Egon began to pace the control room and grind his teeth loudly.

"Your teeth are so loud, Egon!"

Then, he stopped and looked at Henry. He placed both hands on his cheeks and pulled down.

"You have calmed yourself. That is fantastic!" Henry clapped.

Egon frantically looked around until he found a toolkit. Then, he rummaged through until he found some wire cutters, and went racing in the opposite direction through the doors and rooms until he could go no farther – he tore through the radio and sound room, through the officer's quarters and into the torpedo room at the front.

"Egon, what are you cutting?" Henry said, keeping a lookout.

Above the torpedoes was a severe mess of lines around the Unterghar's brain. Egon moved wires out of the way until he found a yellow one and he snipped it straight away. Then, he covered it back up with other wires as though nothing happened.

The Unterghar was still breathing.

"Did it do what you wanted it to?" Henry asked.

Egon ran back into the control room and jumped back onto the box and looked through the periscope. The babies all started to swim away from him and swam normally around the water. Some of them played with the geese. Egon motioned for Henry to look into the periscope to see what Egon was seeing.

"They are leaving him," Henry said. "Did you clip their connection?"

Egon ran around the boat looking in compartments and then finally gave up.

"What can I help you find?" Henry asked.

Egon opened the door to the Unterghar and left.

Up past the water, Egon looked in several rooms to find the

items he needed. There were many storage closets, but no bins. He spotted a sign saying LOADING -----> THIS WAY, so he ran THAT WAY.

Henry followed closely behind. They finally hit an area in loading with the bins Egon wanted. They said, LIVE SPECIMEN on them, and he grabbed two. He wasn't one to ask for help, but Henry noticed he needed it, so he took one from him and followed him back to the water.

The Uberghars we very quietly floating along the water, no longer near the Unterghar. Egon put his container on the ground and opened it up. It was meant for aquatic life and was sealed and partitioned accordingly. There were eight babies and Egon was trying to sort out how to grab them. He tipped the container to allow water in and then set it back onto its base once it had sufficient water in it. Just then, one of the Momma geese took an Uberghar in her mouth and placed it in Egon's container. After seeing her do this, two other Mommas did it too. It only took the three of them doing it a few times to get all eight babies in the container. Egon ran off to find their food flakes, saw the container and put that in too. Then, he clamped the lid down.

The geese went back to swimming in the quiet water. The ones who were flipping glass out of their feathers seemed to be healing in the water.

Egon left the Uberghar compartment there and dragged the empty container into the room where the injured goose was.

"Thank you for looking after him, we need to leave now," Henry said to Ben.

"How would you like to deal with this fellow?" Ben said, pointing to the head goose lying on his table.

"I believe Herr Wolff wants him to leave now. Can you set him in there?" Henry asked.

"Certainly, Herr Wolff. I hope you find him well soon," Ben said.

"Herr Wolff doesn't speak, Ben. I can assure you he is pleased and grateful!" Henry said.

As Ben set the head goose inside this box, he said to Henry, "I believe this goose was a hero today."

"Gänseheld!" Henry smiled. "Do you like this name, Egon?"

Egon squatted down and touched his head. Gänseheld's eye was staring at him. Egon took the cloth and pulled it up near his face to keep him warm and then closed the lid on the box.

Henry lifted this box and took him out to where the Uberghars were.

"Well, they are all ready to go," Henry said to Egon.

One of the geese jumped out of the water and walked over to the box Gänseheld was in. It tapped on the box and let out a kind, low rumble honk.

"I believe he approves," Henry said. "I guess we need to sort out what is next!"

"Ben told me you were here, Herr Wolff," Swartz said, startling them. "Thank you so much for looking out for him, Henry."

"It's my pleasure," Henry said, stepping in front of the boxes. "We were fast friends. He is a great child," Henry said.

"It all happened so quickly! A group of men were ordered by the Admiral to make sure I was protected. I needed to understand where Egon was before heading back to the Heer base as the instruction to look after him comes from the top. It is a responsibility I take seriously," he said, somewhat distracted.

"We came in here as it was farthest away from the fighting," Henry said.

"It isn't safe here anymore," Swartz said. "Everyone on this base is needed on this base. Can you take me and Egon back to my base?"

"I would be honoured to," Henry said.

"I can't even find my own men. It's a nightmare out there," Swartz said, briskly leaving the room, but turned to call out, "Please have your car in the Urchin parking area. I will meet you and Herr Wolff there shortly. I need to speak to the Admiral first."

Ben walked in and heard Swartz tell them this, so he thought everything was fine.

"Do you need my help?" he asked Henry.

"That would be wonderful! Something to set these bins on?" Henry said, assuming his authority.

Ben left and promptly returned with a cart for them. The back parking lot door had a terrible squeak in it, but nobody seemed to be around. Henry kept an air of confidence about him and moved ahead.

"Would you wait right here with Herr Wolff while I get my car? It shouldn't take too long," Henry asked.

"Yes, I will," Ben said.

"Be right back!" Henry said and ran off.

"I must admit, Herr Wolff," Ben said, making small talk. "I was concerned about what you and Henry were doing so I called for assistance. When word got out that the General was looking for you, I let them know you were here. It seems he already knew what you were doing. I apologize for any assumptions."

It was a good thing Egon didn't talk, so he didn't have to acknowledge or dispute what Ben was saying. He just glanced up at him briefly, and then stared forward waiting with the boxes for Henry's car.

It was an awkward wait time as the whole base was still chaotic and busy after the bombings, but Henry didn't make him wait long. He showed up with his Ford Model A and Ben started laughing.

"Where are these going to go?" Ben smiled.

"In the back seat. Egon is small, he can tuck in beside them," Henry said. "The General will ride up front. His base isn't far from here."

It took a few attempts to get them in and they finally fit side by side on the seat with Egon squished against the window. He seemed alright with this as he needed these containers to be with him. The Skelekit jumped in by his feet and Hausratte stayed in his coat.

"You can stand outside until the General gets here," Henry offered, but Egon stayed put and watched out the window.

The rest of the geese stood in the parking lot trying to act natural.

Way up high, Egon could see Düster circling and the geese all watched him too.

13 THE BEETLE-TANK TURKEYS (WAR BY GROUND)

"Very good, Henry!" Swartz said, hurrying into the front seat. "I can always count on you!"

"Never a problem, General. Happy to serve," Henry said, winking at Egon and getting in the driver's seat.

The rest of the geese formed a new V formation without their leader. It was a bit awkward but not a new thing for them to do.

"All set, Herr Wolff?" Swartz said, doing a double-take. "Why do you have live specimen crates in your car?"

Henry already sorted out that story. If any noises came from them, he needed to cover that too.

"Science request from another base," Henry said, and then quickly pivoted. "How are things on your base?"

"We can't get there quickly enough," Swartz said. "Years of preparation is culminating now."

"Do you want me to stay at your base with Herr Wolff?"

Henry offered. "At least until you get this sorted out? I mean, he seems to feel safe with me...and it will free you up and make you feel less stressed."

Swartz was gazing out the window.

"General?" Henry asked.

"Hmmm? Oh yes – my apologies. You want to stay with Herr Wolff?" Swartz said, very distracted.

"You have so much to deal with – I can have someone else cook for the team today. Herr Wolff is a big priority as you noted," Henry said.

"Oh! Of course. I just need him close by right now," Swartz said, rubbing his eyes.

"I think many sleepless nights ahead, General?"

"Oh, son. I joined the service because I love this country. We are embarking upon something I never dreamed of for us, for our children, for the Fatherland. It is not going to be easy. Every decision counts. Every second counts," Swartz said, resting his elbow on the window and stroking his chin.

Egon was behind Henry looking out the window. His thoughts were not articulated like the General's. He was watching the geese flying to try and keep up. They eventually lost speed and fell behind.

"Herr Wolff?" Swartz said, looking back at him. "Are you doing alright son? Make sure he is fed when we arrive."

"Of course, General," Henry said. "He has been very well

behaved. He is sharp."

"His lineage is good. He is fortunate to be who he is," Swartz added. "A muted child wouldn't usually fair well."

"And an orphaned child, if I may add, General," Henry said, which made Swartz uncomfortable. "Do we know much about him? I'm sorry – I crossed a line – that is not my concern," Henry corrected.

"You are a good man, Henry. I am glad I entrusted you with him. I can see your fatherly concern. That is noble," Swartz said, and resumed staring out the window.

"Thank you, General," Henry smiled.

After a few minutes of Henry concentrating on the heavy snow coming down, as one may have predicted - it happened. Someone in the live specimen container made a noise.

"MEEEHHH-----OOOOOO"

"What was that?" Swartz asked, looking back.

"MEEEHEEEE-----OOOOOOO"

"Noisy bunch!" Henry laughed. "Did you ever have pets, General?" he attempted to change the subject.

"I had a terrier puppy once," Swartz said.

"That must have been a lifelong companion!"

"My Father took it away when I was eight," he said, looking back out the window.

"I'm sorry to hear that, General," Henry said.

"He said it would make me soft."

"Did you ever get another one?"

"No time for that," Swartz said. "We're here, Herr Wolff! Take him to the underground bunker on the North side until you hear from someone."

Their car was met with two soldiers who opened the door for Swartz and Egon.

"I will park your car," one of them said to Henry.

"Oh – yes – where will you put it?" Henry said, looking to the back seat.

"You need to go with them now," he replied.

As Swartz swiftly left with one of the soldiers, Henry said to the other one, "I have live specimens in the car. I need to transfer them to another base, so I just need to know where the vehicle will be. Can you leave the key in it?"

"East lot, the key will be in it," the soldier responded.

"Thank you," Henry said, unable to control the situation any more than that.

"You should run to catch up with the General," the soldier said.

"Thank you. Are you coming, Herr Wolff?" Henry said to Egon who was staring at the crates in the car.

Egon didn't want to leave the car, so he sat on the ground next to it.

"We'll find the bunker, General – don't let us hold you up!" Henry called out.

Swartz barely acknowledged that as he was moving swiftly and giving directions to the soldier.

The young soldier who was going to park the car looked lost.

"I was ordered to park your car," he said.

"Let's jump in and park it together. Herr Wolff doesn't speak – so it is hard to know if he understands where our items will be," Henry said. "Is that good, Herr Wolff?"

Egon jumped back in the car, Henry got in the driver's side and the soldier got in the passenger side.

"We have live specimens in the backseat," Henry explained on the way. "They won't survive the cold. Can we take them to the bunker with us first?"

"Uh – I was just told to park the car," he responded.

"Oh for sure, you can drop us all off at the bunker and then go park the car like you were asked," Henry smiled at his innocence.

"You can pull over on the left there by that post," the soldier said.

When they got out of the car, Henry asked the soldier to take one of the crates. Egon was now content to go with them. The soldier set the box just inside the cement building where the bunker was.

"Thank you, that is all. Thank you for parking the vehicle," Henry said politely. "Don't get it stuck now!"

This army base was run by the Heer and was particularly busy today as they were told a Panzer division was heading out for battle. Swartz needed to be back though due to a British bomber that was shot down before entering their airspace which set off a domino pattern of chaos.

The visibility wasn't improving today either. Even the tanks were struggling through big banks of snow and the soldiers were removing their heavy gloves to blow heat into their hands.

"Can you stay here with Gänseheld while I move the Uberghars into the bunker?" Henry said, hurrying away with the first crate.

The tanks drove by Egon while he stood just outside the bunker door. They waved at him and he did not wave back. One of the soldiers shrugged and they kept going. Hausratte was shivering inside his coat. It was so cold out that even the Skelekit was shaking while sitting on his boot. Someone should have knit her a sweater because the frigid December air was going straight through her ribs!

Henry was back quickly to grab the other crate and he called out to Egon.

"I thought you would be waiting inside. Come on in out of the cold!"

Egon followed Henry down into a cellar area. It was clean and surprisingly spacious. It had similarities to the Grunewald Forest bunker. There was a fireplace and wooden table for eating. There were also plenty of chairs and a plain sofa.

"Curl up and get Hausratte some relief – poor little thing. The Wolfsboot was always warm – he will be in shock right now," Henry said, locking the door behind them.

The Skelekit also nestled in and Egon cuddled her too.

"I think we have the place to ourselves! A fire will be nice, yes?"

After Henry had a good fire going, he pulled up a chair in front of Egon and sat backwards on it, folding his arms across the back.

"I know this must be so complicated for you. You must miss someone. I hope that I can be good company for you tonight. Do you know who I miss?"

Egon rubbed his eyes, maybe from being tired or possibly from embarrassment.

"Oh come on!" Henry laughed. "You must admit. She is the prettiest girl in all of Germany, right? Do I seem awkward around her? I think I am awkward around her. My hands get clammy and my face gets hot. I don't know how she feels, but I think about her all the time. Oh come on - don't you have someone you think about?"

Egon reached in his pocket and pulled out the Waffen SS tag. He looked at it for a moment and then handed it to Henry.

"I am honoured you are sharing with me. It must be special to you," Henry said, taking another look at it. "I wish I knew who gave it to you, though. Is it from your father?"

Egon took it and put it back in his coat.

"I think it is," Henry said. "Well, I don't know if he is alive or not, but if he died, I am very sorry."

Swartz was accompanied by two armed men as they knocked on the bunker door.

Henry opened the door to greet him.

"Most attacks happen at night – it is best you stay down here for the rest of today. Someone will bring you more supplies," Swartz said.

"The refrigerator seems well stocked, General – and there is more room than my boat bunker! I think Herr Wolff and I will feel like kings tonight. Thank you," Henry smiled.

"Remarkable," Swartz said. "You are such a good boy. So mild-mannered," he said, sitting beside him on the sofa.

Egon tried to conceal Hausratte who was deep in his coat and shivering.

"I have tried to keep you safe in multiple locations, haven't I?" Swartz said. "But this is war, Herr Wolff. War takes you wherever you need to be. It is not like the history books depict where two sides just show up somewhere and battle it out. There are pockets of problems. And those pockets have pockets. Look at Poland where two of our officers were killed in a restaurant. It caused a small conflict – that brought on an outdoor fight – and that escalated to field combat. Then the two sides go to war again – without considering the battles the leaders have already set into motion. I must constantly pivot. It is a complicated problem we are solving. We may have to move you over and over. But we will! Whatever we need to do to keep you safe."

Swartz got up to leave.

"Just wanted to check in to ensure everything was fine. Thank you again, Henry," Swartz said.

"Never a problem, General," Henry said. "I'm not his father, but I can be a good friend."

His invitation to get more information worked slightly.

"I believe you are a better man than his father," Swartz whispered. "Good Night, Herr Wolff!" he called out as he left.

Swartz had left out 'is' or 'was' at the end of his sentence which was mildly frustrating to Henry.

Once Swartz and his men had left the bunker, Henry locked the door behind them.

"I think our friends can come out, what do you think?"

Egon took Hausratte out of his coat and set him inside the blanket on the sofa. He seemed warmer now and sleeping soundly. Then, he opened the first crate to see the goose sleeping.

"Maybe we leave the lid off to give him some extra air tonight?" Henry said, setting him out of the way. "I wouldn't be quick to take him out if he isn't complaining. He seems comfortable."

The second crate with the Uberghars was trickier. They were squiggly and used to moving around. Whatever Egon did to cut the Unterghar's wire seemed to make them calmer, but that one let out a MEEHH-----OOO when they opened it up.

"There is always one baby who is a complainer in every species it seems!" Henry laughed. "Now, what do we do with them? I mean, they need to come out. They are cramped. Hmmmm..."

Egon wandered into the bathroom and there was a small, plain tub. It had a few bags of potatoes, some guns, and some extra ammunition.

"What is it like in here?" Henry asked looking in the bathroom. "Oh – let me check if the tub works," and he turned the tap slightly.

"Well, water is coming out – want to build them a space for the night? What else do we do? Might be fun!"

Egon immediately set to removing a potato bag. Henry picked up the ammunition and guns and set them aside, then put the stopper in the bottom and turned on the water.

"Oh good, there is warm water coming out so we can add some so they aren't shocked!"

Henry went to grab the Uberghars crate while Egon was busy tearing into a potato bag. One by one, he set them inside the tub until he had a nice pile at one end stacked near the top.

"That is a great idea! They can choose to swim or choose to rest," Henry said. "Good thinking, Egon!"

Henry thought about that for a minute.

"It's sure nice to just call you Egon. I don't think you are partial to 'Herr Wolff', are you?"

After they felt like they had an adequate amount of water in, Henry opened the crate.

"I love doing this with you, Egon. I think we get the same enjoyment out of life. I have to admit, I never saw myself hiding in a bunker with such a great friend putting Uberghars in the bathtub with potatoes - while war loomed up above."

Egon gently introduced the first baby who zipped into the tub happily. He did laps around it and then settled on a big potato along the surface.

"Want to add another?" Henry laughed, as he rolled his sleeves up.

Egon grabbed the second and he mimicked the first – did a fast lap and joined his friend.

"MEEEHHH-----OOOOOO"

"Alright, you cry baby! Let's get you in there!" Henry said, grabbing him out.

"MEH—OO MEH—OO MEH--OO" he said on the way to the tub.

"You'll never enjoy life if you are so stressed out, little one!" Henry laughed.

The cry baby did a lap too and joined his friends.

One by one, Egon and Henry added all eight of them to the tub and had a great time doing so. Once they were all in, they started to settle into their temporary home by casually going back and forth between the water and potatoes.

"Glad you grabbed their food flakes!" Henry said, tossing some in the water.

They saw it and swam after it.

"Want to offer them some?" Henry said, giving Egon the container.

Egon put his hand down near the water and they all swam up and touched it with their snouts.

"That is incredible, Egon! You have your calling!" Henry said, getting up to stretch. "I am going to go feed the fire."

Egon sat by the edge of the tub and raised his hand up to the top of the potato pile. As he did, the eight Uberghars all followed and found resting spots where their snouts touched his hand. After several minutes, they all drifted off to sleep.

"Say Egon," Henry said, coming in but stopping himself. "Oh. That is so precious. They are sleeping. Good work!" he whispered. "Would you like to join me for a hot drink?"

Egon waited until he was sure the last one closed his eyes and then he joined Henry. He moved the goose crate close to the sofa and then sat down to have a hot tea.

"Isn't it nice just the two of us boys hanging out?" Henry said.

Egon set his drink down, and then positioned himself on the

couch with his feet up but left one arm hanging down so he could pet the goose in the crate beside him.

"The goose is still sleeping, still breathing well. The night will tell us a lot. Do you want to sleep on the sofa or the bed?"

Egon was already sleeping. Henry smiled and then covered him and Hausratte with a blanket. He took his tea and settled in a rocking chair with a blanket and eventually drifted off too.

In the morning, a few men knocked on the bunker door.

"Open up, Henry!" Swartz called.

"Come in, General. How was the night?" Henry said, as Egon was waking up and looking for his glasses.

"The night was brutal. I can't even go through the events. New events are overshadowing them. There has been an order," Swartz stated with authority and a sense of disappointment. "...that Herr Wolff join Ernst from our Panzer division in a military exercise."

Henry was struggling to respond in a way that could challenge this authority but not be deemed disrespectful.

"At the risk of talking out of turn," Henry started.

"If you know there is a risk in talking out of turn, why would you pose such a risk to yourself?" Swartz interrupted.

"Because, General. Our orders are to protect Herr Wolff. I am simply taking this duty seriously," Henry reminded him.

"It is a military exercise," Swartz said. "I am under no obligation to give you an explanation. I like you, Henry so I am gifting you an explanation. Our orders to include him in the military exercise come from the same source that requires us to protect him. What would you have me do to rectify this?"

"I don't know, General," Henry said with a defeated tone. "I see we are at war – so I know even military exercises are vulnerable. I felt strong about saying it. That is all."

"I considered the vulnerability but can't challenge the source. Your courage is noted. Your attention to duty is noted. There is no other child in all of Germany receiving this level of protection. Herr Wolff is coming with us now. Is this understood?" Swartz said.

"It is understood." Henry said, sadly. "Could I have five minutes to get him prepared? I think if I spoke to him, you would have someone more agreeable accompanying you."

"We will be outside. Make it half that time," Swartz said, leaving with his soldiers.

Egon was already in the bathroom with the gharials. He looked like he already knew and understood, but worried about his friends.

"You heard," Henry said, kneeling by the tub. "I had a great time with you last evening. It was such a joy to do boy things. I only have a minute – please hear me out. I can see you have a great calling in you. There is something special about you. I can't put my finger on it – and I don't know why you are being shuffled around. All I can say is there will be opportunities for you along the way to make a difference – the kind of difference one can only make when they are hurled into the middle of the fire. You are loved. You are protected. Know this, alright?"

Egon didn't get up with Henry. He had his hand in the middle of the tub with eight little snouts touching him.

"Do you trust me, Egon? You saw me work hard to get them here. Do you think I will give up on them now?"

Egon pulled his hand out and looked up at him. He grabbed the flakes and handed them to Henry.

"Would I say no to your big beautiful eyes? They are important to you, so they are important to me. I will be right here with them. And if I must leave, they will come with me. Alright?"

Egon got up and walked past him to the other room. He stroked Hausratte's head, who was still sleeping and then looked in the crate holding the goose. He bent down and stroked his head just once, and then walked towards the door. Then, Gänseheld finally made a honk. Egon turned and walked back to him. He bent down again and held his beak and face in his hands and kissed his forehead between his eyes. Gänseheld was very peaceful.

Egon walked back to the door, and the Skelekit trailed along. Henry followed him out, and Swartz was glad to see him.

"He really is a lovely boy," Swartz said. "Such a pleasure getting to know you!"

Egon turned to look back at Henry who waved, trying to be strong for him.

It was a short ride to the training area.

"Panzerkampfwagens! Those are beasts barreling through. They have new tracks on them to help with the snow. Would you like to ride in one? It will help you become accustomed," Swartz said to Egon.

"Good to see you, General. Is this Herr Wolff?" a high-ranking officer said.

"It is indeed, Oberst! It is a good time for him to ride along during field testing, no?" Swartz suggested. "Herr Wolff, this is Generaloberst Ernst. He runs this division."

"Right this way, Herr Wolff! We are honoured to have you," the Oberst said.

Swartz reiterated that Egon is a top priority for the base and then he left.

Egon was fascinated by something much smaller which a couple soldiers were toying with. One of the soldiers was kneeling in the snow with a remote control in his hands. Egon walked over and stood behind them. Their handheld remote device had a long cable coming from it and was attached to a mini tank. The soldier controlling it was making it go backwards and forwards on tracks and a few other soldiers started to gather to have a look. The most bizarre part of this was the turkey vulture on top of it. It was fastened in with a body harness, and camouflage was draped around him. The tank itself looked like a giant hard-armoured beetle no longer than the length of a soldier and only came up to his knee. The Skelekit ran up to this mini tank and Egon ran after her.

"WHO ALLOWED A CHILD IN HERE?" a soldier yelled.

Egon picked her up and ran back to them.

"Did he just grab a hunk of snow? What is he doing? WHO IS

THIS CHILD?" he yelled.

Ernst approached them and said, "Herr Wolff. No harm done. He was simply curious."

"Herr Wolff? My apologies," the soldier said, as the men all began to whisper.

"Are you ready?" Ernst asked. "Oh yes, I understand – you do not speak. You have learned the first lesson in communication – to listen! Be attentive!"

The tank he took Egon into only had three crew, so he was number four. The Commander who doubled as a Gunner was there, plus the Driver and the Loader. It was a cramped space but plenty to look at and explain on the way.

They took a long drive out to a field surrounded by woods. The snow was bigger flakes, visibility was normal, but it was one of the coldest winters anyone of them could remember. Lines of tanks, marching infantrymen and several trucks full of men with artillery rolled out. The men controlling the beetle tanks were excited to try them in an open space. When they arrived in the clearing, they began to set up various formations. The turkeys were very noisy, and the men laughed at them. It was a casual exercise day.

Then, something hit the tank Egon was in. Gun fire.

"What was that?" the Commander said.

"Are we under fire?" the Driver asked.

Then another hit.

After looking out the hatch, the Loader announced. "We are being ambushed! Look out and see!"

When the Commander looked out, he almost took a hit.

"Weisser's tank was destroyed! Schumacher's tank is taking heavy fire!"

"Where is it coming from?" the Driver asked.

"Mostly the west!" the Commander said, firing back. "Look out again – I am firing into a white wall. I can't see!"

When the Loader opened the hatch, Egon crawled over top of him and out onto the ground.

"The boy got out!" the Loader yelled.

"Go get him!" the Commander yelled back.

When he tried to go out, artillery rounds fired at him and he dropped back in.

"He has a chance of living, but I will die immediately!" the Loader screamed over heavy rounds. "I saw a tank! Right there between those two trees! How did they know we were coming? This was a secret internal exercise?"

"Well, we're going after it!" the Commander said.

The men who were testing the beetles were hiding behind their trucks and only popped out to drag a wounded soldier back. The turkeys were gobbling away on top of their beetles, unable to leave. Egon ran to each remote and moved the beetles out of the line of enemy fire. He successfully moved over half of them behind the trees, but a few of them were still left out in the open. He would have moved others, but a soldier ran past him and the end of his gun sliced Egon's head on the way by. It was chaos.

The fighting went on for over an hour, and then it fell silent. Egon was freezing now behind a tree with the Skelekit and unable to move from the cold. The tank he was in was decimated. Blood was dripping down his forehead and he stared up into a blank sky.

Then he saw a black spot and there was Düster circling down towards him. He landed at his feet and stayed with him. The field was full of debris. Several tanks were destroyed, dead soldiers were scattered, and the surviving men were busy tending to the wounded ones. None of the beetles they were testing were used in this combat. The turkeys were still fastened to the tops of them and were shell-shocked into stillness. Nobody knew combat was coming.

Not far behind, Egon noticed many more spots coming in and they were honking. It was the group that they left behind at the Kriegsmarine. They would have flown a long way to get there. Their funny feet fwap-fwap-fwapped away on the crispy snow and they honked like a bunch of obnoxious guests showing up late to a party. The goose who took over Gänseheld's position honked for them to focus and look after Egon. Once again, they formed their protective canopy of wings around Egon and he began to warm him up. The geese eventually eased up their wing formation, but they stayed close to him.

About ten to fifteen minutes passed and a man yelled at the geese.

"Get away you dumb birds!" he said, scooping Egon up in his

arms and taking him back to a truck. Egon was non-responsive.

"We must leave now!" the driver of a truck said. "We don't know who is still out there!"

The soldier took Egon into the truck, and the Skelekit hopped in beside him.

Meanwhile, the turkeys were stranded in this warzone. Egon opened his eyes to see a goose undoing the straps and a stunned turkey vulture stepping off. The rest of the geese assigned themselves to other turkeys and set them free. Some hopped off, some fell off, and some slid off.

So now they were free, shell-shocked, and wearing army gear in the middle of the forest, but they were alive. It was hard to discern what they were feeling because turkey vultures don't exactly show a wide range of emotion.

Back at Swartz's office, it was easy to tell what his emotion was. The room was very tense.

"I found him knocked unconscious, General," a soldier said. "He seems to be alert now."

Swartz blew up at everyone around him.

"WHO DID THIS? BRING THEM TO ME! NOW!" he yelled at the top of his lungs.

"I'm not sure any one person did this," the soldier said. "It is war, General."

"WE WERE NOT CALLED INTO WAR! WE WERE

BAITED! FROM SOMEONE ON THE INSIDE!" he screamed and beat the table. "THEY KNEW OUR POSITION! MILITARY TRAINING IS NEVER OVER A RADIO! MAY THE DRILLMEISTER HAVE MERCY ON ANY ONE OF YOU IF YOU ARE FOUND RESPONSIBLE!"

Swartz paced for a few minutes and then put both his hands on the table.

"We are going to get Henry from the bunker. You, go get his car. Bring it around," Swartz said in a much calmer demeanour. "I will meet you there."

"Yes, General," the young soldier said.

It wasn't long until they all arrived at Henry's bunker, and he hurried to the door when they knocked.

"We were ambushed...tricked by one of our own, Henry," Swartz said. "We suffered massive casualties."

"I assume because you are telling me, this has to do with Herr Wolff?" Henry said, concerned and looking around for him.

"He is in the front seat of your car and the engine is running. Here are the directions," he said handing him a piece of paper. "Take him there immediately...and then destroy the directions. Can you handle this?"

"I will indeed, General!" Henry said. "I will leave right now."

"They are expecting you," Swartz said, and then left.

Henry tore down the stairs and immediately started picking out the Uberghars from the bathtub and returning them to their crate. He ran with them up the stairs and out to his running car.

"You and me again! Unfortunately not for long, I am dropping you off – but I proved I could take care of the babies, right? Be right back!"

Henry then zipped down the stairs and grabbed Gänseheld's crate and took it out to the car where he put it in the back seat.

"Lots of room for them – AND you!" he laughed and ran back inside.

The last thing he did was get Hausratte. He bundled him in the blanket he slept in, grabbed a bunch of food on the way out, and jumped in the car.

"Someone is anxious to see you!" he said, handing Hausratte to him. "Oh! EGON! You are HURT!"

Egon had blood on his cheek, and some was seeping through a bandaged hand. He seemed disoriented, but tucked Hausratte in. Even though Henry couldn't see her, the Skelekit was shaking uncontrollably - and Egon was not alert enough to console her.

"The General said you were all deceived today. I am glad you are alive," he said, driving out of the parking lot with a "MEEEHHH-----OOOOOO" coming from the crate.

Up above, there was the V formation, once again...sticking near their leader, Gänseheld – even if he was in a crate, in a car. **They knew he was beautiful once** and remained loyal to his recovery. Henry spotted them and slowed his speed way down.

14 OPERATION: WOLFFKREUZER

Henry's directions took them up a snowy S-bend road lined with a beautiful pine tree forest. Egon stared blankly out the window with Hausratte in his coat and the Skelekit had her front paws up on the frosty glass looking out. Even with the windows up, the smell of the trees and wood burning welcomed them at the main gate of 33 Hoch Road.

"I suppose I just ring the buzzer?" Henry said, looking around – not really understanding what to do next.

When he did, the gate opened, and he drove the car through slowly. Once he reached the estate, his mouth dropped open.

"It's a castle, Egon! Look at the size of this structure!"

Egon was not a boy who was impressed by grandiosities, even though this truly was grand. Most of the buildings in Germany were red brick, but this rectangular fortress was mostly field stone, five floors across and four floors high with two attached towers on each corner that resembled silos. There were armed lookout men in the tops of each of them, who were probably paid well to freeze. Close to the house were horse stables. They seemed nicer than most homes.

The stable door opened, and Egon finally perked up. It was

Anna and she was carrying a grain bucket and horse brush. She walked up to the driver side door and Henry got out.

“Who are you here to see?” she asked.

“I don’t actually know!” he laughed. “General Swartz told me to bring Egon here. Do you know about this?”

Anna’s face lit up when she looked into the car and saw Egon, but she was careful.

“Uh, yes! You can park the car over there. I am sure someone will be right out. Is the boy to stay here? Is that what the General told you?” she said, faking her authority.

“Yes,” Henry laughed at her grown-up attitude. “Do you also stay here?”

“Yes I work for the Festung,” she said.

“Taking care of horses?” Henry asked.

“Yes, would you and Egon like to come see while you wait?” Anna asked. “No sense in staying out in the cold. They take their time coming down.”

“I don’t see why not. Let me go ask Egon.”

Egon was already getting out of the car. He kept Hausratte close to him to block the cold, and the Skelekit ran around, excited to go into the barn.

“You must be Egon,” she said. “My name is Anna.”

“Egon doesn’t speak, but I am sure he is happy to meet you, Anna!” Henry smiled.

Anna smiled at Egon and then said, "This way to the stables."

She took them through and showed them some of the most decorated horses in all of Europe.

"This one is my favourite. That is Renner. The owner paid more for him than a house," she said.

"They are all lovely. Egon, why don't you stay in here out of the cold. I will go wait outside. I don't want to appear as though I am imposing. I still don't know who is greeting me.

"You don't?" Anna laughed. "Wow. That is so funny."

Henry shook his head and went back outside as the children kept walking through the stables.

"What are the chances of us meeting again?" Anna said, grabbing his hands and spinning him in circles. "Are you staying here? Do you have a plan? Are we leaving? Where are the rest of the children? Is Mrs. Winter alright? What about General Kluck? What about Zusa? Oh I miss him so badly, Egon! I sure wish you could tell me!"

Egon rubbed his eyes under his glasses.

"You miss him too...I know. He gives the best cuddles on Earth. I have so much to tell you! So – guess what! The Death Marchers got me in the Forest. I really have them fooled, though. They think I am German. They don't like my legs, but if I keep them covered up, I can stay in the barn. Working with the horses isn't so bad...but it's terribly lonely. Still, it's better than working in the house. He keeps the pretty women as housekeepers and cooks. He treats them worse than his dogs as far as I am concerned."

Egon lifted Hausratte out of his coat.

"Where did you pick him up? You better not let them see him. That is a pest in a horse barn!"

Egon tucked him back in.

"He sure is sweet, though. And we can all use a friend!"

Anna peeked out the door to make sure nobody was eavesdropping.

"You should hear the things I have heard. These people act so proper and high society! They are planning the worst things you can imagine. I would tell the police, but they ARE the police. They constantly talk about this superior race and oh Egon – they are doing this big population movement program – or something like that. I don't think they are just moving people. I saw things. Oh - never mind! I hear voices out there. It's a good thing you and I have blonde hair and blue eyes. But we must help all these poor people, Egon! I just don't know what to do about it yet!"

Anna slipped out of the barn to see who was there.

"Egon! Come out! Come see!" she squealed.

The Skelekit was super excited to see Frecher, and both children loved seeing Kluck!

"I am too old to ride, Egon. I have finally decided this," Kluck laughed, walking the horse near the main steps. "But oh – what a classic specimen Reiter is. If the two of you could have a conversation, he would tell you about his adventures – and you would tell him about yours - and neither of you would believe the other."

Kluck hopped off Reiter with a slippery thud on the snowy stone. Anna was careful not to give herself away in front of Henry, as she didn't know him yet.

"Well, Egon! You are at the Festung Wolff," Kluck said, and then he paused. "Has anyone told you that you have arrived at your rightful estate?"

Egon was confused – or didn't seem to care.

"Oh you will dislike it, but it's yours. Nor will anyone give it to you, but it is still yours," Kluck added.

Kluck noticed Egon's cut on his temple.

"I heard you tried out this war thing," Kluck said. "What did you think of your geese setting the turkey vultures free? Wasn't that fun? The soldiers these days are so devoid of amusement. They have too much time on their hands. They actually thought if they had turkey vultures strapped to the tops of beetle tanks, the enemy would sense motion and then see the vultures and then think 'Oh! That is just a bird, no big deal' and not fire at them. That is the level of intelligence these days, Egon. It's embarrassing."

Egon looked down at Hausratte.

"Oh yes – Hausratte got off that boat. Where are my manners? You must be Henry!" he said, offering his hand. "Heard so much about you!"

"Forgive my manners, I do not know you, uh, Feldmarschall?" Henry said, looking at his uniform.

"Oh I am a drifter...the name is Kluck. You kept Hausratte alive for a long time. That is good news. That is one more for Team Wolff," Kluck said, but thought about what he said. "Team Wolff. Which Team Wolff, though. Hmmmm – interesting. You have company, Egon," he said, pointing behind him.

The large snowflakes were falling onto the heads of white wolves – a whole pack of them. Only the blacks of their eyes and tips of their noses were visible. Without Kluck pointing them out, they may not have been seen.

"OOOOOOOH," Anna said. "I love them! Welcome to the Festung Wolff!" she called out, then laughed.

Kluck smiled at Anna and then turned to Henry.

"Thank you for bringing him here, Henry," Kluck said. "It's good for him to have solid mentors in his life."

"Oh! Is this your place? Did you request him? You have been protecting him this whole time?" Henry asked. "I just do as Swartz asks me."

"I tried not to move you around," a voice said, causing everyone to turn their heads.

"General," Kluck said. "Good to see you again, Kurt."

There was the young, arrogant General from the Berlin-Grunewald Station.

"Hello, Feldmarschall," Kurt said. "We can keep formalities. The children should note the respect."

"Rank, first name, last name, whatever you prefer! You can call me General von Kluck, for instance. And if that were so, what would I call you?"

"General is fine," he said, with a stiff upper lip.

"Tell the children, so they understand. What would I call you then? Please! They are dying to know," Kluck said.

"I already know his name," Anna piped up.

"She is a smart girl but talks out of turn. Why are you here, General? How did you get in? I am a busy man," Kurt said, running out of patience.

"Do you see them?" Kluck pointed to the line of wolves surrounding them.

"I live in the woods. I see lots of wildlife. Or did you bring them here? I do not have time for games, General," Kurt said, anxiously.

"Oh no. I didn't bring them here. I am one of them!" Kluck laughed.

"You are one of them. I see. These games are tiresome. I want to respect your rank, but I fear you have taken a bump on the head – perhaps you are still suffering from the Great War. There is no shame. I can get you the help you need," Kurt said.

"If you are one of them, General – does this also make you – a wolf?" Anna asked.

"Yes! I believe it does! Anna, I am ever so sorry – could I formally invite you to the wolf club? You are lovely and more than welcome," Kluck laughed out loud.

"It is time for this tall tale to end. I have had enough of the madness," Kurt said, walking away.

Kluck stormed up, yanked his arm, and flung him around.

"YOU WILL SHOW RESPECT, GENERAL. I OUTRANK YOU EVEN STILL," Kluck said, blood rushing into his face. "WOULD YOU LIKE TO TALK ABOUT A TALL TALE – YOU WISH TO SPEAK OF MADNESS? YOU HAVE BECOME IMPATIENT WITH THE GAMES? YOU SIT HERE WITH A STIFF DRINK BY YOUR WARM FIRE – ORDERING THE DEATHS OF THOUSANDS. AND YOU? YOU HAVE HAD ENOUGH OF THE MADNESS?"

Kurt motioned for his men to come over to remove Kluck.

"GET YOUR HANDS OFF OF ME, COWARDS. YOU ARE SO GOOD AT INSTIGATING WAR AND FLEXING YOUR WAR MACHINES – THEN YOU HIDE IN YOUR HOLE. SHOW SOME COURAGE AND TELL THE BOY YOUR NAME! OWN YOUR RANK! OWN WHO YOU ARE! -AND YOU BETTER BE A MAN AND LOOK HIM IN HIS EYE WHEN YOU SAY IT!"

Kluck stood back and straightened his jacket, then crossed his arms and waited. Henry had no idea what was going on and stood there frozen.

"How dare you say these things in front of children, old man? You are a lunatic," Kurt said.

"Do you want to tell him you are ashamed of him? Do you

wish to tell your high-ranking officers that a muted boy exists among them?"

The officers looked at each other as though they wanted to duck out of this situation. Egon walked slowly forward towards Kurt. Then he stood at his feet, looking at the ground, petting Hausratte inside his coat. The Skelekit came along for moral support and sat at his foot.

"Lift your head, Egon – and make sure he knows you have eyes. He should know that about you at the very least!" Kluck said, as Frecher stood tall on his hind legs.

Egon was stuck looking at the ground. Anna shuffled along and stood beside him.

"Hold my hand, Egon. Be brave," Anna said, as the Skelekit stayed close.

Kurt looked at the children holding hands, then over at Kluck. He then squatted in front of Egon.

"Like I said, I tried not to move you so many times," Kurt said. "Can you look at me?"

Egon slowly lifted his chin enough to look at the insignia on his jacket.

"Your eyes are so blue," Kurt said.

Then Egon looked back at Kurt's eyes for a moment – which were the same blue.

Kurt looked over at Kluck who just shook his head in disgust.

"Does he know his mother's eyes were not blue, Kurt?" Kluck

said, in a calmer voice. "Does he know you were ashamed of her too?"

"BACK OFF, OLD MAN!" Kurt erupted, and then rubbed his face to calm down.

"I have always tried to keep you safe. I understand you are an A student," he said to no reaction.

"He's really really smart," Anna added.

"I think you may be more than smart," Kurt added.

"General," Anna said. "If you just told him your name, this would be over, no?"

Kurt looked at Anna who shrugged. He fought for many awkward moments but ultimately broke.

"My name -" he said, almost showing emotion but then switched to his arrogant, General's demeanour. "My name is General Kurt Wolff."

"Is that it?" Anna asked. "Is that all you want to say to him?"

Kurt looked at Anna and sternly said, "That is enough, child. I do not owe anyone an explanation."

The stable went silent as everyone waited for Egon's reaction. He stared down at the snow, and then looked up. There was Düster flying overhead. He looked back at Kurt's jacket - and especially the Iron Cross. Then he looked at the black spider on Kurt's sleeve and began to grind his teeth. He looked back up to see Düster flying towards them. Egon took a few steps back and the black eagle hovered in front of General Wolff.

Düster stared deep in his eyes and then he batted both wings straight down causing a powerful current to push Kurt's hat off. Kurt swiped the air to push Düster back, fell forward and found himself belly down staring into the eyes of a black wolf. Egon just pet his rat.

"You have surrounded yourself with the most powerful people in all of Germany," Kluck said, calmly. "You sit at the right hand of the Drillmeister. You think this boy may be "more than smart", you say? Congratulations on knowing something about him! There is ever so much you do NOT know about him. Egon doesn't surround himself with powerful people. Power moves through him. Power follows him everywhere. You see, Kurt – nature only takes so much, but make no mistake! It is watching! It is listening! It is taking notes! You know something about strategy..." he said, walking a wide circle around Kurt and the black wolf. "THEY ARE strategy. You are building these wolfpacks? THEY ARE the wolf pack. They don't go looking for trouble. They cannot help but course correct. You are trying to create something balanced by destroying one side of the see-saw. They are simply restoring the balance. You are fighting a losing battle."

Kurt's embarrassment was turning into rage.

"SHOOT THE WOLF!" Kurt yelled out to his men as Blackguard bared teeth.

One of the men pulled out his pistol and aimed.

"No!" Anna cried out. "PLEASE NO!"

A shot rang out and Anna covered her eyes.

Nothing happened.

Kurt called out again, "You missed! SHOOT! SHOOT!"

The man shot twice – still Blackguard stood there. Frecher and the Skelekit ran behind Egon.

Blackguard moved closer to Kurt and sniffed his head. He began to shake.

"I am glad to see you still have a nervous system. I was beginning to think you were dead," Kluck smirked. "If you are going to proudly profess your name, I would suggest making sure you understand where it came from and the true nature of that beast."

Egon walked over to Kurt and looked down at him. Then he pet Hausratte and walked over to Henry's car and opened the passenger door for Anna.

"Go ahead, Anna. They aren't going to stop you," Kluck smiled.

Anna wasted little time and moved as quickly as her leg braces would allow. After getting in, Egon closed the door for her and then got into the back seat beside the crates. The Skelekit jumped in before he closed the door.

Kluck walked up to Henry and whispered, "Take them to the Grunewald Tower. Anna will guide you once you are there."

"Zusa!" Anna clapped from the front seat.

Kluck opened Egon's door and said, "A boy has a right to know where he came from. Now you can heal."

Henry got in the front seat quickly, and Kluck called into the back seat.

"Oh and Skelekitty – you still don't know your power! You are no different than Blackguard, you know!"

The Skelekit sat up tall on Egon's lap and tipped her head. Egon kept his head down and continued to pet Hausratte. Kluck smiled and waved at them. Henry then nervously pulled out of the driveway with the children. There were the geese in their flying V formation, not far behind them.

Blackguard was still holding his position and the rest of the white wolves formed a tight circle on Kurt and his men.

Kluck walked over and looked down at Kurt who was shaking in the snow.

"For bravery, you said," Kluck said, removing his own iron cross. "You were correct. It changed the entire trajectory of my life too."

He took a moment to look at it, then he chucked it at Kurt's feet.

"You chose ego over country, General," Kluck said, walking over to Reiter who was still at the step. "I told you before - we must remember not to own these awards. No war is won – or lost – by one man."

Then he mounted the horse, Frecher jumped up, and he trotted Reiter over to Kurt.

"Do you know what struck me the most about our conversation at the train station, General Wolff?" Kluck said, looking down from atop of Reiter. "You lied straight to my face when I asked you if you had any children of your own."

"It was none of your concern!" Kurt snapped.

"You could have said it was none of my business. Instead, you lied. But you weren't lying to me. You were lying to you."

Blackguard bared teeth as Kluck said that, and he slunk down on his belly to watch General Wolff.

"I told you – it isn't *my* job to break up your plans," Kluck concluded, and then he trotted off.

The white wolves kept a tight circle on the men while Düster spread his wings and hopped into flight.

In the car, Anna was a chatterbox on the way there.

"You were incredible, Egon! You were so brave!" she exclaimed, looking at the back seat. "Woah – do you have any room?"

"Egon has friends in there! Have you ever seen baby gharials?" Henry asked.

"No! Is that like an alligator?" Anna said.

"They are the Uberghars! They are from India – they have long snouts – we had them in the bathtub last night and Egon made a potato island for them – great fun!" Henry smiled.

"That does sound fun! I can't wait to meet them!" Anna laughed. "Who is in the other crate?"

"A bomber hit the Kriegsmarine. We were there – and the

geese which are currently flying behind us protected Egon. But this one took a bad hit. He is bandaged and healing."

"There are geese following us?" she said looking out the back window. "Well, that is wonderful, isn't it?"

"Indeed!" Henry laughed.

"I just thought you were a horribly slow driver," she laughed back.

"Well, I am mindful in the snow, but yes," Henry said.

"So who are you? Why do you have Egon?" Anna asked.

"I work part-time as a cook on the Kriegsmarine Wolfsboot – but the General there asks me to do various tasks for him. I originally helped Egon's teacher to get him to the first farm he stayed at."

"Helped his teacher, huh? Does the colour in your face always change when you speak of her?" Anna giggled.

Henry shot a hand up to his cheek. "Is it warm in here?"

Anna laughed. "Oh! You like her! Why don't you ask her to go out for dinner or something?"

"Well," Henry said. "I haven't had any female advice so far!"

"Alright," Anna said, sitting up tall. "Do you know her? Like, do you pay attention to what she likes?"

"You mean like flowers or something?" Henry asked.

"Hmmmm – no. I mean, what is in her heart?"

"The whole universe is in there," Henry said, daydreaming. "The stars, the moon, the planets – they are all housed in her heart."

"Then you should write her a poem," Anna said. "Tell her this."

"You are a smart girl, Anna!" Henry said, popping a finger on the tip of her nose.

"I can't wait to see the others again – how about you, Egon? Like Charlotte?" Anna smiled back at him.

Egon buried his chin in his chest and kept petting Hausratte and the Skelekit.

"Same reaction as you," she whispered to Henry.

"You see everything, Anna!" Henry said.

Egon just ignored them for the remainder of the ride. They soon arrived at the Grunewald Tower.

"Here we are, drive in there!" Anna said.

Zusa was sitting on the ground, leaning against one of the posts behind the Tower. He was holding his head when Henry's car drove up.

Henry, Anna, and Egon all got out of the car and Anna went looking for him.

"Zusa!" she called for him, cheerfully. "I am back!"

She ran all around the Tower and saw him tucked in the back. "Your head is bleeding – oh Zusa you have cuts everywhere –

Henry! Zusa is hurt!"

Henry came over to see. Zusa was close to sleeping. He looked like he had been in a fight.

"Zusa – I need to go down and get some bandages or help or something – oh no, Henry, he is the one who moves the statue for us!"

Henry ran up the stairs to the statue.

"Why do we move it?" Henry asked.

"Because it is how we get to our bunker," she said. "You slide it away and open the trap door."

"Maybe if the three of us try?" Henry suggested.

They all tried and were simply not powerful enough.

"We need to wait for Kluck then," she said, comforting Zusa while Henry paced the forest.

It felt like a whole lifetime had passed before Kluck finally arrived.

"I think I see him coming on his horse. Is that Kluck galloping in?" Henry said.

Anna looked, "Yes – that is him. Let's wait. Maybe Reiter can help?"

"The horse? Yes – I agree," Henry said.

They all waited with Zusa who was shivering.

"I have blankets in the car – let me grab them," Henry said.

After a few moments, Kluck arrived on Reiter.

"Zusa's hurt! We can't get downstairs! Can Reiter help us move the statue?"

"Yes of course, I have rope in my saddle bag!" Kluck said.

Kluck tied a rope around Reiter's chest and then around the statue.

"If we all push it from behind, and Reiter pulls, it should budge enough to get the door open," Kluck said.

"There is also the emergency Juggerkampf door," Anna said.

"That only opens with the key for the Juggerkampf and then it only opens from the inside. It's complicated, Sweetheart," Kluck said.

After rigging up the horse and all of them working together, they got the statue to move away from the trapdoor.

When they opened it, there was Miss Winter, and she popped up out of the ground.

"Is everyone alright?" she said, frantically looking around.

"Yes, we are fine!" Kluck said.

"Oh Anna! You are back! So happy to see you – and Egon! Very nice!" she said, still looking around. "But where are the others?"

"What others?" Kluck said.

"Zusa took them for a forest walk – maybe they aren't back

yet," she said.

"Mrs. Winter! Zusa is here and he is severely hurt!" Anna exclaimed.

"Oh no! I told Zusa it wasn't safe, but he kept knocking on the door – he was so lonely! When we opened it, he started grabbing the children one at a time and cuddling them – oh General, they wanted out so badly. I told them to make it short!"

"ARE YOU TELLING ME YOU ARE THE ONLY PERSON DOWN THERE?" Kluck said, furiously.

"I am so sorry!" she said. "Zusa overpowered me on it – and the children were so bored!"

"He is close to death – and they are GONE!" Kluck said, running around the Tower looking and calling for them.

Morris the Woodpecker flew in and landed on the post.

He tapped out "Children – GONE" in Morse code.

Up above, the Golden Eagle Swarm had returned and were circling the area.

"Did you not hear Morris? Never mind now - Anna, Egon... come here," Kluck called. "Go get in the Juggerkampf, children, and get it out of here! This is where they found you, so they will be looking for you. Mrs. Winter cannot go with you. She will slow you down. You will know what to do. Egon will know what to do – go now!"

"How can we know what to do? Do we just hide?" Anna

panicked.

"Sweetheart – do as I say – get in the Juggerkampf and get it out! We don't have time to cover the hole back up. I need to distract them. We must all disperse quickly!" he raged.

Anna grabbed Egon's hand and they went down the hole. The Skelekit ran down too. Frecher looked at Kluck.

"You better go with them – they will need you!" Kluck laughed.

Frecher ran after them - and down the hole he went!

"Henry, help me get Zusa into your car," Kluck said, getting under Zusa's arm. "You must help us, Zusa – you are too heavy! Squish Mrs. Winter into the back seat and drive to Tiefer Bach Road – Egon will need his crates!" Kluck ordered.

"What do I tell the guards?" Henry said, doing his best to move Zusa along. "Come on big boy, lean on me... there you go."

"Find Officer Zimmermann and tell him General Kluck sent you. Only speak with him. It is how I get on the base every time," Kluck said. "Otherwise, be creative with your stories!"

The Swarm was still circling the Tower and Morris the Woodpecker tapped out DANGER.

"Get out of here! I will hold them off until the children are gone!" Kluck said.

Henry closed the door for Mrs. Winter after getting Zusa in and they drove out.

"It is so empty here! And so quiet!" Anna said, walking underground through the room that had the rescued animals still in their cages. "Oh! We can't leave them here!"

Egon climbed up into the hatch and went inside.

"I will round them up. Do you want to work on – well, whatever it is Kluck says you are supposed to do?" Anna said, trying her best to delegate.

Egon opened a bigger cargo-style hatch, and Anna started loading cages.

"Lots of room without the ammunition, right?" she giggled. "Oh, this Beagle girl looks so sad! It's ok, girl, we will get you out of here! **I know you used to be beautiful once**. We will clean you up!"

Egon looked at all the controls.

"When was the last time this thing ran?" Anna asked. "I know Kluck said it would free us all someday. I guess we are kind of late. And what is the point of the elephant trunk? Every time we asked Kluck, he would say, 'oh -for something fun!'"

Hausratte peeked out of Egon's coat with something shiny.

"What does Hausratte have?" Anna asked.

It was the tarnished gold skeleton key he got from Hoffie the pangolin baby. Hausratte jumped out of Egon's coat and placed it near the keyhole. Egon picked it up to look at it again, then he touched the teeth inside the open mouth of the elephant head and began to grind his own.

"Is that what starts this? Egon you are the one to start it! How thrilling!" Anna squealed.

Egon placed the key into the hole and turned. It certainly wasn't a normal way to start such a beast, but what had been normal so far? It fired up and was the loudest thing either of them had heard.

Anna hurried to get the rest of the animals in the back as the door in front of them started to shake. The walls began to show hairline cracks which grew and grew – then the bedrock fell away and exposed a hangar door large enough to go through. As it opened, huge drifts of snow blew in.

"YOU DID IT! HA!" Anna shouted. "WE ARE DOING IT! KLUCK IS GOING TO LOVE THIS! YES, EGON, YES!"

Frecher and the Skelekit hugged Egon's legs, and Hausratte returned to his coat pocket.

"Hold on, I am coming in – oooooooh so exciting!" Anna screamed, and she closed the cargo hatch and jumped in the control area with him.

Just before closing the hatch, she took one last look at where they spent so much time. Then, she yelled "ALL CLEAR!" to Egon and closed the door.

Out of the corner of his eye, Kluck saw the poof of snow in the distance and he knew the children got the door open.

"So," one of the Death Marchers said, confronting Kluck. "You thought you could waltz in and take two children from the Festung Wolff and there would be no follow-up? And here you are exactly where we found Anna. Did you think out your plans?"

"We love this forest," Kluck began. "I thought I would find her back here after they left. Sadly, I was mistaken."

"We thought we would find more children here after finding Anna too," the man said. "Well, we were right! Where you find one child, you simply turn over a few rocks, you find many more. How many did we get today?"

"At least a dozen," another man said.

"Then I suppose you plucked the forest clean," Kluck said.

"They are slippery too – and it makes it harder fighting a gorilla while doing so!" he said.

"That sounds like quite a day for you all. You must be proud," Kluck said, as he went back to Reiter.

"No, that is enough trouble from you, General. You will be coming with us now," the man said, pointing to their car.

Kluck turned to Reiter and yelled, "YAAAAAA!" and clapped.

Reiter took off through the trees.

"Glad your horse knows its way home," the man said, and they all laughed.

"Let's get going then," Kluck said, walking to their car.

"Glad you are good-natured about it. I would hate to mark you up like the gorilla," the man joked.

"Why wouldn't you just shoot it dead?" Kluck asked.

"Oh we tried, but he was holding the children. I finally had to hit it with the car when it jumped back in front of us. At one point, it was holding five children at once! A valiant effort," the man smiled.

"Do you have a Father, son?" Kluck asked.

"I did," he replied.

"He never hugged you, did he?" Kluck asked.

"He wasn't that kind of Father. He kept our house in line. I am a better man because of it," he responded.

"You are exactly the kind of man you are because he kept your house 'in line' as you say," Kluck said. "And for the record, you are NOT a better man because of it."

"GET IN THE CAR," the man stormed.

"That is a fiery reaction! There is hope for you. You aren't completely made of stone," Kluck smiled, and he got into the back seat.

As their car pulled out, Kluck looked out the window to see the tank leaving the forest. Egon and Anna had moved the Juggerkampf through the massive opening and the tank's tracks squeaked on its first trek through the snow.

"Did you get a chance to say goodbye to your Father?" Kluck asked the man.

"I did not," he said.

"Herr Wolff did. Isn't that wonderful?" Kluck smiled.

He looked out to see Reiter chasing behind the Juggerkampf.

"Or perhaps Good Riddance," Kluck smiled.

Henry arrived at Tiefer Bach first but didn't go to the gate yet. He pulled over and waited. Mrs. Winter was crying quietly in the back and Zusa was sleeping in the front seat.

"I know he told me to ask for Zimmermann, but I don't feel very confident," Henry said to her.

"I agree – we should wait," Mrs. Winter said. "But Egon needs these crates – and Zusa should go with them."

"Do you need to go? I still don't understand this bigger plan," Henry said to her.

"I understand," she said. "This is a child and animal mission. We can't go."

"Let's wait for Kluck then," Henry said. "I don't want to mess this up!"

"I doubt we will see Kluck," she said, sadly. "If Egon managed to do what he needed to, we will know what to do next," she said, looking behind them.

It was a long, fidgety wait and Henry was becoming restless.

"I don't think we can stay here. I see a military vehicle coming," Henry said. "Should I move?"

"Oh! No! That is them! That is the Juggerkampf! Egon did it! He got it out of there!

"What is a Juggerkampf?" Henry asked.

"It's a Supertank – well – a special Supertank!" she clapped. "Oh I am so nervous for them."

The tank slowed down on the road beside Henry's car, and then parked just in front of it. Reiter was running behind them.

"Why is Kluck's horse here?" Henry asked.

"He – didn't make it out of there – they must have grabbed him," Mrs. Winter said.

Zusa perked right up and hit his fist on his chest.

"Quickly, Henry! Help me get Zusa out!" she said.

Henry and Mrs. Winter had an easier time with Zusa. Even though he was terribly injured, he mustered up the energy to get out and pull himself up onto the tank. Luckily, it was getting dark now so nobody would notice a gorilla on the side of the road loading into a tank. The hatch opened and there was Anna.

"Look at us, Henry!" Anna yelled above the engine. "Egon had a key! And the engine started and the door in the wall opened and snow came rushing in and we went through it and then we were out on the open road! It is incredible! Want to come in?"

"Zusa is coming in!" Henry laughed.

"Oh! Zusa! Let me get out so you can get in. Wow! You barely fit through the opening!"

"That wouldn't happen in a regular sized tank," Henry laughed.

"This tank never went into production. Wait until the men on base see it!" Mrs. Winter laughed.

"Anna, my instruction was to ask for Zimmermann. He is the only one who will let you onto the Tiefer Base," Henry said.

"That is it?" Anna said.

"I think if he had more time, our instructions would have been better. He said to be creative in making a story," Henry said.

"That is so easy for me! It was how I got out of being put on the east-bound train," Anna bragged. "Where is Kluck?"

"I believe they grabbed him, Anna," Mrs. Winter said.

"I figured. I saw Reiter following us. We will get him back. He got me back!" Anna promised.

Once Zusa was inside, Egon crawled out and stood on top.

"Great work, Egon!" Mrs. Winter said.

"I have your crates!" Henry said.

Egon jumped down onto the snow.

As Henry took each of them and put them inside the Juggerkampf, Mrs. Winter spoke to Egon.

"We will get the children back," she said quietly. "They will just keep taking them until we fix the bigger picture. This is your job. You know what to do!" and she hugged him.

"Alright, you are ready to go!" Henry said.

Egon walked over to him and looked up.

"May I hug you?" Henry asked, and Egon stood and waited for him to.

"I am going to take Mrs. Winter to stay with Miss Kraus. How is that for an idea?" Henry smiled.

Anna overheard him and clapped.

"I agree!" she said. "Don't forget to give her a poem!"

"Thank you for the advice, Anna!" Henry said. "Would you like to ride in the front seat now?" he said to Mrs. Winter.

"Yes, please!" she said, jumping in.

Egon and Anna went back into the hatch, but both popped their heads out to wave.

Frecher and the Skelekit both popped out to be nosey. Then Anna closed the hatch and they moved out.

"Where are we going?" Mrs. Winter asked.

"I am going to take you somewhere you can rest. I think you have been looking after others for a long time," Henry said.

"I worry about the children – but this will keep going until it is fixed at the top," she said. "What about you? Where will you go?"

"I have a poem to deliver to someone that I should have a long time ago," Henry smiled.

Mrs. Winter smiled back, and they left.

The Juggerkampf pulled up to the gate at Tiefer Bach Road. They were met with a welcoming party of about fifteen men with flashlights and guns drawn.

A soldier said to them all, "Wait for my command!" and they all held still. The hatch opened, and Anna popped out and put up her hands.

"My name is Anna Schmidt," she said, not divulging her Polish last name, Nowak. "We would like to speak with Officer Zipper Man, please."

"ZIMMERMANN," he laughed. "- is not here," the man said.

"Where shall we park until he arrives?" she asked boldly.

"You can deal with me. Let me speak with an adult," he said.

She decided to try overconfidence.

"You will only speak to me long enough to tell me where Zimmermann is. Who else is in this tank is nobody else's business. That is Top Secret information. Why do you think a child is speaking to you?" Anna said.

"Spicy little pepper, aren't you?" the man laughed. "Park it there. I will get Zimmermann, but it will take some time. You will need to wait for a while."

"Thank you," she said, closing the hatch.

It was like parking a house. Egon understood the basics, but it wasn't finessed. Inside, Anna was tending to Zusa's wounds.

"Did you cuddle all the children?" Anna asked him, and he pulled her in close. "I love your cuddles," she said.

Egon sat with Hausratte still in his coat, the Skelekit on his foot and Frecher on his knee.

"If we died, wouldn't this be the way to go?" Anna said to him. "Just animals and us?"

There was something so lovely about no adults being there. Zusa breathed in deeply and let out a throaty grunt. He waved for Egon to come over. Frecher jumped off as he got up. With Anna on one knee, he patted his other leg and Egon sat down on it. Zusa curled both the children into himself and he closed his eyes. Both Anna and Egon had their heads just under his arms, near his chest looking at each other. Frecher was jealous and jumped up to cuddle too.

"What do you want to do when this is all over? I mean - when we can walk freely?" Anna asked.

Egon reached in his coat and pulled out his book.

"You still have your book!" she smiled. "Can I see your crocodiles again?"

Egon turned the pages until he reached the four of them.

"Are they like the baby gharials that Henry told me about?"

Egon held his breath...and pressed his head into Zusa's chest.

Anna looked nervously at him...and she did the same. It was dead silent. Zusa's breath stopped too. The two children froze, Anna stopped her breathing too.

"Egon," Anna whispered, her eyes filling with tears. "Egon – show me your eyes."

Egon looked up at her.

"Egon," she said, not moving a muscle. "Tell me you can still hear it."

Egon remained frozen.

"It stopped, didn't it," she said. "Egon – I can't move. Egon – help me – I cannot move."

She began blinking quickly as tears poured down.

Egon got up and stared at Zusa. Frecher and the Skelekit lowered themselves to the floor and sat in the corner. Hausratte climbed out of his coat and joined them below. Anna hugged him tightly and silently cried. It was like the air had been let out of the tank. Having no adults in this situation suddenly became a real problem.

It was hard to know if Egon was more troubled by losing Zusa or watching Anna cry, but he took charge of a foreign situation to him. He found a blanket and stood in front of Anna.

She pulled her head away from Zusa's chest and said, "Yes, he is cold."

She got up and stood back as Egon placed the blanket over Zusa's body.

"Not over his face yet," Anna said.

She reached up and kissed his forehead.

"Do you want to kiss him too?" she asked, barely able to get the words out.

Egon thought about it, then he pulled the blanket up over Zusa's head.

Anna walked to the other side of the tank and slid down into a crouched position and hugged her knees. Several minutes passed where the silence was just terrible. Now, it was just taking too long for Zimmermann to show up. They both had a long day and were running on fumes at this point.

The noise that finally cut the air was a MEEEEHHH-OOOOO coming from the gharial crate.

"Do you think I could see them?" Anna said, wiping her face from her elbow to her wrist.

Egon bent down and opened the crate enough to pull one of the Uberghars out.

"MEEEHH -OOOO! MEEEHHH OOOOOO!" it cried.

"That is like a kitten with a very sore throat!" Anna smiled. "May I hold it?"

A baby gharial is NOT cuddly like a kitten. They are like holding a slippery fish.

"I love them! Oh! I should look to see if Reiter is still there," Anna said. "And I imagine the flock of geese is close if you still have their leader."

Anna handed the Uberghar back to Egon and she lifted the hatch. Reiter was standing close to the Juggerkampf to break the cold night wind. The geese had landed in a nearby field. A soldier was walking towards the tank with his flashlight.

"An Anna Schmidt wanted to see me?" he asked when he saw her.

"That is me," she said.

"Is Kluck in there with you, Anna?" he asked.

"No," she said, as he looked over at Reiter.

"Did the horse come with you?" he said.

"Sadly, yes Sir," she said.

"May I enter your tank?" he asked.

"Yes, Sir," she said, and let him come in.

When his feet hit the floor inside, he was amazed.

"You could fit twenty people in this room!" he laughed. "Such a shame it never went into production. The whole Base is gossiping about it. I heard some men say they hope they can drive it someday."

"It isn't easy, but Egon knew where he was going," Anna said. "We just went in a straight line. Backing it up might be tricky!"

"Well, hello Herr Wolff! I have heard magnificent things about you!" and he looked over to see Zusa's feet under the blanket.

"Is that Zusa?" he said, sadly.

"It is, Sir – or it was, Sir," Anna said, still in shock.

"What a spectacular gorilla. Your poor hearts, children. You must feel extremely exhausted by now. Keep him there – he will finish the journey with you," Zimmermann said. "May I drive your tank?"

"I wish you would," Anna said.

Egon stepped back as Zimmermann began to maneuver them out. He didn't seem to mind, as he was not a boy who was impressed by grandiosities. He appeared agitated and ready to get out now.

Hausratte returned to Egon's coat and Anna sat back down on the floor and hid her face.

15 THE GHOST-DRONES OF JAGANNATHA

The tank moved into the farm.

A young German boy around seventeen years old came out of the chicken coop with eggs. When Zimmermann got out of the Juggerkampf, the boy had his flashlight on him, and his mouth was gaping open.

"Bet you never saw one of these, Max," Zimmermann said from up top.

"Things are getting...uh - bigger," Max said.

"We need to park it for the night – the children need their sleep. Can you make up a bed for them?" Zimmermann said.

"I just arrived today as Irene and Eugen were leaving. So, I don't know where anything is yet – but I can figure it out!" Max said.

"Thank you, Max. I will bring them in shortly," Zimmermann said.

"I am concerned for these Uberghars. They have been in the water crate for a long time now," Anna said.

"Well, that is a concern – where should we put them?" Zimmermann said.

"Henry told me that they put them in tub water overnight with a bunch of potatoes to climb on for an island," she said, shrugging her shoulders.

"Well! I will see if Max can do that!" he laughed. "I must admit, I never saw that coming today!"

"Did you hear that, Max?" Zimmermann said.

"I did – and I think that will be a fun adventure for me!" he said with a wide smile, letting Reiter into the barn door.

Zimmermann then handed Max the crate before moving the tank in between a few sheds where it was out of sight. It was snowing again, so it would be hidden at least until morning.

"Alright children, let's get you some sleep and something to eat if you are hungry," he said to them, but noticed Anna asleep, slumped against the wall in the control room of the Juggerkampf.

"I guess I will carry her in," he said to Egon who looked like his eyes were propped open. "Are you good to walk in, Egon?"

He scooped Anna up in his arms, but Egon didn't want to leave Zusa – and he sat in a ball between the gorilla's legs on the floor.

"I see," Zimmermann said. "I will be back."

While Egon was alone, he began to grind his teeth again. He stood up and took the blanket off Zusa's face. He looked very peaceful. Egon placed both his hands on Zusa's cheeks and pulled down and then did the same on his own face just like Zusa taught him to. He looked down and touched his big hand and then slipped back onto the floor against his legs. He put his hands under his glasses and rubbed his eyes.

Zimmermann returned with several blankets and some pillows for him.

"I don't know how warm you will be in here overnight, but I suspect there is no talking you out of leaving him," he said, placing the pillows on the floor.

"Here, sleep on top of these. I got them from the empty beds in there. They took Eugen and Irene today," Zimmermann said. "Max is looking after the farm now."

Egon curled up on the pillows and Zimmermann placed one under his head. Then he put many layers of blankets on top of him.

"I also grabbed some pumpernickel from the kitchen and some water for you. I will just set them here," Zimmermann said. "I will get you up early, so try and rest now. Tomorrow is a massive day."

Zimmermann went to leave and then turned around.

"Anna is in the bedroom where you were sleeping. I made sure Max knew to be there for her when she wakes up, so she won't be frightened. I would love to be a fly on the wall to see her reaction to the black chicken in her room. Wouldn't that be fun?"

Egon took a deep breath and exhaled.

"Max will take good care of your Uberghars. Good night, Herr Wolff. If you only knew what was waiting for you!" Zimmermann said.

After he left, Egon reached for a drink of water and poured some into his hand for Frecher and Hausratte. Then he took the pumpernickel and shared it with them both. The Skelekit – due to being a Skelekitty – didn't require either one. She was low maintenance. A small honk came from the remaining crate, and Egon took some water and bread over to Gänseheld too. The goose was getting stronger but was still doing an awful lot of sleeping.

Egon returned to the floor under the blankets, and Frecher and the Skelekit joined Hausratte in nestling in with him. He was so exhausted and fell asleep within minutes.

These children needed a good night's sleep badly. The farm was quiet for the night.

In the morning, Anna woke up to Aldo on her legs and a chicken on the nightstand beside her.

"Well, hello, sweet chickee!" she said to Soot, who looked like she had been awake staring at her new roommate all night long. "Why are you in here?"

When she went to get up, Aldo grunted.

"So YOU were why I had warm feet!" she said, petting his head.

She rubbed her eyes, grabbed her coat and boots from the floor, and hopped downstairs where Max was washing a few dishes. Aldo followed along.

"I am Anna. I know I was supposed to sleep here, but how did I get in?"

"Oh, you fell asleep! Zimmermann carried you in. It was my first day and night here too. I was taken off base, now I am looking after the farm," Max said. "Want to find some food?"

"Alright!" she said, rummaging through the refrigerator.

Zimmermann came in and saw Anna.

"Oh good, you are up! Big day for you, little lady!" he said, running back outside.

Anna shrugged at Max, then stuffed some buns and carrot sticks into a cradle in her shirt.

"Thank you for everything, Mr. Max! Good luck on the farm!" she said, running out. "Oh, wait!"

"Yes?" Max asked.

"Uberghars. Did they make it into the tub?" she laughed.

"Oh! Ha! They are funny – go see in the bathroom," Max said.

When Anna walked into the bathroom, they were playing in the water. Max overdid it on the amount of potatoes, but there were plenty of places for them to sit. The can of flakes was on the tub's edge, so she knew they were fed.

"That is so wonderful, Max! You did a great job! Think we should leave them until we know where we are going. It is better than a cramped crate," she said, running out the door.

Zimmermann was speaking to Egon when Anna came out.

"Oh good, Anna – come here," he said. "We only have an hour before Swartz and his crew arrive. This whole farm is going to be transformed to make room for new projects. This means, we need to remove horses, pigs, chickens – whoever else you can think of."

"There is a black chicken in the room I slept in," she said pointing up where Soot was staring at them through the window. "Uberghars are in the tub... oh and a beautiful old hound doggy slept on my leg."

"Oh, that is Aldo – the farm dog. Lovely old soul," Zimmermann said.

"How is everyone going to fit in the Juggerkampf?" Anna asked.

Zimmermann squatted in front of her and held her hands.

"Whoever needs corralling or containing, put them in. I saw you had crates of animals in the cargo section already. Not many else will go in there. There is room for twenty-five men inside, so there is room, but we need to be creative and put them in where we can!"

They spent several minutes planning who would go where. Egon was already on his way into the house where he tore up the stairs to get Soot. When he opened the door, she clucked away and followed him back down the stairs. He went into the bathroom where Max was loading the Uberghars into their crates.

"I have these eight!" he said, and Egon took a quick look. He then briskly walked back to the living room where he patted

Aldo on the head, who also followed him outside.

"You want those two inside?" Zimmermann said.

Soot was a bit more elusive and she wanted to stay with Egon, while Aldo's hound dog sniffer took him in every direction.

"I know what to do with horses! I took care of them at Festung Wolff!" Anna said, running to the barn.

"I heard you were there!" Zimmermann said. "Sorry you had to go through that, dear children."

Egon turned and walked away as quickly as he turned that chapter. His first stop was the pig barn. All the pigs were oinking away, and he went through them to the back door where Blumen and Gras were. What is the best way to get pigs to leave? Egon picked up Gras and walked out. Blumen followed immediately. On the way out of the barn, he opened all the stalls and doors. He had a hold of Gras in one arm and reached in behind the large potato sack and took the plans the Skelekit stole from Professor Wissen. He handed those back to her and she bolted out the door with them.

He then dragged the whole bag of potatoes outside and laid them in the snow. Eventually, the pigs filed out of the barn and began eating them. He set Gras down in the snow and Blumen joined her. Some pigs ate while others rolled around in the snow. It was great fun! While they were playing, Egon ducked into the shop where he met the Professor. Wissen left the jar with the hornet on the table, and he grabbed it. That is what happens when you leave somewhere in a panic. You forget your hornet jars.

He came out and handed it to Zimmermann.

"Well done, Egon," Zimmermann smiled. "You should have seen him leave the base. I am surprised he left with his head - he was so frazzled! I will put that in the tank!"

Anna walked Reiter and Spickz out. She really was a natural with horses!

Aldo walked around slowly and sniffed everyone. It was a foreign feeling for them all to be standing outside like this together, but they were remarkably good!

"How are we going to deal with chickens – or any animal that is walking along?" Anna asked.

As animals started to wander a bit, the flock of geese landed behind them, formed a circle, and honked like crazy to corral them.

"They are herding geese!" Anna laughed. "I will let the chickens out of the coop, then," she laughed.

Egon followed her in and went to the back of the coop.

"GO! GO! GO!" Anna yelled at them, and they chaotically flew out.

Soot was instantly nervous when the white chickens came out and he hid behind the piglet. For the first time, the chickens were not hostile. One of them stabbed a potato with its beak and dropped it at Soot's feet like a peace offering. Soot looked around seemingly in shock and began to peck at the potato.

"I guess cooped up birds are not so aggressive once they are free! They never let her in before. Guess she let them out!" Zimmermann laughed.

"There are a lot of animals to load up. The smaller ones can ride with us, but how far are we going?" Anna asked.

"You are going to go maybe the length of a corn field," Zimmermann laughed.

"The length of a corn field?" Anna said, in disbelief. "We need a Supertank and crates to go the length of a corn field?"

"Yes," he smiled.

"I don't know what we are walking into," she said, shaking her head. "But I am IN!"

"Most of the animals will walk with you. I believe this bunch will make sure of it," he said, pointing to the flock of geese.

Egon ran quickly by them with very full arms and ran into the Juggerkampf hatch.

"What was THAT all about?" Anna asked, following him in.

Egon had the Momma pangolin from the cage and Hoffie who she was separated from. While Hoffie was technically old enough to be on her own, the separation was not planned by her. Certainly, Egon could relate to an unnatural weaning and he watched while they sniffed each other.

"Is that her Momma?" Anna smiled. "Awwww, Egon... they are nice! So, Zimmermann says we are going one corn field! ONE CORN FIELD! Can you believe all of this to take these guys to a new location on the same farm? So funny!"

Zimmermann stuck his head in.

"Oh you got a couple pangolins. The underground is ok for now, too many of the Drillmeister's people are down there. We can't risk unearthing it yet. How did you even get those two out?"

"You better start a long list of "how did you" questions for Egon and save them for another day. He is amazing!" Anna smiled, and Egon put is head down.

"They are all waiting," Zimmermann said.

"We don't know what to do, Egon," Anna said.

"I can't go with you, but here is what I can tell you. Take the Juggerkampf straight down the edge of the field until you reach the apple line along the fence. You will see a silo on another farm field. Beside it is the foundation of a house and barn. They were burned to the ground. Egon will know what to do," Zimmermann said.

"Normally, I would say those instructions lack any instructions," Anna smirked. "But we have had no instructions about instructions this whole time!"

"Adventure contains discovery. It is what makes it so wonderful!" Zimmermann said.

"What kind of fire took their house and barn?" Anna asked.

"The kind where someone hates you and wants to take everything you have," Zimmermann said. "We call it the Forgotten Farm. Nobody was to speak of it after it happened."

"Tap. Tap tap. Tappity-tap tap tap. Tap TAP TAPPITY TAPP TAP TAP!"

"What is that?" Anna said.

Zimmermann looked out and there was Soot tapping the tank.

"Oh! Let her come in! I woke up to her staring at me!" Anna laughed.

Zimmermann picked her up and handed her to Anna.

It took several minutes for them to load up the smaller animals, but the geese were doing a fantastic job of rallying them to follow. Egon started the tank and Anna shouted and waved out the hatch.

"Thank you, Mr. Zipper man!" she joked. "Maybe we will see you soon! Who knows!" and she closed the hatch.

The pigs and chickens were oinking and clucking away, not knowing what direction they were going, but the geese kept a close circle around them. It is not wise to cross a black-headed, grey-bodied goose. Aldo was maybe the slowest of them all, but he was smelling the entire perimeter.

Düster soared circles around the fields against a clear blue sky as the Juggerkampf approached this old farm.

The Juggerkampf's tracks were smooth enough for all the little ones to walk in as they travelled a full field. It didn't take long for them to reach the Forgotten Farm. A painted wooden sign which read 39 Rattenbury Lane was barely legible from years of harsh weather – maybe even from farm equipment hitting it. One half of a wall on one side of the house was still standing, and only a foot of stone from the barn near the silo was there. The bare winter trees lining the property were either dead or taken over by vines. Perhaps it was more picturesque in Summer or Autumn, but for now, it was bleak.

Egon and Anna stopped the tank at the massive stone silo Zimmermann was referring to. Egon shut the tank down and opened the hatch. He hopped out onto the ground and the Skelekit and Frecher followed. He still had Hausratte in his coat. The geese honked when necessary to keep everyone from wandering off and Aldo decided to lay down for a sleep. Anna came out of the hatch and sat on top of the tank and looked around the farm and fields.

"I don't know what we do now, Egon," Anna said. "It's a beautiful stone silo, or **maybe used to be beautiful once**, but I don't know what is next. Do you?"

Egon walked around it as Frecher and the Skelekit skipped through the snow to keep up. The cedar cone-shaped roof was slightly visible through snow, the rest of it was made of field stone with old thick vine growing into the cracks.

Egon took the elephant key out and looked at every crack on the surface. Just behind the silo to the left, he saw movement in the trees. It was the bison from the train station – the one who chased when he went with his friends to Tiergarten. This big beast only made himself visible for a short time and then disappeared into the thick of the bush. When Egon's vision came back into focus in the forefront, there was the crack he was looking for. He dropped his head, closed his eyes, put the key straight out and the tusks and trunk matched the opening. When he stepped back, everything trembled. Stones from the house's wall fell off, the geese starting honking frantically and most of the animals scattered. The silo itself was either experiencing or creating an earthquake and Egon fell to the ground. Anna, amazingly, held onto some steel on the tank and only fell to the next level. The silo had cracked vertically from ground to roof, and the left separated from the right. The cone roof lifted off the top, and fog poured out.

"39 Rattenbury Lane! I heard Kluck talk about this place to us at bedtime! I think most of us were nodding off by that point in the story. I will have to ask him, Egon – but I think he said it could only be visited at a certain time or something – or by certain people. I guess that is today? I guess that is us? Wait until we see him! I have so many questions for him!" Anna said, but then added, "I sure hope he is alright. I don't like that Reiter came back on his own."

Egon walked back to the Juggerkampf and reached up to hand Anna the key.

"Why are you giving me this?" she asked as he walked towards the silo.

Egon went straight through into the fog as Frecher and the Skelekit ran after him. Aldo sniffed a straight line behind them and Gras, the little black pig, got brave and decided to tag along. Blumen oinked and he ignored her. One could easily forgive Gras because of the cute little curly tail bouncing as he ran.

"I guess we wait?" she said, tucking her knees into her chest on top of the tank.

Egon was already inside the silo where the first thing he noticed under the thick fog was green grass. Frecher plucked some immediately and began to chew, while the Skelekit rolled in it – perhaps feeling warm for the first time since September. As they walked, the fog lifted, and he looked waaaaaaaaay up to see tall evergreens that only seemed to end because the sun's rays were cutting them off. They went up forever.

Gras had the most adorable little oinks and they made Frecher and the Skelekit play even more. One of his oinks was echoed back to him and he immediately hid behind Frecher, who in turn, tried to hide behind him! Egon followed the oink-y callback to a tree stump. There was the fantastic forest lyrebird, sprawling his transparent peacock-style feathers out behind him – greeting them or bragging about it.

He looked at Ian and OINKED! Egon's head snapped back reacting to the bizarre combination of bird and pig. It was simply his magician's trick. He could mimic anything in the forest. He moved onto make a capuchin monkey sound – he learned that one quite recently. Frecher, Gras and the Skelekit all hid behind Egon when that happened!

Egon was more taken with the gorgeous salmon hue the sun exposed on its tail when it reflected off it.

"Well, alright everyone! I am driving a tank today!" Anna said fearlessly. "Uh – everyone follow me!"

She got herself down into the Juggerkampf and it soon moved forward.

"I'm doing it, Zusa!" she said. "If only you knew I was doing it," she added sadly.

Once the tank got through, and the animals all entered, the silo closed. As it did, the stone wall nudged the tail feathers on the last goose causing quite a grumpy honk! Up above, Düster made a wonderful call and the lyrebird took great pleasure in calling back. It never missed the opportunity to show off!

Anna stopped the Juggerkampf to get oriented.

"Are we on - grass?" she gasped. "Why isn't it winter here?"

Egon was not paying attention as he was looking intensely at something on the edge of the forest.

"Are we seeing a field of wheat in December?" Anna said, walking up behind him. "That is truly odd! That looks like enough wheat to feed all of Germany bread for a year!"

Egon was looking at this ancient rectangular castle as big as a city on the edge of the ocean. It was a sight to see! It was set high on the rocks and the walls were as tall as the banyan trees to the left of it. This was the only structure he could see, and he looked out at the ocean's never-ending horizon line.

Egon had enough and turned and walked past Anna to sit by the tank. Once he did, Anna began to see what he saw.

"Oh my stars, Egon – are we – home? Why does this feel like home? EGON! ARE WE HOME?" Anna said as she began to jump up and down. "Look at me jumping, Egon! I am jumping!"

Anna's leg braces did stop her from jumping like other children, but she certainly jumped exactly like Anna!

Meanwhile Frecher was on his back legs staring at the ocean.

"We are home, Frecher – want to play in the water? Go!"

Frecher ran into this stone city and the Skelekit stayed with Egon and Anna. The pigs and chickens ran vibrantly ahead and ploughed into the water. It was an instant celebration for everyone. The geese stayed near the Juggerkampf.

Spickz and Reiter trotted along but stopped when they saw Albert, the organ grinder from New York City. He came out to greet everyone. As he walked towards the Juggerkampf, he saw the two children sitting by themselves as animals moved past him.

"Hmmm," he said. "I expected to see August on his horse. Well, hello my boy...and my girl...lovely to see you both," he said patting their faces.

"And who is this lovely hound dog," he said as Aldo stopped for pettings.

"That is Aldo!" Anna said. "Are you British?"

"Well hello beautiful Anna! I am indeed!" Albert smiled. "Welcome to Jagannatha!"

"Am I dreaming this?" she asked.

"No, you are home!" Albert said.

"See? Egon!! We ARE home!" she squealed.

Egon wasn't looking up.

"Now, Anna – where is the adult among you?" Albert said.

Anna's energy dropped.

"I don't know. I believe the Death Marchers took him," she said sadly.

"General Kluck, you mean," he asked.

"Yes," she said. "You know him?"

"He wanted to be here with you, I am sure of it. It is a concern that you are missing an enormous list of children," Albert said.

"It is just Egon and I arriving, Sir," Anna said.

"No Charlotte, no Rita, no Mia, no Edward - nor any other children?"

"No, Sir," Anna said. "I believe the Death Marchers got them all."

"I see," Albert said, solemnly. "Well, I am impressed you children drove the Juggerkampf!" he said, lightening the mood.

"It is easy in a straight line. Mr. Zipper man could back it up!" she laughed.

"Can you drive it right over there and park it beside that large structure?" Albert noted.

"What is that thing?" she asked.

"It's how we arrived – that is the Juggernaut!" Albert said, proudly.

Düster dropped in and landed on top of the Juggerkampf and cried again.

"Egon, your bird angel is noisy today!" Anna said. "I never

heard him before we came here!"

"Hello lovely Düster," Albert said. "He chooses wisely when he speaks."

"Well, here I go - to drive my tank everyone," Anna laughed. "Never thought those words would come out of my mouth. Oh, Mr. Albert, we brought Zusa home," she said, sadly. "He is still inside."

"Oh dear, Anna. I can get some help for that," Albert said, feeling awful for her. "Thank you for telling me."

Egon was visibly affected by that, and he got up to let her pass. Then, he stood on the edge of the forest, petting Hausratte and staring at Jagannatha.

"Hello, Egon. My name is Albert. I am here to welcome you home," he said, smiling.

Egon didn't respond in any way. He was still.

"It's alright, little Makadee. I am not concerned about your non-responsiveness. I know you already. You are Egon Engel Wolff. Oh Engel – how wonderful that your middle name means Angel. I hope you will feel safe knowing that I know who you are."

Egon looked down when he said that and pulled out the Waffen SS tag.

"Oh -that tag. Hmmmm...are you feeling shame in your name lately? You shouldn't. He has no idea what a fortunate father he could have been to a Spider Child," Albert assured him. "You are surrounded by family now. Perhaps you are sick of people talking about you. Would you like to learn about me?" Albert asked. "General Kluck did everything to protect you to get you here. I did something similar for a little Makadee just like you. I am not math smart like you and Kluck. I wrote music for orchestra for years – until they moved me into the streets. I was an organ grinder in New York City for a time -"

Egon's teeth started to grind.

"Now hold on," Albert said, placing his hands on Egon's cheeks and gently pulling down. "Didn't somebody teach you not to do that?" he said, and he winked.

Egon relaxed when he did that.

"You *are* home, Egon. Nothing hurts you here," Albert said. "Would you like to get all your animals out of the Juggerkampf now?"

Egon followed Albert over to the tank.

"I love so much that you are home, Makadee!" Albert said, with his hand on his back.

"Woah! Düster made a crow mother uncomfortable!" Anna said, jumping down from the Juggerkampf, as Egon went in.

"Oh! Everything makes Mother Crow uncomfortable. She had fledgling babies a couple months back and she has been edgy ever since," Albert explained.

"So she should be! Did she come here in the Jugger-nut?" Anna said.

"Ha! The Juggernaut was her home in the woods when we

moved it. She still feels at home there," Albert smiled. "Don't you, Mama?" he said as she cawed back at him.

"Perhaps Düster could be her friend!" Anna suggested.

"Doubtful – but remain hopeful!" Albert said, dotting her on the nose. "So, Anna – besides Zusa, you have quite the crew in there, yes?"

"Well, you saw the horses, the chickens, the pigs. Zipper-man told us to get them off the farm right away. Aldo there, he looks pretty old," Anna said.

"We have doctors and scientists here who should give Aldo a checkup," Albert suggested.

"Oh good!" she said. "The top priority in there is Gänseheld, the lead goose. As you can see, his team won't go anywhere without him. He is in a crate inside. I must tell you, though. There is a perfectly healthy chicken in there who is so clucky, she needs to get out to save the sanity of the others – including ME!"

"SOOT!" Albert clapped.

"Yes – that's her!" Anna shook her head. "She is in love with Egon, I think. I am most concerned about a Beagle in a crate. He looks horrible," Anna said.

"The team will be ready for all of them. I can't wait to introduce everyone to you!" Albert smiled.

"Who is that girl?" Anna asked pointing to Katy in her wheelchair along the ocean shore.

"That is Katy – my Serinetta – one of the loveliest humans I have ever had the pleasure of knowing. Would you like to say hello?" Albert asked.

"Sure!" Anna said.

Albert and Anna walked up behind Katy.

"I saw you coming," Katy said, without turning around.

"I am Anna! Happy to meet you!" she said, cheerfully.

"You as well," Katy said, not turning around.

Albert walked around the front of her and kneeled in front.

"Did you hear my bones crack? Getting old is not for old people!" Albert laughed. "Are you doing ok today?"

"Yes, I am fine," Katy said.

"Anna is here to meet you!" he said.

"I met her," Katy said, glancing at Anna's leg braces.

"Hmmmm, we may need to do eggshell cleanup," Albert said.

"I don't need to do eggshell cleanup," Katy said.

"Am I within my right to do eggshell cleanup even if you have no intention of doing eggshell cleanup?"

"What's eggshell cleanup?" Anna asked.

"It's where we identify that someone in our talking circle is walking on eggshells - and we clean up those eggshells. Everyone in the circle must give permission first, even if you do not want to help clean up the eggshells, you allow others to clean up the eggshells. Make sense?" Albert says.

Anna looked totally confused.

"Go ahead," Katy said.

"Anna, have you ever been so uncomfortable around adults who sweep topics under carpets? Or they pretend something is or is not happening?" Albert asked.

"Yes – all the time!" Anna smiled.

"So, here - we do not allow anyone to be so nervous or uncomfortable with their feelings that they begin eggshell walking," Albert smiled.

"I am neither of those things!" Katy snapped.

"I am so glad! I would hate to think anything made a superhero nervous or uncomfortable," Albert smiled.

"You are a superhero?" Anna asked.

"Why wouldn't I be?" Katy said.

"Can I cleanup some of these eggshells, Mr. Albert?" Anna asked.

"I would love the help!" Albert said, smiling at Katy.

"Are you the only Superhero here?" Anna asked.

"Am I the only one in a chair?" Katy said.

"I didn't ask that," Anna said.

"Yes, I am the only one in a chair – but it's my choice," Katy said. "Don't assume I don't make my own choices in life. I don't want to be fixed."

"Does it hurt?" Anna asked, moving closer but Katy said nothing. "I am in a lot of pain – it is why I ask."

"Where does yours hurt?" Katy softened a bit.

"My back, my hips, my knees – below that, I feel nothing.

"I have pain too," Katy said.

"But you fight through it every single day," Anna said.

"I do," Katy said.

"Do you feel alone?" Anna asked.

"Sometimes," Katy said.

"Me too," Anna said. "People like us have to work harder."

"I helped save a bunch of Zoo animals in New York City. It was harder for me, but I did it."

"That is amazing! You have a great big heart!" Anna smiled.

"I saw you drive that big tank in here," Katy said.

"Look at my hands! They are still shaking!" Anna laughed.

"We don't know what we are truly capable of until we are in it sometimes!" Katy laughed.

"We brought animals too. Do you want to meet them?" Anna said.

"What kinds?" Katy said, turning her chair around.

"Pigs, chickens, horses. Do you know what a gharial is?" Anna asked.

"No! That is new here, right?" she asked Albert.

"They are indeed – like mini crocodiles with long flat snouts," he said.

"Mr. Albert," Anna said, sadly. "My heart can't do this right now."

"What's wrong, Anna?" he asked.

"Zusa is still in there," she said.

"Who is Zusa?" Katy asked.

"Zusa is our Gorilla father. He died while Egon and I were resting on his chest – inside our tank," she said, beginning to cry hard.

Albert walked over to her and rested a hand on her shoulder.

"Have you ever given your tears to the ocean?" he asked.

"No, I never have. How do I do that?" she asked.

"You sit on the edge of the water and think of him. When a tear comes down, you offer it to the ocean," he said.

She wasted no time and went and sat down at the water's edge.

"Let's give her some space, Katy. Will you help me get the other animals? I see Sadar and Kabir," he said. "Can you ask them to start with the Beagle and the other crates in the cargo part of the tank?"

"I will," she said, going that way.

When Sadar and Kabir came outside, Booza zoomed through their legs and out to the ocean. He startled Frecher who was looking inside a shell. He really missed White Cap, who hadn't returned to Jagannatha, and saw a new friend in Frecher. Just behind Booza was Richard, Sally and Emmie all running full boar to the ocean.

Anna watched them from her sitting position.

"That's Richard – he works on boats," Albert explained. "Sally and Emmie are the loveliest souls. Everyone you see has experienced tremendous loss. They will all prove to be great friends to you. I am ever so sorry you had this experience with Zusa. Perhaps, we can give him a proper service tonight? Maybe a campfire by the beach? Would you like that?" he asked.

"I would very much. Oh, Mr. Albert. He cuddled us like we were his. He kissed every inch of our face. In the end, he was trying to save too many. His injuries were too far past, I guess," Anna said, bawling now.

"My heart is breaking for you, Anna," he said. "You aren't German, are you?"

"No," she said. "I miss home."

"I hope someday – maybe not today – but another day – your choice of day – you will feel home here," he smiled.

"Who are you?" Sally said, her braids dripping wet on top of

Anna.

"I am Anna Schmidt!" she said, but then she looked around. "Actually, I am Anna Nowak."

"Yes, you are! You are safe here," Albert smiled.

"Ever played in an ocean?" Sally asked.

"No – but it looks so fun. I don't have swimming shorts or anything," Anna said.

"Your first swim you should just run straight in – clothes and all. It helps you leave your past behind!" Sally laughed.

Anna wiped her tears and gave that some thought.

"I could always THROW YOU IN," Sally said, starting to tickle her ribs...and she laughed out loud.

"STOP! STOP! I will go in! I will go in!" Anna said, fighting her off.

"Last one in's a rotten egg!" Sally said, jumping up and down.

"Oh yeah?" Anna said, boldly.

"Let's see it!" Sally laughed.

Anna rose to her feet and looked at Albert.

"Thank you, Mr. Albert. I am going to go give all my tears to the ocean now," she smiled.

"You give as many as you want," he said.

"Ready?" Sally asked.

"Ready!" Anna said.

"Shall I count to three?" Albert offered.

"YES!" they both said in unison.

"One...two...two and a half..." he joked. "And... THREE!"

They both darted straight for the ocean, and Sally was good enough to stay in pace with her. They both hit the water together. Richard and Emmie greeted her with splashes and squeals.

"I would say Anna was slightly ahead!" Albert called out. "But a remarkably close race!"

Then he said in a low voice to himself, "No rotten eggs there...and no eggshells. Lovely."

Richard stood up in the water and looked out.

"What do you see, Richard?" Emmie asked.

"Fins on the water!" he said, pointing. "Look!"

Albert put his hand to his forehead to block the sun. A line of fins were heading for the aquarium entrance.

All the kids ran back onto the shore and joined Albert. Booza grabbed Frecher's hand and pulled him out of the water.

"What are they?" Anna asked, sopping wet.

"Ghost Drones," Albert said.

That was the thing to catch Egon's attention, and he walked towards the shoreline with the Skelekit. The Drones moved through the currents in single file.

"Is that some sort of army?" Anna asked.

"We don't see them often," Albert said. "When they come – they make their presence known – and then they go."

"I am done swimming for now," Anna said.

It was a day for great arrivals. Just like Max on the farm seeing that Supertank, these children all stood with their mouths wide open. Things were certainly getting...bigger.

16 BACK IN THE ELEPHANT DEN

Kabir and Sadar were busy taking the crates and cages out of the Juggerkampf when Egon jumped back inside. He took the elephant key and returned it to Hausratte on his inside pocket for safe keeping. Then, he took the jar with the hornet in it and went to leave, only to stop at Zusa's leg. He removed the blanket covering his head, put both his hands on Zusa's face and pulled down. Then he did it to his own cheeks. It was the closest connection he had to a father, and his real father was simply terrible. He put the blanket back over Zusa's head and then left the Juggerkampf.

"I spoke with Anna, but I also wanted to check in with you too, Egon," Albert said. "We talked about having a fire service for Zusa tonight. Is that something you would like?"

Egon began walking towards Jagannatha.

"That is never easy," Albert said to Anna. "You are not alone dear souls."

"Zusa loved us – very – hmmmm – I can't think of the right way to say it," Anna said.

"Unconditionally?" Albert suggested.

"What does that mean?" she asked.

"There are no conditions or rules on his love. He just picks you up and loves you," Albert explained.

"Yes, he does that – but then the love he gives you is really BIG. He gave BIG love," Anna smiled.

"With joy!" Albert added.

"Yeah, Zusa wasn't happy to love us. He was joyful," she said.

"And protective," Albert said.

"I think it broke his heart that he didn't protect his children at the end. He may have died of a broken heart. Is that even possible?" Anna asked.

"I don't know, sweet girl," Albert sighed. "I love that your heart thinks about these things, though!"

"Everyone is out," Sadar said. "The gharial babies are healthy. I think they can go straight into the aquarium. They just need space to swim."

"We call them Uberghars. They spent a couple nights in bathtubs on mini potato islands!" Anna laughed.

"In rescue, a lot of animals get through their crucial transitions in bathtubs!" Sadar laughed.

"The Beagle seems like the worst one to me," Anna said.

"The Beagle is very sick, Anna," Sadar said. "Can you come give Kabir some history on everyone?"

"I can try. I don't know where Egon grabbed the pangolins from. The mother looks sick," Anna said.

"We'll go through them all one at a time," Sadar said. "Let's get you some dry clothes too!"

"Sally was right about swimming in your old clothes for the first time. She said it is a good way to leave your past behind," Anna said.

"We have so many clothes that you can pick something you like!" Sadar said.

"Alright!" Anna smiled. "Thank you, Mr. Albert. I wish General Kluck was here."

"We go way back! Our paths always cross – and they will again," Albert said.

The children all went inside, and Frecher followed Booza in. Without Kluck, he needed someone to hang with!

Egon stood and stared at the Elephant head framing the main entrance to Jagannatha.

"You are at the Elephant Entrance – if that wasn't obvious," Albert laughed. "Oh, I didn't say hello to your Skelekitty!" Albert said, as Egon's head turned. "Yes, I can see her!"

Egon pulled out his elephant key. He looked at it and then up at the Elephant head. Then, he stuck his finger in his mouth.

"Do you have any teeth left?" Albert smiled. "You dream about teeth too, don't you?"

Egon looked at Albert when he said that.

"Ah! Thought so," he said. "Your jaw will relax someday. I noticed you took an interest in the Ghost Drones swimming in. Would you like to see our aquarium?"

Albert kicked the sand away from the door in the ground.

"Aren't all the interesting places underground?" he smiled. "Why do you think animals make homes there?"

Egon grabbed the door which was no different than the door in the chicken coop or the door under the statue at the Grunewald Tower, and down the stairs they went.

"If we go right, you can see where the animals went. Let's check in on them later once they get everyone settled. If we go left up a few steps, we can go walk on that rope bridge!" Albert said.

As they began to walk along the wooden bridge, Albert invited him to look down.

"Everything from up here looks down onto glass ceilings. There is the Emergency room, there is the laboratory where the animals are fixed. See there is Sadar who helped bring in your animals. That is Harsha working on your goose!"

Egon stopped to watch that for a minute.

"Little known fact: Geese love children," Albert said, but then he laughed. "I don't know that they love adults, but they love you. When that goose is better, they better stand waaaaaaay back – that's all I can say!"

Egon continued his walk.

"We have geese on the other side of the bridge if you would like to look down. Those are the Opera Drones who need fixing!"

Egon looked over the left rope to see the enclosures below with various birds healing. He took the small jar with the hornet out of his coat.

"I am having a moment here. You will have to forgive me. I stood on this exact bridge a few months ago with a boy like you. I showed him all of this. Do you know what he did, Egon? He pulled out a jar of spiders," Albert said, folding his arms. "May I see your jar? Would that be ok?"

Egon handed the jar to Albert and waited for his reaction.

"Operation: Hornet Nest. I bet someone doesn't know you have her! We need to keep her contained until Kabir can modify her back. She will not be flying for the Luftwaffe! There is a whole hive that is really confused and missing her somewhere. Hold onto her for now, maybe Kabir can put her somewhere she can feel better than a jar. However, Egon - she is not herself right now. So we cannot let her out, ok?"

Egon put her safely back inside his coat.

"She is beautiful!" Albert smiled. "Right on time – I swear I did this before. Here comes Jeet!"

"A new boy!" Jeet cheered. "Hello Albert!"

"Hello, this is Egon!" Albert said. "He just arrived from Berlin."

"You are at the *Encephalon*, Egon. It means brain," Jeet said.

"We oversee Jagannatha's comings and goings from here. I suppose you would like him to see the other Drones?"

"We would indeed!" Albert said. "Egon saw the fins coming in."

"Oh you saw that? They don't come often! That was a really special moment for you then!" Jeet smiled. "Look down over here."

There they were. The *orcas.*

I believe you are the first child to see the Ghost Pod. They show up through the opening to the ocean – a passage that never closes. Every now and then, if we are lucky, we see the pod come check in on the injured orcas. Then, they leave.

"Can you go open the ceiling holes so Egon can hear them?" Albert asked.

"I absolutely will!" Jeet said, going back to the Tower.

"Sit with me, Egon," Albert said, patting the bench beside him.

Egon sat down and was locked on the orca with the metal plated face.

"Torpedo - that is his name. They came for him. He fought them off. You got to see his pod come visit him today. Oh and there is Orzel. Just like I told the children before you. His fin fell – the same people working on your goose fixed it. He was captured for entertainment. It is the sickest practice around. Our King was captured for entertainment too."

Egon looked up at him when he said that.

"The King – the King! He loves you so much, Egon. Someday, you will meet him. For now, look at your key and be reminded of his love. He is why we are all here," Albert smiled.

Jeet came out to join them.

"Listen," he said.

The holes in the glass ceiling of the aquarium were open, and the calls of the orcas were resonating through the tunnel out to the ocean. They were communicating with whistles, jaw claps, and clicks. Albert's eyes filled, and Egon was frozen.

"Those are restoration calls. There isn't a sound on Earth like it," Albert said, taking out a handkerchief and wiping his eyes.

Hausratte peeked out to listen intently, and the Skelekit stood still against Egon's boot.

"I hate to interrupt this beautiful moment, but the Encephalon caught the Tintenfisch on radar," Jeet said.

"Well that is good news! Will it settle into shore?" Albert asked.

"I will know more shortly," Jeet said.

"I think it might be a good time to show Egon those plans. He is well versed in blueprints," Albert said. "When we found out Kluck wasn't going to be here, it changed a lot. We can still accomplish this. I have great faith in Egon."

"The Tintenfisch moves her body around with a central brain. Her arms don't have their brains in them anymore, so they sort of just get dragged around wherever the body goes," Jeet explained, pointing to the paper.

"So the brain is consumed with survival and general movement," Albert said.

"Yes, which isn't a bad thing, except this Tintenfisch used to thrive in a realm of strategy," Jeet said.

"So, explain what happened – so Egon can understand," Albert suggested.

"Well, at one point, she was the Octopolizei – or Octopolice. After the Kriegsmarine captured her, they did extensive experimentation on her at the Sea Urchin. Basically, they ended up killing all eight brains in her arms."

Egon looked at the blueprints in front of him. He pulled out his book and turned the pages to the crocodiles.

"Part of their experimentation made her massive – and every time I see catch her on radar, she is bigger. I am sure she is hundreds of feet long by now. They just tossed her back in the ocean when their experimentation failed. Why use resources to feed a useless fish, right?" Jeet said. "Oh! Those are certainly lovely crocodiles! Yes – we are talking about sea creatures today," Jeet said, and shrugged at Albert.

"What do you want us to know about them, Egon?" Albert asked.

"Yes, I don't understand," Jeet said.

"We may need the Spider Network – or Mita. I don't know yet," Albert said.

Egon took Jeet's pencil to the blueprints and began drawing on each arm of the Tintenfisch. They resembled the crocodiles in his book, but he made the snouts long and flat.

When he got to the sixth one, Albert clued in.

"You are drawing eight of them. But they aren't crocodiles, are they?" Albert said.

Egon drew the eighth one and then put the pencil down.

"Oh! Those are the gharials... what Anna calls the Uberghars!" Albert said.

"Those babies he brought here?" Jeet said.

"Yes! Yes! Yes!" Albert said, putting an arm around Egon. "The little bathtub-swimming, potato island babies!"

"And you didn't see this?" Jeet laughed.

"People like Kluck and me – we are getting old! We need the children to come here – to connect – they are the next generation. I think we will know more once we get Egon connected upstairs," Albert said. "But safe to assume they will be powering her!"

"I have them in a new tank. They are loving it!" Jeet said. "...except the one is crying all the time."

"Hmmm, I will have to check with Anna. If Kluck were here, he'd get this sorted. I can't be expected to do New York AND Berlin," he laughed.

"You are more capable than you think!" Jeet smiled.

"Oh I was – in my day! I forget a lot now," Albert said. "Someday – when the King is made new, we will all be made new. For now, these are my old bones that my brain has to drag around."

"Should we draw some gharial babies on your limbs too?" Jeet laughed.

"Not the worst idea you have had, Jeet!" Albert laughed.

"I was thinking of asking Richard to come assist me. What do you think of that idea?" Jeet asked.

"Richard loves the sea – loves working on the boats. He is an example of a boy who was a sour candy until he found his calling. He would be a great addition in the Encephalon as you need him!" Albert said. "I am going to take Egon down to see Sadar now. Love you, my Jeet!" he said, hugging him.

"Speak soon!" Jeet said, running off with his brain on fire.

"I have something special for you. I have been waiting for two months for you to arrive. I wish Kluck could have been here for it," Albert said, as he started back down the rope bridge to the original door that they came in.

They went to the right of the bridge this time down below where Albert pointed out the emergency room and laboratory. When they walked in the emergency room, Kabir and Sadar were working on several stations. Egon walked over to where they were working on his goose. He let out a small honk when he saw Egon.

"That is the first noise! Isn't that nice!" Kabir said.

"Did you find the problem?" Albert asked.

"So Egon, he broke his wing where it attaches at the body – see, right here? The problem is the bone fractured, and basically jabbed into his body right here. The infection is not good. We are looking at removing the whole wing," Kabir said.

Egon put his hands up under his glasses and rubbed his eyes.

"It would be to save him, my friend," Sadar added.

Albert put his hand on Egon's shoulder.

"He shouldn't have lived through his injury," Sadar said. "Whoever treated him initially did a good job stabilizing him, but now it is about his life."

"If the wing stays on, he will die, Egon. I want to respect you and be honest," Kabir said.

"Can I show you what we would like to do?" Sadar asked. "This would be his new attachment."

Egon picked up a lightweight mechanical skeletal structure that was the same size as Gänseheld's wing.

"We would like to try fastening some of the feathers from his broken wing on it," Sadar said.

Egon picked up the new wing and took it over to Gänseheld. He showed it to him, and he gave a quiet, approving honk. Egon looked it over and then handed it back to Sadar.

"There's your approval," Albert said.

"We will begin immediately," Kabir said, calling in his staff.

"Sadar, I think we are ready to take Egon back now," Albert said pointing to the back room with the spider silhouette on the door.

"I thought that might be happening! It has been a few months!" Sadar said. "Right this way, Egon!"

Egon walked in and stood by a solo piece of furniture - the table in the middle of the bare room. Sadar walked over to the wall with the drawers in it and pulled out a compartment. Just like he had done before, he took out a large copper compass and set it on the table for Egon.

"Go ahead and look!" Albert said.

Egon looked down at the shiny spider-shaped dome sitting a few inches up on its eight legs. He touched his eyeglasses and then touched the glass on top, which had a picture of some fangs on it. Egon's teeth began to grind.

"That is a fitting picture for you, no?" Albert said.

Egon put the compass up to Hausratte's nose who sniffed it. Then, he showed it to the Skelekit, who also approved. He set it on the table, and then took the jar out.

"Oh! Does he already have his -" Sadar started, but Albert cut him off.

"No, this is something else he wants you to see!" Albert said. "Remember we were talking about Operation: Hornet Nest some of the scientists in Germany became entangled in?"

"Yes," Sadar said. "We have all talked about it in the lab."

"Egon has the Queen," Albert smiled.

Sadar's mouth fell open.

"May I see?" Sadar asked.

Egon handed the jar to Sadar.

"This is your jar, I want to be clear, ok? I will give it right back," Sadar said, looking closely.

"Can she be reprogrammed?" Albert asked.

The Skelekit scratched Egon's leg, and it prompted him to take out Professor Wissen's papers. He handed those over too. Sadar set them on the table and they all took a good look.

"This has Wissen's name on it," Sadar noted.

"Professor Wissen?" Albert asked.

"It's scribbly, but I am sure that is who this is. The Luftwaffe professors are the top scientists in all of Germany. It must be him. If it is, they are planning something horrible. I believe you are correct that Operation: Hornet Nest will be coming. Egon bringing the Queen would be an unbelievable gift to us, but you understand what this will mean," Sadar said, sadly.

"The Spider Children are all equipped to take on these tasks. It was the original intention for them. None of them are fearful," Albert said. "You did the right thing by bringing the Queen Hornet here, Egon. He already knows, Sadar."

"It doesn't make my heart hurt any less," Sadar said.

"I love that your heart has the capacity to hurt. It's a nice addition to your stellar intellect!" Albert said.

"Would you like to take the Queen and plans with you, Egon?" Albert asked.

Egon picked up his new compass and left the room.

"It's your move, Sadar," Albert smiled. "We are heading upstairs. Once Egon connects, we will let you know."

"Very good," Sadar said. "Here we go again!"

"And we will again!" Albert laughed.

"Yes," Sadar smiled. "It is a joy to serve."

Albert and Egon headed back up the stairs to the trap door outside the Elephant Entrance.

"We kick sand on top of the door, not because we are not safe here, but the most vulnerable are downstairs and it is just an added layer of safety if there is ever an issue," Albert said, covering it up before heading up the stone steps.

Egon followed along and Albert grabbed the giant iron handle and opened the big door for him. Egon was sort of interested in the structure, but mostly in this new gadget he was given. Albert guided him along the shaky wooden rope bridge and pointed at all the main floor rooms.

"On your right are the gardens and greenhouses. It is a reminder that **life was beautiful once.** They harvested the corn, so it is kind of bare there now. All our friends who work there and, in the kitchen, wear the most beautiful blues and yellows and purples. Those are the people making clay pots for food," Albert said. "On your left are where all the animals live together. Oh, hi Booza!" he said to the gibbon. "Where is Frecher?" he asked – and Booza picked him up like a doll and held him high. "He isn't a toy!" he laughed.

Egon stopped to see some of the animals he brought here mingling with the others.

"Reiter and Spickz will be outside grazing, I am sure," Albert said. "I am sure it has been a while since they saw grass!"

Egon stayed there and stared at the Momma gibbon, who was kissing her baby like Zusa cuddled the children.

"If you need hugs and kisses, go to her!" Albert said.

As he said that, Egon spotted Soot who was following the gibbon around – perhaps waiting for hugs too.

"Oh – Soot!" Albert laughed. "We all know about this chicken. There are some lovely roosters who will love to befriend her down there too – she is a beauty!"

Albert was holding the door open waiting for Egon to stop staring at Soot. The room went into the Assembly of Seven, and Egon was struck by the height of this massive tower with marble floor.

"If you look to your right, you will see seven high-back chairs. Nobody has sat in those. Seems a bit dull and boring, no?" Albert said. "And while that red and gold rug is certainly breath-taking, there isn't much point in it, is there?" he laughed.

Egon kept looking up.

"Sun shining through the roof is a lovely architectural touch, I must admit," Albert said. "Peace will be discussed here one day, I hope. There's an awful lot of dust accumulating!"

They continued along the wooden walkway out of the Assembly of Seven and into The Spider Network, the heptagon room with the Great Copper Spider hanging from the two-story ceiling. Egon's eyes went to the first station on the right – the three-foot pillar with the transparent glass tube reaching all the way up to the Spider. This was the only one which was illuminated. The flat surface on this pillar had the spider named Skull resting inside its imprint.

"You can walk all the way around the room, or you can go to the left," Albert said.

Egon opted to walk around the whole room where he looked in the imprints of each pillar. The post beside Skull's had an imprint of wings with no spider in it. The next four posts had spiders sleeping in them. There was a canine nose, a set of eyes, a set of ears and a paw print. That was Hunt, Scope, Echo and Claw. The last pillar that ended back at the door he came in, had no spider in it. There was only an imprint of a spider with teeth which made Egon's teeth grind.

Albert walked over to him.

"Your spider's name is Fangs. I wish to speak of his bravery. He was the best biter of all the spiders. When they had to go on to fight without him, it was much harder. He is here, but I will have someone else introduce you to him," Albert said.

Egon looked down at his compass while Albert opened the door on the other side of the room.

"Little Makadee, will you come in here for a moment?" he called into the next room.

There was Mita – the girl with the big spider eyelashes.

"Egon is here, Mita!" he said.

Mita went running over to him but stopped at his personal space. She smiled her wonderful Mita smile, then put her hand out and waited. He looked at his compass and then her hand. Then he gave it to her.

Mita looked at it and handed it right back. Then she went to the middle of the room under the Great Copper Spider and lifted the corner on the carpet. In the floor was the jar she had set in a couple months before which had the two dead spiders in it. Egon came over to look and she patted the floor next to her to invite him to watch. He sat next to her to look in the jar. There was Fly and Fangs. She gently lifted Fangs out and offered him to Egon, who put his hand out. Egon looked at the dead spider and back to Mita who was still smiling. She returned the jar to the floor. With his other hand he held the shiny compass with Fangs' picture. Mita put her hand out and he handed the compass back to her. She flipped the side button like a locket, and it popped open. Then she held it flat on her hand for him. He looked at her and she smiled. He gently set Fangs inside the compass and closed the lid.

"You just allowed Fangs to continue his journey. Thank you, Egon. He will always point you where you are supposed to be," the grinder explained.

Egon was really taken with Fangs staying in the same direction even if he turned it left or right. He was always facing the

Great Copper Spider in the middle of the room.

"Would you like to put him in his home?" Albert asked.

Mita went with him to his station and he set the compass into its position. Just like Skull, Fangs started the liquid bubbling in the leg of the Great Copper Spider. The mirrored surface of the Spider where Egon could see his reflection changed to reveal vital information.

The first flashes were of New York City, the carnival of Pollepel Island, the Ringmaster from the Circus on Rabbit Island and he saw the elephant killed in the middle of the tent. Mita put her head down.

"DRILLMEISTER! Look at that!" Albert said, which set Egon's teeth grinding. "Did you see that, Egon? He took them. Is that Professor Wissen that Sadar was talking about with the hornet? Boy, seeing this never gets old! When I was a boy, the visions were never this fancy!"

He saw the Octopus. He saw the gharials. He saw hornets. Then it became too much. Egon walked away from it and stared at the floor. He put both hands on his cheeks and pulled down like Zusa asked him to.

"I don't hear them, Mita," he said, looking up.

Mita also looked up.

"It isn't today. The magpies will let you know, Egon," Albert said.

The Spider Network had two legs lit up and bubbling now. It made the room brighter.

"Won't that be a nice way to welcome others – greeted by two pillars of bubbling spider legs?" Albert laughed.

Egon kept pulling his cheeks down.

"Would you like to come see your room? I suspect no grinding will happen in there," Albert suggested.

Mita jumped up and down ecstatically.

"It's been a few months since you had a new guest, Mita! We'll go in, you come when you are ready," Albert said, as Mita followed him in.

Mita jumped on her bed, sat cross-legged, and waited.

"I love it in here so much. My bunk out there is so plain," Albert laughed. "No worries! It suits me!"

After a few minutes, the door creaked open and there was Egon. He walked in slowly to see the seven dark walnut poster beds covered in deep purple satin bedspreads with the gold and red pillows. Mita came rushing up to him again and stopped on the imaginary line of his personal space. She boldly grabbed his hand this time and took him over to the first bed on the right.

And there was Ian.

"I am to Ian, what Kluck is to you," Albert said. "Ian and I spent time in New York City together...and now we are here. His spider is Skull."

Egon walked slowly over to Ian and stood at his bed. Ian was holding his Skelegroom doll which the Skelekit took a keen interest in, and his two Border Collie angels were sitting on either side of Ian's bed like stone statues.

"Ian still misses parts of his home," Albert said, sadly. "Over half a century has passed – and I still miss parts of my home. It never truly goes away."

Ian stared down at his doll and the two boys had no reaction to each other.

"Ian, Egon met his father. He disappointed him greatly – and they can never be together because of it," Albert said.

Ian thought about that. He moved over on his bed, giving Egon permission to sit down. When he did, Ian handed Egon the doll. The Skelekit jumped up to have a look, and Mita clapped and smiled. None of these children spoke a word – and yet they were communicating fabulously! Egon handed Ian the doll back and held the Skelekit in his arms. Mita grabbed his hand and took him over to the bed on the left-hand side of the door where they walked in. She pointed to the headboard which had Fangs picture on it. Egon reached inside his coat and pulled out Hausratte.

"Ha! He was in there this whole time! Quiet little thing!" Albert said, as Mita smiled.

Egon pulled back the purple bedspread and set Hausratte in there, then tucked the blanket up under his chin.

"I am willing to place a wager – that rat has never slept so well! Welcome, little one!" Albert said.

Egon walked to the middle of the room to the life-sized stone elephant on the square platform. He walked up the ramp and stood beside it. Everyone in the room was alarmed when a trumpet sound happened.

"Oh! That is our little Olly! She sleeps on the platform," Albert said. "She won't leave him."

Olly slid down the ramp and tripped over her own feet. The Skelekit was happiest to meet her and they began to play. Egon walked around this platform to take a better look. He touched the 'I' that was lit up in the stone.

"You are in the Elephant Den. No harm can come to you in here. It is a place of peace...and of rest. Mita and Ian are your family – if you will have them. If you choose to stay - and it is always your choice, Egon - nothing will separate you!" Albert smiled.

Mita clapped and jumped up and down again. Her family was growing – and she loved it!

"So, children...an incredibly special friend of Egon's fought a hard war. We are going to say goodbye to him on the beach tonight. It is open to whoever wants to come. It will begin at bonfire time," Albert said. "Welcome home, Egon."

The three children watched Olly and the Skelekit play as Albert entered the Spider Network.

"The last time I was in here, I only touched the imprint of you," Albert said. "Now you are in there, little Einstein! You were never really gone. You have a great adventure ahead! I trust you will guide our Egon - our wee Engel!"

At bonfire time, the ocean was calm with small waves coming up on the shore. The sun was setting, and the sky was orange and pink. There was enough of a breeze to feed the flames of the fire Albert started, and Zusa's body was a few feet away covered in wildflowers that the women picked from the island.

All the children gathered around Zusa and the fire, except for Egon who sat a few feet back, and Ian who sat far back under a tree. Olly, the baby elephant had a stick and was twirling it near Ian. Mita noticed Ian by himself and went and sat with him. Richard, Sally, and Emmie were there to lend their support, and Anna and Katy sat on either side of Albert.

Suddenly, the silence was broken by a few slaps on the water. There were three women standing in the ocean up to their hips.

"That is the Banyan Forest Women. They are here to play a song for Zusa," Albert said.

The first woman began to slap the water with her hands. Then the second one added a double-time beat to it. The third woman added tiny splashes here and there.

"Did you ever think water drumming could sound like that? They play from their souls," Albert said. "They do this for Zusa to remind him of home."

The women finished their song with three synchronized slaps on the surface and then they sat on the shore.

Albert looked at all the children's sad faces, and then he began.

"Zusa's name means *together* – and so I want to talk about his name.

If we were meant to be alone, there would be billions of

islands.

Even then, someone would fly there, crawl there, swim there to be with us...because we live on a planet that functions by working *together*.

Each grain of sand is not alone, and there are billions of grains. The water droplets of the sea form the ocean that surrounds us...it does so, by working *together*.

A tree seems alone, but its roots will crawl deeper than the tree is high so it may find nourishment – it does so not as one root, but by working *together*. That tree appears to be one, but even the leaves work *together*, the branches seem as though they are trying to grow away from the trunk, but they house birds who make families, insects crawl inside them for shelter and food. Even the cells of that tree are constantly working *together*.

We were not dropped here coincidentally – but born here intentionally. Each of us was created with love...so we are love...so we should move and work in love – and do so, *together*.

Egon...Anna...The reason Zusa loved so deeply, was that he genuinely understood why we need to be *together*. He was stolen from his home, from his country, from his family. He was put into a Zoo to form a new family...only to be put into a separate pen. He left there and found a new home back in the closest thing he could find to a forest - where he could feel the cells of the trees working *together* again. There, he found you. He *chose* you. So, when you say he cuddled you like nobody else, kissed you all over and rocked you in his arms – always remember that up to that point – he did not get to choose...and when given the freedom to choose – he chose you. When you think of Zusa – remember that he chose you. Also remember that death is not final. We are not saying goodbye but see you soon. And so we say, see you very soon, Zusa – and we do not say you *were* loved – we say you *are* loved, Zusa. And we say this – as a group here – his woodpeckers – the Mauerspechte children *together*," he concluded.

There was no break in the silence.

"I recognize that not everyone is here that should be here. I hate that they are not here. I do love that they got to feel the kind of perfect love that Zusa knew how to give. I would count them as exceptionally fortunate to have experienced him. Mita, would you like to give something to Zusa?"

Mita got up and took the yellow snout bean flower from behind her ear and placed it on his chest.

"Anna, would you like to speak?" Albert asked.

"I don't have anything lovely to add to what you said. But it was lovely," she said, quietly.

Katy whispered, "It's ok, Anna – we don't do eggshells here. If you don't have anything lovely, you can always give what you do have."

Anna thought about that and then she got up and stood beside Zusa.

"I am deeply sorry, Mr. Albert. I am currently too angry. I do not think this is fair, Zusa," she said. "You fought off those Death Marchers – and for what? Just to be killed. It didn't even save the others. So, they were not only robbed of your love, they don't even get to be here to send you off!"

"No, it isn't fair," Albert said.

Anna rubbed her whole face – the kind of rub where you just don't want your face anymore.

"I need to go give my tears to the ocean," she said, walking down to the shore.

Egon had four little friends trying their best to console him. Frecher and the Skelekit were nestled into his legs, Hausratte remained in his coat and Soot didn't even know where she was, but she was hanging out. Booza initially came because Frecher was there, but it had to be disturbing for him seeing a gorilla like that.

Ian got up from his tree and went back inside. Mita ran and followed him.

Richard, Sally and Emmie stared into the fire.

"Were you hoping for a better ending that that?" Katy asked Albert.

"There is no ideal ending to things like this. People try to wrap it up in a neat little package, and then put that package in the mail – hoping someone will mysteriously fix it for them. Grieving isn't a ceremony. It is a process. It may sound odd, but tonight ended on a good note," he said, looking into the fire pit.

"How so?" Katy asked.

"With the truth. One cannot heal until they look truth in its eye. I am happy about that. Life isn't about happy endings. Everyone here is so broken, my Serinetta. We all came here, elated to have a happy place we can call home. But nobody came here without dragging their past along in a suitcase," he said.

"Most of us can't even carry it!" she laughed.

"I don't know of anyone who can," he smiled back.

Anna looked over at them and Katy waved at her. She put her hand up to gently wave back.

"Maybe I will go park my chair near her and just be available," Katy said.

"How did you get to be so smart?" Albert laughed.

"Someone once told me that the problem with our world was that we quit caring," Katy grinned.

"Thank you for caring, my Serinetta," Albert said, touching her nose.

As Katy wheeled away, she turned back to ask, "What will happen to Zusa? Will he be burned or buried?"

"There is a special resting place for Zusa on the playground," Albert said.

"That sounds perfect," Katy said, and she left to go sit on the shore near Anna.

"How tired you must be, dear Engel," Albert said to Egon, who was rubbing his eyes under his glasses.

"May we go?" Sally asked, boldly.

"Yes, sweetheart – thank you for being available too," Albert said.

After the children went back inside for the night, Albert spoke with Egon.

"We have a children's playground right near the ocean. Zusa has a place there. If you like, when you wake up in the morning, you can come see it. If you want him somewhere else, that would be fine too," Albert said.

Egon yawned and so did Frecher. Booza pointed at his fur and looked at Albert.

"Oh! He isn't in winter! His white fur will go brown here," Albert said.

Booza clapped, picked him up and took him inside.

"You picked up some strange friends along the way. You have a hound dog and Skelekit at your feet, a rat in your pocket and a black chicken who is completely enamoured with you!" he laughed. "Shall we go to bed?"

Egon yawned again and began to follow Albert inside. He stopped first to look at Zusa. He put both hands on Zusa's cheeks and pulled down – then did it to his own face.

"When you learn a lesson from someone wise, you take it everywhere with you. That is so lovely, wee Engel," Albert said with his hand on Egon's back. Soot stopped to cluck at the girls and Aldo the hound dog trailed along.

"We'll be in soon," Katy said.

The Banyan forest women came over to them and one of them scooped up Anna in her arms. She cuddled her and then passed her to the next woman who also cuddled her...and so did the third. Anna cried a gut-wrenching cry. They formed a circle around her and held hands and sang a song nobody understood...perhaps Zusa did...and somehow Anna did. When she was done, she walked over to Katy's chair and the women disappeared into the forest.

"I don't know where I am sleeping tonight," she said.

"There is an empty bed right beside me. Would you like it?" Katy asked.

"I would very much," Anna said.

The two of them went inside and Zusa's body lay alone near the shore, as the fire's embers burned low.

Mita and Ian were already in their beds and Mita pointed to a nightshirt on Egon's bed that her elderly friend, Lavani placed there.

"I just got him his change of clothes and I am getting them all settled in," Lavani said.

When she left, Albert stood at the footboards of their beds. Aldo sat on the foot of the bed, Soot found a place behind Egon's knees, and Hausratte was cuddled under the blanket with him. Olly was on the elephant riser with all four legs straight up, fast asleep, and Mita was giggling at her.

"Thank you both for supporting Egon tonight," Albert said to Mita and Ian. "And Egon," he began but noticed his eyes were already closed. "Oh," he laughed. "I was going to tell you to be kind to yourself and rest."

Mita smiled and seemed pleased to see another bed with someone in it.

"Friendship – there is nothing like it, is there Mita!"

She smiled and put her head on her pillow.

Albert walked over to Ian.

"You seem preoccupied. You saw some things again?" Albert said.

Ian pulled his blanket up over his ear and cuddled his Skelegroom, which remained the only connection to his Father.

"I did too," Albert sighed. "You are not alone, dear soul. Tomorrow will be busy."

Albert walked over to the door and said, "Good night, my Makadees," and he shut out the light.

17 THE BLITZKRIEG HORNETS

Ian wasn't one to sleep in ever since coming to Jagannatha two months before. He also wasn't big on socializing, but he followed Mita around like a lost puppy dog. Of course, he always stayed two steps behind her – a comfortable distance. Mita liked to hit the playground early in the mornings so she could tend to the flowerbeds during the sunrise which played peekaboo with her over the high garden walls.

The children's playground was between the ocean and the Elephant Den and had everything from monkey bars to slides. Around six am, Mita was trimming some bushes while Ian sat on a nearby bench and watched her. He didn't really use the playground, and he hadn't taken an interest in girls up until meeting her, but she seemed to be his everything.

The playground had a new guest in it that morning. There was a cement box with a flat stone on the lower half. On the upper half, Zusa's body was visible from the chest up, sitting in the sun, seemingly transitioning from chaos to peace...waiting for the children to come.

Mita clipped red and white roses and took them over to Ian.

She handed him a basket and he held it for her while she separated the petals. He held it so still, he was shaking a bit, perhaps concentrating hard on not messing up this task.

Albert arrived soon after with Egon and Anna. The sun was now shining a warm beam onto the playground.

"Are you getting lots of worms, little birds?" he asked. "Look, at who else fell out of their nests early today! Well, the dog and chicken are still on the bed. The rat is inside the sheets. They sure like it there."

Anna walked over to see what Mita and Ian were doing.

"Are those for Zusa?" she asked.

Ian gave her back the basket and she handed it to Anna.

"Rose petals. My Mama grew roses," she said.

Mita gently took Anna's hand and took her over to Zusa.

"Will he be buried?" Anna asked.

"No," Albert said.

"Alright," she said quietly. "May I put the petals anywhere?"

"Of course," Albert said.

Anna sprinkled a few onto Zusa's chest and a few tears came down. It wasn't severe crying like the night before.

"I like that his arms are crossed over his chest like that. We talked about sign language," Anna said.

She turned to Egon and offered him the basket. Egon walked

over and sat beside Ian.

"Alright, Mita. Would you like to place some?" Anna asked.

Mita took the remainder of the petals and made a heart-shape on his chest.

"That is really nice. He was love," Anna said.

"He IS love," Albert said.

"Yes, he is," she agreed. "Mr. Albert – will we see the Banyan Forest women again?"

"Maybe, they really only show up at very special times of celebration and healing," Albert said. "Did you like them?"

"Yes," Anna said. "There was something pretty magical about them. I dreamed about them."

"That is really nice, Anna," Albert said.

"So this is the playground. It is beautiful here," Anna said.

"Oh, you can thank Mita for that. She is our resident groundskeeper," Albert said.

"I had another dream I wanted to ask Kluck about but maybe you know," she said.

"I can certainly try and answer for you," he said.

"Did you come through the silo too?" she asked.

"We came through *a* silo, but on a farm in upstate New York," he said.

"In America?" she gasped.

"Yes, in the Juggernaut parked next to your Juggerkampf," he laughed.

"I have to be honest with you. I am just rolling with it all...but I have questions!" she said.

"Go ahead!" he laughed at her boldness.

"I don't want to overwhelm you, so I will just ask two for now," she said.

"Alright!" he smiled.

"There are three children here who don't sleep with the rest of us. They don't speak, but they know things – and they don't seem at all concerned about anything. Are they alright?" she said in a low tone.

"They are indeed!" Albert said.

"Perfectly normal behaviour?" she asked.

"Yes," he said. "They are the Makadees."

"What does that mean?"

"They are Spider children. They have a special mission and spiders which guide them. Ian here went to New York on a mission with his spider named Skull. Katy went with him," he said.

"I like Katy very much," Anna said. "I guess Egon will also be going," she said, a bit sad.

"If Egon does have to go, would you like to go with him?" Albert asked. "That is, if Egon would like you to go."

Egon took out his book and flipped it to the crocodile page.

"Egon showed me his book the first day I met him. We were fast friends," Anna said.

Mita took Anna's hand and walked over to Egon. She took Anna's right hand and put it in Egon's left hand.

"I believe you will go," Albert said. "Mita knows more than we do."

"Did Mita have a mission?" Anna asked.

"Mita has a unique calling. It isn't time for her right now. If she says you are going, you can be sure you are going," Albert smiled.

"The other question I have is about the Forgotten Farm. It is where we came in through the silo. Do you know what happened there?"

"Oh yes," Albert said. "The Death Marchers burned it to the ground when they found out people from outside the country were there."

"Just like that? They burned it?" Anna asked.

"The farmers were hiding people from Poland there," Albert said. "I am sorry, Anna. But I want to respond with the truth."

Anna really absorbed that.

"If Egon goes on a mission," Anna said in a sharp tone. "I

wish to go."

"That will be up to you, children. I have no say in that," Albert said.

Egon handed Albert the book.

"Oh, you want me to look in it?" Albert said, as Egon put his head down. "I am honoured, Engel."

Egon got up and walked out of the playground.

"Do you wish to spend any time with Zusa?" Anna asked.

"I believe Egon spent his time last night. We will be sliding the flat stone across, Egon - if you wish to see him once more," Albert said.

Egon left.

"He is done, then. Thank you for offering, Anna," Albert said. "Would you like to stay with Mita? I am sure the children will be out soon."

Mita took her hand and began to show her around. Albert followed Egon out, and the Skelekit pranced behind them.

Egon walked towards the Elephant Entrance. He kicked away the sand from the door in the ground and lifted the handle.

"May I come?" Albert asked, and Egon held the door for him. "I figure you wouldn't want to be without your book."

They walked back down to the lab which was tranquil this early in the morning.

"Good morning, Sadar," Albert said. "Up late or up early?"

"Haven't gone to sleep yet! Come see, just finishing up," he said.

Sadar's station looking like a tornado passed through. It seemed every small utensil was being used.

"It smells lovely in here! Is that fresh bread?" Albert asked.

"They just brought breakfast in, help yourself," Sadar said.

"There is fruit - and the bagels are heavenly here, Egon. Want some orange juice?" Albert asked. "Oh a tea, I will have that!"

Egon took a bagel and nibbled away at it while he watched Sadar work.

He had Egon's Queen hornet in the middle of his table with a large magnifying glass on a mechanical arm.

"We have named her Zahnea," Sadar smiled. "Is that a good name, Egon?"

"How did you come up with that?" Albert asked.

"Teeth in German, but then added a nice Queenie ending on it," Sadar smiled.

Egon began grinding his.

"Works well with Fangs, no?" Albert said.

"Come look!" Sadar said, adjusting the arm of the magnifying glass to Egon's height.

Zahnea no longer had just a stinger, but fangs.

"Not completely necessary, but fun to implement!" Sadar laughed.

Egon was pretty taken with it all.

"Turn off the lights, Albert," Sadar said.

When he did, a bright orange glow came from the Queen.

"We need to differentiate between her and the others. Additionally, you will want to see her in the dark," Sadar explained.

Egon really seemed to love that.

"So those are the fun bits, what functionality did you change?" Albert asked.

"Before working on her, she was programmed to locate the enemy that they wanted her to find. In this case, from what I can tell, she was programmed to go after a certain race of people and kill them using a stored chemical component from her abdomen. She had nothing in her abdomen, per say, but there were microscopic remnants of a cyanide-based pesticide. It is some exceptional technology going on to not have her exterminated in the process. No doubt, thousands of hornets like her were killed previously in the experimentation process."

That part made Egon rub his eyes under his glasses.

"When were your glasses cleaned last?" Sadar asked. "May I?"

He lifted them gently off Egon's face, cleaned then and returned them to his nose.

"WOW! Look at your blue eyes!" Sadar said, and then had an

epiphany. "That's it!"

"His eyes!" Albert said.

"Yes!" Sadar celebrated. "Genetics are complicated. How do you program the Queen to know who the enemy is? It is too vast for their extermination programs. It is easier for her to identify who belongs in the hive – and everything else is a threat."

"So they programmed her to think the Aryan race is part of her hive?" Albert asked.

"Indeed! I mean, she still needed to be trained to be offensive. They generally only attack when threatened, but it makes the programming easier."

"So undoing it?" Albert asked.

"We don't undo it completely. There are still thousands of hornets out there," Sadar said.

"In winter?" Albert asked.

"Temperature is a simple thing they adjusted. We don't want to adjust that part – she still needs to fly in winter. Egon is a bright boy. He knew to leave her down here. We kept her in a cold room overnight."

"So – what is her task? What do you hope to accomplish?" Albert asked.

"She needs to be able to go to where her hive is – instruct thousands of them to do what we need them to. They are most likely already filled with this killer extermination pesticide. I am willing to be bet, whoever left this Queen with Egon is scrambling right now to replace her," Sadar warned.

"How do you get around that?" Albert asked.

"We extract a sample of the pesticide still lining her abdomen, as small as that is, and we use it to test another attraction agent that makes them choose her," Sadar said.

"That seems complicated," Albert said.

"And risky," Sadar said. "Are you alright with the risks, Egon? Zahnea is your Queen."

"I feel like the Makadees understand this," Albert said, as they watched Egon leave.

"Speaking frankly, Albert...if Egon doesn't do this, thousands of hornets and thousands of people could die," Sadar said.

"I know. As quickly as you can finish up – whatever you need to do. The magpies haven't dropped the flag... and Mita hasn't created urgency yet," Albert said. "Thank you, Sadar."

"Always a joy, Albert. I won't be long finishing this," Sadar said, as Albert followed Egon.

Egon went up the stairs to reach the rope bridge. He walked briskly to reach the Encephalon where Jeet greeted him. Albert hurried to keep up.

"I am OLD, dear boy!" he laughed.

"Where did you two come from?" Jeet asked.

"We just spent some time with Sadar. He has been up all-night working on Egon's Queen hornet," Albert said.

"Oh, yes. We had a break together in the middle of the night. I was working too," Jeet said. "Would you like to come see?"

"Of course!" Albert said.

They followed Jeet down a ladder beside the Encephalon to the largest aquarium. Inside was the body of an octopus and its arms seemed to be outside, still in the ocean.

"When they designed this place, they were smart attaching it directly to the ocean," Albert said.

"That is the Tintenfisch we saw on radar! This is the first creature which doesn't fit! I always thought the aquarium was open because they wanted the creatures to come and go – and that is certainly true – but now you see my dilemma," Jeet smiled.

"How did you lure her in?" Albert asked.

"Do we lure anything here?" Jeet laughed.

"I suppose not," Albert said. "Do you think she knew she needed help?"

"I believe this to be the case," Jeet explained. "She needed her main brain detoxified and the brain in each of her eight arms was pretty much scrambled."

"Giant lab rat experiment gone horribly wrong," Albert said, sadly.

Then they heard "MEEEEH-OOOOOO!"

Egon knew that noise!

"Come see her new arms!" Jeet said.

When they walked outside, they saw each of the Uberghars on the tips of the Tintenfisch's arms.

"Are they sitting on top or attached?" Albert asked.

"I thought they would need to be attached, but that seemed like some sort of mad-science cruelty. I just put one into the water and it swam to one of the arms. Each one I added, went to another arm," he explained.

"Because they are separated from the Unterghar!" Albert said.

"That is exactly the case," Jeet said. "Sadar and I spoke about it at length and agreed that the reason we are seeing her receptors coming alive is because they are powering her motherly instinct and giving a brain to each arm. It is powerful stuff! And they just want a parent to sit on top of. Something in the Tintenfisch's brain is connected to them. It's a miracle, really."

Egon picked up the Skelekit.

"We all want that connection," Albert said, looking at Egon.

"I am only counting seven gharials," Albert said.

"Oh yes – I think as soon as we add the eighth, she will leave – so I am just holding off," Jeet said.

"And that is why one cries," Albert said. "That is remarkable."

"I know it appears cruel, but I am sure that guy was crying even when he was with the rest," Jeet said.

"There is always one baby who is simply out of sorts," Albert agreed.

"I should tell you why I don't want her leaving yet," Jeet said.

"Oh he knows," Albert said.

"Oh he knows the bigger reason, but I need to tell him my reason," Jeet said. "I want you to always feel safe here, Egon. You entrusted those Uberghars to me – for whatever reason, you trust me. I never want to break your trust. I wanted you to see what happened here – and be ok with it. What happens next is up to you. If you want them removed, I will remove them simply because you ask me to. However, if you would like to add the last one yourself, just know – she will leave with them – I am quite certain of this."

"You know this is just about timing," Albert said.

"I do – but I needed to show Egon respect," Jeet said.

"Love your big heart, Jeet!" Albert said, embracing him. "You are making the right choice."

"Would you like to see how some of the others are doing?" Jeet asked.

"Would you like that, Egon?" Albert asked, but Egon started walking halfway through his question.

Egon sat where Ian had sat before with his feet dangling, watching a couple orcas swim around one another.

"Torpedo and Orzel are doing well – I believe the pod was checking in. They show up periodically and don't really socialize with us," Jeet said. "Molly and the rest of the dolphins basically just have fun all day. They swim hard in the ocean and come in to rest and be nosey, then they leave again...they are all healthy now. Our hammerhead shark pup isn't such a pup anymore as you can see."

Egon was closely watching her.

"Stealth is just about twenty feet now. Without the metal hammerhead that we replaced, she would weigh just under five hundred kilograms," Jeet said.

"Would you tell Egon about Stealth's hammer?" Albert asked.

"We replaced her hammer. She lost her mother to a submarine ramming her. Stealth barely lived. One of our boats witnessed it and brought her here. Part of why we understand the Tintenfisch's growth, is because we have similar technology to make her hammer adjust to the rapid body and hammer growth. We had to replace it completely this time because she simply outgrew it faster than it could adjust."

"She seems more agitated than the last time I saw her," Albert said.

"Everyone is restless today for sure. Something is in the air," Jeet said.

"I would make sure they are well fed... just in case," Albert suggested.

"Good idea," Jeet said. "The good news is we don't have to parade them through a silo."

"Very true!" Albert said.

Egon looked into Stealth's big glassy eye at the end of her metal hammer. They spent several moments silently communicating.

"Are you ready to go?" Albert asked.

Egon got up and walked out.

"Great work, Jeet! I used to be a night owl. Now I require tea and my slippers. My, how life has changed over the years! If I tried to command a fleet today, I would fall asleep mid command!"

"You have earned your right to rest!" Jeet joked.

Egon was walking at a focused, steady pace to get back outside. Anna was walking with Mita back from the playground when she spotted them.

"Hey! Egon! Where are you going in a hurry?" Anna said.

He marched quickly through the Assembly of Seven but stopped at the highbacked chair which had the same imprint as Fangs the spider. He touched the carving and then kept going into the Spider Network.

"Is everything alright, Egon?" Albert asked when he finally caught up.

Mita and Anna followed behind and joined them in the Spider Network. Ian was in the Elephant Den and heard Albert's voice, so he came out to see what was happening.

It was still only Skull and Fangs who had bubbled up the leg of the Great Copper Spider, but Egon stood and stared at it.

"The Copper Spider is quiet, Egon," Albert said. "I know you are eager to go but-"

Just one quick flash showed up in the mirrored surface of the Copper Spider. It was an elephant raising its trunk and opening its mouth. Only Egon caught it.

"Did something just flash? I think I missed it," Albert said, stepping towards the Spider.

Anna cut him off to say, "LOOK UP!"

At the very top of the room, there was that pecking noise once again on the glass ceiling panels.

"ARE THOSE THE MAGPIES?" Anna asked.

Albert ran to the doorway and pulled the rope to open the ceiling panel. The mischief of magpies were back and descended into the group. This time, they were carrying a hand-sewn German flag. It looked like it was hand-crafted the same way Ian's American flag was, patchworked together in rectangles and the material was mixes of satin and heavy stitching. The magpies mounted the flag above Egon's pillar and then they formed rows in front of Egon. He walked among them staring at their reconstructed copper beaks, while others had pewter wings. Ian walked up to Bomber and picked him up.

"You don't want him going, Ian? He can fly!" Albert said.

Since Bomber was shot in New York, it would have been understandable that he sat this one out. Instead, Ian took Bomber over to Egon and handed him the bird.

"That is special, Egon," Albert said. "I believe Ian wants you to know you can take Bomber if you need him."

"He looks like he has had more surgery than the others," Anna noted.

"Hmmm, yes. I don't know that he is the strongest choice for a winter engagement," Albert said.

Mita walked up to Egon and put her hands out. Egon looked at Bomber and handed him over to her. Mita confidently walked the bird over to Ian and gave him back.

"Mita decided it. Thank you, sweetheart," Albert said.

"What makes her decide?" Anna asked curiously.

"Everything goes better if Mita decides," Albert smiled.

Egon walked over to Ian, who was now standing by Skull in the pillar, and he pet Bomber's head. Egon looked at Skull and then back at Ian. Everyone in the room was quietly waiting for Egon's next move. He walked across the room to his pillar and looked in at Fangs.

Egon looked to Albert who simply said, "Your move, Egon."

The magpies started yapping away and caused everyone to cover their ears with their loud caws. Egon looked down at the Skelekit who was simply sitting pretty.

"Mr. Albert, why do some of the magpies have coins?" Anna asked.

"So they do! Travel money, I am guessing!" Albert said, as Mita collected them all.

She handed the coins to Anna.

"Am I – going?" Anna gasped, as she dropped a few.

Egon bent down and picked them up.

"Do you want me going, Egon?" Anna asked.

Egon handed her the coins and walked back to Fangs.

"You are the keeper of the coins, I suppose!" Albert laughed.

"I need to go find Katy! I - AM – NOT - READY!" she screamed as she ran out of the Network.

"No better person to seek advice from," Albert smiled. "Well, Egon? We still have the matter of Zahnea and the Tintenfisch to attend to - if Mita and the magpies believe you need to go today!"

Egon looked down at Fangs in his compass who was no longer pointing at the Great Copper Spider but at the door leading out. Egon gently lifted him out and he maintained the direction. Albert looked down.

"Isn't this magnificent that even a seemingly dead spider can find its purpose?" Albert clapped. "That gives some hope to the rest of us. AND by the rest of us – I mean me. Oh my aching bones!" he laughed.

Egon walked over to Ian's pillar and looked down at Skull. Ian reached out and touched the cracked dome on the top of Skull's surface from his night in New York. Egon had a moment where he may have been thinking this could also happen to Fangs, but he stood tall and walked out. The magpies began their proud party cry and flooded the Assembly of Seven and then flew out the door onto the beach where they parked and waited.

Anna was on the beach chatting with Katy in her chair.

"Look Mr. Albert, Katy suggested I get a toolbelt to put some things in. I got it from Richard at the docks!" Anna confidently yelled.

"That is fantastic," Albert said, hurrying after Egon as he pulled the door up from the ground to go downstairs.

"You need a handier door!" Anna yelled.

"It's an extra layer of protection for the vulnerable animals downstairs," Katy said. "Sadar said they are going to install a ramp for me. Right now, they carry me down if I need to go."

"Could they not just fix you somehow?" Anna asked.

"Do you want to be fixed?" Katy asked.

"If I could throw these braces in the trash, I would!" Anna said.

"Hmmm, let's talk more when you get back. Put this flashlight in your pack too. I find there is always a need to pick a lock, so I am glad Richard showed you how to do that!" Katy said.

"Ok, great! So Katy," Anna said, looking a bit anxious. "How did you shake your nerves?"

"From what I understand, you boldly go wherever you want! Why should you be nervous?" Katy asked.

Anna teared up a bit.

"I don't want to fail Egon," she said.

"Nerves just mean you care. Do you know who has failed? The Death Marchers. They have failed before you have even got there. They failed to be kind, compassionate and loving. They failed the people who thought they would save them. AND they failed this war. They WILL fail, Anna. You will make sure they fail," Katy said.

"Any last words of advice?" Anna asked.

"Hmmmm – I guess I would say, remember the weak – the ones who cannot fight back. When you feel scared, or weak yourself, remember that you are their hope. It keeps you going," Katy smiled.

"I want to find Kluck. He sacrificed himself for us – and if he is still out there, I want him back," Anna said.

"I don't know him, but if it was Albert, I would feel how you feel," Katy said.

"I think he is still alive," Anna said.

"That is faith! That may be what the others are clinging to – and waiting for," Katy said.

"I am going to fight for them. Thank you, Katy," Anna said.

"Make sure you get yourself back here!" Katy said.

"You can count on it!" Anna said, hugging her.

Back in the Lab, Sadar was speaking to Egon.

"Zahnea has gone through zero clinical testing," Sadar said. "We consider her strong, but anything could go wrong. Remain alert to anything potentially backfiring."

Egon looked at her inside a transparent tube.

"This will fit on your inside pocket. When the time comes to release her, you simply remove the cap. If you are ready to go, you can take her now, but I just don't want her staying in our warm weather too long. She was adjusted for winter – so are the other hornets from her hive."

Egon took her and put her inside his coat pocket....and then he walked out.

"Thank you, Sadar," Albert said. "I am going to go with the children until they reach the train station. I can't go with them – but I will wait for them there. I don't know how long we will be gone."

"Did the folks from the kitchen load you up?" Sadar asked.

"Would you go ask them to? Egon and I need to go to the Encephalon first, but then we will be taking the Juggerkampf," Albert said.

"Oh yes, Jeet mentioned this will be primarily a water mission," Sadar said.

"Once I get them to the train station, I don't know where they will go. I mean I have an idea, but you know how this goes," Albert said.

"I do indeed, my friend!" Sadar said, hugging him.

Albert had some catching up to do to meet up with Egon, who was already with Jeet.

Jeet put his finger up to ask Albert to quietly stop.

"He is showing Fangs to Molly and Stealth," Jeet whispered.

The Skelekit was apprehensive and hid behind Albert's leg.

"Hey Skelekitty! Come to me," he said, picking her up. She was pleased that another human noticed her!

The dolphin and hammerhead shark pup both gently touched the compass many times.

Molly made tiny vibrations that sounded like a creaking door and then celebrated by going backwards on her tail. Her sounds increased with more trills, grunts, and squeaks. Outside the aquarium, dolphins began calling back. She jumped out of the air and over Egon's arm while he held the compass and out the tunnel she went.

Stealth stayed at the compass for a moment longer and then went out the tunnel to follow Molly. The sounds of the dolphins outside became festive and very loud! Egon walked over to the ladder that previously took him down to the Tintenfisch. Her body was resting until Egon showed her the compass too. That made her body start to swish back and forth.

"MEEEEEEHHHH-OOOOOOO," they heard from the crate nearby.

The little cry baby was anxious to be moved where he could – probably cry some more.

"I guess it is your turn, little one!" Jeet said. "I sure hope this works!"

"We are going to find out!" Albert said.

Jeet lifted the crying Uberghar from the crate and took it out to where her arms were.

"Would you like to do the honours, Egon?" Jeet asked.

Egon took the gharial baby, who was constantly crying, away from Jeet. He hugged it until it settled down. Then, he put its flat snout down to the water and it raced straight for the remaining arm of the Tintenfisch. As soon as it climbed up on top, the Tintenfisch's arms all went stiff and stuck up out of the water. One by one, the arms created an indentation where the Uberghars sunk in and disappeared.

"Did her arms just absorb the babies?" Albert gasped.

"They did! Not in a bad way. They are now protected inside her arms. Look at it like each baby is inside their own personal submarine where they can now go see the ocean from a small window at the tip of her arm," Jeet smiled.

The Tintenfisch began to move out of the aquarium and towards the ocean, slowly at first, then swooshed under the surface and disappeared.

"I can watch her on radar for a bit, but at a certain point, they are on their own," Jeet said.

"How do you know this stuff?" Albert said, amazed.

"I can't cook or sew to save my life. Can you believe that?"

Jeet laughed.

"We all have our talents, I suppose!" Albert laughed back.

Egon wasn't laughing. He looked super intent on leaving – NOW. He ran down the bridge to the exit and out to the beach. The Skelekit jumped clear out of Albert's arms and tore after him.

"I don't hear the dolphins anymore. Has Molly left?" Albert asked.

"Oh yes, her entire pod is gone. Stealth went with them," Jeet said.

Out on the beach, a loud tubular bell rang above the Elephant Den. There was Mita hanging on a rope ringing it. After a half dozen rings, the Opera Drones assembled on the beach.

"Katy said we are their hope," Anna said to Albert.

"She is right! You ARE their hope – but you are NOT responsible for how it is received or if it simply doesn't work. There are people out there doing nothing. Be content that you are doing something. If things don't work out, feel good with your full effort. Give all of yourself – so that later you can say, I gave my full self," Albert said.

"I will give my full self, Mr. Albert. I don't know what that means yet," she said.

"Isn't that beautiful?" Albert asked.

"How so?" she asked.

"The fire in your belly!" he said.

"I might throw up," she laughed.

"You are Anna! You were made for this!" Albert said.

Egon looked at Anna's work belt and then looked in his own pockets.

"I think Anna has the right idea on these adventures. We must come up with something more effective than pockets," Albert said.

"I really wanted a superhero outfit! My chair did carry a lot last time!" Katy said.

"Yes! You had sick animals, flashlights - and I believe seahorses at one point?" Albert laughed.

"Sea horses?" Anna said.

"Oh no, I passed them off to a kangaroo – who knows where he went with those!" Katy laughed.

"Kangaroo? Running around New York?" Anna asked. "Is New York beautiful?"

"**It used to be beautiful once**!" Albert said.

While they were carrying on, Egon was already inside the Juggerkampf.

"My ride!" Anna said. "Gotta go! Wish us luck!"

"I will get you to the train station," Albert said.

"Who told you we can't back that thing up?" Anna laughed.

Albert saw Ian standing at the door of the Elephant Entrance.

He had both the Border Collies on either side of him. When he sat down on the step, so did they.

“Angels,” Albert said to Katy. “Do you miss it?”

“The adventure?” Katy said.

“Yes,” Albert said.

“Yes and no,” she said. “I think about it fondly, but I don’t miss Jackal House.”

“I don’t think Ian does either,” Albert said, looking at him. “I don’t think that place bothered him the same way. I think the sheer amount of incoming information is what overwhelms him. He knows this isn’t done. I think he is perpetually tortured by it not being done.”

Ian didn’t wait to see them off. He went back in and the dogs followed.

“Mita will keep him calm,” Albert said. “Love you, Serinetta. Be back soon!” Albert said, kissing her forehead.

He hurried to join Anna and Egon in the Juggerkampf. Anna was there to help him in.

“I will bake Kluck a cake if he can get inside this thing without assistance. There is no way!” Albert laughed.

“Hey here comes Frecher!” Anna pointed.

He was running as fast as he could to catch up...and up and in he went!

“Alright, let me back this up!” Albert said.

"How do you know how to do that?" Anna asked.

"1914-1918 taught me fifty years' worth of lessons, my dear!" Albert said.

"I bet it did! We just read about it in books," Anna said.

Frecher perched on Albert's leg.

"Frecher belongs to Kluck. I think he wants to find him too!" Anna laughed.

"It's good to have a wee friend again. I had a little capuchin monkey in New York," Albert said.

"What happened to him?" Anna asked.

"His name was White Cap. It's a classic love story, really. He fell for a girl monkey named Sapajou and ran off with her," he laughed.

"That is funny!" Anna giggled. "And such a monkey thing to do!"

"And such a White Cap thing to do!" he smiled.

"Frecher's coat has been turning brown in the heat. I wonder if it will go white again when we are back in Germany," Anna said. "Germany. It's going to be hard to be there after being at Jagannatha."

"You brought lots of warm clothes?" Albert asked.

"Yes, Katy really prepared me," she said.

"Pop your head out and see if the lyrebird is there," Albert said.

"Oh I see it!" Anna said. "It is stretching its beautiful tail!"

"Oh isn't it lovely? Transparent with those salmon-pink edges! Gorgeous!" Albert smiled.

The lyrebird made the same creaking door noise that Molly made.

"Was that a dolphin?" Albert asked.

"I saw the noise come straight out of its mouth!" Anna said.

"Fantastic!" Albert smiled.

The Juggerkampf moved through the foggy forest and up to the silo, split open and waiting for them...and the big tracks slowly moved through.

"Are you ready?" Albert asked.

Egon was sitting quietly, and Anna was still perched up top.

"I see the Forgotten Farm again. Wow is it ever cold!" she said, bundling her jacket up and closing the hatch.

"Just settle in and center yourselves until we get to the train station," Albert said. "You are in for a very long evening - and possibly night ahead of you!"

The Juggerkampf moved down the field, through the farm and stopped at the exit of the Base where Zimmermann greeted them.

"That's Zipper Man. He helped us before!" Anna said.

"Well hello again," Zimmermann said to Anna up top. "You have someone with you to back it up?" he laughed.

"As a matter of fact – we do!" she smiled back.

He opened the gate for them to pass through.

"Thank you for everything, Mr. Zipper Man!" she waved, and he just shook his head at her and closed the gate.

"That was ridiculously easy!" Albert said.

"Yeah, I am pretty connected!" Anna said.

"Alright, we are on open road for a while until we reach the train station. There is food if you want to eat – or you can just rest for a while," Albert said.

Anna grabbed a peanut butter and jelly sandwich from the food box and Egon didn't want anything. They stayed quiet until they arrived.

"So, the train station is just ahead, but I think we need to park somewhere this is hidden. It will be your job to get back here once Egon is ready to come back, ok Anna?" Albert said.

"Are you going to drive it around to kill time?" Anna asked.

"Oh, I can sleep for a whole day, if you let me!" Albert laughed.

"Alright! What are you doing Frecher?" Anna smiled.

Frecher jumped up onto her shoulder.

"Well, that is decided then!" Albert said.

Egon jumped out and the Skelekit followed him. He checked on Zahnea in her tube in his coat and then started walking towards the station.

"Wait for us!" Anna called, as Frecher held on tightly.

"Get yourselves back here!" Albert said, sharply.

"Thank you, Mr. Albert," she yelled, as Albert waved.

The train station was still busy from the holidays. Lots of people were coming and going. Egon looked at the spot he left Rosa and her dog Eisbär.

"Where do we go?" Anna asked. "What does Fangs say?"

Fangs took a minute to adjust to the cold – or to the fact that he was dead and running a compass. He eventually stabilized on a direction and Egon started going that way.

"Here we go, Frecher!" Anna said.

Fangs brought them to a bench near the ticket area.

"I can't let this year end without telling you how I feel," Henry said, sitting on the bench with Miss Kraus.

"Egon! There he is!" Miss Kraus jumped up and hugged him.

"Oh! And Anna is with him!" Henry said.

"So happy to meet you!" Miss Kraus said, hugging Anna.

Anna smiled, loving her hug instantly.

"Henry, what are you doing here?" Anna asked.

"Swartz told me to come get Egon. I asked Miss Kraus here to come along and surprise him!"

"Do you think that is a good idea after everything that has happened?" Anna said.

"He is ashamed, Anna. He is ever so ashamed," Henry said.

"Do we go Egon?" Anna asked.

Egon looked down at Fangs, who was pointed right at Henry.

"Looks like we do!" Anna said.

"I think about you every day," Miss Kraus said to Egon, as she put her arm around him as they walked.

Egon was distracted as he saw Düster flying overhead. He landed on the stone eagle that was still there and gathering snow.

"Did you give her a poem?" Anna whispered to Henry.

"I have tried a hundred times! Mrs. Winter is staying at her place, so I have been there," he said. "The timing is never right, or I lose my nerve."

"You need to do this, Henry!" she scolded.

"I will! I will!" he laughed.

"This is our train," Henry said.

"WAIT! I have money from the magpies!" Anna said, reaching in her belt.

"Oh we can get it, Sweetheart!" Miss Kraus said.

"No, I can pay! This is mission money!" Anna said.

"Well, I don't know what that means, but alright!" Miss Kraus smiled.

"Frecher! Get inside my coat!" Anna warned, and Frecher agreed. "The Lokführer might kick you off!"

"Where are we heading?" Miss Kraus asked Henry.

"I have an address – I honestly don't know. We just get off here," he said, showing her the paper.

"I don't know it," Miss Kraus said.

Fangs was pointed in the direction the train was going and Egon watched Düster preening himself on top of the stone eagle. He set his head on the glass and waited until they arrived. Along the way, he saw a quick glimpse of the bison in the snow again. He closed his eyes and just waited it out.

The train ride was long, and it was getting dark.

"Candy bars?" Miss Kraus offered.

Egon didn't want it, but Anna sure did!

"Thank you!" she said, loving this lady more and more.

"Well, this is our stop, everyone," Henry said, as they exited the train. "I see Swartz waiting. Let me go talk to him first. You all wait here."

"Thank you, Henry," Swartz said, shaking his hand. "Looks like the timing worked out. Who is the girl?"

"Anna Schmidt. She is a friend of Egon's," Henry said.

"Egon's father is here, Henry," Swartz said.

"Is that who sent for him?" Henry asked, realizing he made an incredible error.

"It is," Swartz said.

"You said yourself that he was a horrible father," he whispered. "Let us leave... look the other way, General. I beg you."

"I can't do that," Swartz said. "You need to take the woman and child and just get back on the train now."

"Sir, General, please. I trusted that you had Egon's best interest at heart," Henry pleaded.

"Henry, turn around and go now," Swartz warned as his soldiers stepped forward.

"Alright," Henry conceded, knowing he was outmatched.

"Thank you as always," Swartz said. "I know Egon likes you and trusts you. Your job is done now."

"Thank you, General," Henry said. "Egon, you need to go with General Swartz now."

Miss Kraus leaned into him.

"What are you doing?" she scolded.

"Look what I am up against!" Henry snapped back.

The soldiers came on either side of Egon. He looked down at

his compass and it was pointing towards the entrance...so, he started walking that way.

"That's it?" Anna snapped. "That is our journey?"

"Our train left," Henry shouted out. "We'll have to catch the next."

He ushered Anna and Miss Kraus over to a bench to wait.

"It's good to see you again, Egon. Do you still have your flashlight?" Swartz asked.

Egon reached in his coat and pulled it out, trying to hide his compass.

"A boy and his flashlight," Swartz smiled, as though that was the only tool Egon knew about.

"Herr Wolff is here, Sir," Swartz said, bringing Egon into a living room where Kurt Wolff was sitting behind a desk.

"Please, have a seat," he said formally. "That is all, Swartz."

"Very good, Sir," Swartz said, closing the door as he left.

Egon preferred to stand.

"I asked you to sit," General Wolff said, so Egon did. "I felt like we needed to clear the air – without Kluck and his wolves. We are at war, son. I have tremendous responsibilities. I am making decisions quickly. I cannot be distracted by parenting. Therefore, I have asked Swartz to consistently track you down – to hide you from danger – to keep you protected. You understand? But you cannot live with me. People simply – how do I say – don't know about you. Your mother was not my wife. I am a highly respected General. If word got out – let's just say word cannot get out. Even if I cannot love you in the conventional father way, you should know the highest form of love is protection. I can do this for you. I know you cannot speak to respond. This works a bit in my favour – so I can tell you things which you then cannot repeat. It is important for you to know what is happening in the Fatherland. I need to begin to show you the harsh reality of our future. I need you to see who the enemies are and who the traitors are. You are still a Wolff. You still must know."

Egon reached inside his pocket and pulled out his Waffen SS tag and he handed it to him.

"Where did you get this?" General Wolff said, shocked. "You can't answer me. I will get to the bottom of that. I was just a boy. You can keep it."

Egon looked at it and put it back in his coat.

"Well, that is a good sign you want to have it. I think it is time for you to come see some reality and consequences now," Kurt said, guiding him out of the room.

General Wolff took him outside and the cold air smelled of a fire burning.

"You saw me at my home. You didn't get to see me at work," he said, sternly.

The whole area had barbed wire and fences with lightning bolts on them.

"Don't touch those, you will get electrocuted," he warned.

They walked past several wood cabins with no windows, but he saw small holes where eyeballs were looking out. Anyone in there would be freezing for sure. Then they heard some quiet whimpering and moaning, and the General slammed a nightstick on the door and yelled "SILENCE!" which did, in fact, silence them efficiently.

They entered a small cabin-style building that had people in beekeeper suits.

"Just stay back here at the door. The Professor will come and explain what we are doing here," Kurt said.

"Egon, good to see you again!" a familiar voice said.

It was Professor Wissen who visited Eugen and Irene's farm.

"Did you know Eugen and Irene stole the Queen that I showed you?" he lied. "We shut the farm down. I let the General here know it wasn't your fault. I did, however brag about your knowledge of hornets and he suggested you come work with me here! What do you think about that?"

Egon held his coat closed so nobody would see his compass or Zahnea in the tube inside his pocket.

"I think a bee suit for the boy. We are dealing with some dangerous environments here," Wissen suggested.

"Whatever you need to do," Wolff said. "I must go now. I trust he will be of good use to you."

"Oh, I am certain of it," Wissen agreed.

"Alright, the challenge will be to find a smaller suit!" Wissen laughed. "Come with me!"

Meanwhile, Henry, Miss Kraus and Anna were sitting on the bench trying to figure out how to get Egon out of there.

"Henry – uh – is that Blackguard? The wolf from Festung Wolff?" Anna asked.

"It is," Henry said, surprised.

"I think we should follow him – doesn't it seem like we should?" Anna asked.

"I don't have a better plan," Henry snickered.

Blackguard took them to the back of the cabins. The fencing was high and had skull and cross bones on it.

"Nobody touch that," Henry warned.

"Certainly not," Miss Kraus agreed.

Blackguard sniffed under the snow and when they cleared it away, he showed them where he began to dig under the fence.

"We would have to really dig it out to get in," Henry said. "The ground is frozen."

"Maybe Frecher could go in and report back?" Anna said.

"Does he speak to you?" Miss Kraus laughed.

"Well, no... but he is super quick and may alert someone. If nothing happens, we know it is clear," she said.

"Where did he go?" Henry asked, catching the black tip of his snowy tail disappearing into the hole.

"He is way ahead of us! Let's see what happens," Anna said...and they waited.

"Hey," a young voice whispered. "Is that your weasel?"

"Did you hear that?" Anna said with her ear pinned.

"No, what did you hear?" Miss Kraus asked.

"Frecher!" the voice whispered.

"That is Kluck! He is here! Frecher must have smelled him!" Anna said.

"Now what do we do?" Miss Kraus asked.

"Even if Blackguard dug a deeper hole, he is too tall to get out...and it is too risky," Anna said.

"Do you suppose *they* could help?" Henry pointed into the woods.

White wolves.

"From the Festung Wolff," Anna said. "They must really hate that guy!"

"Egon's father?" Henry laughed.

"Yes, maybe he is a disgrace to their name!" she smiled.

Egon's beekeeper suit was miles too big on him and his glasses kept fogging up.

"You look smashing!" Professor Wissen said. "Would you like to meet the Queen? It goes easier if she likes you."

Egon walked over to the main hive and looked in. The Queen was sitting in the middle and the workers were busy around her.

"After speaking with you at the farm, I made some modifications. It was easier to start with a new Queen anyways. She will be flying tonight. Nighttime is better. I am thrilled you are here. I need an assistant!"

Blackguard dug a hole big enough for Anna to get in, and she squeezed through. It was a bit trickier for her with her leg braces, but she did it brilliantly. She ended up in a cabin with Kluck, Eugen and Irene.

"Anna Nowak! Look at you!" Kluck whispered.

"Look at me getting up like a stiff tin man?" she said.

"I thought you were going to invent better ones!" Kluck joked.

"Yes, well, I am busy saving the world right now!" she said.

"I am teasing you!" he said. "Are you wearing a toolbelt?"

"Yes, I spoke with Katy at great length about her mission and she said I would need it to improve the process," Anna said, matter-of-factly.

"Katy? Where did you see her?" Kluck asked.

"Who is this?" Eugen asked.

"A friend of mine," Kluck said.

"Jagannatha... Egon and I drove the tank there," she said. "We went through the Forgotten Farm and -"

"On the back of our farm," Irene said.

"I missed it!" Kluck said, disappointed.

"Well, you are kind of busy, right?" Anna smiled. "Why are the three of you in here?"

"General Wolff is housing anyone who was involved with his son here. He doesn't want another incident like the white wolves at the Festung Wolff," Kluck said. "He is going mad, Anna."

"I worked for him for a short time – he went mad ages ago," Anna said.

"And what process are you improving with this belt?" Kluck asked.

"Superheroing," Anna said. "Or superheroin-ing – is that a thing?" Anna said.

"It certainly is!" Kluck said. "But Anna, who are you here with?"

"Henry and Miss Kraus – Egon is inside - with General Wolff," Anna said. "What is this place?"

"Think of it as a jail in the woods," Kluck said, petting Frecher.

"It is the main place Wolff comes to meet with his scientists," Eugen says. "Sometimes, we hear the hornet's buzzing. It is such an odd sound for winter."

"How many people are jailed here?" Anna asked.

"I am guessing a lot," Irene inserted. "The Scientists require people to experiment on. I believe that is our fate too."

"Not today," she said. "So you mentioned the white wolves? They are here. Blackguard is on the other side of this hole with Henry and Miss Kraus."

Back at the beehive, Wissen was speaking to Egon.

"We have test subjects quarantined. They are not from the Fatherland. If they can understand this, they can handle any enemy that comes our way," Wissen explained. "Just keep your suit on!"

Dr. Wissen transported the main hive in a cart outside and wheeled it to a nearby building. Egon was struggling to get a hold of Zahnea's tube inside his coat while wearing this heavy suit.

"Can you unlock the door for me?" Wissen said, handing him the key.

Egon unlocked the door and held it open for him as he wheeled the hive in. It was a dilapidated building and smelled like prisoners were there for a long time.

They walked down the hall and Wissen announced, "Second door on the left."

Egon showed him the key and he nodded. He put the key in the lock and opened the door. What he saw was horrifying. There were at least two dozen children laying on cold cement shivering. Egon hid his face when he caught a glimpse of Rita among them. Wissen wheeled the cart in and asked Egon to close the door behind them.

The children looked as though they had been shocked and frozen into a nervous state. None of them moved, unless trying to disappear into the wall or floor was movement.

"So, here is what will happen," Wissen whispered to Egon. "As soon as the Queen is threatened, they will attack. We can't be in here when it happens. We want to get them to a place where they don't attack us. But that isn't today. Today, we see if the mass attacks provide the effects we are looking for."

Egon walked boldly up to the hive and looked at Wissen.

"I was hoping you would volunteer," he said, like the complete chicken he was, and he stepped outside the door. "You are German, son. They *shouldn't* touch you."

That wasn't comforting.

The Skelekit sat loyally at his feet. She wasn't going to abandon him in this moment, even though a bee sting of any potency was not a threat to her.

"What do you all have in that work belt," Kluck asked Anna. "Anything to unlock a door?"

"This boy Richard who works the docks at Jagannatha taught me to pick a lock!" Anna smiled.

"There is no better skill to acquire!" Kluck said, but then looked to the hole in the ground which was getting bigger. "Digging frozen ground is noble too!"

"I feel useless out here," Henry said. "If we do get them out, then what?"

“I’ll stay here, you go see if you can find a vehicle,” Miss Kraus said.

“Good idea,” Henry said.

“Oh and Henry,” she said.

“Yes?”

“Be careful!” she said. “It’s New Year’s Eve tomorrow – and I don’t want to spend it alone,” she smiled.

“You got it!” he said, now with an extra bounce in his step.

Frecher hugged Kluck tightly when he saw a wolf snout emerge from the hole. It was a small white wolf who looked at them and then began digging on the inside of the wall. The same intensity of digging was happening on the other side. As dirt was flying on Anna while she was picking the lock, Kluck was laughing at her.

“I am trying to save the day here, do you mind?” she snipped at them.

“Frozen ground can take some time,” he said.

Once the hole was done, the whole pack poured into their cabin. It was the same white wolf pack from Festung Wolff, and Blackguard was the last one.

“I got it!” Anna said. “We need a plan, though.”

“I think he is our plan,” Kluck pointed.

“Oh – Blackguard! Good!” she said, and then stuck her head into the hole.

"Miss Kraus? Henry? Are you still there?" Anna whispered.

"I am here," Miss Kraus said. "Henry is looking for a vehicle."

"Our getaway car!" Anna laughed. "Yes, alright – good!"

Egon had his back to Wissen and glanced at him. Then he found an opening in his beekeeper suit and pulled out the tube with Zahnea in it.

"Don't be too hesitant, that is only a small portion of her hive. We lost a lot through experimentation. And they are out there - somewhere," Wissen laughed.

When Egon took Zahnea out, she began to glow, so he had to keep he covered as she entered the hive. As soon as she did, there was an instant battle between her and the replacement Queen.

"What's going on?" Wissen said. "Uh – I will be back here!"

Zahnea darted for the Queen and they tussled into a fury. The whole hive began buzzing in a frenzy and swarmed the room. The children began screaming and covering their heads. Egon did his best to keep them away from the children, but the hive was confused by mixed messaging.

Once Anna had the door unlocked, Blackguard and the wolves strayed out into the open. Most of the guards were either sleeping at their post, or killing time chatting with others. It was a chore just to stay warm, so most of the soldiers were bundled up to avoid the increasingly heavy blowing snow.

Blackguard approached the closest group that was guarding the cabins and he bared teeth. One guard took out his gun and shot – which did the same thing as it did at the Festung Wolff – nothing. The shot however alerted everyone. The white wolves poured out of the cabin and circled Blackguard giving Kluck, Irene and Eugen a chance to run out of the cabin with Anna not far behind.

Finally, Zahnea emerged the winner and claimed her spot in the middle of the hive. Her orange glow radiated throughout the room and the hive was still taking time to settle back down.

"Why is it orange in there? What went wrong?" Wissen said from his safe spot in the hall. "Once they settle, we need to go back to the drawing board. Knock on the door once they are all in," Wissen said.

After the hornets had settled in, Egon gently took Zahnea's empty tube and scooped one of the hornets into it. Then he showed his face to Rita.

"Charlotte," Rita whispered. "That is Egon!"

Egon motioned for them to be quiet by raising his finger up to his facemask. He closed the hive and knocked on the door. When Wissen opened it, Egon wheeled the cart out and Wissen stood way back down the hall. Once he left the room, Egon released the hornet from the tube, and it buzzed around Wissen's head which sent him running.

Egon pointed to the children and Charlotte and Rita took charge of getting the others out.

"Edward! Mia! Julia! Illia! Ivan! Philip! Go! Go! GOOOO!" they said, and the children ran outside.

Egon was tripping over his long beekeeper suit as he pushed

the bee cart through the heavy snow.

The wolves each picked a guard and cornered them until Kluck, Irene, Eugen and Anna could escape. General Wolff came running out yelling.

“Guards! Don’t let them leave!”

Egon was pushing the cart behind the children, and Swartz was waiting at the exit.

“Go now!” he said.

“Swartz?” Kluck said.

“Before I change my mind!” he said, pushing them through.

“I see Henry in the truck!” Kluck yelled. “Go children,” he said. “Get in the back!

Henry and Miss Kraus had commandeered a big cargo truck and the children jumped in the back. Eugen and Irene lifted the bee cart in and then assisted Egon.

“Your Christmas holidays are a nightmare, Wolff!” Kluck yelled to Kurt, as Blackguard, once again, had him pinned against a wall.

“You won’t get far!” General Wolff yelled back.

“Thank you for believing in your boy! There is hope for you yet!” Kluck laughed and jumped in the back of the truck.

Henry put his foot on the gas and trudged through the blowing snow. Guards ran out shooting at them.

All but one child didn't make it into the truck before it left, and she was left running into the bushes.

Egon was digging through his beekeeper outfit frantically to find Fangs who was pointing in the direction Henry was driving. Egon slunk back against the side of the truck.

"You saved us, Egon!" Charlotte said, putting her arm around him and kissing his face. He sat back and watched her for the rest of the ride. He hadn't taken an interest in girls up until meeting her, but she seemed to be his everything.

18 THE NINE BRAINS OF THE OCTOPUS

"They were shooting at us," Mia said.

"Better than staying there!" Julia said.

"Sometimes, you need to just go for it. Being on the run is better than giving up," Anna said.

The truck did well with a load full of children to get through the heavy snow, until Henry started to struggle with it.

"Is it out of gas?" Miss Kraus asked from the seat beside him.

"I think a tire was hit by a bullet," Henry said, pulling it over. "I can't get through the snow with it like that."

"Then we get out and start walking," she said. "We aren't far from the next train stop, and they will be looking for this truck."

"We don't even know where we are going to take these children. Let me get out and talk to Kluck. We need a plan," Henry said, getting out and opening the back.

"What happened?" Kluck said.

"They blew the tire out...may I speak with you?" Henry said.

Kluck jumped out of the back and closed the door so the children would stay warm.

"The children are not dressed for it, but we need to walk to the next train stop. I don't see another option. They will be coming for us," Henry suggested.

"It's sure death or possible death," Kluck warned. "We need to walk. The children, if given the choice of going back to that Hell or walk to potential freedom, will choose to walk."

"The good news is the snow works in our favour to cover the tracks," Henry said.

"Then it's settled. I saw some soldier overcoats and tarps in the back. Let's see how much we can bundle them up and we'll head out on foot," Kluck said.

Henry put his head in the front door to speak to Miss Kraus.

"Kluck said there is random material. We can improvise and bundle the children as best as we can," Henry said.

"I will help," Miss Kraus said, jumping out.

Charlotte, Rita, and Anna were like miniature mothers who took charge to help bundle up the others. Irene and Eugen helped a bit, but they were still emotionally despondent from what happened.

"Is this a tarp?" Mia asked as Anna wrapped it around her.

"It is the latest in German fashion!" Anna joked.

"You look dazzling!" Rita laughed as Mia spun around.

Egon stood there with his full beekeeper outfit on, headgear and all, standing beside the bee cart. The bottoms of his pants were accumulating ice and snow, making it heavy as he walked around the truck, but he was certainly ready for the elements.

"If I could only snap a picture of you all!" Charlotte laughed. "Egon the beekeeper and his war gang of drifters! What a sight we are!"

"That's the spirit, Charlotte! Keep your humour about you!" Kluck said. "Keep tightly knit and walk quietly. We don't want to bring attention to ourselves."

They stayed close to one another as they walked in the bushes close to the train tracks. Some held hands, while others interlocked their arms. Egon walked much faster ahead, dragging the beehive inside the cart, and kept a close eye on Fangs.

"Could we sing something?" Rita said, after many minutes of walking.

"If it isn't too loud," Kluck said. "I would love to hear something."

"What about our name-game?" Charlotte said.

"What is that?" Anna asked.

"We made it up to pass the time," Charlotte said. "My name's Charlotte – starts with C. I have a friend who starts with E."

"My name's Edmund. I like pie. I have a friend who starts with

I," Edmund added.

"My name's Ivan, I laugh all day...I have a friend who starts with J!" Ivan laughed.

"My name's Julia, I love to read.... I have a friend who starts with P!" Julia said.

"My name's Philip, taller than them... I have a friend who starts with M!" Philip said.

"My name's Mia, I love to play! I have a friend who starts with A!" Mia pointed at Anna.

"My name's Anna..." and she paused. "...gave my tears to the sea..."

All the children looked at her and were quietly listening.

"I have a great friend. Starts with E," she added.

Everyone looked to Egon who was marching ahead, snow crunching under his feet. When it went silent, he stopped and so did they. He turned around and looked at them all through his beekeeper mask.

"His name is Egon," Charlotte said, interrupting the silence. "A hero --- and a friend," she said, tearing up. "This rhyme ...and this war ...must come to an end."

Egon looked at them all, then turned and resumed walking, dragging the bee cart behind him.

It was quiet after that.

After many minutes of stomping through deep snow, Egon

noticed Fangs was pointing left. The visibility was poor, but he saw a small train station along the way and began walking toward it.

"I am just happy to sit for a minute," Anna said. "Anywhere would be fine!"

"My bones agree!" Kluck said, with Frecher deep in his coat.

"Let me check the schedule," Henry said, going inside the station.

The children all huddled together on a bench and stayed quiet. Miss Kraus cycled through them, adjusting their coats to keep them warm. Irene and Eugen kept to themselves.

"Fifteen minutes – a train will be passing through," Henry announced. "Listen, I know it is bitter cold out here, but there are a few people staying warm inside who we probably don't want to alert."

"I am fine!" Anna said.

"Me too," Charlotte said. "We are NOT going back."

"Yes," Philip said. "No matter what!"

"Here is a mint candy for you all," Miss Kraus said.

"Oh," Rita said, holding it in her mouth. "It tastes like heaven!"

They all sat content, and nobody complained.

When the train's light came barreling in the direction of the station, Kluck stood up to speak to them.

"If we encounter anyone, let me do the talking. I keep this horrible hat on my head to get me through most uncomfortable scenarios," he said.

Miss Kraus kept them in single file as they boarded, while Henry helped Egon with the bee cart. Kluck went last.

"Odd group of children, Feldmarschall," a lower ranking Death Marcher said.

"Who would like to know?" Kluck said, pulling rank.

"Not my business, Feldmarschall. Just making conversation," he said.

"Good night to you, soldier," Kluck said, joining the children.

"Good night, Feldmarschall," he replied.

"That hat is disgusting – and very handy!" Anna laughed.

"I am surprised one of the Opera Drones haven't scooped it off my head by now!" he laughed.

"I met them today. They followed the Juggerkampf here," Anna said.

"You really went ahead without me!" Kluck smiled. "Is there anything left for me to do? Or do you have it all sorted?"

"You have a lot to catch up on. Try to keep up!" Anna smiled back.

As the train pulled in, Kluck looked at Egon's compass and asked the children to huddle in close to him.

"This is the end of the line for some of us," Kluck began. "Egon and Anna are staying on the train."

"By themselves?" Charlotte asked.

"Well, with Frecher and the Skelekitty," he smiled.

"The whattakitty?" Philip asked.

Frecher gave a "who, me?" look up on his hind legs.

"Oh! Hmmmm, you don't see him. It's Egon's little, uh – friend," Kluck said.

"Oh yes – his *friend*," Rita said, looking around. "I see!"

"Maybe like an angel, Rita," Charlotte added.

"Kind of like that," Kluck agreed. "And yes, Frecher – you are heading out with Egon and Anna."

Frecher jumped into Anna's lap and curled up like a croissant.

"How will Egon get away with looking like a beekeeper child on a train? There is no story that can fix that!" Rita chimed in.

"I am getting good at creative story-telling," Anna smiled at Kluck.

"This is their mission now, children," Kluck says.

Anna leaned in to whisper to Kluck.

"The Juggerkampf is parked in the bushes back behind those buildings. Albert is in it waiting for us."

"Then you better do your work and get back to him as

promised!" Kluck said.

"And back to you," Anna said.

"Yes, come back to me, Anna," he said hugging her.

"He said he was going to nap!" she giggled.

"NAP! Oh, we'll wake him up!" Kluck laughed.

Everyone else exited the train and Anna changed seats and sat close to Egon. Henry put his hand on Anna's shoulder.

"I am ever so proud of you!" he said with a big smile. Then he leaned into her ear to whisper, "Klein is the Captain, Prentzel is the Admiral and Ben could be of assistance to you at the Aquarium. Fire off a few of those names if you need names. Alright?"

"Thank you, Henry," she said, hugging him. "You know where we are headed?"

"I have done this route plenty of times," he smiled, and stepped off.

"You have money?" Kluck asked from outside the train.

"We do," Anna said, taking a deep breath.

"What about courage?" Kluck asked.

"Do I have time to assemble that?" Anna laughed.

"A few minutes," he laughed. "Sometimes we get hurled into situations without it – and we do just fine."

"I am going with or without it!" Anna said.

"That is courage!" he smiled and waved to her as the doors closed.

Kluck stood for a moment watching the train leave while the group waited for his instructions. It was dangerous for him to be caught up in his thoughts for so long, but the enormity of the situation suddenly affected him.

"Kluck, we should go," Henry said. "KLUCK!"

"We need your guidance, General," Miss Kraus added.

"Yes! Indeed. Henry, do you have a vehicle?" Kluck asked.

"My car is here, in the train station parking lot," Henry responded.

"Eugen and Irene are viewed as traitors. They will be shot on sight. You may be too, for that matter. Can you drive them somewhere safe?"

"Mrs. Winter is at my place," Miss Kraus said. "Nobody has me tied to any of this except Swartz – and he let us go. Eugen and Irene can come there."

"Get going then," Kluck said. "Thank you, Henry."

"What about the children?" Miss Kraus said.

"Let me think," Kluck said. "How many can you take with you?"

"One can ride in the front between us, two would fit comfortably between Eugen and Irene," Henry said.

"Someone can sit on my lap, plus a couple on Eugen and

Irene's lap," Miss Kraus said.

"Great, if I take eight with me, that will cover everyone," Kluck said.

"Do you need help?" Henry asked.

"Charlotte, Rita, Edward, Mia, Julia, Ivan, Illia, Philip – come with me!" Kluck said, and they took off on foot.

"Alright children," Henry said to the remaining six. "This way!"

Miss Kraus helped Eugen and Irene along. They were frozen with fear.

Kluck and the children didn't take long to get to the Juggerkampf which was well-hidden except for the elephant trunk on the front which Kluck recognized.

"Wait here for a moment," he said, climbing up to the hatch.

It was open. He knew this machine intimately and so he also knew how to get in. Ever so quietly, he tip-toed over to Albert who was napping with the pillows and blankets Zimmermann provided for Egon.

"ATTENTION!" he said sternly, which scared Albert half to death.

"KLUCK! You're alive!" Albert said, rubbing his eyes and jumping up to his feet. "And still brutal!"

"That's more than I can say for you, old man! Napping while we are at war. Must be nice!" Kluck joked.

"I see you are still as grumpy as ever!" Albert laughed.

"I see you are still in love with sleeping!" Kluck joked.

"Are you jealous?" Albert said.

"I kind of am!" Kluck laughed. "I am bringing the children in."

"How long was I sleeping? They are all done?" Albert asked.

"It is the Grunewald children. Egon and Anna just left for the Sea Urchin," he whispered, guiding each child in.

"Come in children!" Albert said, greeting them. "I have food and blankets. Kluck made this thing the size of a house – plenty of room!"

"How does it drive?" Kluck asked.

"Beautifully. Everyone should have one for winter driving!" he joked. "So what happened with the hornet?"

"He has the whole hive with him on the train with Anna," Kluck said.

"It's heart-breaking they must go alone," Albert said. "Ian and Katy's mission was the longest night of my life."

"You napped through it," Kluck said.

"You don't know that," he laughed.

The children were thrilled to see all the food Albert had. Some of it, they didn't recognize.

"Some of those pastries were made by a little girl like you named Mita," Albert said.

"Mita bakes heavenly cookies," Edmund said.

"So, did the hornet get swapped out?" Albert asked.

"From what I can tell, but I was only with him for a short time," Kluck said. "I guess we wait."

The children couldn't decide if they were more tired or hungry. It was that brutal of an experience. They all curled in next to one another and didn't say much else.

"Have the children talked to you yet about what happened to them?" Albert whispered to Kluck.

"They are surprisingly in good spirits, but it may hit them later," Kluck said.

"And what about you?" Albert asked.

"It's heavy," Kluck said. "I will feel better when tonight is over. How are Ian and Katy?"

"Katy talks about her feelings quite a bit with me. She is on a good path to healing. Ian is not content. He is restless and doesn't sleep well."

"It took me years to rest," Kluck said. "When you see certain things nobody else sees, it becomes a burden you cannot shake. The children with our same burdens are too young to manage them."

"Ian never celebrates small victories," Albert said.

"Is he looking for the big one?" Kluck asked.

"No, these children don't think that way. They have jobs to

do...the jobs aren't done, so they remain unsettled," Albert said.

"I agree. Egon will remain unsettled too," Kluck said.

"And so we wait!" Albert said.

"And so we nap!" Kluck added.

"And so we nap," Albert agreed, and they settled in with the children.

Back on the train, a middle-aged German couple was gossiping about Egon and Anna.

"I wish you could tell me about this hornet's nest," Anna whispered to Egon. "People are looking at us funny. Hey! Watch this!"

Anna sat up tall and crossed her legs. Then she put on her best adult voice.

"I guess I have to explain this – yet again – doesn't it get tiring, Egon? All the people staring?" she said rolling her eyes. "You are probably wondering what two children are doing with a buzzing hornet's nest on a train. We are heading to the Lab with them. We take this route all the time."

"But – you are children," the woman said.

"Wunderkind children – isn't that what they call us?" she said looking at Egon. "Yes, something like that. We skipped school and were homeschooled – then straight to work. It's a gift – or whatever they want to call it."

The woman furrowed her brow and stuck her nose back in her

book.

"Yes, that is where your nose belongs," Anna muttered.

"I beg your pardon?" she said.

"Oh I was asking my friend 'where are those three prongs?'" Anna said.

"Prongs?" she said.

"You wouldn't understand. It's over your head," Anna snapped.

She smiled at Egon – and was getting joy out of her 'creative storytelling'. Fortunately, the civilians had all left the train a few stops in. Unfortunately, the train started filling up with Kriegsmarine workers heading to their base - and that story was just practice.

Egon stared at Fangs the whole route. He remained pinned in the direction the train was going.

"We just have to act like it is totally normal," Anna whispered to Egon. "We are supposed to go there just like they are supposed to go there."

Someone from the Kriegsmarine base walked over and stood beside Anna.

"You must be heading to the Aquarium or Lab," he said calmly, to her surprise.

"Yes, we have work to do at both of those," she said confidently.

"I see a lot of weird people come and go in the science sector," he smiled.

Anna bit her tongue even though she didn't like that they were viewed as "weird".

"Science is weird, Sir," she said, keeping it short.

"So, you have a beekeeper suit on – how does that protect the rest of us?" he said, nodding to Egon.

"He doesn't speak, Sir," Anna interjected. "It doesn't. It is our recommendation that you keep your distance so as not to introduce any new vibrations they are not used to."

That made the man think.

"Oh, probably a good idea," he said, standing on the other side of the train. "It is a bit disgusting that adults now transfer these tasks to children."

"We are happy to do it," she responded, taking a deep breath.

"So who are you working with there?" he asked.

Anna didn't know his name, nor did she know who he knew.

"I don't think that is my place to say, Sir," she said, petting Frecher.

"Well, I will ask you again in five minutes when I take over the shift at the main gate," he smiled.

Five minutes was five minutes...and she took it as a gift.

"You understand, it is top secret. We are mindful of who here has clearance to know," she said, fairly proud of that response.

"Fair enough," he said.

She began quietly reciting the names Henry threw at her as the train slowed to a stop. Fangs took a forty-five degree turn inside the compass and pointed at the doors.

Egon stayed seated while crew left the train.

"We have to exit the train, but after, let's wait a minute until that man takes his post. I already know his personality. I would rather not start again with a new one," she whispered.

When she saw the man switching shifts with another man at the entrance, Anna let Egon know.

"Ok, he is there," she said.

"So, are you ready to answer my questions?" he said.

"Of course, Sir," she said. "We are here to see -"

"I have other questions," he said, throwing her off. "Names?"

Anna scrambled for a moment and then said, "Ian and Katy."

"Ian and Katy who?"

"Ian Klein...Katy Pretzel," she made up on the spot.

"Prentzel?" he questioned.

"Yes, sorry, night air is cold on my throat," she quickly corrected.

"Oh, I see how you got your jobs," he said, disgusted by it.

"The rest of us work for decades and are still at the door."

"I'm sorry, Sir... you must work hard," Anna said, spreading it on thick.

"Head on in," he said.

"Uh, thank you!" she responded, wasting no time. "Come on, Ian!"

Egon quickly pushed the bee cart through, and they stood there while Egon checked his compass.

"Weren't you here before?" Anna asked.

Fangs directed them to a building attached to the Aquarium.

"I guess this will be the Lab – we need to do something with this hornet's nest!" Anna said to Egon. "Ok, a Captain won't run it ...an Admiral won't run it. Henry said Ben was the Aquarium man. I guess I say Ben. That is all I have, Egon."

When they walked into the Lab, Anna asked for Ben.

"Ben is in the Aquarium. You will want Jakob," the security guard said.

"Whoever it is, please tell them Katy Pretzel and Ian Klein need a room to work in," she said as Egon looked down at Fangs pointing to the right.

Egon started walking without permission.

"Oh, thank you – he already knows where he is going. He doesn't speak, so it can get confusing for me. Sorry about that!" she said, following him.

The guard just shrugged and went back to reading his paper.

"Well, that was easy," she laughed, following Egon into a room.

Frecher jumped out of Anna's arms and onto the lab countertops to explore.

"I'm not afraid of bees, I just know very little about them," Anna said, standing way back.

Egon took his book out of his coat and set it on the table. He flipped it to a page with scribbles of lab compounds.

"Is that like a recipe book for scientists?" Anna smiled. "I saw your crocodiles, but I don't understand the rest of it. Is it like your book of ideas – like what poets have?"

The Skelekit jumped onto the table and sat there watching them. Then, she slipped inside Egon's coat pocket and pulled out the plans that Dr. Wissen had. Egon looked at Anna to see if she noticed the Skelekit, and she didn't. So far, only Albert, Kluck, Mita and Ian had acknowledged her.

After looking at the plans Wissen had, and his book of ideas, he began to assemble a workstation of lab utensils. Frecher was a wonderful little helper who seemed to have done things like this before. Certainly, hanging out with General Kluck would have given him many life experiences!

Egon searched through cupboards and drawers to mix the solution he wanted and then he took an eyedropper and sucked up a tube full of it. He walked over to the bee cart and dripped it throughout a beat-up hive **that used to be beautiful once**. The hornets began to buzz which made Anna slightly nervous.

"Are you upsetting them on purpose, Egon?" she asked. "And why the bright orange glow?"

Egon closed the lid as they began buzzing in harmony. He removed his beekeeper mask and rubbed his eyes under his glasses.

"Let me clean those," Anna said, taking them off his face, as Egon removed the rest of his outfit.

"You were sweating under there! You must have been roasting this whole time! I would have passed out!" Anna said. "Now what?"

Fangs was pointing to the door now. The Skelekit returned the plans to him, Egon grabbed his book, and the bee-cart, and walked out.

"Let's go, Frecher!" Anna said. "I think our work begins now!"

Anna held Frecher in her arms and followed Egon to the door of the Sea Urchin. He stood behind the bee cart and looked back at Anna.

"Shall I knock?" she asked. "Alright, I am going to knock."

She was greeted with, "Hello, oh hello, young lady."

It was Ben. When he saw Egon, he said, "Herr Wolff!"

"Uh yes!" Anna chimed in. "Herr Wolff is here."

"Come in! Come in!" he said, looking around, then closing the door behind them.

Egon started down the hall as quickly as possible as the Skelekit and Anna with Frecher followed. He frantically eyeballed the empty aquariums and walked faster.

"Wow, look at this ceiling! Isn't it breathing? Spectacular! Were there supposed to be creatures in these compartments?" Anna asked.

"There were up until an hour ago. Then we got a message to transport everyone – all at once," Ben explained. "Are those bees?" he asked.

"Yes," Anna said.

Egon looked to Fangs for clarity as his brain was churning like a hamster wheel. He ran with the bee cart straight for the Unterghar.

"Oh yes, he is still there," Ben said. "They abandoned him after you left. They said it was broken and would revisit after this next wolfpack mission."

They heard voices in the corridors of the Urchin, and Ben ran out.

"I will head them off, you do what you need to," he said, rushing off.

Egon looked straight at him when he said that and ran down to the entrance of the Unterghar. He tried to drag the bee cart with him and was having a rough time of it.

"You open it, I can get the cart," Anna said, as Frecher jumped on top.

Egon placed his hand on the scales of the Unterghar and opened the door.

"Well, that is the best thing I have seen all day!" Anna said, dragging the cart behind her.

Once inside, Egon grabbed the toolkit where he had found the wire cutters. Then, he went racing back through the radio and sound room, through the officer's quarters and into the torpedo room at the front. He spent a few minutes playing with the mess of wires until the Unterghar inhaled a very deep breath and gently exhaled. He returned to the control room and sat in front of the periscope.

"If this is anything like driving the Juggerkampf, we should be fine, no?" she laughed. "May I look out?" she said.

Egon let her sit in front of it.

"It looks dark. I don't see anything," she said.

Outside, a crowd of men had gathered by the docks as an entourage full of important men showed up. They were all dressed better than everyone else and had the black spider on their red arm band. They were the type of group who were not on the ground fighting but would show up for ribbon-cutting ceremonies and to address large crowds. The security was over-the-top and the main man in the middle was predominantly protected. All the men were similar-looking German figureheads, but this man was tall, dressed in full German war attire with iron cross and power-spider armband...but he was a skeleton. This made it feel more ominous, because it was immediately apparent that the security was for show. Who was going to hurt or kill someone who was clearly already dead?

He walked to the edge of the dock by the Wolfsboot and folded his boney arms across his chest.

"Would you like it to begin, Drillmeister?" Admiral Prentzel said.

"Show me the main wolfpack with their corresponding assistants," he instructed in a monotone voice.

Some of his men were heavily guarding a case.

"Would you like your package taken inside, Drillmeister?" Prentzel asked.

"Were you instructed to do so?" he responded, not even looking at him.

"I was not, Sir," Prentzel said.

"After your demonstration, which I am certain will be perfect, this case needs to go to the Elefanteufel. I trust it was transported here without incident?" the Drillmeister said.

"It was, Drillmeister," Prentzel said.

"I will leave it where it is and await further instruction," Prentzel said.

"Yes, you will," he replied.

Egon looked out the periscope and couldn't see anything either. Nighttime would be tough if they didn't soon find a light source. Egon moved to the controls and managed to get the Unterghar to move slightly.

"Do you suppose I press this button that says 'DOOR'?" Anna asked, but Frecher beat her to it. He pounced right on top of it and they heard a big creaking noise way out in front of them.

"I don't know what that was, Frecher," Anna laughed. "I am guessing any movement right now is good movement!"

Egon wheeled the hornets to the torpedo room and the Skelekit followed.

"Do I drive? Is it anything like the Juggerkampf controls?" Anna asked.

The Skelekit jumped on top of the hive, and Egon returned to the control room.

"I don't even know what you are doing – but this is FANTASTIC!" Anna squealed.

"You will see each Wolfsboot has a beneficial partner," Captain Klein explained to the Drillmeister. "The Sea Pens have grown well over two meters and are stationed in various ports around the base. They are the first to alert incoming boats. The Frilled Shark is extremely sensitive to microscopic activities of prey. It has been programmed to detect specific movement from thousands of miles away. We send it deep into the waters. The Winzig Panzers underwater tank division will pierce thousands of small holes in enemy ships. They won't know they are hit until they find themselves sinking. The Leafy Sea Dragons suck up bits of enemy cells for us to analyze. The Vampire Squid returns the overall data back to us. Each creature was programmed to work with their corresponding boat. They fall under the command of each Wolfsboot Captain."

Not being powered by any motors, the Unterghar moved as the Kriegsmarine intended. They expected him to be silent, and if seen by the enemy, they would not expect a sea creature to be a war machine. He slithered out the door and into the ocean.

"Is it still dark through the periscope?" Anna asked, and she looked through it.

As they moved blindly through the dark waters, Egon caught a small spot of glowing orange in his view. Then, another...and another...and another. Egon showed Anna and then he ran towards the torpedo room.

"My father had a telescope – and we would watch the stars. It looks like that!" Anna said. "Egon? Where did you go?"

She followed him and there was the Skelekit sitting proudly on top of an empty hive.

"How did they get out?" Anna asked, and she ran back to the periscope.

Egon and the Skelekit followed.

"Look out!" she directed him.

The sea was full of hundreds and hundreds of glowing underwater hornets. They were so bright, that it caused a bright orange glow in front of the Unterghar.

"How do you do things like that, Egon?" Anna said in amazement. "So, we can see in front and above? Is that how this works?"

The glowing hornets dispersed through the sea, and it became dark again.

"Where did they go?" Anna said, looking through the scope.

Each of the hornets had transformed since Egon inserted the solution into their hive. They had this lovely orange glow, but they were hyper-focused on a target now. They basically became like Zahnea, complete with fangs in addition to a stinger.

"Enough explaining, get them into the water," the Drillmeister ordered. "We have work to do inside."

He remained on the edge of the dock looking out, while his men had formed a secured circle around this mystery case, and it was obviously the bigger priority.

Just then, the air raid sirens went off on the base.

"Is that part of the drill?" the Drillmeister noted.

"That is real, Sir," Prentzel responded. "Our Frilled Shark has detected an enemy combatant. It is far out yet, but it is on its way here! Klein, deploy the full Untersee Wolfpack and Untersee Winzig Panzer Division. Whatever this enemy is remains unidentifiable right now. We need to be prepared for anything. Make sure the Dragons and Squid accompany them for data collection upon annihilation."

"Nothing like real action to test the technology," the Drillmeister said. "Let's hope you also pass this test."

It wasn't long after the deployment of the Urchin creatures, that the hornets sharpened their focus. The Untersee Winzig

Panzer Division was the first set of targets. Each of them was small – no longer than the Drillmeister's boot, but there were hundreds of them, and their shells were difficult to penetrate. The hornets had to target the soft underbelly if they were going to make an impact. The Panzers also spread out and coupled with the U-boats, and so they had some cover.

The weakness was that each shell still had a creature inside who had wild instincts to protect themselves. The Hornets knew this and could swim circles around them. They began in a wide glowing circle to corral them like a Border Collie with sheep. The goal was to drive each Panzer away from the U-boats. Pockets of Panzers began separating from the wolfpack and would try to hide. There was no hiding from a hornet who had the good fortune of being repeatedly messed up by science. They were fully featured and angry.

Once the Hornets rounded up an adequate number of Panzers, they swooped in and simultaneously stung the underbelly and bit a chunk out. After a hornet did their job, their orange light burned out ...and they sunk.

The Panzers did not sink but began turning on the Wolfpack of U-boats. They put hundreds of holes into them, and the boats began filling with water.

Anna and Egon watched as much as they could see through the scope, but Fangs was redirecting their route.

"I am glad for your spider, Egon," Anna said. "I don't know how we would know what to do next!"

The Unterghar wasn't interested in sticking around for the Wolfpack catastrophe that the team was witnessing through their radar detection, and then relaying to Prentzel and the Drillmeister. It was already heading deeper out to sea to greet the enemy the Frilled Shark detected.

As they ventured out, they were suddenly rammed in the side and both children plus Frecher and the Skelekit fell onto the floor. It was the emotionless, robotic Frilled Shark and it wasn't connected in any way to the Unterghar – so it viewed them as an instant enemy.

"The Shark rammed another combatant," Prentzel said. "The Luftwaffe is on standby."

"What do we do, Egon?" Anna screamed. "We are being attacked – and we have NO light!"

The Unterghar gained speed to get away from the Frilled Shark which was now chasing it. The Wolfsboots were sinking like rocks and the unidentified enemy was showing up closer and closer on Klein's radar.

"What does Fangs say?" Anna asked.

The Unterghar stayed on course with Fangs' deep-sea direction until it finally met up with the incoming enemy and slammed into it. The sides of the Unterghar were hit, and Frecher and the Skelekit slid to the far end. When Egon steadied himself, he saw Fangs change direction and he did his best to guide the Unterghar to go that way. It finally stabilized and was heading back into shallow waters.

Overhead, the Luftwaffe had deployed bombers on standby at Klein's request. They were losing the entire Wolfpack and required assistance.

"Level the entire harbour," the Drillmeister called out to Prentzel.

"We still have men down there," Prentzel called back.

"Your men are dead regardless. You still haven't identified that massive incoming vessel and you have no underwater defense," he argued. "MAKE THE CALL!"

Prentzel radioed to his Luftwaffe counterpart and simply said, "Level it. Go."

Egon and Anna were in the middle of the target zone and were now helpless sitting ducks.

Just then, the unidentified enemy arrived at the shoreline. It was the Tintenfisch with the Uberghars inside each arm. In one solid swoop, it cut through the icy waters and slammed four of its arms onto the docks, slicing truck-length chunks out of the area they were standing on. Men were running everywhere, screaming over the air raid sirens.

The turbulence caused Egon and Anna to slam off the sides of the Unterghar once again when it jumped out of the water and grabbed the Drillmeister's case in its snout, then turned and headed back out to deeper seas. The Tintenfisch did one more leap out of the water way above the docks, the remaining men screamed and ran for cover, and four of its arms slammed down with a thunderous crash on the docks slicing bigger chunks between the chunks. The whole dock was collapsing into the harbour and the Luftwaffe planes could be heard in the distance.

Düster was circling in the night sky and soon the Opera

Drones were overhead. With precision nose-dives, dozens of them pierced the water and grabbed as many Winzig Panzer tanks as they could and flew off with them.

It wasn't clear if the Tintenfisch got out of the way when the bombers dropped the final explosives on the harbour, but the area was obliterated.

Back at the Juggerkampf, there was a knock on the hatch. Kluck was sitting awake with Albert while the rest of the children slept.

"Henry, come in," Albert said. "Why are you here?"

"I know why you are here," Kluck said with a straight face.

"I got a message from Ben at the Sea Urchin. The harbour was completely decimated," he said.

"And where were Anna and Egon," Albert said.

"They were in the harbour, Albert!" Kluck said. "Weren't they, Henry?"

"They were," Henry said, sadly.

"Do we go there?" Charlotte said.

"Charlotte," Kluck said. "You are supposed to be sleeping."

"I can't sleep," she said.

"It's a complete perimeter lockdown," Henry said. "We would never get in. If they were in the harbour like Ben said – in the Unterghar, there is a chance they survived it."

"If they did," Kluck said. "They wouldn't be coming home by train or with us."

"Ben said he will communicate again in an hour or if the Unterghar returns to the Urchin. He says it is chaos there now, but the Urchin is still alright," Henry said.

"What do you want to do, Kluck?" Albert asked.

"We've waited this long. Let's wait for another update from Ben," Kluck said.

"Alright, I will go and wait for his call," Henry said.

"How are the other children?" Albert asked.

"They are thrilled to be with Miss Kraus," Henry said.

"Who wouldn't be, right Henry?" Kluck teased.

"I'll call you as soon as I hear anything," Henry said, leaving on that embarrassing note.

"And we wait, dear friend," Albert said.

"Thank you for not giving up," Charlotte said, crying.

"This isn't over," Kluck said, touching her head.

Back at the Urchin, Ben was pacing the floors when he heard a knock at the door. There was Egon and Anna, sopping wet, the Skelekit shook like a wet dog, and Frecher was shivering in Anna's arms like a drowned rat.

"We abandoned ship, Ben," Anna said, her teeth chattering and her skin blue.

"Get in here! I will run and get blankets," Ben said, bolting off.

Egon sat on the ground and poured water out of Fangs' compass, and then out of his boots.

Ben returned with blankets and wrapped them up.

"Come into my lab, it's warmer in there," he said, rushing them down the curly corridors. "I need to put a call into Henry."

"Did we fail?" Anna asked.

"Oh sweetheart, there are only survivors of war. There are no winners," Ben said, calling Henry.

Egon was flat on his back with his knees drawn up and both arms across his face. He seemed defeated. The Skelekit stayed close.

"You heard what Ben said, Egon," Anna said. "There are only survivors in war. We are alive."

There was no consoling Egon at that moment, and Anna knew her words were useless.

"Alright, children. I spoke with Henry," Ben said. "He will let your friends know you are alive and alright. Here is the challenge. This entire base is at war. We are on lockdown. There is no coming or going. I have a way to get you out, but we are going to have to wait it out – not too long - or they will find you. You are a wanted boy right now, Herr Wolff. I got the wire about you earlier. Your father is furious."

"I worked at the Festung Wolff," Anna said. "He will be

thrilled to find out Egon is with me!" she added, sarcastically.

"Nobody will know, if I can help it," Ben said.

A solid hour went by and the kids had dried off somewhat.

"I have a window to get you back on the train. Henry will meet you at the station you departed from, but we have to go right now," Ben said.

The children got up and followed him out the back of the Urchin.

"We must walk to the station, but as you know from coming in, it's quick. We have darkness on our side," Ben said, as they all headed out.

Ben successfully got them on the train.

"I can't help you after this. Be ever so careful," he said. "Stay low, don't draw attention to yourself."

"Thank you, Mr. Ben. I love you and your Sea Urchin. I sure hope you get away someday," Anna said.

"I am alive. I don't even know where I would go," Ben said.

"Want to come with us?" Anna asked.

"Oh – Don't worry about me. I will leave here at some point," he said. "Was glad I could be here for you two!"

"Sometimes, you need to just go for it. Being on the run is better than giving up," Anna said.

19 THE ASHES OF THE LIONS

Anna held Frecher tightly in her coat while the Skelekit was inside Egon's. They faced each other on the train ride back and tried not to draw attention. It was a long, cold night and they were still damp. This early morning train had very few people on it, thankfully.

"That was the craziest night of my life, Egon," Anna said. "That last blast made me lose my hearing in one ear – unless I just have water in it. Does your face hurt?"

Egon was having a hard time seeing as he lost his glasses and the side of his face had a big cut from his eye to his jawbone.

"Maybe someone in the Kingdom can get you new eyewear. How is Fangs?" she asked.

Egon couldn't see him very well and passed him to Anna.

"It looks the same – he seems to still be pointing the way we are going. I think you are meant to carry him, but I can tell you which way he is going. Is your vision really that bad?"

Egon rubbed his eyes and then closed them.

"You rest, I will keep watch. I feel remarkably good," Anna said.

That wasn't entirely true. The blast they experienced had shoved a piece of metal from Anna's leg brace into her outer thigh, and it was beginning to swell. She was just keeping her superhero spirit going and attempting to be strong.

The sun was coming up strong on the horizon line to greet them and the overnight snow had stopped. Anna watched the sparkly crystals on the trees and cuddled Frecher to sleep. For a hurt little girl, she seemed plenty proud of herself.

"What are you doing to bring in the new year?" a woman asked her.

"Oh! What day is it?" she asked.

"December thirty-first," she laughed. "Did you sleep through the holidays?"

"I must have," she smiled. "I am starting a new life tonight."

"That is quite a reset!" the woman laughed.

"If you say it – it is more likely to happen," Anna smiled.

"I may adopt your attitude!" the woman said, going back to her paper.

"Do you believe all of that?" Anna asked.

"In the paper?" the woman asked. "It just passes the time."

"You could always pass the time by getting inside giant sea creatures and then go out to explore the ocean," Anna suggested.

"Well," she smiled. "That seems considerably more exciting than this boring paper. Perhaps I will kick my New Year off with such a suggestion!"

"I highly recommend it," Anna smirked, and then looked out the window again.

The train pulled into the Anhalter Bahnhof station, and Anna woke Egon up.

"We are here, sleepy boy. Let's go between adults so we don't look like strays," she suggested.

When they exited, Anna looked around to see if she recognized anyone.

"I guess we head back to the Juggerkampf," she said, tugging Egon's coat. "It's this way."

Egon was trying to see Fangs but was struggling.

"Let me see," Anna said. "Hmmmm – it is pointing over there. Alright, I guess we go there?"

There was nothing down the platform that applied to them, and they stood there for too long looking lost.

"We should just go back to the tank then, Egon."

Egon sat on a bench and waited.

"It is really risky for us, just hanging out like this," Anna warned. "You stay here – I am going to go get help."

Anna started running back to the Juggerkampf with Frecher, and Egon pet his Skelekit and waited.

"Did you lose your glasses again?" a familiar voice said.

It was Rosa, standing in front of him, eating a cookie.

"Wasn't I eating the last time we spoke?" she smiled.

Egon rubbed his eyes and touched the side of his face.

"Where did you get a gash like that?" Rosa whispered. "You all left me, you know."

Egon was confused.

"When you loaded up the truck. You left me," she said. "I ran for hours – in the woods – caught the train finally back here by stowing away. I have skills, you know."

Anna jumped up onto the Juggerkampf and tapped the hatch. As soon as it opened, Frecher jumped inside.

"Anna!" Kluck chirped. "You are back!"

"Egon won't come. His compass is staying at the station," Anna said.

"Well, let's go see what is happening then!" Kluck said, coming out. "Yes! Yes! Missed you too, Frecher! You funny little weasel!"

Frecher stood up and stared at him.

"STOAT! I know, you aren't technically a weasel. WE ALL KNOW!" he laughed.

"Kluck, I don't want to announce it, but my leg really hurts," Anna whispered.

"Anna, your brace is pierced in your leg," Kluck said.

"I'll get to it – but right now, Egon is vulnerable sitting there," she said.

"Yes – let's go see what is going on with him – and then we go home, alright?" he said.

"Home. That sounds like a dream," she said, hobbling along. "We got in the Unterghar, but had to abandon ship," she began.

"I see," Kluck said. "Where did he go?"

"He took a massive hit from the Luftwaffe blast – not direct, but enough that we had to get out," she said. "I don't know where he went after that."

"Did you see the Tintenfisch?" he asked.

"It was so dark," she said. "I did catch one of the arms smashing the harbour, but that is all I saw. I am not good at that periscope thing like Egon is. The last thing I saw was the Unterghar snatching something off the dock... some box – I don't know, it was dark."

"A box you say," Kluck said. "Could you describe it?"

"I can't, I am sorry – it all happened so fast. Maybe things will come to me when I have some sleep."

"You did well, Anna," Kluck smiled. "Wait until Katy hears of your adventure!"

"I have SO many things to tell her!" Anna said. "My work belt is great!"

Egon reached in deep into one of his inside coat pockets and pulled out Rosa's book. Then, he handed it to her.

"My art," she gasped. "How did you get this?"

The Lokführer saw the children talking.

"Rosa! I see you and Egon reunited!" he clapped.

"How did he get my art back? Do you know?" Rosa asked.

"Oh that? He wrestled the Death Marchers for it," the Lokführer smiled.

"That works for me," Rosa laughed. "They took my dog," she said, sadly.

"I checked on that," he said. "Mr. Ziegler from Ziegler's Shoes has him."

"They actually took him there?" Rosa asked.

"One of the Death Marchers followed up with him. He told me that you and him already had this plan," the Lokführer said.

"Thank you for looking out for me," Rosa said.

"We've become good friends since the Blitz, Rosa. You can't live here forever, though," he said.

"Nobody will have me but you," Rosa said.

"That isn't true, Rosa," he said.

"We will have you," Kluck interjected.

"I don't look like you – why would you want me," Rosa said. "You all left me back there."

"We were all prisoners, Rosa. It wasn't on purpose," Kluck said.

"Did you know I nearly froze out there?" she said.

"But you didn't," Kluck smiled.

She thought about that.

"No, I didn't," she said.

Kluck kneeled to speak to her and held her hands.

"It just happened so quickly. I couldn't count fast enough. I am so sorry. I can assure you it wasn't on purpose," he said.

"I've been through worse," she said.

Egon stood up and gave Fangs to Anna.

"What's happening?" Kluck asked.

"Fangs is pointing to the Juggerkampf now," Anna said.

"Then, we go!" Kluck said.

"Come with us, Rosa," Anna said.

"Your adventure doesn't end here," the Lokführer said.

"It isn't about adventure," Rosa said. "I just can't miss -" and she cut herself off.

"Oh, you think you might see her," the Lokführer said.

"Who?" Kluck asked.

"Rosa's father was shot in the Poland Blitzkrieg. Her mother was taken. She may see her pass on a train someday," the Lokführer whispered.

"I see," Kluck said. "Your risk is high here – and you know it is. Your heart is big – and you can survive a lot. I can't make you come, but I am willing to bet if your Mama shows up, the Lokführer would let us know, right?"

"I absolutely would," the Lokführer agreed.

"Do you know why I am so happy I got my book back?" Rosa said.

She reached in the back and pulled out a photo of her parents. She handed it to him.

"Can you keep it, so you know what she looks like?" she asked.

The Lokführer took it and had a good look.

"I have a steel-trap memory. I got it!" he said, pointing to his temple, and he handed the photo back to her.

"You will let me know right away?" Rosa asked. "How will you let me know?"

"Kluck and I go way back. You would find out right away," he said to her.

"RIGHT AWAY!" she said boldly.

"IMMEDIATELY," he smiled back.

"Alright," she said, kind of sadly.

Rosa deep down knew she had to move on, but nobody wants to. It isn't a natural thing to do, especially with no closure.

"There is an ocean!" Anna said, putting her arm around Rosa. "And a playground! You can sleep in my room! The walls look like a castle!"

Rosa walked over to the Lokführer and hugged him.

"Thank you," she smiled.

"Happy New Year, Rosa," he said.

As she walked with Anna, Kluck said to the Lokführer, "He met his father."

"And?"

"It set everything into motion," Kluck said.

"I knew it would," the Lokführer said.

"Happy New Year, my friend," Kluck said.

"And to you!" the Lokführer smiled.

Egon was at the stone eagle. Düster was sitting on top.

"Do you suppose he is upset?" Kluck asked Egon. "His friend is trapped in stone – misrepresented – used for something he wasn't created for. He will be free – someday."

Egon looked down at Fangs who was changing direction, and

Düster flew off.

Kluck looked at Fangs.

"He is pointing back to the Juggerkampf. Düster is also flying that way. Shall we go?"

Egon touched the stone eagle for a moment and then turned to follow Kluck. He was very tired.

"What is THIS thing?" Rosa asked.

"It's the Juggerkampf!" Anna said. "A Supertank! Kluck was on the team who made it for the war – but it never went into production – isn't that right, Kluck?"

"Close enough," Kluck said. "It fits approximately thirty crew, or a crazy bunch of misfits like us."

"My Mama called us mutts," Rosa said.

"Mixed bag – aren't we? There is nothing wrong with variety!" Kluck laughed. "Come on in! Meet the others!"

Rosa followed Anna in and was met by lots of hellos. Düster flew to the left of where they needed to go. Kluck looked up at him.

"Hmmmm, Düster isn't done," he said. "What is Fangs saying?"

Egon showed him the compass.

"Same direction," Kluck said. "Looks like Tiergarten. Well, come in and we will follow Fangs then."

They got inside the Juggerkampf and Albert was elated to see Egon.

"Welcome back, Egon! Everyone is waking up – you look like you are ready for sleep!"

"Fangs is pointing towards Tiergarten – I am willing to bet that is where we need to go," Kluck said.

"We are rested and ready – it's whether Anna and Egon want to go," Albert said.

"Do you have any food left?" Anna asked.

"Of course! Cinnamon buns and fruit?" Albert asked.

"Did you just offer me heaven?" Anna smiled.

"I bet you are hungry," Albert said. "Bread for you little one?"

Egon took it and broke off some for Frecher, then nibbled at it himself.

"Always worried about the critters," Kluck laughed. "Help yourself, Rosa!"

She took a bun and some juice and sat close beside Anna – happy to have a girlfriend or possibly a sister.

Anna nodded off for the tank ride to Tiergarten. That was exactly where Fangs was pointing, and Düster circled the whole way. It took a long time to get there due to it being a tank and not a train, but it gave the children a much-needed break. Anna and Rosa slept, although Egon was not ready for sleep. He did rub his eyes a lot due to having no glasses.

"We will get you new glasses when we return," Albert said. "No doubt you are due for new ones anyways. I doubt anyone has helped you sort out your eyes for a long time."

"When they don't speak, they don't always communicate what they can see or not see," Kluck said.

"This is true, but that is why he needs a detailed exam of his eyes. He shouldn't have to suffer when technology exists," Albert said.

"Very true!" Kluck agreed. "I believe we are finally here!"

The Juggerkampf parked at the Elephant Entrance of the Garden.

"I bet many of you would like a good stretch!" Kluck said to the children.

"I slept better than the night before!" Mia laughed.

"That was perfectly awful," Philip said.

"Well, go on – go get the stink off of you," Albert laughed, and the children ran into the bushes.

"I love watching children run," Kluck said. "What about you, Rosa?"

"I'm fine," she said. "I'm good watching them."

"Me too," Anna said.

"Don't stay for me," Rosa said. "You can go run with your friends."

"I haven't slept, they have. I will stay with you," Anna said. "They will be your friends too."

Egon started walking in the bush which alerted Anna.

"I guess I am going! Come with me," she said to Rosa, tugging her arm. "You can see how Egon's spider works!"

When Egon got to the edge of the bush where Fangs took him, he stopped and rubbed his eyes.

"Let me look at Fangs for you – OH MY STARS!" Anna gasped.

"Oh no," Rosa said, cupping her hands around her nose and mouth.

"I don't know if Egon completely sees that," Anna said. "Egon?"

Egon started marching forward and then it turned into a jog and a run. There he found himself in the middle of the Aquarium – which was reduced to rubble.

"What happened here?" Rosa yelled.

"What was this place?" Anna asked.

"I think it was the Aquarium," Rosa said. "At least that seems to be what the partial sign says."

Egon collapsed like he had become dizzy and passed out.

"EGON! Get some snow for his face," Anna said.

"He fainted," Rosa said, patting snow on his forehead and

cheeks. "Someone dropped a bomb. This is a disaster!"

"Who would bomb an Aquarium?" Anna said, looking around. "Oh, it's everywhere! Look!"

The pile of rubble they were standing on afforded them the view of the surrounding gardens. The entire forest on that side was wiped out too.

"I think I may pass out," Anna said.

"Not you too!" Rosa said. "Look I think he is coming around."

"Egon, can you hear me? Yes, his eyes are opening. Egon! Wake up!" Anna said.

Rosa began to walk around the perimeter of this pile.

"Anna, there are bodies," Rosa said.

"Like what kind of bodies?" Anna asked, holding Egon's head.

"I think that is some sort of reptile...I might throw up," Rosa said.

"Seriously! Ok, Egon, wake up...why are we here? Why did Fangs bring us? WHY CAN'T I GET A BOY WITH ME WHO SPEAKS!" Anna said, becoming enraged.

"You are tired, he didn't do this," Rosa said.

"WE JUST RODE AROUND IN THE BELLY OF A GIANT GHARIAL, GOT HIT BY A BOMB, AND HAD TO ABANDON SHIP! I HAVE HAD ZERO SLEEP! I'M A BIT IMPATIENT RIGHT NOW!" Anna fumed with tears pouring down.

"I know, but be mad at whoever did this," Rosa said.

Egon sat up and got up on his feet. He looked at the rubble and started to slowly walk around.

"Did Fangs show us this for a reason?" Anna asked him.

As Egon walked down to the sidewalk, there were four dead crocodiles.

"Alright, I did NOT need to see that," Rosa said.

"Egon," Anna said. "May I see your book?"

Egon dropped his head and gave it to her as the Skelekit smelled the crocodiles.

"Look, Rosa!" she said, turning to that page. "Four crocodiles. Exact same positioning."

Up above, a black funnel of vultures began circling. There weren't ten, fifty or even a hundred. There were hundreds and hundreds of them. They turned the white winter sky black as they spread out to land.

"I'm not sticking around for that!" Rosa said.

Egon calmly stood back, as they surrounded the crocodiles. Some of them were the shell-shocked, turkey vultures that were left wearing army gear in the middle of the forest during the Beetle-tank Ambush. They circled Egon a few times and then moved in on the crocodiles. They gently picked up each crocodile and flew off.

"What level of strength is that?" Anna asked.

"Strength in numbers," Rosa said.

Egon watched them fly off and looked in the woods to see the wild boar skeletons approve, then they ran off. Egon looked back down at Fangs.

"Let me see, Egon. Which way now?" Anna asked.

"That sign says the Elefantenpagode," Rosa said.

"That is flattened too. Oh Rosa. That is a dead elephant," Anna said. "That is too horrible."

"Hey, Anna – didn't *they* help us get out of that jail?" Rosa said, pointing to the woods.

"Woah – it's Blackguard, yes and the white wolf army," Anna said.

"I don't think they want anyone near that elephant. They are forming a circle around it," Rosa said.

Egon walked towards them, and straight up to Blackguard. He bared teeth and Egon kneeled and put his head down. Blackguard sniffed his head, then passed by him. Egon slowly got up and walked toward the dead elephant. He looked down and then touched the bridge of its trunk. Then he looked around at the ruins this bombing had caused.

"Who did this, Egon?" Anna asked. "I wish we understood."

"There isn't much to understand about war," Rosa said. "In September, the tanks rolled into my city in Poland and took us down. Out of nowhere."

"I know, I was there too," Anna said.

"You are from Poland?" Rosa asked.

"Yes," Anna said.

The white wolves drove the children away from the elephant, and Egon marched off.

They ended up at the bison statue. This was the one where the hunters with hounds had an arrow deep into the side of the bison.... except, the bison was gone. Egon looked up and around and there was the bison that kept appearing to him but had a female bison with him. They looked at Egon for a moment and then disappeared.

When Egon went to the lion statue, it was completely decimated. The lion that was once standing by his dying lioness and cubs was now dust with his family.

"Look! There are more Opera Drones, Egon!" Anna pointed out.

Hundreds of blackbirds landed on the pile and began pecking away at it.

"Are they eating it?" Anna asked.

"There are some things we simply don't need to see," Rosa said.

Egon just watched them and was calmer than the girls.

"The ashes of the lions," Kluck said, appearing at the edge of the forest.

"What does that mean?" Anna asked.

"It means they are free," Kluck said.

"Everything was destroyed! Where is the freedom?"

"In some places, natural fires happen. And those ashes feed the new growth. These statues represented the killings throughout hundreds of years of senseless hunting – not even for food, but sport. That lion statue was an accurate representation of the pain families went through because of their families being broken up. Now, they are free."

"You compare this to a natural fire?" Rosa asked.

"Oh, no. Certainly not. Some disasters are for the good of the future. Sometimes, you must find the good in the bad kind of disaster. This was a shameful target," Kluck said.

Egon looked around for the Skelekit. She was nowhere to be found.

"She's over there, Egon," Kluck said, pointing to a nearby tree.

There was the Skelekit reunited with its Mama. When Egon looked at the hunting statue that had been holding up the dead fox, the fox was gone from there and back with its wife and baby. The Skelekit had its family back. She stopped running around her Skelefox parents and came back to Egon. He kneeled to touch her nose and she jumped up to nudge his finger. He picked her up and hugged her and then released her to her family.

"Beautiful," Kluck said.

"What is?" Anna asked.

"Yes, I don't see anything," Rosa said.

"It is hard to explain right now," Kluck said. "You may already be seeing that Egon has a unique connection to this world. People think he cannot communicate. On the contrary, he communicates like *them*."

Egon stood up and walked over to Kluck and looked up at him.

"You have that 'can we go home now' look," Kluck smiled, and grabbed his chin. "Thank you for bringing her home. Among other things, I think she saved you from some hornet stings by releasing them, didn't she?" he whispered. "That is the beauty of being a Skelekitty!"

Egon looked down at Fangs who was pointing back to the Juggerkampf. He began to slow-walk his way there. Anna took Rosa's hand and followed.

Albert saw them coming back and called for the children. When they came back, they all talked at once about the bombings and the forest landscape. They talked about birds overhead and climbing trees as they poured into the Juggerkampf.

"Are we done here, Egon?" Albert asked.

Egon jumped up on the Juggerkampf and went inside.

"That is one exhausted boy. Reminds me of a boy I saw in New York in the Fall," Albert said.

Rosa went inside and Anna climbed up behind her. Before going in, she turned to look at the forest, and then to Albert and Kluck.

"I didn't see this forest before, but **I bet it was beautiful once**," she said.

"It will be beautiful again," Albert said.

"It's peaceful, Anna. That makes it beautiful right now," Kluck added.

She thought about that.

"You are right. It is quiet," she smiled, and she went in the Juggerkampf.

"Well, you must be ready for your mid-day nap now!" Kluck said with his arm around Albert.

"You are just jealous," Albert laughed, as they both went inside with the children.

"Frecher!" Kluck called. "Time to go!"

Frecher jumped up and in and they left Tiergarten.

Egon was wide awake still, but at least he was horizontal. He had a blanket high up under his chin and over his ear. He became accustomed to the Skelekit hanging out with him, and now there was an empty place beside him.

Anna and Rosa were under blankets against the wall of the Juggerkampf saying nothing. They looked overwhelmed. The rest of the children were equally as quiet. It was as though the reality of what happened to them all was starting to infiltrate their thoughts which often happens after trauma. Kluck just looked at Albert who looked at the children. They also said nothing. It was a time for peaceful resetting. The tracks of the Juggerkampf made a soothing rotation that was lulling everyone into a daze. Even Frecher knew to be quiet, but he was making the most noise nibbling bread bits.

By the time they reached Tiefer Bach Road, almost everyone was asleep.

"I'll get out to speak with Zimmermann," Kluck said quietly to Albert.

The Base was unusually quiet. Zimmermann greeted them.

"Oh! I usually have to ask for you," Kluck said.

"Nobody is here, they were all deployed," Zimmermann said.

"The bombings are ramping up," Kluck said. "We saw some of the destruction. Some of the children were at the Kriegsmarine when it was hit."

"They bombed themselves," Zimmermann said.

"They did what?" Kluck asked.

"Yes, they called in the Luftwaffe. Apparently, an underwater enemy bigger than anything they had ever seen destroyed the harbour, so they called for self-obliteration," Zimmermann explained.

"I heard bits and pieces. That makes sense. The children are safe," Kluck said.

"Glad to hear it," Zimmermann responded.

The Juggerkampf moved into the farm where Max greeted

them.

"Hello Max!" Albert called out.

When Egon heard that, he exited the tank and ran for the empty chicken coop.

"They are gone Egon! Remember – they went with you!" Max yelled.

Egon turned around and looked at them.

"Do you need help?" Kluck asked, and Egon waited.

"Alright children! We need extra hands. Follow Egon, please!" Kluck said to them.

Egon lifted the floorboard and went down the stairs. He had no key, but the door was wide open.

"What is this place?" Charlotte asked.

"No idea," Rita said.

Egon took out the flashlight that Swartz commending him for carrying and walked down the hall with the pangolins in cages on one side and the pangolins in an enclosure on the other side.

"This is disgusting!" Charlotte said. "The smell is really extreme!"

Egon quietly opened the door to the labs where Professor Wirdstaub worked, but nobody was there. It was abandoned. He kept walking through where the workers and prisoners were. They were all gone, and it was quiet. He was startled by one voice.

"You aren't allowed to hold the livestock," the boy said, hiding behind a barrel. "Don't eat them. You need to quit looking at them. Say no to the livestock."

It was Noah. He was down there by himself.

"They left him here?" Anna asked, as Egon shone a flashlight on him.

The light hurt him so badly.

"Here," Charlotte said. "Have my coat," and she put it on his shoulders.

"He can have my hat," Philip said. "He'll need to stop the light outside if we take him out."

Philip and Charlotte put their arms around Noah and took him down the hall and out. The rest of the children followed Egon back to the pangolins.

"I guess we all grab one?" Anna asked.

"That's what I am going to do," Rosa said.

The pangolins were remarkably calm – like they just gave up.

"Poor things," Rita said.

"No time for emotion," Anna said. "We are almost home."

"Where is home?" Mia Asked.

"Can't wait to show you!"

The children emerged from the ground with arms full of pangolins.

"They just left them there! What a bunch of cowards!" Anna said.

"Love your big, passionate heart, Anna!" Albert said.

"I didn't know about them," Max said. "I was preparing to leave too!"

"Where will you go?" Kluck asked.

"North of Berlin with my grandparents. They need me," Max said.

"Alright, be safe out there, Max," Kluck said as Zimmermann approached with his hand out.

"I can't thank you enough, my dear friend. You are so brave," Kluck said, shaking his hand and then he hugged him.

"You have a great team, old boy!" Zimmermann said. "Now, get out of here!"

Kluck smiled and then called the children to get back inside, and they made their way through the field and back to the Forgotten Farm.

"It feels like we could rescue with no end in sight," Anna said.

"It can feel that way for sure. We must always look at who we can save, not who we didn't," Kluck said.

People like Egon and Ian were unable to do this. Their mission never seemed to end even after missions seemed to have ended. Egon remained unsettled.

"That was definitely the craziest night of my life, Egon," Anna said.

20 WHAT WAS IN THE SHARK'S MOUTH

Egon jumped out and looked at the ground beside him.

Still no Skelekit. It was the first time he was alone, and he took a minute to breathe. He didn't look like a boy who was successful. He seemed disheartened. He looked at the distressed sign which read 39 Rattenbury Lane and then took the key with the elephant head and tusk and put it in the hole in the silo as passively as putting morning toast in a toaster. The other children peeking out of the Juggerkampf hatch were awestruck that this enormous silo split open and had fog coming out. Egon walked through the split and Frecher jumped out and off the tank to join him.

"Frecher either knows Egon is alone or he is anxious to get back with Booza!" Albert said.

"He made a friend, did he?" Kluck asked.

"Oh, straight away! Fast friends!" Albert said.

"Any sign of White Cap returning?" Kluck asked.

"No, that monkey was made to be in the thick of it all. I am guessing he is watching over Jackie," Albert said.

"Jackie still won't come?" Kluck asked.

"Jackie needs to keep sticking it to the Mayor," Albert laughed.

"He always said you just have to show up!" Kluck laughed.

"He shows up even where he is not welcome," Albert laughed. "It's a great skill!"

Albert looked up.

"The last time we came through, the Opera Drones came with us," Albert said. "They finally don't need a door!"

"Their mouths were full – they needed to get home," Kluck laughed. "The children will have a lot to see today. They don't need to understand everything those birds take back to base right now."

The Juggerkampf moved through the forest, past the lyrebird and parked beside the Juggernaut.

Sadar and Kabir were waiting at the Elephant Entrance the same as when Ian came home. The children poured out of the tank like an interrupted anthill and they stood with their mouths open.

Richard, who was soaking wet from playing in the ocean, came running up to Anna.

"How was the belt? Did you use the tools?"

"I picked a lock – we set all these kids free!" Anna said.

"Were they at Jackal House too?" he asked.

"Oh! That is where you were right? In New York? No, these people were stolen by Death Marchers in Germany," Anna said.

"GERMANY?" Richard yelled. "But that door in the silo comes from New York!"

"How does that work?" Anna asked Kluck.

"Our silo is from Germany," Kluck said.

"WOAH!" Richard said. "Could kids come here from all over the world?"

"I wish that were possible!" Albert said. "I would fill an ocean with troublemakers like Richard!"

"Hey!" he said, furrowing his brow, and Albert messed up his wet hair.

"When you come here," Sally piped up. "Just make a clear run for the ocean!"

"Why?" Mia asked.

"Your first swim you should just run straight in – clothes and all. It helps you leave your past behind!" Sally laughed.

"Oh, Mia – just do it!" Anna said. "She may throw you in!"

Mia gave that about two seconds of consideration and then ran as fast as she could and slammed the water hard with a squeal. All the other children followed, and it soon became a frenzy of children bubbling the water like piranha.

"Who are the animal guests this time?" Sadar laughed.

"Pangolins!" Kluck said.

"Oh that is terrific!" Kabir said. "Have we done pangolins before?"

"I have two that Egon brought in," Sadar said.

"WHERE?" Kabir asked.

"Oh! The Mother Gibbon is currently tending to one of them, the other is in intensive care," Sadar laughed.

"I can't keep up with the comings and goings anymore," Kabir laughed.

"But we love it!" Sadar said.

"But – we love it," Kabir smiled. "I'll go get help bringing them in. Let's let the children play."

"Kluck!" Sadar said, hugging him. "You made it!"

"I heard I missed a lot," Kluck said.

"The ceremony for Zusa was lovely," Sadar said.

Kluck's head snapped to Albert.

"WHERE IS ZUSA?"

"We better go to the garden," Albert said.

Kluck followed him, leaving Egon and Anna to stand alone. Katy rolled up in her chair.

"Egon lost his glasses, Sadar," Anna called out.

"Oh! So you did. Come downstairs when you are ready, and we'll get you sorted," he said, going inside.

"Hello, Anna!" Katy said. "So happy you came back. Albert said Germany is super dangerous right now!"

"And cold," she said as Egon sat in the sand and put his arms around his knees.

"Are you hurt?" Katy asked.

Anna moved towards Katy and tears started to come.

"I am really hurt," she said. "I want to be brave like you, but Katy – what do I do right now? I am in massive pain."

"Where? Can you show me?" Katy asked.

Anna showed her the brace jabbed in her leg.

"Anna – that is an emergency! You need help!" Katy said.

"You said you didn't want to be fixed – that you have pain – I just thought it was part of being a superhero," she cried.

"I do have pain – but not the kind that could be life-threatening! Look at your wound! That is infected!" Katy snapped.

"I know, it's bad," Anna said. "Everything is just so much bigger here – and more magical and I don't understand what I am supposed to do."

"You go get it fixed so you can keep going!" Katy said.

"Ok, I don't wish to announce it," Anna said.

"Of course, it is personal," Katy said. "I can see your heart is still big and beating fine!" she smiled.

"Thank you, Katy," she said hugging her in her chair.

Kluck and Albert were in the gardens of the children's playground.

"Hello, Mita! Look who is here!" Albert said.

Mita ran over to Kluck and hugged him around the waist and then went back to gardening.

"Mita!" Kluck said. "Your roses are exquisite!"

"This is her happy place," Albert said. "She made Anna feel very welcome here and helped her with Zusa. He is over there."

"Uh, thank you Miss Mita," Kluck said, removing his hat and walking over to the stone box Zusa was in. "How did it happen?"

"Anna said his heart stopped beating when she and Egon were laying against his chest in the Juggerkampf," Albert responded.

"And you had a nice ceremony?" Kluck asked.

"Maybe we should have waited for you," Albert said, apologetically.

"No-no," Kluck said. "The children needed that."

"The Banyan women came," Albert said.

"They did?" Kluck said. "That is marvelous."

"Anna cried half that ocean you see – and they held her and cuddled her," Albert said.

"*I gave my tears to the sea*," Kluck said.

"What's that?" Albert said.

"Anna said that to the children after we escaped Wolff's camp," Kluck said. "Now I understand. You told them it wasn't forever?" Kluck asked.

"Of course," he nodded.

"He would be so happy to know that most of them are here now," Kluck said.

"I know you loved him too," Albert said, patting his back.

Egon and Anna were down in the Lab. Sadar was examining Egon's eyes in a chair, and Kabir was looking at Anna's leg on a bed beside them.

"So let me understand," Sadar asked. "You were riding inside a giant gharial, it was hit by a bomb, you abandoned ship, swam to shore in frigid waters and ended up at an aquarium."

"Oh - the night didn't end there," Anna laughed.

"Anna, do you want something for pain? I am going to remove your brace. It will hurt badly," Kabir said.

"I can take it," Anna said.

"This is not an insult to what you can mentally overcome, your body will react badly," he explained.

"Please take it out – it is throbbing badly," she said.

Kabir cleaned the area and then gave her a tree branch.

"What is this?" she asked.

"Banyan tree, put it sideways in your mouth and bite down," Kabir said.

"Oh Banyan! Like the women who cuddled me in the ocean," she said, and then put the branch in her mouth but tried to keep talking while it was in there. "Dey kssd mu n dey cudow – OOOOOOOOOOOH!"

"Ok, it is out!" Kabir said.

Anna began to cry those deep tears that were part relief.

"I am going to hold intense pressure on it for a minute or so...deep breaths, sweetheart," Kabir said.

"Kabir! That is SOOOOOO BAAAAAAAD! You should have forced me to take medicine first!" she cried.

"Drink this," he said. "It has some pain-relieving herbs in it – and will make you feel calm."

After a few minutes, she settled down.

"So Egon's eyes," Sadar said. "He was probably not seeing well with the glasses he had before. Children's orphanages don't have great resources for this – mix that with him not telling them if it was working or not, made him basically have reading glasses when the issue is worse than that."

"Well, orphanages hardly have the equipment we have here,"

Kabir laughed.

"True," Sadar said. "I am going to go get his glasses ready. I really only need an hour or so."

Sadar left to deal with that and Kabir kept chatting with the children.

"How did Zahnea do?" Kabir asked.

"I don't know who that is," Anna asked.

"The Queen hornet that Egon took with him," he said.

"Oh, did you guys do that to her? They were spectacular! They were set loose into the ocean – and we looked at them through the periscope and they all glowed orange!"

"They *all* glowed orange? That is great! So you swapped out the main Queen then, Egon!"

"He dripped something into their hive too," Anna added.

"We only gave him the Queen in a tube," Kabir said.

"He made it himself in a lab," she said. "I don't know what that did."

"I see," he smiled. "You did good, Egon!"

Egon dropped his head and stared down at Fangs. He wasn't happy.

"You don't seem to be the type to be proud, Egon," Anna said. "But you should be."

He rubbed his eyes and waited in his chair.

Kabir finished wrapping Anna's leg and grabbed bandages for Egon's face.

"You make quite a team!" Kabir smiled.

Sadar returned with Egon's glasses in a little less than an hour and the children left the Lab.

"Hi Egon! Welcome back!" Jeet called from the rope bridge above. "Hello Anna! So glad you made it home safely!"

"Home!" Anna smiled. "Yes! Happy to be home!"

She liked the sound of that.

"Molly and the Pod are here, Egon," Jeet said. "If you want to see."

Egon ran up the steps and onto the bridge. Anna hobbled along quickly behind him.

"Look down," he said.

Egon and Anna looked in the aquarium and there was Molly and her pod of dolphins cackling away playfully with objects in their mouths.

"They are giant snails mixed with crabs, best I can tell," Jeet said. "Are those presents for me, Molly?"

"Oh! I think I saw a hornet bite one of those through the periscope when we were at war," Anna said, choking on the word war. "I never wanted to go to war."

"For the peacekeepers, war is thrust upon us," Jeet said. "You saved a lot of creatures and people from what I understand!"

A bleep went off on Jeet's radar.

"Excuse me, children," he said, returning to the Encephalon.

Anna and Egon sat with their feet dangling, watching the dolphins. Egon's eyes danced with the Pod.

"Oh! Can you see better?" Anna smiled. "So glad. Say, Egon...did I do right by you out there? I would go again if you needed me to."

Egon handed her Fangs. She ran her hand along the scratched-up dome.

"Pretty good for, you know, not being alive and all," she smiled. "Maybe he is, what do I know?" she laughed, handing it back.

"Big object coming in on my radar, children!" Jeet called out. "I am going to go get Albert and Kluck!"

The dolphin pod raced out to sea and disappeared into the ocean.

"I wonder if Jeet would let me work here. It's an exciting place, right?" Anna said.

Egon stood up and went into the Encephalon and looked at Jeet's radar. Then, he ran back out and down the ladder to where he originally saw the Tintenfisch.

Soon, Albert and Kluck returned with Jeet and they both looked at the radar.

"Where have Egon and Anna gone?" Kluck asked.

"Oh, I see them down the ladder," Jeet said.

Albert and Kluck went down the ladder slower than the children but made it.

"Can we put in better accessibility for old men?" Albert laughed.

"LOOK!" Anna shouted.

Coming into shore was the Tintenfisch. It was moving at a steady pace but was dragging a long object behind it.

"What on Earth?" Albert said.

When it got close to shore, it hurled itself into the outdoor aquarium area like it was a Doctor who finished an eighteen-hour shift at the hospital and threw itself into bed. Something was still hanging off one of its arms in the ocean. It expanded itself and then seemed to exhale - and all the Uberghars came out of its arms and swam around in the pen.

"Why were they in there?" Anna asked with big eyes.

"Long story, short... they acted as a brain for each of the Tintenfisch's arms. I can explain more later," Jeet laughed. "Can you help me bring them inside?"

"Hold on a minute," Kluck said. "Look out there."

On the tip of an arm was the traumatised Unterghar. The Tintenfisch's appendage was wrapped around the neck like a leash, and it appeared to have dragged it all the way back.

"That is what we were in!" Anna clapped. "That was it! Oh no, is it dead?"

"We will send a team out to look," Jeet said.

Egon handed Fangs to Anna and had already jumped in the water and swam out to it. It was floating on top of the water and he touched the side to open the door. Inside, he went to the control area and hooked the wire back to how he originally found it.

"Oh wow – look there," Albert pointed.

Egon came back out and treaded water and watched. The Uberghars started swimming out to the Unterghar and circled it. It let out a big breath and then submerged. The babies assumed their position on top of him.

"Amazing," Jeet said.

"He's really hurt," Anna said.

"Yes, that is a big project. I need massive help with the Tintenfisch and the gharials," Jeet said.

"I know a little bit about them," Anna chimed in. "And what I don't know, I can learn!"

"I would love to have you. Can you show up for work at nine am tomorrow?" Jeet smiled.

"I can be here at six!" she said.

"Happy to have you, Anna!" Jeet said, patting her shoulder.

Egon swam over and looked at the snout and then looked around the water.

"He didn't get it," Kluck whispered to Albert.

"I know," Albert whispered back. "Not every mission is going to work out perfectly."

"It's alright, Egon," Kluck called out. "You did well."

Egon stormed back out of the water and straight past them all, put his hand out to Anna, who handed him his compass and he went back up the ladder.

"He can feel disappointed. Let's give him some space," Kluck said.

"I don't know how we failed," Anna said. "Then again, I don't understand the mission."

"You showed up," Albert said. "A friend of mine reminds me that is important."

Jeet stayed with the Tintenfisch while the others all went back up the ladder and inside.

"I understand they didn't get the Elefanteufel operating," Kluck said to Albert.

"Oh, their secret weapon?" Albert said. "That is fine news."

"Lots of success, just a lot still unknown," Kluck said.

"Progress isn't perfect," Albert said.

Egon was in the Spider Network when Kluck found him later that day.

"We all decided to give you some quiet time," Kluck said.

Egon was sitting under the Great Copper Spider with Fangs in his lap.

"You two had quite an adventure together, no?" Kluck said. "Is he tired?"

Egon looked at him closely.

"New glasses! I don't think you really saw his Fangs on his abdomen before, did you? How does his dome look? Just a bit scratched. Did you ever see the crack in Skull's? I think yours came out good considering!"

Egon got up to look at Skull in Ian's pillar.

"We are doing New Year's Eve on the beach tonight. You are welcome to join us," Kluck said. "So happy you are home," he said, and he walked out.

The door to the Elephant Den opened and there was Ian. He shuffled quietly over to Egon in his stocking feet and stood beside Skull's pillar. Egon handed Fangs to him and he looked at the scratches. Then he pointed to the crack in Skull's dome. Both boys took deep breaths.

Egon walked over to his own pillar and Ian shuffled behind him. It seemed that Egon needed Ian to be there when he put Fangs in. The leg of the spider began to bubble up and Fangs was home again.

Everyone at Jagannatha came together to prepare a finger-food feast and the big serving table beside the fire was like a hive with honeybees. The children were laughing and telling jokes and roasting marshmallows by the bonfire.

"Everyone sit on the shore and wait," Albert announced.

The children had their mouths full and sat patiently. In the distance, they heard tribal chanting. It was the Banyan women that were water drumming at Zusa's ceremony, but they were very celebrational now.

Anna, who was sitting beside Katy, lit up like a Christmas tree when she saw them.

"I love them," she whispered to Katy as they banged handmade drums and stomped the sand before entering the water to do their big water drum performance.

When they were done, the children all clapped and ran into the water. The women scooped the children up in their arms, held them high, splashed with them and played. They just loved it.

"The Mauerspechte are loving it here," Kluck grinned.

"Look!" Charlotte called out.

The Opera Drones had returned and soared past like a military show and headed towards their Air Force base. These were the birds that scooped up bits of ocean fighters at the Kriegsmarine, and other flocks who gobbled up the ashes of the lions.

"They are bringing the dead home," Kluck said.

Egon spotted the vultures flying toward the Encephalon and he slipped away from the party to go see them.

Jeet was with several workers tending to the Tintenfisch when Egon came down the ladder.

"Why aren't you at the festivities with the other children?" Jeet said. "These creatures are fine tonight. We are stabilizing and doing some testing."

Egon looked up to see the vultures against the moonlit sky. They were coming into shore...hundreds of them. They were carrying the four crocodiles from Tiergarten and Egon ran down to greet them.

"Because we don't have enough to do, right?" Jeet laughed.

As he walked over to Egon, he noticed they were still breathing.

"Oh they are alive!" Jeet smiled. "Ah, rescue. Never a dull moment! They are welcome here!"

The workers got busy assessing and loading the crocodiles up for transport.

"Didn't you have four in your book?" Jeet smiled.

Egon followed the men in who were transporting them. They took them to a nearby water pen and Egon stopped to see Molly who had returned and was making a lot of noise. When he looked in the water, he noticed the bottom of her mouth was hooked in something. She jumped up on her back fin and danced for Egon. It was his akkordion case and she set it on the edge for him. When he opened it, he seemed a bit disappointed that something was missing. The abboardion was in there.

Right behind Molly was Stealth, the hammerhead shark pup who had accompanied the dolphin pod to the Kriegsmarine. She swam up to Egon and looked at him with the glass eye coming out of the left side of her hammer. She got close and then opened her mouth. Egon looked thoroughly and then reached up inside her hammer and started pulling things out and shoving them quickly into his akkordion case. It was a tight fit in the case, but thankfully because it was currently the skeleton boar instead of the instrument, there were empty spaces in the ribs. He closed the case quickly and ran back through the Assembly of Seven, past the Spider Network and into the Elephant Den.

He rushed in so quickly, Mita and Ian both sat straight up in bed. Neither one of them celebrated on the beach with the other children. Perhaps they were waiting for Egon, but they were in bed for the night.

Mita smiled her big flashy smile and got out of bed to greet him. She picked up his case and set it beside his bed. Then, she hugged him. He exhaled and seemed more at peace. She handed him his night shirt and pajama bottoms and he left to go change and use the bathroom. Mita sat on the side of Ian's bed and moved the hair out of his eyes and off his forehead. They looked at each other for a moment and she checked for his Skelegroom doll. Then, she wound the bottom on the music box beside his bed and it began to play the rhythm that helped him sleep every night. Ian's Border Collies never left his side. They were his angels for life.

When Egon came out of the bathroom in his pajamas, Mita ran back to his bed to show him how Aldo the hound dog and Soot the chicken had curled up together on the foot of his bed. She picked Soot straight up and showed Egon that she had laid an egg. She giggled and set Soot back down. It was going to be difficult for Aldo to move when his belly was warming a nest!

"Soot!" Kluck laughed as he came in. "You finally have a warm location for your egg!"

Egon gently got into bed.

"I came to say good night – and thank you, Egon. You won't want the thank you, but I am going to offer it anyways," Kluck laughed. "I love this room so much. The purple bedspreads and gold and red pillows. Oh and Olly – Albert told me she sleeps every night by the elephant on the riser. Adorable."

Then he walked over to Ian's bed.

"Can't wait to catch up with you and Mita tomorrow as well, Mr. Jefferson," he said to Ian. "I know none of you are the New Year's type, but Happy New Year to you all. This year will be more trying than the last, but we are getting through the missions – one at a time," Kluck smiled, and left the room.

He stopped briefly at the door and looked at Egon.

"I see someone brought you your Abboardion," he smiled. "That is excellent news."

After he left, Mita ran around to tuck Egon in and he reached down for his case. She opened it for him and began pulling the objects out.

They were teeth. *Elephant teeth.*

She took a couple of these fossil-like bricks in her arms and placed them on the elephant riser. Ian was sitting straight up watching them. Then, she returned to Egon's bed and handed him the other two and she waited. He slowly got up and took the other teeth to the riser and ever so carefully, placed them at the feet of the stone elephant.

As soon as he did this, a light appeared in the stone like it did when Ian gifted him the tusks. Ian's was the letter 'I', Egon's was at another corner and was a bright letter 'E'. Just like Ian, he waved his hand in front of the light and watched the beams of light shine through his fingers.

Mita smiled and returned to her bed. Egon followed her lead and jumped under the covers of his own bed. Ian pulled his covers up too.

After several minutes of silence, the heavy steps came off the riser and walked up behind Egon. Ian's Border Collies made the high whimper noises again but Aldo the dog was completely silent. Soot let out mildly concerned clucks but stayed on her nest. The elephant's trunk pulled back his covers and returned the teeth to him. Then it turned with heavy feet and returned to its position on the riser and let out that same throaty exhale once again. Egon was frozen.

That was Mita's cue to put a blanket back on loyal little Olly and the stone elephant, and then she tucked Egon in. She stopped at Ian's bed to wind up the music box that peddled on those same three to four notes. This prompted Ian's Skello to join in and it woke up Egon's abboardion. It wasn't loud, though. It was a sweet lullaby that they all needed – and deserved, to hear.

Aldo got up to do a few circles as dogs often do before they sleep, and Soot clucked at him to settle in as she protected her egg.

Egon touched every curve on the teeth and finally began to get sleepy. As his eyes became heavy, he looked out the window and saw the two bison. His angels were much bigger than Ian's

– and they seemed to prefer being outside.

The children's secrets were growing, and still – nobody was about to hear any of them.

The rest of the children were winding down on the beach and Rosa was teaching Anna her hand-games. The Beagle from the Grunewald forest was improving and was becoming attached to Anna.

"POLISH SWINE!" Rosa said, sitting cross-legged in front of her. "Push your nose up with your finger when you say the word 'swine'!"

"Proud to be a Polish pig with you, Rosa," Anna said.

"My friend Olcay and I called ourselves Hand-game Pigs!" Rosa laughed.

"Hand-game Pigs it is!" Anna laughed.

"I had a dog once," Rosa said, looking at Anna's Beagle. "I believe he is safe with a friend, but I miss him."

"What was his name?" Anna asked.

"Eisbär – a little polar bear!" Rosa smiled. "What will you call your Beagle?"

"Spotz, I think. Do you like this name?" Anna asked.

"She sure is spotty!" Rosa laughed.

Meanwhile, Albert and Kluck were chatting when Mita's elderly friend walked by.

"Heading to bed, Lavani?" Albert asked.

"I need to go spend time with Noah," she said.

"Thank you, Lavani," Albert responded. "How is Noah?"

"Catatonic. He is staring at a wall in his room," she said.

"Trauma. It takes time. Thank you for loving him," Albert said. "When you think the time is right, Kluck and I can come speak with him."

"We certainly will," Kluck added. "He needs some gradual light therapy too. He lived underground for a long time."

"They don't want to join us?" Albert asked, looking towards the Elephant Den.

"The Makadees? This isn't their style," Kluck said.

"It's past my bedtime too!" Albert laughed.

"Noon is past your bedtime," Kluck joked.

"Alright old man. I made you a hot tea. Just look at us. Sipping tea," Albert laughed.

"Nowhere I'd rather be tonight, dear friend," Kluck said, clanking their cups.

Then he removed his fur hat.

"How do you still wear that thing? You know the Opera Drones keep eyeing it up," Albert said. "You are receding like me!"

"It's a helpful costume at this point," Kluck laughed, slicking back his mess of white curls. "Hey, did you see that?"

"See what?" Albert asked.

"Through the trees. The wolves are carrying something," Kluck said.

"Where were they last?" Albert asked.

"Tiergarten," Kluck replied.

"Well then, we know what they are bringing home," Albert said.

"Do you know what? We'll go look tomorrow," Kluck said, yawning.

"Or we won't," Albert laughed, clanking his cup against Kluck's.

"Cheers to that," Kluck clanked back.

"You know, I stood out here after tucking Ian in a few months ago. I reflected on how things **used to be beautiful once**. They are beautiful even still...and if things do have to get ugly again, the beauty always returns."

"Yes it does. It will heal," Kluck smiled.

"Speaking of healing," Albert said.

"I know, I can't wait until she comes," Kluck said. "She has no idea what she is walking into at 39 Rattenbury Lane!"

"Oh, I think she may. But won't that be fun to witness?" Albert asked.

“Yes! And Claw is alive!” Kluck smiled.

“Right!” Albert remembered. “Claw *is* alive.”

ABOUT THE AUTHOR

Karen Stever is a Canadian author & musician.

Her award-winning first book, **KING JUGGERNAUT: NYC** is one of seven in ***The Rattenbury Chronicles*** and is a companion piece to her concept record, **Idiot Savant**.

To learn more, please visit **karenstever.com**

LOOK FOR THESE BOOKS

1 KING JUGGERNAUT – *NYC*

2 KING JUGGERNAUT – *BERLIN*

3 KING JUGGERNAUT – *TOKYO*

4 KING JUGGERNAUT – *ROME*

5 KING JUGGERNAUT – *CAIRO*

6 KING JUGGERNAUT – *MANAUS*

7 KING JUGGERNAUT – *BOMBAY*

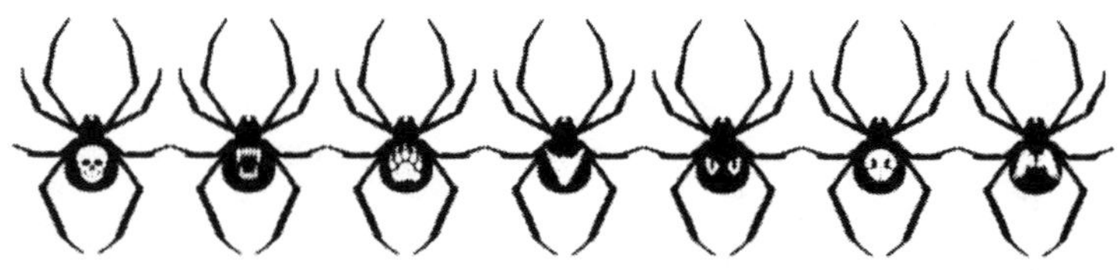

KARENSTEVER.COM

Made in the USA
Middletown, DE
28 October 2020